PRAISE FOR *PAYDAY*

'With complex female characters spiralling out of control,
Payday is tense, full of twists, and impossible to put down'
HELEN FIELDING

'A fast-paced psychological thriller and a feminist unpicking
of the issues that unite and divide women. I adored it'
GILLIAN MCALLISTER

'Modern, intelligent and totally gripping. Nicole
Kidman TV miniseries is written all over it'
SUNDAY TELEGRAPH

'The final twist genuinely blindsided me'
Reader Review ★ ★ ★ ★ ★

'Fearless, stylish, suspenseful and immensely entertaining'
LOUISE CANDLISH

'A cracking feminist revenge thriller that rips
along, full of tension and drama'
DAILY MAIL

'Seductive. Intelligent. Should have a 'must read' advisory on it'
JANE CORRY

'The thriller of the year'
Reader Review ★ ★ ★ ★ ★

'A runaway train ride of a thriller'
SUN

'Absolutely gripping from the start'
Reader Review ★ ★ ★ ★ ★

'A mystery that's as thought-provoking as it is compelling'
MAIL ON SUNDAY

PAY DAY

CELIA WALDEN

SPHERE

SPHERE

First published in Great Britain in 2021 by Sphere
This paperback edition published by Sphere in 2022

1 3 5 7 9 10 8 6 4 2

A CIP catalogue record for this book
is available from the British Library.

ISBN 978-0-7515-8315-1

Typeset in Minion by M Rules
Printed and bound in Great Britain by
Clays Ltd, Elcograf S.p.A.

Papers used by Sphere are from well-managed forests
and other responsible sources.

Sphere
An imprint of
Little, Brown Book Group
Carmelite House
50 Victoria Embankment
London EC4Y 0DZ

An Hachette UK Company
www.hachette.co.uk

www.littlebrown.co.uk

For Ed Victor

Richard and Judy tell us why they love
***Payday* by Celia Walden**

Richard writes:

This is stirring stuff for any woman who's ever had the misfortune to work for a nasty, abusive, bullying, throughgoing b****** of a male boss. And almost at once it begs the question: 'What would YOU do?' Indeed. Moving beyond the normal revenge fantasies most would legitimately enjoy after yet another day working for such a vile man, Celia Walden moves into the enticing possibilities of direct action. Or, put more accurately, the sweet satisfaction of revenge.

We know the outcome from chapter one – the hated boss in question is found on a building site, impaled on iron railings, a brutally sharp spike running directly through his stomach. But how did it happen? Why did it happen? Was it suicide? And if not, who is responsible?

Richard

Judy writes:

Three women working at the same company have one thing in common. They all loathe their boss, Jamie Lawrence. He is superficially attractive. 'Pretty-boy looks, still there beneath the extra stone he now carried around his jowls and waist . . . the height from which he inclined his head to hold your gaze that bit too long . . . that marauding smile that made you feel lucky to be in on the joke with him.'

But, without giving any plot spoilers, those three women have very powerful but separate reasons to want to punish Jamie. At an office party they pool their experiences and make a pact: together they will find a way to make him pay for the shameful way he has treated them.

But those plans begin to spiral out of control. And then Jamie is found dead. What happened? You'll enjoy finding out – and stand by for a terrific twist!

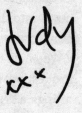

PROLOGUE

'You forgot the brown sauce again.' Terry inspected his bacon roll, sighed and took a bite. 'These have to be done by the end of the day.' Indicating the adjacent pallet of concrete blocks, he eyed his crew without much hope. 'Hey.'

But they were assembled around an iPhone, watching one of their YouTube clips.

'Come on. Where's the mixer? Let's get going.'

Picking his way around the piles of bricks and timber, Terry trudged to the back of the site. There in the corner, in the shadow of the vast disused building the site backed on to, lay his mixer.

'Useless wankers,' he muttered. Then he saw the man.

Terry took in his suit – 'poncy', his wife would have called it – his shoes – the kind of suede loafers those braying Chelsea lads wore, but distinctive for the gold chain links across the tops – and the iron railings that he was impaled upon. Bread and bacon paste flew from his mouth. 'Steve,' he heard himself say, registering the flower of flesh pushed out by the railing running through the man's abdomen. And then in a holler that sounded shrill, feminine: 'Steve!'

By the time his foreman reached him, Terry was patting down the pockets of his hoodie. 'Your phone, mate,' he managed, without taking his eyes off the body.

And when all Steve could do was repeat 'Fuck me. Fuck me,' Terry took it from him and dialled 999.

Only after telling the impassive voice on the phone, 'There's a dead guy on our building site', after running his eyes from the corpse on the spikes up the full height of the blank façade behind, after realising and telling the operator, 'He must've fallen' – only then did Terry see the man's foot twitch.

CHAPTER 1

JILL

ick up, pick up, pick up.

Sitting in her driveway in a blouse, work skirt and fleece-lined slippers, Jill stared at the single letter on her iPhone screen. 'A'. The initial felt like an admission of guilt. As her employee it would have been natural for Alex to figure in her scroll of contacts, professional and personal. Only nothing about Jill's connection to 'A' was legitimate, let alone justifiable – and as of half an hour ago, she had everything to hide.

Welcome to the O2 messaging service. The person you are calling is unable to take your call.

People don't tell you that chaos has a sound: a churning,

3

crashing, intravenous beat. And it's deafening. They don't tell you that once you've invited that white noise into your life, there's no way of turning it off.

Terminating the call – leaving a message was too risky, and with the four previous attempts to reach Alex, Jill had already taken the precaution to hide her caller ID – she slumped forward to rest her forehead on the steering wheel, forcing herself to breathe. In, out; in, out – slowly now, slowly. Each exhalation misted up the winged chrome logo at the centre of the wheel, and she watched it dissipate in hazy patches before breathing out once more.

The police said they'd be in touch. That was what Paul had said. It could be hours. Or it could be minutes. And she couldn't have that conversation without having spoken to Alex.

'Where *are* you?' Out loud, the words were startling. Imperious. And she wondered what the neighbours would think if they saw her sitting in her car, talking to herself. She wondered whether Stan, inside, had noticed her absence yet, and how much a human being could withstand before, like an overloaded electrical system, they cut out.

The buzz of her phone brought her to, but it was only another message from Paul. *It's on the news.* With fumbling fingers she slotted the key into the ignition, switched on the radio and sat numbly through an amped-up exchange between an LBC presenter and a vegan campaigner before, finally, they cut to the news. Jamie was third on the bill. Only he was no longer Jamie, but 'a forty-six-year-old man, found impaled on railings on a north-west London building site'.

It was only a matter of time before the office found out that the dead man was their boss, and as a reporter 'at the scene' delivered details she could never unhear, Jill pictured the news spreading in startled cries and wild, unpunctuated emails from desk to desk. She saw hands clamped across mouths, tears of disbelief: mayhem. As Jamie's partners, it was up to her and Paul to make an announcement; 'manage' the fallout. But going into work was also unthinkable – until she'd spoken to Alex. Then there was Nicole.

Her colleague's name wasn't disguised by an initial, although it should have been, and the sight of it on her phone screen made Jill feel no less toxic. Her own name would have a similar effect on these two women, she realised. They were bound by that, now.

You've reached Nicole Harper. I can't come to the phone right now, but you know what to do . . .

That both women were going to voicemail, despite repeated attempts, wasn't right. But then none of this was right, and what could Jill do, but try, try, try again?

'Hello?'

Nicole's voice sounded artificially bright, as though put on for her benefit. Then Jill remembered her withheld number. 'It's . . . ' She cleared her throat. 'It's Jill.'

'One sec.' A party blower blared in the background, followed by a discordant jumble of childish joy. 'Sorry, who?' She heard the jingle of a door swinging shut, all jollity sealed off behind it.

'It's Jill.' She closed her eyes.

'Sorry, I'm at a kids' party with my daughter – they're about to bring the cake out. Can I call you back?'

'No.' She had to stop Nicole talking and make her listen. 'Jamie's dead. They found him this morning. The police want to talk to me. They'll want to talk to you, too.' The words came out in a rush. 'And Nicole –' she heard her own voice dip down '– I can't get hold of Alex.'

There was a muffled clunk at the other end of the line, followed by silence. Then another clunk, and a whisper: 'How?'

'They don't know yet. He was found by the Vale Theatre early this morning. There's a building site behind—'

'He was at the theatre?'

The change of tone made Jill sit up straight. It wasn't just alarm, but recognition.

'If you know something . . .'

At the end of the line Nicole let out a faint moan. Then there was a choking noise. And as Jill waited she saw her own slippered foot tapping impatiently by the pedals. There wasn't time for this.

'We've got to find Alex.'

Silence.

'Nicole, are you there?'

'The theatre . . . there's this little glass hut on the roof . . .'

The rap of knuckles against glass made Jill jump, every synapse now on high alert, every word Nicole was saying drowned out, and she looked up to see Stan's face peering in at her.

CHAPTER 2

~✦~

ALEX

Three Months Earlier

The pink onesie had been a mistake. So had taking the bus. When she'd left the flat half an hour ago, Katie strapped to her chest, Alex had felt passable: soft dough of stomach and thighs reined in by the maternity jeans she could no longer envisage living without; engorged breasts disguised by a floaty blue top bought especially. Katie had looked pretty and pristine in her striped onesie too – until they'd reached Hammersmith Broadway, where she'd thrown up over them both.

By the time Alex had found the public toilets, scored her bag for a 50p coin she didn't have and waited in line behind two Italian teenagers counting out their change in

Tesco Metro, much of the excitement she'd woken up with had evaporated.

It had been building for over a week, that excitement, ever since Jamie's email had come in. Because although her boss had kept it brief – 'You thinking of popping by with the new addition? Good to catch up sooner rather than later' – Alex had always been able to read between his lines.

The maternity cover wasn't working out. She'd guessed Ashley wouldn't last the course by the end of their handover session. It wasn't so much that she was too young and had started a couple of their email exchanges with 'Hey!', as the pre-emptive corner-cutting. Alex had never understood that 'what's the least amount of work I can get away with?' mentality. And before you were even in the job! Where was the pride? The quiet satisfaction of knowing that you had every eventuality covered, so that when your boss forgot the file or figure, you could produce it. When, ever anxious to please the client, he double-booked himself in a meeting – 'Thursday morning it is!' – you were the one to correct him: 'Actually, Jamie, Thursday a.m. won't work, but we could find a window that afternoon?' There was power in that moment: in being the gatekeeper of Jamie's calendar and anticipating his needs so efficiently that he would be lost without her.

Not that Ashley would have understood any of that. And on the day of that handover meeting, after a few too many questions like 'Do I really have to answer every email within an hour, like you said in your handover file?' (Answer: 'Yes – every email needs to be acknowledged within the hour, even if a full response can't be given until a later date.') And: 'When are we actually off? You know, no longer expected to be reachable on the phone after work?'

(Answer: 'Never – even when Jamie was on a two-week break in the Maldives I was answering his calls past ten at night, scanning and sending documents and retrieving his wife's online shopping from their local Parcelforce depot.') Alex had swivelled her chair around to face her cover and asked a question of her own.

'Do you want this job?'

The girl retracted her chin into her neck, taken aback by the tone of this woman she'd assumed would be complicit in her skimping.

'Course I do. I mean it's a stopgap for me, you know? What with you only planning to take six months' maternity – least that's what Jamie told me. But maybe he was—'

Alex had cut her off there. Yes, she was only planning to take six months. Why was everyone so convinced that women would change their minds and either take the full year or not come back at all? And there had been judgement in that twenty-three-year-old girl's eyes, she was sure of it. Based on what? The kind of smug schoolgirl certainties you could still hold on to at that age. That when you met someone you liked, which you would, he would like you back. That you'd both be ready for marriage and children at the same time, and that when you had those children, you'd feel the way a new mum should.

After the turmoil of the past few months Alex didn't have many certainties left. But she was sure of one thing: when Jamie asked her to come back to work early (and he wouldn't ask, she knew, so much as 'suggest' it, with a contrite expression and a little speech about him 'fully appreciating what a special time this is, but . . . ') she would say yes. Yes to having a reason to get dressed in the morning. Yes to structured days. Yes to being needed for something she knew she excelled at, being back on full pay, and having the weight of her mum's loan lifted sooner than it had to be. Not that she was going to say as much to Jamie, who would appreciate the sacrifice that little bit more if she told him she needed a few days to think it over. And as Alex turned on to Black's Road and saw BWL's blue mirrored façade rising up before her, she felt some of her earlier excitement return.

'Ready to see where Mummy works?' she murmured into the silken muss of her daughter's hair. 'I think you're going to like it. And I know you're going to love Mummy's boss.'

Five days a week for just under a year she'd pushed through the revolving doors of BWL's bright white atrium, latte in hand. And the memory of that one free hand – a hand with which she could open doors, wave hello to Lydia at reception, brush the hair out of her face, reach for a travel card, hitch up trousers or scratch an itch – highlighted everything Alex had lost in motherhood. She would never be carefree or just plain free again, and the thought of that made her want to do another half lap in the revolving doors and go straight home. But Alex had watched enough new mums parade through BWL – look what I made! – to know what she was supposed to do, and although most waited until the baby was at least four or five months, she was aware that today wasn't really about Katie. In any case, Lydia had already seen her.

'Oh, oh, oh . . .' Ignoring the ringing phones, her colleague ducked out from behind the curved walnut reception desk inscribed with BWL's ubiquitous motto – 'History. Heritage. Preserved' – one hand clamped to her mouth. 'I can't bear it.' A clicking of heels on marble as she trotted over. 'Is this . . . little Katie? Yes it is! It is!'

Before having her, Alex had found the wide eyes, baby voices and constant repetition funny. Now she just found it annoying. But she was pleased to see a friendly face and anxious to show her daughter off the way the others had.

'Course she puked on the way here. It's the excitement of seeing where Mummy works, isn't it, Katie?'

'I just want to eat her,' Lydia threaded a finger through her daughter's curled fist. 'And you, lovely, how are you doing?'

'Well I'm not getting much sleep. This one's got her mum's appetite, that's for sure. And quite the pair of lungs. But we're doing OK, aren't we?'

Lydia's head was slanted to one side now: a mix of pity and curiosity in her eyes.

'Still, hard doing it all on your own? Although I bet your mum and dad are all over her.'

'*All* over her.'

Alex was used to the jolts of sadness these casual assumptions prompted, and had long ago decided that it was easier to play along than try to explain why her parents were not like other people's.

'Maya came in with little Elsa the other day, who must be what . . . almost exactly the same age? Two months?'

'Three.'

Alex had yet to meet her boss's wife, but on a couple of occasions during the course of their simultaneous pregnancies the two women had commiserated over morning sickness and swollen ankles on the phone.

'Thought it was close. Anyway, Maya said little Elsa's been good as gold, and already sleeping six hour stretches at night.'

'Great.'

'Sorry! If it makes you feel any better, she also said she'd forgotten how hard it all was. And with Jamie doing such long hours here ...'

'No change there. He must be thrilled, though?'

As she said it, Alex remember how ardently her boss had wanted a boy.

'To be honest I think he was a bit ...'

'Disappointed? He'll get over it. We girls aren't so bad.'

'Too right! And if I know Jamie, he'll already be planning a third.'

Lydia rolled her eyes but couldn't suppress the small smile that often accompanied the mention of Jamie's name by a certain kind of woman. 'You should've seen him and Hayden down at the Firkin last week. They were three pints in and ...'

Lydia stopped short, wincing at her own tactlessness.

'Sorry Alex, I didn't mean to make you feel ... I didn't want to sound disloyal.' With a shake of the head, she moved on. 'Hayden knows, does he, that you're coming in today?'

'He does and he's conveniently "out at a meeting".' Alex was trying her best to keep the bitterness out of her voice. 'So today won't be the day Katie gets to meet her dad.'

Lydia stared.

'Hayden hasn't met her yet?'

'Nope.' Alex kissed her daughter's head in reassurance. *You're never going to be made to feel like I did.* 'He's made it pretty clear he doesn't want to be involved.'

'But he's her dad!'

Alex debated telling her that even this was in dispute, the idea of confiding in someone, anyone, after what felt like months of conversations with herself, being more appealing than anything she could think of. But this wasn't the time.

'And Al – you two are going to be working in the same office: he can hardly pretend you don't exist.'

'I know, I know.'

She was keen to extricate herself now, climb onto the escalator beckoning her upwards beyond the security gates and have the conversation she was here to have. Sensing this, Lydia handed her a visitor's pass that felt absurd dangling from her neck, and zapped her through.

'You'll give me a bell when you're ready for a few G&Ts, won't you? Oh – and you've got Joyce's leaving bash in the diary? Week after next?'

Up on the top floor, heads were down, low-level phone conversations were being had, and meetings were taking place in glass boxes. Alex wasn't sure what she'd expected, but it wasn't this sense of invisibility in a community she'd been such an integral part of just a few months earlier.

She'd walked out of this place on a high: with a gift hamper of organic baby products and a 'Mum To Be' helium balloon. And maybe that was it: the pregnancy had made Alex feel remarkable for the first time in her life. UPS men, coffee baristas, clients, even partners like Jill and Paul had noticed her once she started showing, asking when she was due, what she was having and how she was feeling. But Alex was starting to understand that whereas pregnancy made you remarkable, motherhood rendered you invisible. And as she scoured the office floor for any of her office friends and colleagues, she felt a few glances rest briefly and incuriously upon her before moving on.

Sat at her desk – a desk that Alex had always kept free of personal clutter but was now overrun with tubes of cosmetics, miniature cacti, magazines and a small teddy bear wearing a heart-shaped bib with 'Just For You' scrawled across it – was Ashley. And Alex was working out how to greet a woman who was her replacement when Katie revved up into a full-scale wail, solving the problem for her.

Within minutes she was surrounded by women, with Joyce – at sixty-five the longest-serving member of staff by decades – jiggling Katie up and down in an attempt to stop the crying.

'Where's Jamie?' Alex managed over the noise.

'He's just finishing up a meeting with the Energy and Sustainability team,' cut in Ashley.

Alex looked over at the main conference room. Her boss's broad back was just visible through the glass, where he was talking to the company's special projects supervisor, Nicole. 'I don't want to bother him. I can always wait . . . or come back.'

'Don't be silly,' Joyce tutted. 'He'll be done in a sec.'

'I know he can't wait to meet this one!' Ashley again, smiling up at Katie from her chair.

Although Alex forced herself to smile back, she couldn't help noticing how full her cover's in-tray was. On the desk partition behind it, a photo booth collage had been assembled, every strip a palette swatch of light to dark blondes, every face leaning in towards the camera with a Spice Girl snarl. How had this girl lasted as long as she had? Alex wondered – before immediately feeling guilty at the thought. OK, so Ashley wasn't exactly vying for employee of the year, but she clearly had no idea her days were numbered, or she wouldn't have turned her desk into her bedroom. Knowing Jamie, it might even fall to Alex to do the deed . . .

'I like the teddy,' Alex volunteered. 'Seriously, though, if it's better for me to come back in a bit . . . ?'

'You're not going anywhere.' Balancing Katie on one arm like the grandmother of four that she was, Joyce bashed out three numbers on the nearest phone. 'Jamie, dearest, we have ourselves a visitor. Two, actually.' A wink. 'Well, one and a half.'

Whatever Jamie said in response made Joyce laugh in an uncharacteristically girlish way, reminding Alex that Jamie's appeal was always broader than she imagined. Was it his pretty-boy looks, still there beneath the extra stone he now carried around his jowls and waist? The height from which he inclined his head to hold your gaze that bit too long? The marauding smile that made you feel lucky to be in on the joke with him. Alex wasn't sure. But she'd seen everyone from Botoxed businesswomen to chippy millennials get giggly after a few minutes with Jamie.

For her, at least, her boss's appeal had always been clear: Jamie saw you. Which sounded stupid, but over the years Alex had worked for men and women who managed to spend eight hours a day looking over and to either side of her. And from the moment Jamie had beckoned Alex into his office for an interview just over a year ago, she'd felt more substantial: a real person with opinions and stories worth listening to.

'Al!' Here he was now, slow-motion jogging across the floor towards her. Out of the corner of her eye Alex saw women's bodies straighten and fingers comb through hair. 'Look at you. And look at *you!*'

Peering down at Katie, still in Joyce's arms, Jamie pulled a goofy face.

'Want a cuddle?'

'Thought you'd never ask.'

'Not me, silly – Katie!' Alex laughed, and it felt good to have slipped back into their old banter.

Jamie held up his hands, regretful.

'Best not – been shaking hands with developers all morning. And we know what a grubby bunch that lot are. There isn't enough hand sanitiser in the world. But Al, she's so tiny! How much did she weigh? Elsa's a great big lump.'

'Five pounds, seven ounces – so yeah, on the small side. Elsa looks such a sweetie, Jamie. So blonde! Congrats.'

They nodded at one another, both conscious that baby talk could only be extended so long – and that this wasn't the real reason Alex was here.

'How's Maya getting on?'

'Great, great . . . you know. It's easier second time around.'

Joyce had somehow managed to stem Katie's tears, and as all three gazed down at her gurgling daughter Alex felt the knot of tension in her stomach relax for the first time that day.

'She really is gorgeous, Al. Nicely done.'

Glancing down at the pale circle of skin on his right wrist where his watch had once been – a TAG Heuer anniversary present from his wife that had caused them both a few sleepless nights when he lost it – Jamie motioned towards his office with his chin. 'Want to pop in here for a quick chat?'

'Sure.'

Alex was struggling not to smile. The whole thing was so transparent. They could have had this conversation on the phone, without poor Ashley peering in at them from her desk and fearing the worst. But she couldn't lie: the idea of Jamie feeling nervous about their meeting, maybe even rehearsing the speech that might entice her back – that part Alex was enjoying. With a mouthed 'thank you' she took Katie back in her arms.

But Jamie wasn't moving. 'Do you want to –' he scratched at the back of his head, eyes on Katie '– maybe leave her with Joyce?'

'Don't worry.'

'Really? Might be easier if . . . '

'Jamie!' Alex laughed, starting towards his office. 'Relax, she'll be fine.'

The last time she'd sat in here, on the anthracite Roche Bobois sofa that was her boss's pride and joy, Alex had been feeling a different kind of nervy. Worried about breaking the news of her pregnancy to Jamie and pleased for the first time in her life to have the extra weight to hide behind, she'd left it later than she should have to tell him. But on a quiet Wednesday afternoon at just over five months gone, Alex had blurted it out as he was dictating a portfolio report. It had been an accident, she'd stammered, conscious as she did so both that this was too much information and that it wasn't entirely true. And even though she hadn't planned to end up a single mum at twenty-nine, Alex had assured Jamie, she was planning to get good childcare sorted early on and be back at work as soon as possible. Her only mistake had been assuming that Jamie already knew, from either Hayden or the office grapevine, the identity of the father.

'Hayden?' A flash of something between amused incredulity and annoyance. 'Our Hayden?'

It had come across as 'my mate Hayden'. 'Sorry. I thought you knew.'

Jamie's smile was tight. 'Because?'

'Well, I know you two are ... close.' Picking at the varnish on her thumbnail, Alex had pushed on. 'And people, I mean – well they seem to know about us. Although I did try and—'

'Great.' Jamie had sat back hard in his chair. 'Well in answer to your question: no, I didn't know.'

Alex had been taken aback by her boss's reaction before remembering how much he hated being kept out of the loop on anything BWL-related.

'When I say "people", I don't mean it's—'

'Honestly, I'm just surprised you waited this long to tell me.' He'd cut her off. 'You say you're five months?'

As his eyes had dropped down to her belly, Alex stifled the shades of shame she felt, as though they'd been zapped back a century and she were some loose woman bringing them all into disrepute.

'Yes. A little over.'

'And Hayden – how does he feel about this?'

'We're not actually ... together.'

Alex was aware that men didn't tend to discuss their personal lives in the forensic way women did but couldn't help feeling a little stung that Hayden hadn't even mentioned their relationship – or its demise – in passing. 'But listen, if you're worried about any weirdness in the office, please don't be. We're both grown-ups, and it won't affect my work in any way moving forward, Jamie. I can promise you that. I love this job,' she'd ended, breathless at this point. 'And I hope you know that I'll always go above and beyond for you.'

After a slight pause, Jamie had been quick to reassure her that he did ('everyone knows you're a machine, Al – and you know I'd be lost without you'). He'd seemed surprised but relieved too that she had her return date already worked out, and grateful when the handover came that Alex had been as thorough as she had. And yet despite the comprehensive file she'd put together and the full afternoon she'd insisted on spending with Ashley, she had left unconvinced her cover was anywhere near as adept at the software BWL relied upon as she should be. Which seemed as good a place as any to start their conversation today: Jamie looked like he needed a little prompting.

'Listen, I meant it when I said that I was around to help with anything Ashley didn't quite get, Jamie. I know she was struggling a bit with the intranet.'

'Alex,' Jamie cut in, passing a hand over his forehead. 'The problem isn't Ashley. The problem's you.'

Hoisting Katie to her shoulder, Alex began to rub her daughter's back. There had been no signs of gassiness, but Alex was aware of a pressing need to do something with her hands – pretend, at least, that all peripheral sight and hearing hadn't been blocked out, with only the words Jamie's lips were forming in her tunnel line of vision. And a memory chimed somewhere deep within her. Bad news, life-changing news, delivered oh so matter-of-factly by a man: you always guessed it a millisecond before – just as she guessed it now.

'Alex, we're going to have to let you go.'

CHAPTER 3

JILL

'What do you mean they went in an hour ago?'

'Mr Ho got here early,' Joyce explained. 'Jamie thought rather than make him wait, they'd get going.'

'Right.'

It wasn't uncommon for Jill's PA to have a whole conversation without once taking her eyes off her screen, but something in the tightness of her boss's tone made Joyce glance up.

'Sorry. I tried to call you, but your phone was off.'

'I was at the hospital.'

'I know. And I told Jamie you'd probably rather he waited – but when I couldn't get hold of you . . .'

'Of course.' Jill fingered a surveyor's report on Joyce's desk. 'I did remind Jamie's temp yesterday that I wouldn't be in until just before the meeting.'

'Hmm.'

'What's her name again?'

'Ashley? She's just been made permanent. You know –
with Alex gone.'

A burst of laughter from inside the conference room,
where Jamie was gesticulating in front of the scale model
of the Lots Road Hotel Jill had spent the past fortnight
working on with their model maker in preparation for
today's meeting.

It wasn't easy to get a smile out of those Malaysian
businessmen. In all the years Mr Ho had been her client,
Jill could only remember a couple of real 'eyes and teeth'
moments when a long, drawn-out deal had finally been
rubber-stamped. But whatever Jamie was joking about now
had Ho and his colleagues all lit up, nudging and repeating
the punchline to one another. Even Paul – sitting back as he
watched his charismatic partner do what he did best – was
laughing, somehow still enjoying a show he must have sat
through a thousand times.

That was the thing about Jamie: he was a performer.
Alongside his rare ability to connect with anyone from any
social class or walk of life, this was the reason she and Stan
had brought him in as a cocky thirty-something looking to
move from corporate property to something 'meatier': his
word – and one with predatory undertones she'd been worried by at first. But the projects of architectural significance
she and Stan had set the company up to protect were dense
with history and culture – so yes, something to sink one's
teeth into. And when her husband had decided to retire,
they'd both known that there was only one man capable of
filling his shoes.

'Listen, I might catch the end of it. Mr Ho will be wondering why I'm not there.'

It was as though she were asking her PA's permission. And Joyce, back to her typing, just nodded, leaving Jill to wonder at the tentative quality of her statement – and the fact that she still wasn't making any kind of move in the direction of the conference room.

In the three years Jamie's name had sat alongside hers and Paul's on marble walls and stationery, software and presentation screens, they'd never had cause to regret their decision, she thought, eyes back on the protégé who had long outgrown any need for his mentor. Oh to have that energy! Jill had always been confident, vibrant even when she needed to turn that side of herself on for a boardroom full of people, without once suffering from the 'impostor syndrome' so many women whined about. But Jamie's capacity to buoy up clients into making ambitious, expensive and sometimes reckless decisions – she'd never had that. Not in her twenties or thirties and certainly not now, when what little life force she'd managed to claw back post-menopause had plummeted after Stan's diagnosis. And if anybody in that room had been expecting her, she was forced to concede, they weren't any longer.

Never mind that she was the one who had persuaded the Malaysian conglomerate to sell the power station in the first place. Or that it was thanks to her that Mr Ho had sold his Chelsea barracks for a little less than twice the asking price five years ago. Now that she'd lined it all up, maybe it was natural, right, that Jamie should be doing what he did best and whetting her client's taste buds with a smorgasbord of prospective buyers.

'Jill?'

'Yes?'

'Can I take your ... ?'

Following Joyce's eyeline, Jill realised that she was still in her summer trench coat, handbag hanging from an inner elbow. In a series of brisk movements, she shrugged both off and handed them to her PA.

'Thanks.'

But now that she'd decided it might be better to miss the meeting than go into that conference room and be forced to play catch-up, she resented that decision. 'Better' really meant 'less humiliating', and the impotence she felt looking in at those men in their glass box from the outside was horribly familiar. It brought back memories of identical scenes decades earlier, when – in cheaper suits and with naturally blonde hair – she'd regularly been made to feel insignificant: surplus to requirements.

'Joyce?'

'Hmm?'

'What *did* happen with Jamie's PA? He didn't go into it.'

'Alex? I didn't even know you could do that: sack someone on maternity leave. I get that what she did was wrong—'

'Because ... ?'

'Sorry.' Her PA bashed out one last sentence, pressed 'return' and turned towards her. 'So yes, apparently she'd got Jamie to sign off on a due diligence file without all the documentation in place. Key things like the solicitor's confirmation on money laundering checks were missing. Which would be unthinkable at the best of times – but when your buyer is some Georgian developer we've never done business with before ...'

'That Khalvashi man,' Jill murmured.

'It could have blown up big time if Paul hadn't clocked it.'

Jill had her post in her hand and could have been in her office opening it and starting on her morning calls, but she felt a curious inability to do either.

'What's weird is that Alex was great. Way more efficient than the previous one.' Joyce frowned back down at her screen. 'Maybe it was "pregnancy brain", as Jamie said.'

'He shouldn't be saying stuff like that. And is it even really a thing? I'm not best placed to say.'

'You can get a bit foggy,' her PA chuckled. 'But the way men go on about it, you'd think we all get lobotomised the moment we conceive.' She paused, frowning. 'I was a bit surprised. He'll be hard pushed to find someone as meticulous as Alex. She'd drive all the Addison Lee drivers bonkers, asking them to call her as soon as Jamie was "on board" so that she could text whoever was expecting his arrival-time updates – as though he were the PM or something.'

'Bet he loved that.'

Papers were being gathered in the conference room and files closed, indicating a near end to the meeting. The Malaysians were standing now and dipping down into their little bows. 'She never really crossed my radar – except that whole business with Hayden. That went around the office, didn't it?' Jill dropped her voice. 'I've got to say: I know I'm a geriatric – but casually getting pregnant by a co-worker?'

'Don't say it would never have happened in our day.'

'Well, would it?'

Joyce stopped typing long enough to throw her boss a

disbelieving look. 'Pretty sure that's always happened at office parties the world over.'

'And it happened at our do?'

'BWL's fortieth – least that's what I heard.'

'God. I used to be the first to know these things. When did I get so out of the loop?'

The answer hung there, unspoken: *when your husband got cancer.*

Jill ran a hand through her hair. She'd always felt proud of how few greys she had, even as her sixtieth approached. But over the past few months she'd seen and felt the colour and texture change, and with everything she and Stan were going through, it felt like a spiteful little twist of the knife on the part of Mother Nature.

'I feel grim,' Jill murmured, more to herself than Joyce. 'Need to wipe the hospital off myself. Can you do me a favour and—'

'Americano and an apricot Danish?'

'You're a lifesaver.' Jill smiled. 'How am I going to manage without you?'

'Don't. All these years I've been dreaming of this moment and now the thought of ticking the "retired" box on forms makes me want to cry. Never mind you – what am *I* going to do all day?'

Jill shook her head. 'Post pictures of the grandchildren on Facebook—?'

Male voices drowned out the end of her sentence, and as everyone began to file out of the conference room, Jill smoothed down the Jaeger skirt that she'd bought in every colour – something she did once every couple of years with office staples – and strode towards the group of men.

'Mrs Barnes.'

'Mr Ho. Good to see you, and so sorry I couldn't join you. I hope Mr Lawrence here explained that I got held up.'

'It's really no problem. We've got a whole marketing strategy sorted – isn't that right? And Mr Lawrence here seems confident that he'll be able to get us a sale by June.'

'That's in three weeks.'

'He says it's doable.' Reaching up, Mr Ho rested a hand lightly on Jamie's back. 'And Mrs Barnes, I hope you'll send your husband my very best. I had no idea he'd been so unwell.'

Jill's smile froze.

'My brother went through the same thing.' He nodded sympathetically. 'He came through it, but, well ... prostate: one of the worst.'

As Mr Ho took her hand in his, Jill felt the rage rise up and block her windpipe. One thing – one thing stoic, undemanding Stan had asked for from the start: 'You'll make sure none of the clients ever find out, won't you, love? I know the partners will have to, and the office top tier – but having anyone else know, all the clients I've worked with over the years ... well, I don't think I could stand it.'

'Thank you,' she managed.

'I'm surprised you're here now,' Ho went on. 'I hope you didn't come in especially, Jill, for me?'

'Oh I'm still very much—'

'Because Jamie tells me you've been spending as much time as possible at home, which is where you should be. Not here in the office. And I'm being taken care of by this good man here.' Smiling, he nodded in Jamie's direction. 'But do give Mr Barnes all our very best wishes for his recovery.'

With another little bow, her client started in the direction of the lift, flanked by Jamie.

'Mr Ho ...' A horror of the kind of women who were forced to trot to keep up with men meant that Jill always kept her heel height to two inches or lower, and yet the two men were walking so fast that she was struggling to keep up. 'Whilst I'm confident Lots Road will appeal to a good many of our buyers, we've still got a few hurdles before we can even start showing – the hurdles I pointed out to you earlier in the year. So when we say June ...'

'I know. But Mr Lawrence here says they will be biting ...' Swivelling on the heels of his tiny, shiny brogues, Mr Ho turned to Jamie.

'Biting your hand off. They will, Mr Ho. They will.'

'Jamie's thinking, as you people say, "outside the box". We like that. I'm told by my friends at the Hong Kong office that he's a bit of a rising star.'

'Rising?' Jamie made a face.

'Risen!' Mr Ho laughed. 'Risen, Mr Lawrence ...'

'Jamie.'

'Jamie – let's keep in close touch.'

As the little troop of men in neat, identikit suits filed into the lift and disappeared from view, Jill headed back across the floor to her office, where Joyce was already waiting with her forgotten post and handbag. But before starting on their decades-old ritual of confirming the day's schedule, Joyce paused, pressing her lips together.

'What?'

Joyce blinked: 'I didn't know Stan was OK with clients knowing.'

Without taking her eyes off Jamie's self-congratulatory

back, without bothering to mask an emotion that had been muddied until today, when it had become crystal clear to Jill that her partner wasn't just insensitive but deliberately undermining her, she murmured: 'He's not.'

CHAPTER 4

NICOLE

'The mouldings. I mean look at those mouldings!'

In the pause following a client's exclamation of awe Nicole had learned to stay silent. Let them revel in the sun tunnels, roof-lights or Juliet balconies. Don't break the spell with your waffle. Not that Rupert Jones was your typical client. She was willing to bet he knew more about the finer points of neoclassical architecture than she did.

Brutalism was her thing: to Nicole its clean, egalitarian lines weren't just more in line with her politics but rousing on a deeper level, whereas the Vale Theatre – however awe-inspiring in its faded grandeur – somehow failed to reach her senses. And by the end of the minute she and Rupert had stood staring silently up at the theatre's ceiling, the swirling trellis of fruit, foliage and flowers had begun to seem faintly ridiculous.

'Obviously there's some restoration needed,' Nicole ventured. 'But if you picture this as the central atrium and maybe imagine a bar here and another one there ... '

The three money men Rupert had brought with him were nodding, but it was the billionaire in jeans and scuffed Converse she cared about.

'It's certainly way more workable than I thought it would be,' said her client eventually. 'And Jamie tells me that in principle the council doesn't seem to have an issue with it being turned into a members' club?'

'Apparently not. I know he looked into it before we got in touch.'

There was so much more to show and tell Rupert about the property. Nicole was particularly proud of the architectural peculiarity she'd found buried in Historic England's dense report.

Up on the roof of the Vale theatre, invisible to all but passing birds and planes, was a small octagonal glass dome that had once allowed in additional light before being concealed by a trapdoor in the heavens at a later date. The structure was present in only a handful of historical buildings across the country, and Nicole had found it so fascinating that a week earlier she had braved the Jacob's ladder leading up above the stage to the heavens. All alone she had marvelled at the view of north-west London – and the rusty hatches that still opened out onto the roof after all these years. Yet something – perhaps as simple as keeping it her secret a little longer – prevented Nicole from telling Rupert about it now.

'Where is Mr Lawrence, by the way? I thought he was joining us.'

'He is.' Nicole checked her phone.

'Or should we be calling him "Deal Don Lawrence"?'

'You saw the *Property Week* piece.'

'Hard to miss.' Rupert tipped his head back to take in the proscenium's full arch. 'What was it – five, six pages? Not that he didn't deserve it: eighteen-mill sales don't happen as often as they used to. BWL must be pretty chuffed with their golden boy.'

'They are.' Nicole nodded, feeling as though her smile might crack. 'Anyway, he should be here any minute. So he can fill you in on exactly what discussions have been had with the council.' She paused: less was more with Rupert. 'But you were the first person I thought of when we took on the Vale.'

'Well, you've nailed it in the past. Now are we able to access those boxes?'

Nicole had always enjoyed her dealings with Rupert. She was aware that he had logged her attractiveness, but only in the objective, passing way one does a person's sex or ethnicity – not with a view to profiting from it, like most men. Softly spoken, punctual and polite, the hotelier also wore his success lightly, which was rare in the brittle, competitive world she inhabited, and something Nicole liked to think she would be able to do when she finally got where she wanted to be.

'I'm going to need a coffee,' announced her client once they'd finished the tour. 'Urgently. How about you call Jamie and get him to meet us at Lytton House in ten?' One of Rupert's boutique clubs, she remembered, was just down the road. 'I'll get them to sort some refreshments in the upstairs dining room, if you can tell him to meet us up there?'

As her client gave out instructions down the phone, Nicole

tapped the 'shortcuts' key on hers and watched her thumb hover over 'Jamie', hoping against hope that her boss would pitch up before she had to make the call. Why did he even have to be here today? The theatre was Nicole's project.

'All good?' Rupert raised an eyebrow at her and, reluctantly, Nicole pressed the little green phone.

'Hell-o?'

Hate shot up like a firework inside her.

'Jamie,' she kept her voice level. 'We're done at the Vale, and Rupert was thinking we could meet at Lytton House to run through the details.' Nicole threw her client a smile. 'The man needs caffeine.'

'Sure. In traffic but should be with you in twenty.'

Jamie made it in less than that, pushing through the double dining room doors with a whole host of explanations nobody could care less about – least of all her client, surely? And yet there they both were, immediately engrossed in their London traffic woes. *You're not stuck in traffic, you* are *traffic*. Nicole dug a nail into her thigh beneath the table, waiting for it.

'Well you know what they say,' Jamie concluded with a click of the tongue against the upper palate. '"You're not stuck in traffic, you *are* traffic."'

Boom. Predictable as cancer.

'So the numbers on page five of your prospectus are the ones we're looking at,' she murmured, leaving the pair of them to it and leaning in towards the money men. Two of them began flicking through the pages immediately, but the third and most personable had the good grace to smile first. 'Hope you didn't spend that sunny Sunday working. Hotter than Barbados, they said on the news.'

The weather had been freakish for mid-May, the blossom on the horse chestnuts lining the park pathways as upright as ice-cream cones against the wide bulk of their new foliage. That Sunday had been the warmest day yet. But Nicole had secretly been pleased to have a reason to leave early. They'd been wandering along the busy banks of the Serpentine when Ben had suggested hiring a pedalo. Chloe had been ecstatic, but Nicole couldn't face the queues, disclaimers and hiring of lifejackets. Logistics always seemed to leech the joy out of family outings.

'Mummy's got to head back and do some work now,' she'd crouched down to tell her daughter. 'But why don't you and Daddy go out on one of the little boats, and we'll have a nice supper when you get home?'

Released at last and light headed with freedom, Nicole had walked back fast through the park towards the Bayswater Road, weaving in and out of the families splayed across pavements with their prams, scooters and runaway toddlers, and casting furtive glances at the parents who, unperturbed by the pandemonium, didn't appear to be feigning their enjoyment.

Was she the only one for whom weekend jollity so often felt forced? Did none of those women feel as exhausted at the end of family occasions, both formal and informal, as an actress must after that final curtain call? Then again her mum was always telling Nicole she expected too much. Compromise, she liked to point out, was 'neither giving in nor giving up: just life'. And maybe she was right. But in a career context compromise had no upside, which was another reason why Nicole found her professional life easier to navigate, and why she sometimes felt more comfortable sitting around a table

33

of businessmen like this one than she did opposite Ben at home. Even when Jamie was one of those men.

Although they'd left a seat at the head of the table for Jamie, her boss had chosen to sit across from her and was leaning back in his chair now, one Tom Ford suede loafer-clad foot perched on the opposite knee, the trouser leg ruckled to expose two inches of pale ankle. Nicole tried to avoid looking at him wherever possible, but the bright Britishness of that ankle was like a flare in the muted maroons of the room, willing Nicole to raise her eyes. When she finally did, Jamie was staring straight back at her.

'Nicole has explained all the Vale's Grade II restrictions, I think. Nothing if not thorough, our Nic.' A small smile – intended to what? Embarrass her? Intimidate her? Either way it wasn't expecting a response, which was why she came back with a too bright, 'Thank you Jamie,' adding, 'Listed buildings come up so rarely, even for us, and the history of this one is just mind-blowing.'

'We'll let Rupert read up on all that in his own time,' Jamie cut in, grinning ingratiatingly over at their client.

The tall, arched dining-room windows had magnified the mid-afternoon heat, but whereas the other men had taken off their jackets at the start of the meeting, Jamie had kept his on, and speckles of damp now dotted his light blue shirt-front. As he raised a hand to his neck to loosen his collar, Nicole felt her breathing grow shallow, as though the oxygen supply in the room had been reduced.

You like this? You want more?

Same shirt? Same spattering of spots. Only, the spots had been inches away from her face and his hand raised not to his own throat, but hers.

34

I can feel how much you want it, Nic.

In rams his finger. And it feels like an expletive, the kind that made her hit back with an expletive of her own. Only, when she did, pushing back with all her strength against Jamie's damp chest, he just flipped her easily around, shoving her nose against the conference room wall – fingers still tight around her neck, wedding ring cold against her clavicle.

'Nicole?' A row of male faces were staring over at her, expectant. 'The garden walls?'

'The . . . ?'

'Do we know whether they can be knocked down – or moved?'

'Again, I'm afraid we won't know until the planning authorities get back to us. But we'd certainly hope that might be a possibility.' Her hands were trembling and her cheeks tight. 'Anyway –' she nodded at Rupert '– you'll be the first to know when we get those details.'

Keeping up the chatter for the remainder of the meeting helped Nicole recover a semblance of composure. But as she pointed out facts and figures, never allowing herself to be drowned out by the men or stay silent for too long, she felt Jamie's eyes linger questioningly on her. He'd read her mind, she felt, and enjoyed her discomfort. Now, he was irked by her recovery.

'Right.' Rupert stood and the money men followed. 'We'll pick this up next week once we've got all the details?'

'Absolutely.' Nicole wanted to be the first to reassure him.

As Rupert and his men filed out of the room, Nicole gathered up her papers as quickly as she could. But Jamie, ever the gentleman, had already stationed himself by the door.

'Am I going to see you at Joyce's leaving do on Thursday?' he asked in a low voice, as she approached.

'I'll be there.'

The doorway had been narrowed by Jamie, who stood solid, immovable and smiling to one side of it, arm outstretched, and she hesitated.

'After you.'

Imbued in those two words were so many things: power, primarily, and also challenge, along with a basic schoolboy merriment at the discomfort he was causing. And despite every effort at composure, Nicole felt herself hold her breath as she passed, as though she could somehow shrink into invisibility, and ignore Jamie's thumb – under the pretence of guiding her through – rub lightly, caressingly, up and down her spine.

CHAPTER 5

ALEX

The first glass of rosé had knocked her sideways, and Alex was grateful to have the bar to lean against. From her position in the corner of the pub, she could also keep an eye on the steady flow of BWL arrivals, her pulse quickening and slowing every time the door swung open to reveal someone ... who wasn't Jamie.

'Stop it.' Fresh from her cigarette outside, Lydia had reappeared in a breeze of peppermint tobacco.

'Stop what?'

'He may not even come.'

There was no doubt in either of their minds that 'he' wasn't Hayden, who was safely at a conference in Oxford.

'Jamie'll be here – he loves Joyce.' It was early but Alex guessed the number of people who had come to see off her colleague was already nearing fifty. 'Look at all these people: everyone loves Joyce.'

'OK so he'll probably come,' Lydia grudgingly accepted. 'But the place is rammed. Just stay out of his way.' Eyeing Alex's empty glass, she frowned. 'And careful with that. You know what they say about new mums: it's like being a booze virgin all over again.'

Alex had no intention of avoiding Jamie. And she sure as hell didn't feel like being careful. Energised by an anger she hadn't felt in years, not since that final conversation with her father ('Your mother and I think it's best' – as though asking your sixteen-year-old daughter to move out were regrettable, but nothing personal), she'd had her shoulder-length hair cropped and highlighted that morning, and squeezed herself into her first pair of non-maternity trousers in almost a year.

'You look fab,' Lydia grinned. 'I'm just glad you came.'

'You can't believe I came.'

'That too.' She shook her head. 'I know I keep saying this but, Alex, I'm so sorry – I still can't get my head around it.'

'You and me both. But Lyds, you've kept it to yourself, haven't you? Jamie's agreed to keep it quiet, you know, tell everyone it was my decision. Which I need people to think if I'm going to get another job.'

'Well that was big of him. Dickhead. I wouldn't have blamed you for sitting this one out.'

Alex shrugged. 'I told Joyce I'd be here.'

Which was true. But not why she'd gone to the trouble of weaning Katie onto the bottle just for tonight, booked her daughter her first sitter, spent money she didn't have on a hairstyle that would give her the confidence she'd need, and made the trip from Acton to Ravenscourt Park. No, as fond as she was of Joyce, tonight was about something more important: cornering Jamie, and getting him to make good on his promise.

'You still haven't told me what happened. One minute you're all smiles and off upstairs with little Katie, the next you're coming down that escalator in a right state telling me he –' Lydia didn't bother lowering her voice '– telling me he fucking fired you!'

Alex winced, wishing for the nth time that she hadn't blurted the truth out to her colleague as she'd left the office in tears a fortnight ago.

'You're firing me?'

Jamie hadn't liked that word, either.

'I'm letting you go.'

As Alex had tried to take in what her boss was saying, her first thought had been: this is what that hesitation over her bringing Katie into his office was about. This was why Jamie had wanted her to leave her daughter with Joyce. And while the ramifications of his words tipped into one another like dominoes in her head, she'd kept coming back to that. This was the last time she'd set foot in the office that had become a second home to her: a safe space where she knew that her efficiency, loyalty and discretion were noted and appreciated by all. There would be no more of the client meetings she loved to attend, no more falling asleep to the silent run-through of Jamie's schedule, the following day, in her head. What would she tell people? What would they think of her? And her mother's loan. Jesus, the loan. Without a job there was no way she'd be able to repay her by the end of August, as sworn. But Jamie hadn't wanted to fire her in front of her baby – why? Because of the guilt. Because of the lies. Because none of what he'd said to her in his office that day was true.

'You told me that file could be signed off!'

Alex had been so taken aback by the baldness of those lies that she'd dropped her respectful tone.

'No.' A frown. The twitch of a smile, as though it were awkward, embarrassing really, that she should be questioning this. 'You must have misremembered. And listen, if you got confused … but we're not here to debate how this happened.'

'I know how it happened!' Having what she knew to be true so easily dismissed had made Alex feel as though she were trapped in a nightmare, impotent against some greater force that kept pushing her back. 'I remember because I didn't feel right about it at the time, Jamie – not without the solicitor's checks in place. But no: "I'll sign off on the Khalvashi file," you said. "I'll pop the last few documents in once we have them."'

'Alex.'

'I remember querying that. I remember. And "Don't they call it due diligence for a reason?"' Because wasn't that the whole point of all that international transparency stuff in the papers a while back? So that men like Levan Khalvashi – 'import–export' moguls who were vague about what it was they either imported or exported – had their money vetted before they poured it into the country?

'Alex, I'm as gutted about this as you are. Honestly, it's going to feel like losing my right hand. I won't hold it against you, though. You had a lot on your plate at the time with, um, the pregnancy and so on.' One eye had been drawn to his screen at this point, and his mouse discreetly clicked. Was Jamie checking his emails *as* he was firing her? 'Clearly this was a mistake, and I can see that you feel terrible about it, but you know we've got to be airtight on due diligence. If it hadn't been spotted we could all have been in the shit. And it very nearly wasn't.'

'So are you going to tell me what happened?'

Alex poured herself another glass from the bottle in the cooler on the bar. 'It's an open bar until ten. Drink up.'

'Fine. We don't have to talk about it tonight. But you're not allowed to take off as soon as Jamie gets here.'

Again the door swung open – and Alex held her breath. But it was only a gaggle of women from marketing.

'Alex! You won't take off?'

'I won't.'

Quite the opposite. Alex wasn't leaving this pub until she'd had the conversation she'd been trying to have with Jamie for the past two weeks, only to be fobbed off and put off on the phone and via email by both Jamie and, still more humiliatingly, Ashley. Every time he'd either been 'in a meeting', 'out at a viewing' or, earlier that week when the excuses had clearly run out, 'busy'.

Still, Alex trusted Jamie to have stuck to the agreed line of her leaving BWL to 'spend more time with the baby'. Just as she trusted that there would be 'no mention of this "oversight" on the paperwork, which will simply state that you resigned'. But more than anything she trusted him to deliver on the job he'd promised her. 'I've already bigged you up to a mate at JLL who is looking for a new PA. More than bigged you up. So it's basically just a question of me putting you two in touch so that you can get the formalities out of the way – and sort a start date.' Why did she trust him? Because he knew as well as Alex did that she was being scapegoated. Jamie owed her.

'You remember Danielle, don't you?'

The girls from marketing had joined them at the bar, shrugging off their jackets and helping themselves to wine, and Alex smiled and nodded her hellos.

'You came!'

She didn't like the surprise in Danielle's voice – or the wide eyes.

'Ye-es.'

What she said next, Alex liked still less.

'I'm really sorry about what happened.'

'Sorry?'

'Being let go.' Glancing from Lydia's wide eyes back to Alex, Danielle struggled on. 'And when you were on maternity leave, too. But he'll have a tough job finding anyone as good as you.'

Conscious that the conversation wasn't flowing as it should, Danielle moved away, leaving Alex very still, eyes downcast.

'What the … ?' Lydia squeezed her arm. 'It wasn't me. Alex, I swear I haven't told a soul.'

'I know.'

'You do believe me, don't—'

Alex didn't hear the rest. A burst of shouting and slow handclaps drowned it out.

'He made it!'

'Better late, eh mate?'

'Finally!'
Jamie had arrived.

As the pub filled up, and the hierarchical cliques formed at the start of every office party broke up – partners and department heads falling into easy conversation with everyone from IT personnel to interns – a few more people wandered over to express their regret at Alex's sacking. Not that they used that word. It was mostly 'let go', and one 'moved on', which made Alex feel as though she'd died. And as the extent of Jamie's treachery became clear, she felt her anger raise her up into a quasi-levitating state. Jamie hadn't expected her to turn up any more than anyone else had; he'd assumed they'd safely seen the back of her.

But she needed to calm down before she made her approach. All that mattered now was that JLL job. So as Jamie finally took off the stupid padded Patagonia 'power vest' she'd had to order in from Mr Porter after he'd seen Jeff Bezos wearing one – four hundred quid for something you'd find for forty at Snow+Rock – as he drank, laughed and flirted away on the other side of the room, Alex tried to lose herself in small talk, showing the pictures of Katie when asked, smiling in response to the cooing, and assuring concerned faces that she actually already had 'another job lined up' – all the while keeping one eye on Jamie. Until she couldn't any longer.

'Back in a sec, Lyds.'

Ignoring her colleague's worried glance, Alex began to thread her way in a purposeful diagonal through the crowd towards Jamie.

'Hello.'

43

At over a foot taller than her, Alex's former boss hadn't seen her coming, and it took him a moment, she noticed, to rearrange his features in a convincing impression of civility.

'Alex,' Jamie blinked, sucking the beer foam from his top lip. 'You came.'

'I did.'

Picking up on the awkward body language, the broker Jamie had been chatting to took off, leaving them hemmed in by the crowds, and uncomfortably close.

'Like the hair.'

'Thanks.' Alex didn't smile.

'Listen, I was going to reply to your last email,' Jamie assured her, his eyes roving the room for some form of escape.

'And the one before, Jamie – were you going to reply to that one? What about the three messages I left on your mobile?'

Alex was surprised by how easy it was to talk to her former boss in such a combative tone – enjoyable, even. But she had to rein it in: until she was safely ensconced at her new job, she still needed Jamie.

'Listen, I get it. I know your schedule, remember? And, of course, you've just got rid of the best PA you'll ever have,' she added evenly.

'Alex . . .'

'It's doesn't matter. Just that I've still not had the paper-work through.' She paused. 'And I really don't want to miss the window on that JLL job.' She forced herself to keep eye contact. 'I need that job, Jamie.'

Draining the dregs of his pint, Jamie waved at someone over by the bar before turning his attention back to her.

'OK, so here's the thing, Al. I may have got my wires

crossed about that. And I was going to drop you a note to explain but I've—'

'Wait.' Alex closed her eyes, shook her head. 'What do you mean "wires crossed"? Your friend's already found someone?'

'Well, I thought he was on the lookout, but it turns out that . . .'

Alex stared.

'Was there ever a job, Jamie? Or was this about making sure I go quietly? This, and your promise – because you promised – that we'd say it was my decision to leave. And yet everyone here seems to know I was sacked.'

He shrugged, shifting his weight from one foot to the other. And feeling like her glass was now a dead weight in her hand, Alex set it down on a nearby table.

Someone hollered 'Jamie, mate!' from the other side of the room and he looked over, trying to locate the source and dropping any pretence now that the two of them were enjoying a cordial chat.

'I'd better—'

'No wait.' She had no recollection of putting it there, yet her hand was on his forearm. 'Wait.' She swallowed, the implications slowly percolating. 'What am I supposed to do now?'

He pulled a face. 'Honestly, I would have loved to help you out, Al. And of course I'll keep an eye out for you – give you a shout if I hear of anything.'

Another holler from across the room: 'Jaaamie!' Jill's speech was about to begin.

'Sorry.' His hand was on her arm. 'I'm needed. But something'll turn up.' Was that a wink? Did he actually just wink at her? 'I'm sure of it.'

Up by the bar, beyond Jamie's retreating back, she saw Lydia beckoning her back: speech time. And in a daze Alex wove her way through the quietening crowds back to the other side of the pub.

'How did that go?' Lydia whispered, once Jill's speech was over, the applause had died down and normal chatter had resumed. 'What did you say to him?' Then, without waiting for an answer: 'Two o'clock. Are you seeing this?'

They'd turned the music up and over by the fireplace, Harry, BWL's head lawyer, had broken out into a set of staccato dance moves. People watched, amused and appalled, as the sixty-two-year-old tossed his jacket onto a nearby chair and rolled up his shirtsleeves. This was going to be taken to the next level.

'Last time this happened poor old Harry had a TIA,' came Jill's voice from beside them at the bar. 'You waiting to be served?'

They were, alongside everyone else. But neither Lydia nor Alex was about to tell the company founder to wait her turn.

'You go ahead.'

There was a moment's discomfort as the barman uncorked another rosé, and the two women waited for her to leave. But Jill didn't seem to be in any hurry to get back to the throng, turning, instead, to lean her back against the bar.

'Need to sit,' she said to no one in particular. 'That table taken?'

Alex followed her eyeline to a corner table that was empty, aside from a tray of fried finger food.

'Don't think so. Wouldn't touch those, though. They've been there a while.'

Only then, as Jill took her seat with a grateful sigh, did she appear to register who Alex was.

'Alex, isn't it? How are you?'

She had had a lot of that tonight. Mostly it came with a cock of the head.

'OK.' Aware that as a partner and the woman who was known to have mentored Jamie throughout his rise, Jill was unlikely to be sympathetic to her plight, Alex waited for Lydia to fill the silence, but her friend had excused herself 'for another cig', and when Jill gestured at the chair opposite, she couldn't think about anything but the relief of being off her feet.

How many glasses had she had now? Three, four? Enough not to feel the throbbing of her toes, crushed into the points of her pumps – until that moment. She needed to get out of here and away from that man. She needed to go home.

'Better?' Jill smiled.

'Much. That was a good speech, by the way. I had no idea Joyce had been with you and your husband pretty much from the start. Must be quite a wrench.' Then, eyes still on a dancing Harry and conscious that she needed to keep the conversation going at least for a minute or two, until she found a way to get out of there: 'What's a TIA?'

'A tiny stroke. And I shouldn't joke about it because honest to God the St John's Ambulance men took him off, right there in the middle of our Christmas party a couple of years back. Which is not all that surprising: the man's got a couple of years on me, but I'm not about to start tweaking—'

'Twerking.'

'I'm not about to start doing either.'

Surprised and flattered that Jill should be happy to spend any length of time with a mere former PA, especially after the heinous crime she was supposed to have committed, Alex leaned back in her chair to get a full view of the action. Harry had been joined by a handful of people on the makeshift dance floor now, and as Jill sat and watched, eyes crinkled in amusement, Alex snuck a look at her.

She must have been approaching sixty and was good-looking in the way that only a woman who had never been pretty could be in middle age. Her fine cashmere jumper and pleated trousers were expensive but discreet – Jaeger, or maybe Hobbs – and the short ash-blonde hair spun into an efficient, immovable style and the light down on her top lip showed a lack of interest in anything beyond what was needed to appear smart and professional. But her expression was warm and there was a stoicism in Jill's eyes that reminded Alex of a private grief she'd heard Jamie mention: her husband – that was it.

'Sorry. Didn't think to get you a drink.' Jill smiled, and the connection between them – so unexpected – made Alex want to cry.

'Why don't you two stay put and I'll get us a bottle?'

Alex looked up to see Nicole standing there. Harder and glossier than usual in an oxblood dress and high-heeled ankle boots, she was clearly there to make up to Jill. Along with 'gorgeous', 'hungry' had been the word most commonly used to describe Nicole at BWL, and Alex remembered how many times, thinking she was the last one to leave the office, she'd caught sight of Nicole working late into the night at her desk. A tête-à-tête with Jill was clearly too good to pass up, and Alex sighed inwardly at the prospect of sitting there in silence as the two women talked shop.

'We've never really . . . I'm . . . '

'Alex,' slurred back Nicole. She took half a step back. 'It's the hair,' she said eventually. 'You've cut it.'

'And coloured it.' Alex smiled, flashing back to the rare moments a 'cool' girl at school had deigned to talk to her.

Nicole nodded impatiently, as though this last part were beside the point. 'But you were . . . you're no longer with us, I hear?'

'Sacked,' Alex replied. No use sugar-coating it. 'Yeah.'

Pulling a chair out, the special projects supervisor sat down. But instead of crossing her legs, Nicole kept them slightly parted in a way that struck Alex as self-consciously masculine.

'I don't think it's table service,' she murmured, as Nicole made elaborate gestures at the barman to bring them over a bottle of wine.

'What?'

Nicole was staring hard at her now and, feeling a hundred tiny judgements being made, Alex racked up a few of her own.

Nicole's expensive outfit was at odds with her nails, which were unpainted and bitten to the quick: a grafter's nails. Her trademark cherry red lipstick leached her pale skin of any remnants of colour, and it had bled into the tiny twin verticals at the corners of her mouth, pushing her assumed age up to around forty. But she was still, by any measure, a beautiful woman.

'I said I don't think it's . . . '

But one of the barmen was already on his way over with a bottle in an ice bucket, and Jill chuckled into her wine.

'It is when you look like Nicole.'

Visibly pleased by the comment, Nicole began to fill their

glasses. She'd predictably turned the conversation around to work when a tinkle of metal against glass silenced the room for the second time that night.

'Jill may think she's got it covered when it comes to Joyce and the reasons we're going to miss her,' Jamie began, 'but I'm not sure she has ...'

'Why's *he* making a speech?' Nicole mouthed at Jill. By the set of Jill's mouth, Alex could see that having her straight and sincere goodbye tailgated by what would doubtless be a far more colourful performance was galling. With no choice but to listen, however, the three women sat in silence as Jamie made it all about him.

When Jamie had sprayed Sprite over a humourless conservationist intent on blocking a sale of luxury flats in Olympia, he told the room, it was Joyce and the wet wipes she always kept close to hand that had rescued the situation. When Reza Farhat, the Iranian It-boy who was as capricious with his properties as his wife was with her Birkins, had requested some kind of deep-fried rosewater cake to be served at their afternoon sales pitch, it was Joyce, again, who had scoured the far corners of Shepherd's Bush market for the 'zoolibia ... zooleeva, zoo ...' Alex hated that when Jamie laughed at his own jokes it was charming.

'None of us could pronounce it, could we, Joyce? Let alone bring ourselves to eat the things.'

'You got a few down though, didn't you!' someone heckled.

'Anything for a sale, mate. But jeez – they tasted like that stuff my wife leaves in bowls around the house. Isn't that right, Paul?'

'Potpourri!' squealed a woman up at the front.

There was laughter, and more heckling. It didn't take

much to get people going at that stage of the night, and Jamie wasn't one to leave a drop of limelight unsqueezed. But over at their corner table, Alex, Nicole and Jill were grim-faced.

Jamie didn't know she was still there, watching, and doubtless cared even less, leaving her free to pick apart the mannerisms she'd grown as familiar with as a relative's in the seven months she'd tended to Jamie's every need.

Had some ex-girlfriend once told Jamie that the rueful back-of-the-head scratch with which he followed up all his punchlines was charming – sexy? The whole shtick was route one Hugh Grant, and so patently disingenuous. How had it taken her this long to see that her boss was a fraud who specialised in making even insignificant people like her feel special – one of the clan – until they became expendable?

From her first day at BWL, Jamie had done just that, assuring her the company was like 'one great big family' – admittedly 'a dysfunctional one'.

Even when she'd come clean about the pregnancy and he'd got over the initial annoyance of having to find maternity cover (an annoyance she'd actually enjoyed, because it meant she was good, maybe even irreplaceable), he'd been sweet about that, too, buying her a packet of the ginger chews Maya had found helped with the nausea, and recommending a 'baby whisperer' they'd used with Christel when his firstborn still wasn't sleeping through the nights six months in. And when, a month into motherhood and sleep deprived to the point of tears, Alex had googled the woman to find she was 250 quid a session, she hadn't been as put out as she should have been. That was Jamie: in his own charmed bubble, but he always meant well.

'If it helps,' Nicole said, without looking up from her phone, 'I hate him almost as much as you do.'

CHAPTER 6

NICOLE

The surprise on Alex's face was gratifying, and Nicole broke off from the email she'd been tapping out to drink it in. It had felt good to say that out loud; even better to discover that she wasn't alone.

'I don't—'

'Yeah, you do. And I don't blame you. So go on then: what's the real story?'

'With ...?'

'Why did Jamie get rid of you? 'Cause you got pregnant? 'Cause Hayden was his mate? There's been talk.'

From Alex's darting glances at Jill and back to Nicole, she was aware she'd overstepped the mark. But something beyond the alcohol in her blood pushed her on.

'Come on. I think we all know golden boy's been known to cut a few corners when it suits him.'

Nicole badly wanted Jill to be aware of this, she realised. So much so, that she was willing to risk speaking out in front of her boss. Because although Jill and Jamie had always been close, she had above all always struck her as a fair and professional figure. If her protégé had done something out of turn, it was only right that Jill should know about it.

'For what it's worth, Joyce always said you were brilliant.' Jill's usually serene, low voice rose higher, wavering with alcohol, and it occurred to Nicole that in all these years, she'd never seen her drunk before.

BWL's founder was part of that old-school breed who never show any chinks of vulnerability in the office. Nicole had never even seen Jill reapplying lipstick in the Ladies. Fair and steady in the operation of a company that she and her husband had set up to preserve history rather than destroy it, Jill was proof of what women who weren't held back by men could accomplish. Which only made the need to remove the scales from her eyes greater.

'Is Nicole right?' Jill went on gently. 'Did you feel Jamie had some, well, other motive for terminating your employment beside the due diligence business?'

Nicole watched Alex assess the situation – and decide she had nothing to lose.

'I wasn't going to say anything, but the whole Khalvashi mess-up wasn't mine – it was Jamie's. He specifically told me to leave the paperwork unfinished. Why, I don't know, but I reckon it was because he knew Khalvashi wasn't legit and wanted the sale to go through regardless. *Property Week* had just done this big piece on him and maybe the pressure to keep up his whole "Deal Don" image got to him.' She paused. 'Then when you and Paul spotted the incomplete file, he pinned it on me, and used it as an excuse to get rid of me. I wasn't going to say anything, because Jamie promised to make it up to me – that he'd get me another job. And like an idiot I believed him.'

As Jill took this in, Nicole observed her boss closely. She was taken aback, but not shocked. 'He's been cutting the odd corner recently. Behaving, I don't know . . .'

It was Nicole's turn to be surprised. 'I thought he could do no wrong in your eyes.'

'Oh?' Jill gave a dry laugh and, taking two sips of wine in quick succession, looked over at Jamie, who had finally stopped talking and was getting a massive round in at the bar. 'No. No, I wouldn't go that far.'

All three were woozy by now, but Jill's neck seemed to have lost its ability to hold her head steady, and Nicole wished Alex weren't refilling the older woman's glass quite so soon.

'I know that Jamie has always looked up to you,' Alex volunteered, and although Jill nodded, her eyes remained sceptical. 'And I mean, after all you've done for him, I'm sure he always will.'

What started out as reassurance sounded a little like goading now, as though Alex were pushing Jill to acknowledge what a monster her mentee had become. Or perhaps he'd always been one in disguise. 'You brought him into the company, didn't you?'

'Years ago, and he's always been a little cocky . . .'

'But now it feels like something more?' Alex pushed on. 'I felt that, too. Even before I went on maternity leave, there was something about his attitude . . . a lack of respect.'

'Towards me?' Jill looked up sharply.

'Don't take this the wrong way ...'

'Go on.'

'But he'd make these comments – about you being late. Or at the hospital with your ... husband.' At this Jill flinched. 'Just little asides: "Oh, Jill's sitting this one out again," or "Jill was a no show."'

Alex *was* goading her. This young woman wasn't just upset at having lost her job, she realised, but distraught, and something about the intensity in her eyes troubled Nicole, but being equally keen to prolong this conversation, she shuttered off the thought into a corner of her brain.

'What really bothered me,' said Alex, leaning forward, 'was when he spoke like that about you in front of the clients.'

'He said those things in front of clients?'

'Sometimes. And it just seemed a bit insensitive. Your husband ...'

'The big C.' Jill fingered the stem of her glass. 'Stan's been getting treatment. He's always wanted to keep his health concerns private for a number of reasons. Not least that it's nobody else's business. But you'd heard ... from Jamie?'

'Yes ... I ... he mentioned it in passing.'

'In passing.'

'I'm really sorry Jill, but –' she glanced at Nicole, as though checking whether she should go on – 'he'd tell most people. It always made me feel uncomfortable. As though he were using Stan's ...'

'Stan's what?'

'Well sort of using your husband's ... illness to sideline ...'

'To sideline me?'

'Well, to push himself forward. At least that's how it came across to me.'

'Right.' From the rapid rise and fall of Jill's chest beneath her oatmeal jumper, Nicole could see how hard she was struggling to contain her outrage.

But Alex wasn't done.

'Then there were the jokes,' she murmured. 'About women. About older women.' She threw Jill an apologetic look. 'And yes, about you.'

'Well, Jamie's always had an inappropriate sense of humour. I've told him, more than once, to rein it in.'

Jill was trying to claw back some sense of control. This was all so undignified. But from the look on Alex's face, things were only going to get worse.

'I know, and look: most of the time I'd find it funny. But then he'd say this stuff,' she went on hesitantly, 'about what he called ...'

Nicole knew what Alex was about to say. She'd heard Jamie make the same joke. And she was torn between wanting Jill to hear it and hoping she'd be spared.

'... your "RBF".'

'You've lost me.'

'Resting Bitch Face.' The words were said so quietly that for a second Nicole wasn't sure Jill had heard. 'It's a social media term for women – for that aggressive look they can ... we can all ...'

'I get the idea. And what? I'm supposed to have ... that?'

'He'd say you had it in meetings – sometimes. That it had got worse, as you, well, had got older. That it was off-putting for the clients.'

'OK.' Jill gave a terse nod.

'He'd say ...'

'Go on.'

'He'd joke that for your sixtieth, he'd send you to Harley Street "for a bit of refreshing".'

Jill closed her eyes. 'Right.'

Conscious that with the speeches now over, the noise levels had decreased, Alex lowered her voice further. 'Sorry, Jill. I know this is . . . harsh. But what the hell's happened to him?'

'Because he was such an upstanding guy before?' Nicole angled her body towards the wall to have a covert puff on her vape. This drew an almost comical look of alarm from Alex, who glanced from her to the bar staff and back again. 'What are they going to do, arrest me? Relax.'

But Jill was oblivious, caught up in her own thoughts. 'Jamie's never exactly been Mr Sensitive. I mean he's one of the most competitive men you'll ever meet – but that's what makes him so good at his job. And his humour . . . But I always thought he had a good heart.'

'Then I wonder how well you've ever known him.' Nicole spat out the words through a mouthful of water vapour.

On the other side of the pub, someone hollered out 'last orders!' and only when neither one of them reacted did Nicole register the curious turn things were taking.

'What does that mean?'

'It means that I . . . shit.' She glanced up. 'He's coming over.'

As Nicole bent back over her phone, she felt Alex fumble for the shoes she'd slipped off earlier beneath the table, in readiness, she assumed, for escape.

'Alex. Still here?'

You'd think there might be a glimmer of embarrassment before this woman he'd just sacked – but nothing. He was here to talk to Jill. People were only of interest to Jamie while they were useful. After that, they ceased to exist.

'Like the speech?' he asked his partner.

'Loved it.' Jill was stony-faced. 'We weren't sure you were ever going to stop talking.'

Nicole gave a snort and Jamie narrowed his eyes.

'Do you think you girls may have had enough? School night and all that?'

There was a millisecond's pause.

'Not sure you're allowed to call us "girls" any more, Jamie,' Nicole murmured, eyes still fixed on her phone. 'Not least because we're all over thirty. And FYI, "ladies" – another favourite of yours – is also out.'

Alex looked from Nicole to Jamie and then Jill, suppressing a smile.

'Well I'm going to leave you *women* to your feminist symposium. It's getting late.' He shrugged on that padded gilet of his and left.

Once the door had swung shut behind him, the three women's laughter was so loud and immediate that a handful of remaining revellers turned to look at them.

'Do you think you girls may have had enough?' Nicole growled, her voice carrying across the pub. But while the other two women's laughter died down quickly, Nicole couldn't seem to stop, and only when the mirth on the two women's faces was replaced with alarm did she realise that her eyes were wet.

Jill's hand wavered cautiously behind her back. 'Are you OK?'

'Yes.' Nicole cleared her throat noisily. 'No. No, I just … there's something …'

'What?'

'I thought I could put it behind me. I mean, look at me:

I'm hardly that woman, am I? I'm forty bloody three, I've got a pretty decent sense of humour. I'm a flirt and I ...' As the last remaining people headed towards the door and all three women smiled and waved, the conversation was paused. 'I give as good as I get. Always have. But Jamie's behaviour ...'

'Nicole,' Jill's voice was stern now. 'Whatever it is, just spit it out.'

After a long inhalation, Nicole began: 'It was just stupid, harmless flirting at first. Professional flirting, you know? To keep things moving along ... make the day go a bit quicker. Anyway, I guess he thought I was game. Everyone knew about Ian, right?' She glanced over at Jill, hoping the acknowledgement of her stupid, brief office affair years ago wouldn't affect her prospects at BWL. But of course her boss had heard the rumours – everyone had. 'It was way before your time, Alex. He left the company years ago. Still, I'm guessing even you heard about it.'

Alex paused, then gave a slight nod. 'Listen, I'm hardly in a position to judge,' she murmured. 'I'm the girl who got herself pregnant with a guy from work, remember? A guy who by the way couldn't run fast enough.'

'I heard. And I'm sorry that Hayden's been such a ...' Nicole swallowed. 'Best never to expect too much of men, eh? But at least neither you nor Hayden was married.' A crackle of laughter. 'At least you're not the scarlet woman.'

Alex and Jill waited.

'Well, anyway, Jamie clearly saw me as "game". He'd say stuff about what I was wearing – nice stuff and then less nice stuff, and then one day, while we're waiting to go into the conference room, he comes out and says, 'You look very fuckable today, Nic.'

'Woah.' Alex was taken aback, but Jill had actually frozen in shock, her glass suspended in mid-air.

'He said *what*?'

'Then he moved on to a more direct approach, coming to look over project plans on my computer and pressing up against my back so that I could feel him ...'

In any other context Jill's face, slack with disbelief, would have been funny.

'Nicole,' she managed eventually. 'Don't take this the wrong way, but is there any way you misunderstood this? That he was joking? Or that you, well, made Jamie think that it might be something you wanted?'

'"Led him on", you mean?' Alex cut in, and Nicole was glad for the interruption. 'I know that things were very different twenty years ago, but "leading on" is kind of out as a defence now.'

'OK.' Jill held her hands up. 'Listen, I had to ask. And things weren't so different ten, twenty or thirty years ago, for that matter. Much as everyone now likes to think they're the first to call men out.'

'Right – so you can imagine what this must have felt like for Nicole.'

'I don't have to imagine,' Jill snapped. 'It was pretty much the air we breathed back in the day. And it wasn't just that side of men we had to contend with, either: do you have any idea how many times I was underestimated and sidelined on my way up? How many stupid comments about my looks and clothes I had to ignore? How much harder I had to work than every man to prove myself?'

'So you get that this is not about anything Nicole did. You understand that it's about Jamie; that it's harassment.'

Jill blenched.

'Jesus.' Alex contemplated Nicole. 'I always thought he had a thing for you. I mean, I could see him following you with his eyes across the office sometimes, but he wouldn't have been the only one. And I never thought he'd do anything, well, like that.'

Both women watched in silence as Nicole picked at a hangnail, deciding whether to go on. It was madness to have said as much as she had. But there was no going back now.

'Why didn't you report it?' Alex said softly. 'We don't have to put up with this stuff any more, do we? I mean isn't that the whole point of being a woman in the age of Me Too?'

Nicole threw her a watery smile: 'Right. But I didn't want to make too much of it. Plus I'm married and everyone knows I've slept with a co-worker in the past, so I very much doubt I'm going to get much sympathy from HR. God knows it wouldn't make me appealing to future employers, either.'

'But that's got nothing to do with it!'

'I know, I know, but listen.' Nicole ducked to take another drag on her e-cigarette. 'I'm not going to report him. End of.'

'Good.'

Both Nicole and Alex turned to look at Jill. Judging by her very different tone – clear and pragmatic now – she'd moved into damage limitation mode.

'I mean, as Nicole says, I get why reporting him isn't necessarily going to help.'

'Not going to help the company either, is it?'

Drunk or not, Jill seemed to have decided that she'd had enough of being spoken to like that.

'That's not the point. Whatever's going on with Jamie, the bullying and belittling and now this: it all ends here. I don't care if he's a partner. There will not be harassment of any kind in my company. I'll ... I'll talk to him.'

'Because that's really going to make my life easier?'

'Well, it would make him stop.' Jill put down her glass with a clatter.

'He'd stop and then he'd find a way to make me pay, wouldn't he?' Nicole shook her head. 'I couldn't sit there in meetings with him after that. I'd have to leave. Then there's you – the position you'd be left in, now that you know. Because if you don't report him, you could be accused of covering stuff up.' Jill hadn't thought of that. 'Then again, for all I know you've been covering up for Jamie for years.'

In a matter of minutes the conversation had turned from sisterly to antagonistic. Jamie had left the premises and somehow he was still causing trouble.

'Hey,' Alex cut in. 'Maybe there's another way of stopping this – of stopping him.'

Nicole and Jill stared at her, the same thought in both of their eyes: *but you're no longer a part of this.*

'I could have let this go, if he'd done what he promised and got me another job.'

'Oh, Jamie'll say whatever he needs to in the moment,' Nicole spat out, not caring if she sounded bitter – she *was* bitter. 'And he doesn't care who's made to pay for his mistakes so long as it's not him. Because in the end, women are either convenient to Jamie or expendable.'

'But we can't just let him get away with it? He lied to you, to Jill, to me.'

Faced with these bombshells about her one-time protégé, Jill looked shaken. As the most senior of the three, she would know that it was up to her to try and make this right, and

Nicole saw her window: 'If Jamie was trying to do that with Khalvashi, what's to say he hasn't with other clients?'

Jill nodded in agreement. And when the barman announced that it was 'time to drink up now', she did something surprising.

'I'm going to give you this,' Jill told the lad, handing him a folded fifty-pound note. 'And in exchange I want you to give us one last bottle of rosé – and another hour.'

Only when the pub doors had been locked and a fresh bottle of wine brought over did Jill turn back to Alex.

'Go on.'

'What I'm saying,' Alex resumed, encouraged by the two women's attention, 'is that he needs to be put back in his box. He needs to pay.'

'And how are we supposed to do that?' Bored with the subterfuge, Nicole was now openly vaping away.

'Well, you're right that you and I can't go down the formal channels. Me because I'd lose an unfair dismissal suit in a heartbeat – he's sewn that up nicely – and you because . . . '

'Ian would be dredged up if I made a complaint? Because as much as we've been told to shout these men's names from the rooftops, as much as we've been told we've got the power, nobody much cares if Me Too-ing turns us into professional lepers afterwards, do they?'

'Right.' Alex paused, clearly enjoying the second she held them both there. 'Well, I say we find another way. Because there are different kinds of power – and maybe ours is—'

'Please don't say "soft power",' groaned Nicole. 'I hate that expression.'

'Me too.' This was Jill now. 'Like that's the best women can do.'

'You're missing the point. I'm talking about bringing Jamie down in a way that could never be traced back to us, a way he'd manage on his own if he weren't always being covered for and protected.'

From the corner of her eye Nicole saw Jill blink twice in quick succession, taking this as a dig at her.

'All I'm talking about is giving him a little push. Not so much soft power . . . '

'As stealth power.' Beneath the sneer, Nicole was serious.

'And it wouldn't be hard,' Jill murmured, 'given how reckless he's got.'

'No, no – it would be easy.' Alex leaned forward. 'The things I've seen. The things I know. Just think of what we've all found out tonight? I'm betting that if we start digging, Jamie'll turn out to be so far from the person everyone thinks he is it's not even funny.'

For a moment Nicole feared Alex might have gone too far – lost Jill, at least. But after a small hesitation, her boss asked: 'And these things you saw while working with him – you think they can help us?'

Of all the unforeseen events that night – the wine, the nervous flit of Jamie's eyes as he took in the scene at their table, and the revelations of these two women Nicole had only ever exchanged professional words with before tonight – that 'us' was somehow the most pleasing. Nothing bonded, she thought wryly, quite like hate.

'Between the three of us there must be so much that we can use.' Alex paused, bit her lip. 'It's just a question of working out where Jamie's weak spots are.'

For a moment, all three women sipped their wine. Then Nicole inhaled sharply.

'The D-list,' she said to Jill.

Jamie's 'D-list' was an inside joke with senior management at BWL. A compilation of every structural flaw and weakness that might make a property less sellable, including a detailed prediction of everything likely to go wrong moving forward, the document was basically an anti-sales pitch – to be expunged from the office hard drive the moment the deeds were exchanged.

More than once Nicole had heard Jill pull him up on the cynicism of this document in private company meetings: 'Just knowing it's there makes me jittery,' she'd said. And Nicole secretly felt the same. But Jamie had always laughed off her concerns. As a reminder of what not to make the client aware of unless legally obligated to, the D-list was a crucial part of his selling process. 'And if no one but me is ever going to see it,' he'd protested, 'where's the problem?'

Jill held Nicole's gaze. 'You mean . . . '

'I mean, what if Jamie's D-list were to be made public in some way. That would be embarrassing, wouldn't it?'

Jill chewed at the inside of her mouth. 'Ye-es. But to us, as well as him.'

Nicole had to admit she had a point: 'True.'

'Sorry,' Alex interjected, 'but the "D-list" is . . . ?'

As a PA, Alex wouldn't have been privy to the kind of meetings Jamie's dodgy dossier had come up in, Nicole realised, and the young woman's eyes widened as she explained it to her.

'But there might be other ways we could . . . well, give Jamie a bit of a warning?' Jill pushed on.

'Or even a full-scale wake-up call.' Alex's cheeks were flushed. 'Because otherwise men just get away with it, don't they – all of it? And every time that happens, they know that they can push things further the next.'

Fleetingly, Nicole wondered how deeply Alex's dislike of men was rooted. Had it consolidated over years, like hers, or been prompted by something far worse than both Hayden and Jamie's treatment of her?

'So it's just a question of finding the right opportunity to catch Jamie out and show him up,' Alex concluded. 'Really we'd be doing him a favour.'

'We'd be doing women a favour,' cut in Nicole, inviting them, with an upward swing of her glass, to toast the man who had for too long behaved with impunity: 'To Jamie.'

Alex raised hers: 'To putting a not-so-good man down.'

CHAPTER 7

JILL

5 AUGUST
KILBURN POLICE STATION

'You say Mr Lawrence was very highly thought of.'
'Yes.'
'By his clients and colleagues?'
'Yes.'

'More than just popular, he was something of a celebrity in your world – the property world.'

It was more of a statement than a question, and unsure whether she was required to add anything, Jill just nodded.

'He won awards, got write-ups in industry mags.' Flicking through his file, the detective inspector found what he wanted, gesturing to a cutting in front of him. Even upside-down, Jill recognised the portrait taken of her colleague in a BWL conference room the previous year. He had complained about it at the time, claiming the harsh lighting had made his face look 'like a *Spitting Image* puppet'.

'Jamie was a very good broker. He has –' she swallowed '– he had a way with people, which is a big part of the job. He brought in a lot of high-profile clients; got us noticed.'

'Only it wasn't all good publicity, was it? In fact, over the past two months there were a few very negative bits of press involving Mr Lawrence: a wrangle with conservationists over a protected property that was destroyed, and a couple of mentions in property gossip blogs about professional mishaps that must have been embarrassing for the company.'

Jill glanced at the empty plastic cup on the table, willing someone to refill it with water.

'Mishaps we've had corroborated by employees we've spoken to, who told us –' more sifting through his file '– yes here it is, that Mr Lawrence had "been different" over the past few months, "distracted" and "behaving oddly".' That he'd been "messing up repeatedly".' One of your colleagues even describes him as "flailing".'

'It's true that he wasn't himself.' Jill's voice sounded oddly high-pitched. 'Sorry. I'm ... we're all reeling.'

'Of course. Take your time.' A pause. 'Then we have the more serious internal allegation that we've just been made aware of.'

Again, Jill just nodded. The room smelt of Ajax and her need for water was now so all-consuming that when the DI opened his mouth to speak again, she was forced to lip-read: 'How well do you know Nicole Harper, Mrs Barnes, and Alex Fuller?'

CHAPTER 8

JILL

Two And A Half Months Earlier

'You're going to have to try and move yourself over a bit.' Jill felt something twang in her lower back as she wedged her husband's sun-lounger into the last rung. 'There. That's as far as it'll go. Any better?'

It had been such a good idea – a late lunch on *Lady J*'s roof-deck. Stan's, surprisingly. And when he'd called her at the office to check on her hangover and suggest she come home early, Jill had immediately shut down her computer and jumped in a cab.

For almost a year everything in their lives had revolved around the three military Ps – proper planning and preparation – and aside from the odd properly planned and over-prepared dinner, they'd scarcely left Blomfield Road. In all that time, neither had even considered crossing the road to tend to the canalside garden they'd taken so much pride in over the years, much less climbing aboard their narrowboat.

Lady J was robust. With her engine drained for winter, she could sit there quite happily for months. But left to its own devices, the garden had turned into a tangle of weeds, curling protectively over and around the cans, cartons and fast-food wrappers Little Venice tourists had thrown over the railings. And once they'd established that climbing up onto *Lady J*'s roof-deck was way too ambitious for Stan, they'd been forced to settle for a spot of gardening and a canalside picnic instead.

It was all going so well until Jill tore open the mackerel pâté, prompting her husband to throw up right there on the baking concrete. Along with the nausea, the Prostap injections had given Stan a heightened sensitivity to smells – which Jill knew, but had somehow overlooked in her excitement at being 'back to normal'. And the incident had left her feeling both guilty and unfairly angry at her husband for reminding them why the simple joys of their past life were no longer permitted.

Settled at last on his chair, a smear of factor 50 across his hairline, Stan had now nodded off, leaving Jill to enjoy the view they'd revelled in every summer for just over two decades. Closing her eyes for a moment, she tried to lose herself in the anaesthetising heat of the sun, but snippets of the previous night kept floating back to her – phrases Jill couldn't quite believe she'd uttered herself.

That she should have said as much as she did about Jamie, been so indiscreet, was baffling to her. Yes, she'd been blindsided by Nicole and Alex's revelations, but Jill didn't do indiscretion. That wasn't who she was. She wasn't a big drinker, either, and yet last night she'd had this unquenchable thirst – as though actively seeking to find herself in an altered state that would allow her to listen, say and agree to things she wouldn't normally. And Jill couldn't deny that it had felt good – right up until she'd climbed into bed and been hit by the weight of the responsibility she now bore these two women. Would it all be a mirage come morning? With everything that had been said unspoken, and all she'd heard forgotten?

Remembering Jamie's face mid-speech now, however – the faint alcoholic bloom of his cheeks and showman-like expansiveness of his gestures – something hardened inside Jill, just as it had last night, when the feelings she'd been trying to avoid naming for months, if she was being honest with herself, had condensed into loathing.

Never mind that this was a man she'd known for years, a man who had dined at their house, on more than one sozzled occasion – before Maya and the kids were around – passed out in their guest bedroom, and visited Stan in hospital. Jamie was someone whose faults – weaknesses, she'd thought of them, indulgently – were familiar enough to be amusing. He was someone she'd felt confident she could rely on, should the moment come. Only, when that moment had come, her protégé seemed to have taken every opportunity to 'push himself forward', as Alex had put it. And for him to have undermined her and Stan in front of the clients when they both felt so very reduced already, was deplorable.

Was that what this was about? Some displaced anger at what her life and marriage had become? 'It's not easy being a carer,' the radiotherapy nurse had said last week, giving Jill's arm a little squeeze. And it wasn't so much the obviousness of the statement and the empathetic tone that had grated as the dowdiness of that word – a word Jill didn't want to be connected to. Over the years she had watched motherhood reduce her friends, and when it became apparent that she would never be one, she'd secretly felt thankful. At least she'd be able to forge ahead, uncluttered by some little person's overwhelming needs. And that's what she'd done – until now. So no, as it turned out, being a carer wasn't easy.

Jill scanned back over the years and saw Jamie in his early thirties, when she and Stan had brought him into their company: just as cocky but skinnier, harder working, and with more hair. That barrow boy aggressiveness had served him well in the Essex-based company he'd come from, and made him stand out from the other candidates who'd applied for the job. But it had also worried Jill at first: was that brashness really going to win over BWL's high-end clients? And yet they'd taken a chance on Jamie and within days of him starting had understood the extent of his reach. There weren't many people who could disarm men and charm women. But the real surprise was that Jamie wasn't just about playing to an audience. He could do the one-on-ones, too. Not just with clients, either, but with his colleagues and underlings – with Paul and with her.

They'd promoted him quicker and more frequently than anyone in the history of the company, but in that time she'd never noticed his deference towards her eroding. When had that started? When had Jamie gone from looking up to her, to down? Because, now that she thought about it, there had been signs well before Stan was diagnosed: phone calls to Jill that Jamie had somehow intercepted; meetings he'd stepped in and taken 'because you've got bigger fish to fry'; project summations she'd have been sketching out only to find Jamie had written up days in advance. At the time she'd interpreted this as keenness. And when a few clients of hers had started gravitating towards her junior, she hadn't always minded. But often it had grated.

There was the pompous Milanese developer who had never quite got over the queasiness of doing business with a woman. 'I just feel more comfortable with Jamie – like we have more in common,' he'd finally come out and said, as though it were as acceptable to declare an anatomical preference for the person one wanted to do business with as it was to request tea rather than coffee in a business meeting. And perhaps Jamie hadn't been quite as appalled on her behalf as he should have been. He'd come back quickly – too quickly? – with 'Well, whatever it takes to make the sale, right?' So Jamie was an opportunist and a misogynist. But a predator who would trade in every ounce of loyalty to her and Stan for his own glory?

'Stan?' Jill knew she should let her husband sleep, but she felt an urgent need for him, and she hadn't let herself need him in months.

'Mmm ...' Opening one eye and then shutting it again, he murmured, 'How long have I been out?'

'Long enough to get a little pink.' She smiled.

Perching beside Stan on his lounger, Jill rubbed more cream into his temples before turning to gaze out at the packed Prince Regent floating restaurant as it passed.

'You OK, darling?'

'Better than I was this morning. What a good idea this was.'

Taking his wife's hand, Stan began to trace the lines of her palm the way he did when she was tired or overworked. 'How's the headache?'

'Almost gone.'

He nodded, patient.

'And everything else?'

Straightened up and with a bit of colour in his cheeks, he looked like the old Stan – like someone strong enough to confide in. Because they'd never had any secrets, not in thirty-five years. And not telling him about last night was giving her indigestion.

'Joyce's do was a bit ... odd.'

'It was always going to be tough saying goodbye, love. She's been with us long enough.'

'It wasn't just that.'

They were both sitting back in their chairs now, eyes on the canal, and the slow-moving scenery – the gliding boats and squabbling ducks – was going to make this easier.

'You remember Nicole – our special projects head? You will have met her at the Christmas bash.'

'The one with the legs?'

'Pretty sure they all had legs,' she said with a chuckle. Maybe this was all going to be OK.

'We got talking. And Christ, Stan: she says Jamie's been making advances. Not just saying things – appalling things – but, you know, touching her, in the office.'

Jill heard the creak of the sun-lounger's springs as Stan turned to stare at her, but she couldn't bring herself to meet his eye until she'd finished.

'She says he's been harassing her, and that it's been going on for months.'

'Do you believe her?'

'Well, she's got a bit of history. She's married with kids: one or two, I can't remember. And she's had a couple of office flings since she's been with us. One that I know of for sure. Remember that Ian chap?'

'Yes – it's coming back to me now.'

'We all heard whispers about it at the time, didn't we?'

'All of which means . . . ?'

'Maybe nothing. I'm just telling you what kind of a woman she is.'

'I'm not sure that does, love. And either way it doesn't make what Jamie's been doing all right.'

Stan had always been the bigger feminist of the two. It used to make them laugh, but today his automatic swing to Nicole's defence touched a nerve.

'I know that. I'm just filling you in on her . . . background. I mean we don't actually know that Jamie's done a thing.'

'Oh, I think we do.'

Stan's disbelieving laugh – a low rumble at the back of his throat – was the last thing Jill expected to hear. Her husband was someone who always saw the best in people. Swinging her legs off the chair, she turned towards him.

'You think he's one of these predators they talk about in the papers?' She swatted a fly off her shin. 'One of those Me Too men?'

'I don't know, but . . . '

'What?'

'Well, I never said anything at the time, but you remember that PA, way back – the young one who was only with us a couple of months, the one he took to that Lisbon conference?'

'Porto.'

'Right.'

'She went back to college.'

'No she didn't. She went over to Curtis & Hawk.' Stan rubbed at the back of his neck. 'And she told everyone there that Jamie had tried it on – pretty aggressively.'

Jill sat up, pushing her sunglasses up to her forehead.

'You never said anything.'

'I didn't want to worry you. And luckily for us she never made a formal complaint. But I didn't like the idea of her putting that about. We can't have people thinking that stuff goes on at BWL.' A picture of the young girl, of deep-set blue eyes and freckled cheeks, formed in her mind, and it came back to them in unison: 'Jessica.'

'It went away, thank goodness, so I never spoke to him about it. But harassment.' Stan gave a silent whistle. 'That's going to be a problem.'

It wasn't the only problem: there were also Jamie's indiscretions about Stan's health. And although Jill couldn't bear to tell her husband that he was the subject of idle chat – worse still, a sympathy he didn't want – she had to tell him about Khalvashi.

'There's something else: something that could be equally damaging to BWL's reputation. Alex, Jamie's former PA, is claiming she was fired for something he did. She's saying she knew that a due diligence dossier on a Georgian developer I had my doubts about was incomplete, but tried to push the sale through anyway.'

'What?'

'Yup.'

Stan frowned. 'But again, it's her word against his?'

'It is. But I tell you, Stan, he's got . . . I don't know, sloppier recently – more entitled, too.'

'This girl, Alex, has quite a grudge though.'

'Well, yes: she got fired.' She hated the parallel lines scoring her husband's brow. 'But maybe you're right. She's probably just angry and lashing out.'

'She could be.'

'Anyway, I don't want you to think about all that. You've got enough on your plate. Nicole doesn't want to report Jamie's behaviour, so that's something. And maybe everything just descended into a bit of a bitchathon last night. Maybe all they –' she didn't say 'we' '– needed was to air their grievances. But if you think he may actually have form with the ladies . . . ? Poor Maya.'

Both fell silent, and Jill was grateful for the distraction of another passing cruise boat. Staring back into a row of Japanese faces – impassive behind sunglasses – she saw their privileged existence through other people's eyes. 'Imagine having that life,' they'd be thinking. And for all those years they would have been right.

CHAPTER 9

~≫≪~

NICOLE

'As a gateway site, gentlemen, of over three acres, I can honestly say I've never seen anything quite like it in Central London.'

'I'd have to query whether Gunnersbury really qualifies as "Central London", Jamie,' pointed out Patrick O'Ceallaigh good naturedly.

His brother laughed. 'I'm with you there.'

'John.' Swivelling forty-five degrees, Jamie smiled down at the broader-faced of the twins at the head of the conference table, and Nicole marvelled – as she did every time she encountered the power property duo – that these two could ever have shared the same womb. 'Back me up here. If Shepherd's Bush is Central London, Gunnersbury can't be far off. Hell, Richmond will be Central London by this time next year. Am I right?'

'You are. And it's true that we're looking at a very low pass rate, easy access to the M4. Obviously until we see the total site plan it's hard to picture how much work Minerva would need, but I'm sure Pat will agree that we're keen enough to ask you not to show this to anyone else for the time being.'

'That I would,' nodded his brother, looking down at the map of every sizeable mall within a ten-mile radius they'd painstakingly put together. 'It's exactly the kind of size we've been looking for. And certainly with the nearest multiplex over three miles away in Shepherd's Bush, we'd have, what, the whole of Chiswick, South Acton and Kew sewn up?'

'All of which are filled with the kind of prime high-end shopaholics who are currently schlepping down to Westfield to flex their husband's Amexes,' Jamie went on. 'God knows the wife spends enough time and money there.'

Nicole was glad her hollow laugh was drowned out by the male guffaws. She could fake laugh with the best of them – hell, she might have made that joke herself had she been doing the pitch. 'You know what we're like: give us a shoe shop and our husband's Amex and we're happy.' Never mind that right now it was Nicole's Barclaycard in her old man's wallet, and that she'd later be able to track his week's movements online – movements that were always disappointingly predictable. Little Monkeys, the Corner House Play Room, Waitrose and that awful little pottery café full of screaming children he'd once dragged her to: those were the main staples, with the odd couple of hundred quid spent every other month at The Kit Room. More filming equipment for jobs Ben would never get, to be stashed away in the spare room when they became too uncomfortable a reminder of his professional failures. Still, it was easier to stick with the accepted narrative that women were all dependent on men, wasn't it?

'What I'd add, Jamie, if I may –' Nicole didn't wait for her boss's nod '– is that Minerva Industrial Estate could also conceivably be broken up into two separate entities: say, the mall and cinema complex you were after, and a separate state-of-the-art gym. And, as Jamie has pointed out, your lack of immediate competition within the surrounding area is really quite unique.'

'Right,' Jamie agreed. 'Thanks, Nic – and actually I was going to show you how two adjacent developments might work on the site plan. Now if I can just pull it up for you …'

Jamie tapped away at his tablet until the first page of Minerva's property plan appeared on the display screen.

'Right – so this one here gives you a good idea of the building's specifications. It's category … two? Nic?'

She knew the answer, having read through the prospectus just that morning, but it was impossible to sit there opposite Jamie without feeling his every question was a taunt – the upturned corners of his mouth forcing her into a kind of complicity she wanted no part of.

'You needed that, didn't you?'

From that angle – and still pinned to the wall by his weight – Nicole caught the metallic gleam of a filling in the recesses of his jaw.

'I could feel it. I always know what you need, don't I?'

Peeling the damp flesh of his thighs from hers, Jamie pulled away, and for a moment Nicole feared that released, finally, from the pressure of him, she might slide to the ground. Closing her eyes she listened to the process of him putting himself back together – the zipping and buttoning and buckling – surprised by the banality of those noises.

'*You planning on staying like that?*'

Looking down she saw that her skirt was still bunched up around her waist, her knickers looped around one foot. Beneath her open shirt her bra had been pushed up and wedged above one breast. She must have looked comical, grotesque. But she didn't care.

'*No.*'

'*Good. We've got a meeting at four.*'

And as he'd let himself out of the conference room into the darkened office, Jamie had started whistling.

From somewhere up above her the hum of the air conditioner seemed to grow oppressively loud, all those men's eyes prurient, the smiles conspiratorial – as though they all knew, as though they were laughing at her. If she opened her mouth to speak, would any words come out? Nicole pictured herself standing up and walking out of the room. She could explain later: tell them she felt sick.

'Category two.' Her voice was low and filled with shame, just as it had been with her husband when she got home after that first time, betraying nothing. 'That's right, Jamie.'

'Thought so.' He nodded, eyes lingering on her warily.

'And if we call up our plan of the east wing, Jamie ...'

'What the ... what the hell's this?'

Pat's voice, the Irish brogue no longer affable but stung, made her look up from her files. That wasn't the east wing up on the screen: that was ... shit. That was Jamie's D-List.

'"Inadequate foundations",' Patrick read out. '"Unreinforced masonry." Jamie, is this some kind of a joke?'

'Wait.' Jamie's face was white, his middle finger stabbing

at the tablet in a desperate attempt to get this aberration off the screen.

'It's not . . . it's not supposed to be . . .'

'Part of the sell? Yeah, we got that much, mate.'

Every set of eyes in that room was on that screen, unable to tear themselves away from Minerva's horrifying hidden list of inadequacies, bolded and blocked in red, just to make things worse.

'Pat, are you seeing this?' said gentle John, not so gentle now. '"Unbraced cripple walls"? Did you really think we weren't going to find all this shit out?'

'Patrick, John . . . of course I was going to bring all these points to your attention.'

But the twins weren't listening, transfixed by a new image filling the screen. Because however bad what they'd just seen was, this was far, far worse.

The email exchange was short, to the point – and blown up to a grotesquely large font.

Subject: Minerva – A Heads-Up
From: HugoMears@JLL.com to JamieLawrence@bwl.com

Just to confirm that Westfield have pushed the button on our Kew site over the bridge, mate. Sale won't be signed off/made public till early July but in the interest of transparency you'll want to alert the buyers you mentioned that any plans for a multiplex are therefore problematic.

From: JamieLawrence@bwl.com to
HugoMears@JLL.com

Appreciate that. Will keep them in the loop.

The email was dated just over a month ago: two weeks before Jamie had pitched Minerva to the O'Ceallaigh brothers.

'Pat, John. I can honestly tell ...'

'I don't think you can honestly tell us a bloody thing, mate. And listen – we've been in this game a long time. We're not so naïve as to think you guys are going to put the subsidence right there on the prospectus. But this? You knew what we wanted to do with the site, you knew about Kew, and still you came to us? You let us think ...'

'No, no, John.' Jamie put his hands together in what looked pathetically like an imploration or a prayer. 'I've always been straight with you. And listen – when has a bit of competition ever been a bad thing, right? This could even be good for the both of you. This could bring ...'

At that moment the screen finally decided to do as it was told, flipping back to the white on graphite grey BWL logo. But somehow this only made things worse, like pretending you'd never said words patently overheard.

'Pat.' Pushing his chair out from the table and urging his brother with a deft dip of the chin to follow suit, John O'Ceallaigh headed towards the door, with his brother right behind him. Making no attempt to stop them, Jamie watched as they crossed the floor towards the lift. Along with everyone else, he was well aware that this was past saving.

Visibly relieved that they hadn't been the ones responsible for what would clearly go down as one of the biggest gaffes in BWL's history, people began drifting back to their desks. But for a good five minutes, Jamie stood outside that room, stooped and still. And as Nicole watched him from her desk, she felt her mouth twitch into a smile so broad she had to turn away, lest someone should see.

The plan they'd drawn up in the pub – the one that had vanished without a trace, with no word from Alex since or even the most cursory acknowledgement from Jill of the conversation having taken place – was being put into action by one of them. It wasn't Nicole. And it couldn't be Jill, who had ruled out the use of the D-list that night. Which left only Alex. But Alex was no longer at the company, so how on earth could she have pulled this off?

CHAPTER 10

ALEX

Why did milk boil so much quicker than anything else? How could it, in a matter of seconds, go from trembling and trimmed with lace to bubbling and spitting at her like it was now? Alex watched, mesmerised, as angry white dots hit the back of the oven, disappearing into the grease and food splatter that had built up since Katie was born. She watched as the tidemarks forming along the inside of the pan went from nicotine to sepia, and the liquid reduced itself to coagulated soup. Then she switched off the hob. She didn't want a hot chocolate anyway. All she wanted was a good night's sleep – and her job back.

From her play mat Katie gurgled, and Alex turned, guilty at having forgotten her daughter's existence even for a minute. 'What if you leave the house and forget the baby?'

she'd asked Joyce when pregnant. 'It's not like your keys,' her colleague had laughingly replied. 'The baby's at the front and back of your mind, twenty-four-seven. They're proper little people, remember, even before they can talk.'

Only, Katie didn't seem like a little person. Looking up at her mother now, her beautiful blue eyes blank, she seemed more like an alien creature, silently judging her for all her failures.

'Having fun down there?'

Crouching down beside her and blocking her nose to the all-permeating smell of baby powder, Alex jiggled one of the little monkeys hanging overhead. She'd picked up the £80 'play gym' for £15 from Fara Kids, a bargain that only made sense days later when she'd discovered that the electronic elephant with light-up ears could only manage one of the '20 merry melodies' advertised on the battered box. Thanks to that malfunction, 'The Wheels on the Bus' was liable to start up its sickly melody unasked – once even waking both her and Katie in the early hours – just because it could. Three months on Alex found herself clenching her teeth as the first notes rang out through the flat, and she reached out now to switch it off.

How could something so tiny need so much stuff? She'd got it all as cheaply as she could, from charity shops or eBay, but already the seven grand her mum had lent her was gone, and Alex was all too aware that within months there would be a whole new list of necessities: the Moses basket would have to be swapped for a baby bed with a new mattress, and soon she'd need a high chair and a bath chair, safety rails and booster seats.

She thought about the August deadline her mother had

made her swear she'd meet. Alex had to pay back the money she'd borrowed by then – or her father would find out.

'He mustn't know,' her mum had whispered down the phone.

For as long as Alex could remember, her father had always been referred to with that fearful 'he'. And this one was more fearful than most. 'I took the money out of the new account we set up, so he won't notice it's missing until we have to transfer the deposit.'

'Deposit?'

'On the new house.'

Alex didn't point out that she'd never even seen the old house; that she'd never been invited – and that most people didn't have to wait for an invitation from their own parents.

Equally fearful of what 'he' might say, Alex hadn't even been able to bring herself to tell her mother she'd lost her job, allowing herself only a moment's honesty: 'I need you, Mum. I want you to share these first few months, share Katie with me. I didn't expect Dad to be on the first plane over . . . ' But what kind of man doesn't let his wife meet her only grandchild?

Usually so good at defending her husband – 'he's tired', 'he's tetchy' and the one-size-fits-all 'he doesn't mean it' – Alex's mum had fallen silent at the other end of the line, before offering a resigned 'You know what your father's like.'

Alex knew. She just wasn't expecting the other men in her life to be as bad.

Pulling her phone from the pocket of the bathrobe she'd slung on top of her jeans and T-shirt instead of a cardigan, Alex scrolled down to Hayden's number and exhaled deeply. His face – disbelieving, then horrified – when she told him.

His voice, cold, suspicious: 'How can you be sure it's mine?' She couldn't do it. Not when her last words to him had been: 'If you want no part in Katie's life, I'll do this alone. I promise, I'll never ask you for anything.' Not when she'd made the same silent vow to her own father thirteen years earlier, the little parenting he had done having been terminated, with contractual abruptness, before she was even old enough to vote.

On she scrolled, down to J: yet another spineless male waste of space, to add to lover and father. 'Jamie home', 'Jamie mobile', 'Jamie Devon house'. She had more numbers for the man who'd been her world for the past year than she did for her own parents – and a deep reluctance to call any of them. Looking from those numbers to the blinking clock beneath the telly – 5.24 p.m. – and back to Katie, Alex willed her daughter to give her some kind of a sign, but there were only those blank blue eyes: bottomless pools of need. She was the only one who could answer that need, and feeling the last of her dignity drain away, Alex tapped the phone and put it to her ear.

Jamie picked up immediately. 'Al, I'm in the middle of something.'

Alex heard the distant drone of pub music and the clink of glasses, the rise of a joke being told and the fall of a punchline. Even by his standards this was an early start at the Firkin.

'I'll be quick.' She spoke with eyes closed: 'I'd had a bit to drink – at Joyce's party. And I might have come across a bit . . . strong.' But not nearly as strong as I'd have liked to, you useless, treacherous piece of shit. 'Anyway, I realise it wasn't the right time for us to have had that discussion. Sorry.'

She felt physically nauseous apologising to him, but it

had been over a week now, and there was still no word from either Jill or Nicole. If there was still a chance – any chance – that Jamie could help her out, it would be worth it. 'But that job – I was really counting on it . . . ' Reaching for her daughter's tiny foot, she squeezed hard enough for Katie to scrunch up her eyes in a pre-wail grimace, before letting go. 'I really need that job, Jamie. I'm nearly out of money. And so if you really don't think your mate needs anyone . . . ' She took a breath. 'I mean, is there . . . could there be anyone else who might? Or would it be possible –' she cringed at what she was about to ask '– given we both know that what happened wasn't my fault. Given you owe me, Jamie . . . I'm just a bit stuck, you see. All I need is enough to tide me over.'

'Alex.' Jamie sounded more bored than annoyed and she pictured him standing by the pub door, where it was quieter, motioning at all his boozing BWL colleagues that he'd be right back. 'Like I said: there is no job. Got my wires crossed. And look, I really am sorry and I wish you well. I hope you know that. You've got little . . . '

'Katie.'

'You've got little Katie now. And in the end family's what matters most, right? Now I've really got to go.'

At the click, Alex pulled the phone away from her ear and stared at it in disbelief.

'You little shit!'

Alarmed by her mother's tone, Katie hiccupped into a high-pitched complaint. It was too early for her feed and the NHS health visitor had warned darkly against 'overfeeding', but Alex pulled up her T-shirt. 'Take it. Take it!' Again, Katie refused to latch on, jerking her head away just as she had ever since the night of Joyce's leaving do.

Alex wasn't superstitious, but she had started to wonder whether taking her breast away for that single night and allowing herself to be consumed by the hate that now ran through her veins like poison had soured her milk.

The morning after the party she had woken up hung-over and sleep-deprived but buoyant. She hadn't been the only one conned by Jamie, and as shocking as Nicole's revelations had been, they were the validation she needed. Alex had done nothing wrong, but Jamie? He was wrong to the core. And with BWL's founder now aware of who her protégé really was, Alex could breathe easy, knowing his payday was coming. Only as that day had passed and then the next, without the expected text or call from either Jill or Nicole, Alex's exhilaration had faded into doubt. Had she exaggerated the two women's anger in her mind? Imagined their complicity in the plan? No. This wasn't about her playing anything up. This was about their self-preservation.

Pointing her engorged breast at Katie with one hand, and wiping away tears with the back of the other, Alex hissed: 'You want the bottle? Have it.' And too tired to fight, she got one ready, laid her daughter in her lap and held her breath until she saw the muscles in Katie's cheeks slow their mechanical suction down to nothing, and her eyes flutter shut.

How did stay-at-home mums cope with these endless days? Alex had worked long hours at BWL, and in the build-up to a conference or a big sale the work could be gruelling – but not like this. Nothing like this. There wasn't an employer in the Western world who didn't let you pee when you needed to. Although of course if you had a man there, a co-parent, things would be different. There would be some form of human interaction, for a start.

Who had Alex spoken to since she'd woken – been woken – just before 4 a.m.? Her GP's harassed receptionist in a conversation that had lasted all of thirty seconds. An automated voice on her parents' answer machine. 'Why won't Katie take the breast any more?' she'd so desperately wanted to ask her mother. 'Why? When it's the one thing I know how to do.' And yet she hadn't left a message, knowing that her father might intercept it and hear the desperation in her voice. The guy in the 7-Eleven had somehow managed to carry out their whole transaction that morning without even nodding, sick to death of human interaction, probably, or vaguely repulsed by the dribbling baby attached to her chest. The way some people looked at you when you sat down next to them on the bus or Tube, like you were diseased. And Alex didn't blame the ones who moved away, rolling their eyes at Katie's screams. Babies were messy and smelly and loud – even your own.

Her laptop was tantalisingly close, poking out from beneath an old coffee-ringed *Metro* on the coffee table, and Alex did the quick risk assessment every mother of a sleeping infant is forced to make in order to secure herself a few precious minutes of freedom. Having successfully transferred Katie from her arms to the sofa, she clicked on the inbox she'd been checking a dozen times a day in the hope of finding a conciliatory message from Jamie – sucking in a breath when she saw the email.

Nestled in between her Tesco Clubcard newsletter and an eBay reminder to 'pay for your baby sleep sack' was a message from one Ashley Bucknall; subject header, termination of contract. And immediately something didn't feel right. For a minute, Alex's finger hovered over the message, and when she did double click on it, she was surprised to see that there was no cover email, only a Word document attached. Opening up what turned out to be just three pages, Alex scanned the first, a letter:

Dear Ms Fuller, as we discussed in person on 4 May of this year, please be advised that LWB are terminating your contract which began ... As she scanned down, Alex's nails dug into the sofa: *Please find enclosed details of the full and final maternity leave payments. This should bring us up to date. As is usual with a serious misconduct dismissal* ... Here the words began to bleed into the screen. 'Serious misconduct'? She looked over at Katie, as though her sleeping baby could help make sense of this. Only of course she couldn't. Nothing could. And the full extent of Jamie's duplicity opened up before her. Nothing he'd said in that meeting had been true: not the 'misconduct' she was supposed to have committed, not the promise to keep her sacking quiet and have the paperwork 'simply state that you resigned'. How was she supposed to get another job with that on her record? But the biggest lie of all had been the JLL job, dangled like a carrot in order to get her to leave quietly – then withdrawn as soon as Alex was safely out of the way.

Funny how close love is to hate; how strong the desire to see that person's face is, when caught in the vortex of either. Like a teenage girl, Alex pulled up Google images, chewing at the insides of her mouth as she moved from image to image of warm-eyed, duplicitous Jamie. In all the time she'd worked for him, she'd never thought to look at Jamie's social media – the intricacies of her boss's life being her daily bread. And it would have been hard for most people to work up much curiosity about a man who overshared as much as Jamie did with a pint inside him. Even the most transient drinking partner at the Firkin would hear about everything from the marital bust-ups prompted by his secretive smoking bouts ('I swear she can smell them on me from a mile away') and tendency to leave his wedding ring lying about ('If I ever do lose it, Maya's going to freak'), to the exorbitant cost of the Antiguan beach-front suite he was 'about to push the button on' for New Year. But when she scrolled down to find Jamie's Facebook and Instagram pages now, it felt like uncovering virtual gold.

There, at her fingertips, were ten years' worth of Jamie's life: a treasure trove of birthdays, anniversaries and marital mini-breaks, pub nights and date nights and everything braggable in between. And as she clicked through a series of 'family man' posts, Alex found herself increasingly intrigued by the woman who had been so taken in by this fraud that she'd married him.

Alex had seen enough pictures of Jamie's model-esque wife on both her ex-boss's office shelves and phone to be familiar with the pleasing contrast of dark brows and honey-blonde hair, sharp cheekbones and full lips, and because he'd always talked of his wife's looks as though they were a credit to him, she'd dismissed them. But zooming in on Maya now, she was forced to concede that something about this west London trophy wife elevated her above the rest of the breed.

Hers was a clean, catalogue-style beauty that managed to be both cosy and alienating. But it was the freshness – the sort very few women possess much past twenty – that was most disconcerting. Maya was a good few years older than

Alex, and yet everything from her hair and lips, bare but for a slick of coral pink gloss, to the lightly tanned skin of her arms had an untouched quality to it, a newness – as though life had either failed to rub off on her or Maya had been sheltered from anything unpleasant enough to leave a mark.

Alex found herself returning to one Instagram image in particular. Taken a few months earlier, exactly sixteen days after she'd given birth (Alex worked it out), it featured Maya standing in their Bedford Park back garden in jeans and a sweatshirt. As Maya had outstretched a gardening-gloved hand towards whoever was taking the photo – Jamie, presumably – her mouth open in rueful protestation, that sweatshirt had risen up to expose a few inches of lower stomach. 'Come on!' Alex could almost hear her telling her proud husband. Because although it looked eerily perfect to Alex, without a blue vein or stretch mark in sight, in Maya's head she hadn't got her body back yet. Jamie would have known how his wife felt. She would have told him that morning when he rolled, breathless, off her, pinching the tiniest inch of abdomen between her thumb and forefinger and pouting: 'Look what you did to me.' And Jamie would have laughed, telling Maya she was as gorgeous as ever, maybe even bending down to kiss her stomach.

Jamie had only posted once more since that day. A west London park scene from the first weekend in May. The plaid rug was there, but this wasn't your usual picnic debris: no Scotch eggs and cocktail sausages for this family. Instead there was something quiche-like in a brown Daylesford paper bag, a peeled and quartered pomelo, and the glinting green neck of what must have been a Sancerre or a Chablis – both favourites of Jamie's, she knew – poking from a cooler.

Little Elsa asleep on Maya's chest, Christel making a face behind her father: 'My girls.'

Those two posts took Alex down a Maya-shaped rabbit hole. Jamie may have been a liar, harasser and very probably a cheat, but there was no doubt he was still entranced by the woman he'd married. And if Maya was one of the things Jamie valued most beside his job, then Alex was going to need to get a little closer – and work out how she could make use of this.

Her fingers moving at lightning speed across the keyboard, she googled 'Maya Lawrence' before starting on some full-blown social media stalking. How had she never thought to do this sooner? Maya's Facebook and Instagram had started way back when she was Maya Juhl, 'interior designer', pictured leaning against a design board in her Copenhagen studio in ripped boyfriend jeans. Too pretty to be taken seriously, she'd taken to wearing heavy black-rimmed black glasses and a challenging expression over the following months: always perched on the arm of some absurdly minimalist sofa or crossing her arms in the foreground of a monochrome hotel lobby we were supposed to believe she'd designed herself. But something had happened when she moved to London – Jamie? And Maya had become a softer, more playful woman; a woman who wore sundresses and plimsolls, sucked beer foam off her top lip and took selfies of herself kissing a younger, slimmer Jamie.

The baby period – Christel and then Elsa – had come next, and Alex marvelled at the self-indulgence of the photogenic Lawrences, forcing image after image of their perfect progeny down people's throats in what was billed as a display of selfless love but was in fact extreme narcissism. As were the endless pictures of their lush Bedford Park back garden and conservatory, the tomato plants Maya was at pains to make people believe she'd grown herself, and a Stepford Wife post, the previous week, of one of those rainbow 'days of the week' pillboxes rammed full of virtuous-looking capsules. 'Putting the husband on a vitamin schedule!'

The most recent post was of some kind of Mummy and Me class. Pictured in a circle of pampered and laughing Chiswick mums, her spandex-clad legs angled out in a diamond before her, Maya was focused intently on Elsa's little head, supported by her feet. And as Alex zoomed in on the caption – 'Little Gym class at Bumps & Babies. Great place to make new friends!' – her stomach dipped at the realisation of how different two women's experiences of early motherhood could be.

The whine and groan of a scooter breaking outside snapped Alex out of it, and going to the window she gazed down at the familiar hooded figure on the corner, his shadowy customers emerging from cars and doorways to place their nightly orders, the cross-body Fila bag briskly and repeatedly delved into for coke, weed and whatever else people needed to stock up on with alarming regularity. It was past eight now, and because she'd let Katie go off far too early, her daughter would be up all night. But she'd be up all night anyway. She always was. And although Alex felt hollow with tiredness, she was still too worked up to sleep – almost as worked up as she'd been in the early hours of the morning after Joyce's party, when she'd discovered how easy that pub plan would be to implement.

The 'mis-filing' of the D-List, along with Hugo Mears's email, had been an experiment. If it came off, and unsettled

Jill and Nicole at the same time, all the better. Alex hadn't expected her old BWL intranet access code to work – the one she'd used to change Jamie's meeting times and flights, book the Addison Lee cars she could follow on the office database from pick-up to drop-off, and edit documents when out of the office. And, sure enough, it hadn't. The idea of busy Jamie bothering to get IT to change it had rankled in the moment, then a joke he'd made over an *Evening Standard* article on the least secure phone pins came back to her. 'Who seriously still uses their birthday as a pin?' Alex had tittered. 'Guilty,' her boss had grimaced. And she'd had to tell Jamie off for being unsafe. He wasn't stupid, but he was lazy – and when Alex had tried '123456' – the code IT always provided under the proviso you immediately change it – BWL's portal had opened up before her.

A list of staff members in charge of each project was available on the main portal, alongside documents detailing the week's viewings, deals and passes, but another password had been needed to access Jamie's email and calendar, and this hadn't proved so easy. Jamie's wedding day no longer worked and Maya, Christel and Elsa's birthdays all bounced, with and without a '1' at the end. The little red words 'forgot password?' taunted her. How many more tries before she would be locked out? One, two? Staring out of the window at the row of dishevelled Victorian townhouses opposite, Alex had forced her mind to go blank, something she did on the rare occasions she forgot her credit card pin number. Then she'd typed in six letters: 'NICOLE.' 'Fucking predator,' she'd muttered as Jamie's inbox had opened up before her.

Alex had known what to do the second she spotted the Minerva pitch meeting with the O'Ceallaighs in Jamie's calendar. If the D-list was such an in-joke at BWL, with both Jill and Nicole in on it, then there would surely be people with access to the file. And when a quick keyword search of his inbox had unearthed Mears's email advising 'transparency' – something Alex was now well aware her former boss wasn't a fan off – she'd decided to throw it in for fun: for that extra twist of embarrassment. Just a few clicks had transferred both documents into Jamie's Minerva presentation file, one she was confident he wouldn't be bothered to review on the day: Jamie never did. But however much she'd enjoyed reading the 'Minerva fuck-up'-themed email exchanges that were still doing the rounds days later, Jamie already seemed to be wriggling out of it.

In the days after Joyce's leaving do Alex had been desperate for any form of acknowledgement from Nicole or Jill. Now, it was clear that they had erased her from their minds – along with the plan. But Alex couldn't. She wouldn't. And a little professional embarrassment clearly wasn't enough. Not for Jamie – and not for Alex. Opening up her laptop once more, she bashed in 'Bumps & Babies'. What was it he was always saying, unaware of the pang it caused her? 'Family's what matters most'? And after just the smallest hesitation, she clicked on 'Book a class.'

CHAPTER 11

JILL

'I don't know how much clearer I can be on this.'

Jamie was speaking slowly, elongating the vowels and punctuating each clause with a nod, and Jill was tempted to point out that she was neither his child nor his PA. 'I honestly don't know how this happened. I had the site plan right there on my tablet and I'd been through the Minerva presentation file the day before. It must have been misnamed. Or maybe even some kind of bug?'

'It must have been' was a favourite phrase of Jamie's, his default reaction to any oversight or bungle. But this time Jill suspected his wide-eyed wonderment might be genuine. Was this Nicole's doing? Alex's? Or both of them putting into action a plan she'd dismissed as drunken bravado?

'Listen, we've been over and over this. We're all clear I'm to blame, right? Do you see me disputing that?'

Cocking her head to one side, Jill scrutinised her colleague. His body language was still languorous, entitled: long legs outstretched, hands interlinked behind his neck. And Jill wished they were having this conversation in her office, where the power dynamic would be weighted in her favour. She also wished Jamie were being more sheepish and less combative.

'It's not about blame, Jamie.' Glancing at her watch, she sighed. 'It's about making sure that when the O'Ceallaigh brothers are shown up in less than two hours' time we really are ready.'

'I am,' he insisted. 'I'm going to go in there, level with them about every single weakness on Minerva, explain that the reason I didn't mention the sale of the JLL site nearby was because I wasn't convinced it would actually go through . . .'

'Lie, you mean.'

' . . . and then sell it to them all over again. Tell them having a Westfield just over the bridge would bring more business, not less, yada, yada.' He leaned forward. 'You think I don't know how important this is? I'm a big boy, Jill.'

'So you're sure you don't want me to sit in?'

'Yes.'

'Just that it's taken a lot of convincing to get them back in.'

'I'm aware of that – largely because I'm the one who has spent the past week making it happen.'

'A week in which we could have been showing Minerva to other people, Jamie. But you insisted we hold off.' She shrugged. 'For all we know, the O'Ceallaighs have given up on us and already started sniffing around JLL, our more "transparent" counterparts.'

'Jill! I can fix this. Weren't you the one always telling me, way back when, not to go running to people when you've made a mistake: "Just fix it"?'

'I was.' She was pleased he'd remembered. 'And the vintage Glenlochy was a masterful touch.'

'Thank you. It's almost as though I know what I'm doing.'

'Christ, you're so defensive.'

Jamie took a deep breath, swallowing whatever it was he'd been about to say. 'I just need you to stop micro-managing. I've got this sorted.'

'OK.' She smoothed her skirt. 'That a new picture of little Elsa?'

Jamie swivelled his chair around to take the framed family photograph off the shelf behind his desk.

'Isn't she gorgeous?' Running a thumb across three bright white smiles and the blinking bundle at the centre of them all, he passed the photograph to Jill.

'Lovely.' She'd got good at those tenderised tones over the years, even if she never felt that squeeze in her gut, the way she imagined a mother would. 'Maya thinking of going back to work at some point? She mentioned something about it a while back.'

'Oh, I don't think so. It's not realistic right now. We've got help, but I'm not having my kids brought up by some stranger.'

Jamie put the photo back on the shelf, beside an old one of his wife looking trophy-tastic on a beach somewhere equally trophy-tastic. And although Jill had seen the picture a million times and taken in the cut-offs, sheer shirt and row of bangles glinting white in the sun, although she was well aware that in terms of male desirability, this woman was basically a blueprint, the word that popped, unwelcome, into her head as she headed back towards her office was 'fuckable'.

'You look fuckable today.' Wasn't that what Nicole claimed Jamie had said? Banishing the memory with a shake of the head, she picked up the phone to make the first client callback on the list the new PA had left on her desk, dismayed if not surprised to see that Kellie with an 'ie' had the writing of a primary schoolgirl.

'Edward, it's Jill. I just wanted to see whether you had any thoughts about the Portland Road property?'

Edward Dinnigan liked a chat and after sticking him on speaker, Jill checked her mobile for messages from Stan before moving on to her emails. By the time she had answered all but the last three, Edward was still showing no signs of wrapping up a description of his week's yachting trip in Èze.

'Dammit,' she cursed as she clicked too fast on a message that looked like spam.

'What's that?'

'Nothing – you were saying you were glad you had the stabilisers.'

Raxugdy@sharklaser.com; subject heading: WITH FRIENDS LIKE THESE. This wasn't good. She'd get Tara in IT to see if she'd gone and given herself a virus. But the message wasn't asking her to click on a link – or do anything. No, it seemed to be the forwarded thread of a back and forth that had taken place in January between Jamie and Paul. The subject heading was CLARENDON CENTRE, a 150,000-square-foot retail property they'd reluctantly sold for far less than the asking price the following month, and the thrust of the exchange was the difficulty BWL were having in selling it. Only when she reached the third email, from Jamie, did Jill understand why the conversation had been forwarded.

Thinking we take care of this one ourselves? YKW pretty out of it these days. Senile sixties on top of it all? Could be . . . either way not sure she's the kind of image we really want to be projecting right now. And anyway shouldn't she be taking some time off to be home with Stan?

'Edward?'

'Sorry. I'm rabbiting. Now about Portland Road—'

'Sorry,' Jill could feel a wave of heat rising cartoon-like up her face. Only there was nothing comical about either that or the feeling that the room's proportions had changed. 'I've got someone on the other line who's being most persistent.' Her voice sounded like it belonged to someone else. 'Can I give you a call back?'

Had it not been for the age reference, Jill thought, as she reread the email thread, slowly this time, noting and appreciating Paul's refusal to engage with the worst parts of Jamie's email – *She's had a tough time of it, but I get the feeling work has been a help, not a hindrance* – she might have been able to convince herself that the email wasn't about her. As it was, Jill could be in no doubt that she was 'You Know Who', and that if Jamie really had written these words, he wasn't just the predator and opportunist revealed to her that night in the pub, but something far worse.

CHAPTER 12

~≈~

NICOLE

'Why didn't you wake me?'

It was gone nine by the time Nicole padded downstairs to the kitchen. And although Ben always let her sleep in on a Saturday, it was rare that she managed to beyond eight.

'You looked like you needed it.' Her husband smiled and leaned in for a kiss.

'You smell of coffee,' she murmured blearily, because he did, she wanted some, and when he went to make it for her, which she knew he would, Ben would be forced to relax the grip he had on her shoulders. Nicole had always found her husband's need for early morning contact slightly stifling.

'Is it the nice stuff? From the Charleville Road place?'

'Yup. I told Mama Anna you thought the other one was too weak.'

'Not weak, too nutty . . . or something. Where's Chlo?'

'In there.' Ben gestured with his chin towards the adjoining room, where the helium shrieks of SpongeBob could be heard. 'Chlo, come and say good morning to Mummy!'

'I'll go.' Tucking a rogue strand of hair behind her ear, she rubbed her eyes. 'Just give me a second. Who's Mama Anna again?'

Ben laughed. That she couldn't identify which of the genial Italian deli ladies was 'Mama Anna' might seem odd to her husband, who was on first name terms with most of the baristas in the area, but in Nicole's mind it was Ben's interest in these peripheral people's existences that was weird.

'The owner! The one whose husband, Rocco, died last year? Who always gives Chloe those Baci chocolates?'

'The old bird who fancies you?'

'They all fancy me,' he threw back with a wink.

They probably did. Six-foot-five, long-limbed and long-faced, with lashes Nicole would kill for and a smile that went all the way up to the slightly mournful diagonals of his eyebrows, Ben had always been a hit with the grannies and mums. Hell, even the babysitters seemed to linger a good twenty minutes too long at the end of the night, intent on asking her husband for advice on how to frame their Instagram posts.

Safe and kind and brought up in a house full of women, Ben wasn't so much a grand seducer, however, as the guy you sought solace with when you were dumped – and ended up falling for. 'Mr right in front of you': that was her husband, and exactly how the two of them had got together, *When Harry Met Sally*-style, in their third year at Bristol.

'Anyway this one's fortissimo, according to Mama Anna, *come tua moglie.*'

Nicole raised an eyebrow.

'Like your wife.'

'Ah.' She took a sip. It was strong and bitter and Nicole tried not to extend Mama Anna's simile in her head. 'Hello, sweetie.'

Pushing through the double doors that separated the kitchen from the playroom, repainted pink by Ben just the week before, Nicole set her coffee down on the floor and pulled Chloe onto her lap. The back of her four-year-old's neck smelt of Burt's Bees, and in that moment nothing else mattered.

'What are you watching?'

'SpongeBob. He's fighting with an eel.'

'Is he?'

'Can you eat eels?'

'You can. They're not very nice. Bit slimy. These new PJs?'

Eyes glued to the screen, Chloe nodded, and Nicole didn't much care that her daughter wasn't in the mood to talk. She secretly liked it when Chloe was engrossed in something other than her. It was when she ran up to greet her mother as soon as she walked through the door on a weekday evening that Nicole found hard. Not being able to kick off her shoes, sit down for a minute and breathe as that hot little body wrapped itself around her.

Then there were the questions; so many questions. Not just from Chloe but Ben too: how was her day? Any sales? Where did she go and who did she see? Like she was a pigtailed schoolgirl who couldn't wait to tell them both everything she'd learned about the Great Wall of China, but also, somehow, the great decider. Should we have the beef or the salmon? Did she have a chance to look at the school forms he emailed over? And by the way, how about an office shed at the bottom of the garden? She was in control at work, a kind of domestic CEO at home, and sometimes she fantasised about relinquishing all that control, having someone tell her what she wanted and needed, giving herself over to that.

Welded together, the weight of Chloe and Ben's expectations was often enough to send Nicole straight off upstairs for a shower. The advice her mother had given her on her wedding day – 'Just remember always to give Ben a drink, something to eat and half an hour's quiet when he gets home from work' – only seemed to apply to men. The implication was that working women were already getting their 'me time' at the office, that being allowed to work was their indulgence.

Pulling her daughter onto her lap, she whispered, 'What do you want to do today?'

'Playground! Daddy said! Daddy said!'

'I did.' Ben appeared at the door, faintly apologetic with a steaming cafetière in his hand. 'But Mummy's going to need caffeine if she's going to brave the playground.'

Over Chloe's glossy dark curls they locked eyes and Nicole felt a surge of guilt and love – the two so closely intertwined where Ben and Chloe were concerned as to be almost indistinguishable. She'd barely seen either all week and there was no reason they should be tiptoeing around her. 'But it's gorgeous out, I've got zero work to do and the playground would be fun, wouldn't it, ladybird? Shall we go upstairs and get dressed? If we get there early maybe there won't be too many of those big bully boys on the wobbly bridges?'

'Actually the council took the bridges away last month,' said Ben. 'Some health and safety thing.'

'They did?'

It wasn't a slight – one of those pointed little reminders of moments she'd missed in her daughter's life, from clothes she'd never seen before to fads Nicole sometimes only caught on to once they were over. But she always felt the sting, regardless.

'You don't think this room is too pink?' she murmured as Chloe bounded up the stairs.

'No,' said Ben. 'You do?'

'I'm just . . . wary of the whole pink thing.'

'So you've said.'

'Seriously, though, there was a piece in the *Guardian* the other day about behavioural conditioning, and I just don't want Chloe feeling she has to grow up according to some set of rules society laid out for her centuries ago.'

'Is that how you feel when you come home to your house husband?'

'Stop it.' She gave Ben a play punch. 'You're not a house husband. It's just been a dry period. The work'll come in.'

'Actually,' he said with a smile, 'it looks like it already has. Get dressed. I'll tell you on the way.'

When he did, showing her an email on his phone from a renowned Notting Hill-based interior designer interested in getting Ben to shoot a brand film for use in the US, Nicole tried to sound upbeat. But she doubted that Oscar, who was famous and self-regarding enough to be known by his Christian name alone, would see the point of Ben's discreet style. And there had been enough professional near misses over the past three years to make Nicole wary of getting her husband too excited.

'Did you send them the promo you shot for Afshin?'

'No, Chloe, not too close to the road please! You think I should?'

'Well – yes.' Why did her husband find it so hard to push himself forward? 'That would have been the first thing I'd have shown him.'

They'd reached the park, and as Ben unlatched the gate, allowing Chloe to be pushed into the playground by a sudden influx of children behind her, she could see the tension in her husband's face: a hardening of his top lip and refusal to meet her eye.

'Anyway, do whatever you think,' she soothed, relieved as she so often was that they both had Chloe to look at. 'You know best.'

'Apparently not. If I knew best I'd be getting the work, wouldn't I?'

'No Ben … God, that's not what I meant. But don't be, you know, worried to big yourself up – that's all I'm saying. You're so talented, and there's so much shit out there. It's just about making people see that.'

One of the only three much-coveted benches in the playground was empty and they sat in silence for a few minutes, Nicole angling her face away to tug on her e-cigarette.

'Wish you wouldn't.'

'It's better than fags.'

'Nothing would be better still. Anyway it stinks.'

Reluctantly, she slipped it back into her bag.

'Vanilla.'

Nothing.

'I'll help you put together a new portfolio tomorrow if you like? And we can make sure the Afshin promo film is right at the top?'

'Yeah?' He shot her a sideways glance.

'Yeah. Let's do it. The old one's what ... two years old?'

'Three. Maybe four.'

'Ben.'

'I know ...'

Nicole took Ben's hand and gave it a squeeze, calling out 'Stay to that side' as Chloe worked her way nimbly around the rope climbing frame towards the posse of Adidas-clad older boys clambering up the other side.

'She's all right.'

'It's those little shits I'm worried about.'

'They're eight-year-old boys, Nic.'

'Did you see them deliberately rocking the rope bridges last time we were here? Eight-year-old boys can be little shits.' Nicole stood up.

'What are you doing?'

'I just want to keep an eye on them. I'm not having her bullied, Ben.'

'For God's sake.' Grabbing Nicole's hand, he pulled her back down.

'They're not bullying anyone. Look.'

He was right. The boys had parted to allow Chloe to climb up to the top of the frame.

'Even the other day, they were just ...'

'Being boys?'

'Yeah. Jeez – I wouldn't have wanted to be on the same climbing frame as you as a boy.'

'No, you wouldn't have.'

She loved to picture her younger self through Ben's admiring eyes. He would never have imagined that she hadn't come into the world with the hard shell she prided herself on today. That it had taken years to stand up first to the three older brothers who discounted her from their games and derided her opinions at the dinner table as a child. That every casual misogynistic comment she'd forced herself to ignore in meetings over the years took her back to the teenage schoolboys who had tried to drown out her answers in class with heckles of 'I can see Nicole's bra strap!' Because little shits grew up to be big shits.

Conscious that Ben was still frowning at her, Nicole cracked a smile. 'Look at Chlo. Fearless, isn't she?'

And they both had what felt like the first easy laugh of the morning.

Was this what happy felt like? Sitting on a bench with your husband in the early morning sun, watching the little human it took five years and two rounds of IVF to make grow into someone capable and strong? Laughing at your daughter's determined little face as she tried and failed and tried again? That resolve was all her mother's, Nicole knew, and she alone would have to cultivate it in her daughter, pushing her to disregard the doubts and climb ever higher.

That she could have jeopardised all this for someone as meaningless as Ian didn't so much seem wrong, all these years later, as strange: the actions of someone else. Then again, her need for sex had never cohered with the rest of her – with her principles, with her disdain for men. And when, years ago, she'd chanced upon a magazine article on 'erotic friction' by some famous American psychiatrist, the phrase had struck her as exactly right. Because her physical desire for men ran counter to that other logical side of Nicole – it bred an itch beneath her skin that needed to be scratched. This wasn't just inconvenient but humiliating, and she'd hoped that marriage would be a balm. Apart from anything else, you weren't then allowed to give into those impulses, were you? But perhaps it had been as simple as Nicole wanting an affair, and feeling she deserved one after years being pumped full of hormones and the eventual arrival of Chloe.

Certainly it hadn't been about Ian. Transferred from the Nottingham office to manage their corporate estates, he'd simply been there – and willing. And the first surprise had been how minimal the guilt was; the second how improved she'd been as a human being in virtually every area of her life. At work her energy and efficiency had been heightened, and at home Nicole had found herself more patient with Chloe and loving towards Ben. But they hadn't been careful enough, and when Ian's wife had found out along with one or two of the BWL staff, when the rumours had spread and he had moved away, she'd felt both relieved for herself and grateful that Ben had never found out.

Nicole tugged hard on her vape as she remembered the awkwardness on Alex and Jill's faces when she'd mentioned Ian. Reminding people of something that had dwindled from general knowledge down to rumour over time had been stupid; she would never have done it sober. She would never have said what she had about Jamie, either. That had been dangerous. But Nicole was still so angry.

'You're not like other women,' he'd told her the second time. 'I knew that the day you walked into the office in those slutty shoes.'

'They weren't slutty.'

He'd ignored this. 'You're tough. You can take more than other women.'

'Jamie, you're hurting me.'

'But you like it.'

'No.'

'No?'

And just like that he'd released her hands from where they'd been pinned, above her head on the cold tiled floor of the office gym's changing room. Then, looking dispassionately down at her exposed stomach, where her T-shirt had ridden up: 'Still got a bit of a mummy tummy, haven't we?' He'd grinned. 'Weird. I can never picture you as a mum.'

'Mummy, Mummy! Look at me!' Her daughter's voice reached her from the top of the climbing frame. One bunch had fallen out and Chloe's face was partially obscured by a dark curtain of hair, but the half smile Nicole could see almost reached her ear.

'Look at you, ladybird!'

'Sweetie, you're too high.'

'Ben, she's fine. Well done! Now hold on tight on your way down.'

Nicole was quiet on the way home, content to lag behind Ben and Chloe, semi-soothed by their prattle. Having ascertained that her father had never climbed either a mountain or the Eiffel Tower, her daughter had adjusted her expectation levels accordingly and was now working her way down from Big Ben – which he'd assured her you weren't allowed up – to their house.

'Once?' she asked, dismayed.

'Only once have I been up to our roof?' Ben laughed. 'Yes. Sorry to disappoint again, Chlo. Just the once to clean the gutters.'

'Gutters? And Mummy?'

'Hmm?'

Father and daughter had turned towards her, mid-laugh, but Nicole didn't look up, slowing now almost to a halt. A group email from Jamie – MINERVA UPDATE – had just pinged in and she was transfixed by the tone of it. Pompous and self-congratulatory, it described the previous day's meeting with the O'Ceallaigh brothers as 'a last-minute save' and predicted 'a move on Minerva' by the end of the month. Signed off 'Onwards and upwards!', it somehow managed to make light of one of the biggest cock-ups of Jamie's career, if not the history of BWL. And already the laudatory emails were coming back: 'Nice one, mate!'; 'You might just have pulled it out of the bag!' Had any woman made a blunder on that scale, she would have been out by close of play. But it took more than one or two strikes to impact a man's career, and true to form Jamie was somehow going to emerge unscathed.

'Have you, Mum?'

'Have I what?'

'The roof, Mummy – have you ever climbed onto our roof?'

'No, ladybird. Why would I do that?'

They reached the house in silence, Nicole's distraction somehow having killed the mood. And while Chloe constructed an elaborate fortress for her My Little Ponies, Ben made a start on lunch.

'You're going to have to stop doing this, Nic,' he said eventually, without looking up from the chopping board. And actually she was relieved. It was her husband's silences she dreaded most.

'Doing . . . ?'

'Just not being here when you're with us. Being on that –'

115

he pointed the tip of his knife at the iPhone beside her on the sofa '– when you should be interacting with her.'

'Interacting? Have you been spending too much time on Mumsnet again? She knows I have a job, Ben. Sorry if it doesn't always confine itself to the hours of nine to five but there's not much I can do about that. And actually I think it's good for her to see her mum working: understand that women are more than just mothers and . . .'

But Ben was shaking his head. 'I'm not sure she cares about gender equality right now,' he whispered, looking over at Chloe. 'She just wants her mum to listen to her when she's talking. She just wants a bit of banter with you.'

'Right.' Nicole kept her voice level. 'It was one email, Ben, and a fairly important one. Shall we not turn it into some big deal?'

Over lunch and afterwards, as they watched *101 Dalmatians* with a shared tub of Häagen-Dazs and revelled in their caramel-smeared daughter's giggles, the two of them did a convincing job of burying any resentment. It was only once Chloe was asleep and Nicole emerged from as long and hot a bath as she could feasibly manage to find Ben still awake and scrolling through photos on his laptop, that any residual tension was acknowledged.

'You're a great mum, you know,' he murmured, turning out the light and pulling her heat-reddened body into his. And maybe it was the sense that Ben needed that reassurance more than she did that rankled. Or maybe it was the realisation that her husband's comment, like everything else, would only take her back to Jamie – 'I can never quite picture you as a mum' – who had tainted today just as he would every day until he was out of her life.

'Ben,' she started, and her voice sounded too loud in the darkness. 'Sorry if I've been a bit out of it. Work – it's ...'

'Getting you down?'

'Yeah.'

'Leave.' A rustle of sheets as he raised himself up on an elbow. 'Just leave. We'll be OK.'

Nicole said nothing, grateful he couldn't see her face. But her husband was right. If the things she'd heard herself saying that night in the pub proved anything, it was that either she or Jamie was going to have to go. And Nicole was ready to do whatever it took to make sure it wasn't her.

CHAPTER 13

ALEX

She was half an hour early. Despite Katie's extended meltdown in the bowels of Hammersmith station, the unpacking and repacking of the baby bag on a platform bench and an extensive search for a bin in which she had no wish to plant explosives, just a very ripe-smelling nappy, Alex had still managed to get to Bumps & Babies half an hour early.

As she pushed through the door, Katie had finally stopped whimpering and fallen asleep in the Babybjörn, heavy with formula, and Alex sank down onto a chair in the large reception area, too grateful for a moment of nothing to ask herself what she was doing here.

Sandwiched between a homeware boutique and an 'artisanal' coffee shop on Chiswick High Road, the club was light, airy and overdesigned. The reception was styled to look like a provençale kitchen, all crackled tiles, gullwing-grey fittings and rustic farmhouse furniture, and by the row of self-consciously battered French enamel pots labelled 'Café', 'Thé' and 'Sucre', a sign read: 'Mummies and Daddies Help Yourselves.' On the solid pine table at the centre of the room sat a tray of homemade flapjacks that Alex desperately wanted to get stuck into but didn't dare.

Through an open door off the main corridor she glimpsed a coterie of pregnant women rolling up their yoga mats, their Chiswick honking audible from where she sat.

'Can you imagine bidding on an auction prize you couldn't afford?'

'Jules must have been mortified.'

'I would be.'

As they walked past her the women threw Alex an appraising glance, the smiles coming as an afterthought. And she couldn't help noticing that even when about to pop they looked sleeker and better put together than she did.

No staff member had appeared yet and the realisation that Alex could just walk out of this place where she shouldn't be and didn't belong sent a shot of adrenaline through her veins. There would be some way of clawing back the membership deposit she'd rashly committed to that night, when she'd signed up as 'Lexie' – which they'd insisted on calling her in her computer science class at Norwich, to distinguish her from the prettier Alex. Only standing up so hurriedly woke Katie, and as Alex pulled open the front door, desperate to make her exit before anyone appeared, there stood a honey-blonde woman with a baby of almost exactly the same age enveloped in a crimson scarf-like sling: Maya.

'Whoops – sorry! You go first.'

Aside a flatness to the vowels and a faint rolling of the Rs you would never have guessed that English wasn't her first language. This, Alex had already logged from her handful of brief phone conversations with Maya. But she couldn't have known without seeing Jamie's wife in the flesh how empathetic her green eyes were – how deeply they seemed to see into you. And having quashed any last-minute worries earlier about this woman she'd never met somehow still recognising her, Alex felt a renewed terror that Maya might frown and ask: 'What are *you* doing here?'

'Oh dear. Someone's not happy.'

'Sorry?'

'Your baba.'

'Baba,' 'bundle': Alex wasn't sure which she hated more.

As the two women did a doorway dance, swaying awkwardly from one side to the other, Katie's grizzles descended into a full-scale meltdown.

'She's a bit colicky,' Alex murmured, trying to plug the dummy in her daughter's mouth. 'Least I think that's what it is.' With a whinny of irritation, Katie sent the dummy flying.

At this point Alex just needed to get out of there. Humiliated, again, by the disparities between her and this kind-faced blonde who could pull off mesh-panelled leggings four months out of a pregnancy, she tried and failed to retrieve the dummy from the floor. This wasn't going to be possible – not with Katie strapped to her chest.

'You go back in.' Maya laughed. 'I'll grab that. Not in a rush, are you?'

'I'm ...' Giving up, Alex backed into the reception area and sat down again.

Parted from Maya for a moment by a stream of mums, Alex tried to work out a line that would get her out of there quick. But by the time the women had passed Maya had scooped up her daughter's dummy, laid Elsa down in the play gym in the corner and was coming towards Katie, arms outstretched.

'Want me to give something a try?' she asked, elevating her voice above Katie's screams. 'My first had terrible colic, and there's this thing Danish doctors always tell you to do. Oh ...' She shook her head, laughing, and there was nothing contrived about her dizziness. 'I'm Danish. My husband's always saying I start conversations halfway through. Rewind: I'm Maya.'

'I'm ...' Alex's shoulders hunched at the ragged anguish of Katie's cries. 'I'm Lexie. Sorry about this.'

'Number one rule of motherhood: don't ever apologise about things that are beyond your control. Your first?'

Alex nodded.

'Hand her over.'

Alex did. Because there was nothing else for it. Because she'd always been cowed by bossy women, and because she'd caught a sinewy brunette over by the flapjacks wincing at the noise.

'Shall we do something about that sore tummy? Shall we?'

Watching Jamie's wife handle her child should have bothered her more than it did.

But Maya was gentle and precise with her movements, carrying Katie over to a cushioned bench in the corner of the room, where she laid her on her back and began pedalling her daughter's legs backwards and forwards until she stopped crying.

'It helps release the pressure on their stomachs,' she explained, running the flat of her palm over Katie's tummy. 'I sometimes wish someone would do this to me.' She looked over at her, and Alex felt a laugh bubble up.

But Maya was looking at her questioningly now. 'Lexie? That's you?'

And Alex turned to see a pixie-cutted redhead with a print-out looking around the room: 'Lexie? Do we have a Lexie?'

Jamie's wife had stopped stroking her daughter and was standing upright, staring straight at her. 'Busted.'

Alex felt her throat close up.

'I . . . sorry?'

'You were about to slope off, weren't you? Nearly did exactly the same thing the first time I came. Not really a "Mummy and Me" person, either. But listen, it's actually quite fun.'

'I'm sure . . .'

'Lexie's here,' Maya called out.

There was no way out now.

'OK. Looks like we've got everyone. Yoga Tots are on at noon, so Studio One please and let's get baby gymming!'

The class was every bit as cringeworthy as Alex had feared, and yet she was surprised to find herself enjoying it, even forcing back a fit of giggles when Maya had pulled a face at the instructor's talk of 'a skin-to-soul parenting approach'.

'Which way are you headed?' As everyone began gathering up their things, Maya's question caught her unawares.

'We're off home.'

'Home being?'

'Being . . . Stamford Brook.'

There was no reason why anyone who lived in Acton

would be a member of Bumps & Babies. And Alex was familiar with Stamford Brook, having spent a summer house-sitting for a friend off the Shepherd's Bush Road.

'Love it down that way!' Maya seemed in no hurry to be anywhere, which was making Alex nervous again. 'We looked for a place around there, but I so wanted a big garden. Anyway, we ended up in The Park – Bedford Park – so I can't complain.'

Tucking the still serene Elsa into her sling, Maya grabbed two complimentary bottles of something billing itself 'alkaline water' on the way out, passed one to Alex and fell unselfconsciously into step beside her.

'The instructor's a bit much, but I've met a couple of nice women through B&B over the years.'

'Over the years?'

It came out scornful, the implicit 'that's really how you fill your days?' all too obvious, and a flicker of hurt crossed Maya's face.

'Well when you have two, it sort of adds up. They're only twenty months apart, so not much recovery time.'

Alex pictured the airy Norman Shaw house she'd scrutinised online, with its neat, rectangular back lawn. She imagined the help Maya would have on tap: the mother-in-law Jamie never stopped bitching about, the supportive girlfriends and the nannies. How much 'recovery time' could be needed?

'I mean I'm lucky,' Maya admitted, as though reading Alex's mind. 'We have a great nanny. But my husband works long hours.'

'In . . . ?'

'Property. He's a partner at BWL, and there's quite a bit

of travelling involved so the poor guy's always feeling guilty about not spending enough time with the kids ... '

All that boozing in luxury hotels around Europe with his mate Hayden, and Jamie still finds the time to feel guilty?

' ... and then he'll get his head bitten off when he's too tired to do all the things I've planned for us and the kids.' Maya shook her head with ... no, surely not. Yes: this gorgeous woman actually felt ashamed about the kind of wife she was ... to Jamie! The same Jamie who never missed a chance to tell everyone what a devoted and involved dad he was.

'But, well, it's understandable that those things aren't quite so important to him.'

'Maybe they should be.' As she navigated the busy lunchtime pavements of Chiswick, Alex tried to keep her voice light.

But Maya was frowning at her. 'You've got some super-dad husband, haven't you?'

'Guilty.'

'Lucky you. I always feel bad for adding to Jamie's workload. I mean, when I need an "in" somewhere, I'll ask him to help out. Stupid things like Christel's nursery school interview this week ... '

'An interview for nursery school?' Alex regretted it the moment she'd said it: of course women like Maya would send their children to the most elite places West London had to offer.

'Well, you know, Greenleaf – so not just any nursery.'

'Right.'

Even Alex had heard about Greenleaf, with its supermodel mums, hedge-funder dads and endless waiting list.

'And they interview Christel?'

Maya laughed. 'You're funny. Can you imagine interviewing a two-year-old? She's actually quite happy at our local nursery for the moment, but obviously Greenleaf is the Holy Grail.'

'Obviously.'

'Anyway, the whole thing's been so stressful, what with all the groundwork you have to put in and the grovelling. They have so few spaces. But I finally got us this interview, and I'm counting on Jamie to do his charming thing and win them over.'

Tiny buds were sprouting in Alex's mind. This was the kind of information she'd come for.

As Alex took a swig of water, Maya glanced at her hand.

'I leave my wedding and engagement rings at home for classes,' she pre-empted.

'I should probably do the same. You've got to be sure you remember where you put them, though. My husband's forever fiddling with his and leaving it in random places around the house. It's my "pet peeve", as you guys call it. Your husband – what does he do?'

Alex dodged a double buggy heading directly for her. 'He's in the city.'

She was pretty sure she'd never heard anyone follow up on that, very few people apparently either understanding or caring what went on there.

'And you, Lexie?'

This was less easy. But they were approaching Turnham Green Terrace now, where Alex was hoping Maya might veer off home, and her eyes went to a woman laughing shrilly on her phone outside Space NK.

'Marketing – beauty.' As soon as she'd said it Alex realised how stupid it was. People who worked in the beauty industry didn't look like her. 'But I'm on the tech side of things,' she explained, gesturing down at herself. 'As you can probably tell.'

The two women had stopped walking now, having reached the top of the terrace, and Alex felt conflicting emotions: relief that the questions she was finding it increasingly hard to answer would stop, and annoyance at the realisation that she'd been enjoying Maya's company.

'Why do you do that?' Unperturbed by the jostle of people heading out to lunch, Maya was standing on the corner, eyes narrowed. 'Put yourself down all the time. You've been doing it all morning.'

'I just . . .' Alex gave up trying to find a flippant brush-off. 'I don't know.'

'Sorry. Danish people – we're direct.'

'No.' Again, Alex felt that Maya had a curious ability to see into her, spot the equivocations and the bravado. 'Direct is . . . good.'

They were in everyone's way, and probably absurd to look at, facing one another with babies strapped to their chests, but Maya didn't move.

'I was a pretty successful interior designer,' she said. 'You know, before.' And this piece of information – with all the vulnerabilities it contained – hung there for a moment.

'I could see that.'

Maya blinked twice. And shot through with sunlight, her eyes were a khaki green that was almost synthetic in intensity. She wasn't just catalogue beautiful, Alex realised. There was more to it. And this too annoyed her. Jamie didn't deserve anything rare or different.

'I was planning on going back to work before this little one came along. But once you've been off for three or four years you've got to ask yourself what you've really got to offer people.'

'I bet you've got plenty to offer.'

It felt like a long time since Alex had stood opposite someone who wanted something more. Only it wasn't a man holding out for a kiss at the end of the night, and just before Maya opened her mouth to speak Alex realised what it was she wanted.

'I'm starving. You don't fancy lunch ... at mine?'

'Oh.' This was so unexpected that Alex couldn't think of a quick get-out.

'That's such a nice idea, but actually I have to be some-where and Katie's going to need her nap ...'

Always just the one excuse. Wasn't that what people said? Two and it sounds like lies.

'Of course.'

There was that same flicker of hurt again, quickly covered up just like the first time. Which left Alex baffled. Maya could hardly be lonely, could she? Disappointed in the shit she married, maybe. But lonely? 'Sorry. Next time!' Alex had already started to walk away, but what she really wanted to do was run: away from Maya and her freakishly non-reactive child, away from the stifling wealth of these cafés and delicatessens selling dried turmeric and consolation prizes for their absent, cheating husbands. Away from her own pointless lies.

But Maya wasn't giving up that easily. 'Wait. Lexie.'

So she did, listening as Maya breathlessly begged her to 'come back to the house and have lunch and a glass of rosé in the garden with me. Because it's the nanny's day off, and the truth is that as much as I love this little one, I'm going to lose it if I don't get some adult conversation.'

And when she was done, Alex smiled. It was risky and wrong. It was insane. Yet she heard herself say, 'OK – I'd love to see where you live.'

CHAPTER 14

JILL

'Can you keep your voices down?' Jill hissed at the small group assembled outside her office. 'I'm on a conference call to Doha and I can't hear a bloody word.'

'Sorry.'

Paul had the good grace to apologise, but Jamie just threw her an irate glance. 'Or speak as loud as you want,' she muttered, shutting the door, 'but maybe in your own offices?'

It was clear that something had gone very wrong, though, and as Jill wound up the call, inserting the only line of Arabic she knew as a slightly flubbed final flourish, she had a grim realisation what it must be: Minerva.

They've passed? she emailed Jamie. And his reply pinged back within seconds: *Yup.*

Jill stared at the unapologetic one-word message

wondering when and why the man she'd thought of as both a loyal colleague and a friend for years had not only lost all respect for her, but decided she was the enemy.

It had been a week since Jill had received the anonymous email, and in that time she'd examined and re-examined every word and turn of phrase, even getting up in the middle of the night to cross-reference the dates and times on the message thread with the meetings on BWL's intranet calendar. Neither Jamie nor Paul had been in meetings at the precise times those messages had been sent. Another quick search through her inbox had also revealed that Jamie had never used 'YKW' in conversation with her.

There was one last option: Paul. But looking across the floor into his office now, where her partner was bent over a site plan, Jill felt reticent. Just showing him the exchanges would make her look insecure in his eyes – as though Jill secretly feared she had been struck down by the 'senile sixties'. It might even plant the seed of her being past it in his mind. The two men were buddies, too, and had become closer since Paul's marriage had fallen apart, with him preferring to run over the torturous details of his divorce with Jamie than with her – something Jill had welcomed, until now. If he did recognise Jamie's vicious words as those emailed to him months ago, would he even admit to it? Or would he remain loyal to his male colleague?

Having ricocheted between absolute conviction that the email was genuine to the certainty it was either fake or doctored and back again over the past few days, Jill had decided to end the madness earlier that morning and call Tara from IT into her office.

'It's a bit of a sensitive one, this, so it's going to have to stay completely between us,' she began hesitantly, before launching into it – the whole business had already taken up too much of her time. 'You'd better just come over here and have a read.'

As the young woman stooped over her screen to read the email thread, Jill watched her reactions. Her mouth twitching a little with embarrassment at the words she'd read, Tara straightened up and turned to her boss: 'You want to know who sent this? Because that's not going to be easy.'

Jill flashed back to Alex's feverish eyes that night in the pub – 'All I'm talking about is giving him a little push' – and Nicole's semi-smile as she murmured the words 'stealth power'. With either or both women surely behind Jamie's D-list humiliation, wasn't it possible that the email was a similar stunt? But if it had been written and sent to remind Jill of the pub pact she'd reneged on, they were going about this all wrong. Far too much had been drunk and said that night, and although Jill was still in shock over what she'd learned about Jamie and aware that she couldn't now ignore his behaviour, there had to be a better way of dealing with him than the puerile plan they'd come up with.

'All I really want to know, Tara, is if it's genuine: if the messages were written as they appear, or whether they could have been, well, edited.'

'That I may be able to do. You'll give me a couple of hours?'

The phone rang and for a moment she hoped that it might be Jamie calling to apologise and assure her she'd misjudged him on this and everything else. 'But the number on the phone display, she realised, was her own.

'Stan – everything OK?'

'Yes and no, love. But I don't want you to worry. There's

been a fair amount of pain and dizziness since early morning. Dr Jacks seems to think the best thing is to go down to the hospital.'

'Since this morning? Why didn't you say?'

'I'm telling you now, love.'

Stan had always been unflappable, and perversely the cancer only seemed to have made him more so, imbuing him with a sort of fatalistic tranquillity that, far from reassuring Jill, secretly drove her mad.

'OK. Give me forty minutes and I'll be there.'

'No, no, please don't come. I promise I'll call as soon as we're done, and actually on the Prostate UK site it does say that this can happen.'

'I thought we said Dr Google was off limits?'

On the far side of the office, Jill spotted Jamie coming out of the lift with one of the blended iced coffee drinks he liked. All these years she'd logged his sweet tooth with fond amusement. Now that he should be keeping his head down and desperately trying to make up for his mess, it struck her as outrageous that he should be idly nipping out for a frothy treat.

She watched as Jamie wove his way through the marketing section, stopping by the desk of a pretty, almond-eyed brunette in a cornflower-blue summer dress. She had an Italianate surname, Jill remembered, something sexy and exotic, and one of those hoisted upper lips that kept her mouth in a kind of permanently sensual semi-gape. But instead of looking pleased by Jamie's attentions, Jill noticed, the girl looked uncomfortable.

'I'd rather be at the hospital with you.'

'I know you would. But I'm telling you, I don't want you to come, and the cab's here so I'll call from the hospital.'

'Make sure you do. Make sure you call the second you're . . .'

But Stan had hung up.

Jamie was still chatting to the brunette, every so often reaching for something from a packet on her desk – throwing it up in the air and catching it, seal-like, in his mouth. Without taking her eyes off him Jill filled a glass with Evian from the bottle she always kept on her desk and downed it in one.

Looking at Jamie now was like looking at someone in one of those 'face warp' apps her teenage niece had once made her and Stan try. There he was: familiar yet ghoulishly twisted. And was he preying on that girl, just as he had Nicole, right there in front of everyone? Had she really been so blind all this time?

Propelled by the force of her anger, Jill yanked open her office door, striding past a surprised Kellie – 'You've got the valuation guy calling in two minutes!' – and headed in an unwavering diagonal towards Jamie.

The girl spotted her before he did, and the unwelcome image of herself as some kind of aged schoolmarm on the warpath did nothing to calm Jill down.

'Jamie?'

He turned, surprised but also, she thought, slightly defiant. 'Jill.'

'Do you have a moment?'

She'd been in some testing professional situations over the years and until now had always found it easy to keep her cool. That it was somehow deemed OK for young women to behave emotionally at work these days, as though their sex alone excused it, was baffling to her. Jill could count on one hand the times she'd raised her voice in the office, and she'd certainly never allowed any further physical signs of upset to show.

Just the other week she'd thrust an *FT* article about crying in the office being an 'acceptable human reaction most often succumbed to by high achievers' beneath Stan's nose, and they'd both laughed at the idea of her openly weeping in the conference room. 'You've never been a crier even in private,' he'd said. And whilst it was true that she hadn't shed a tear when he was first diagnosed, Jill was glad Stan hadn't seen her the day after all his tests. He'd been laid out in his hospital bed, his waxy face turned towards the window as the oncologist talked about the 'multidisciplinary team' that would be a part of his life moving forward, and the immediate side effects of both his medication and the radiotherapy: the initial 'tumour flare' he might experience, the bone pain, back pain and blood in the urine to watch out for. And she'd nodded and joked her way through it before 'nipping to the loo' where she'd leant her forehead against the tiled wall and cried out a single sob so violent it had left her shaking.

'I do indeed have a moment,' Jamie came back with, his smile tight, and Jill was glad for that at least. If he'd said they couldn't talk now, in front of the girl, Jill would have taken it as a challenge.

'Looks like your honey-glazed almonds have been spared.' He smirked down at the girl. 'Although I may just nick one last one?' Tossing it up in the air, Jamie extended his neck, catching the nut in his mouth. Then he took a small bow. 'Jill, have you met Sophia? She joined us from the Manchester office in March.'

But all of this was somehow power play that Jill didn't have time for. Giving the girl an impatient nod, she motioned towards her office. 'Shall we?'

Nothing more was said until they reached the conference room, where Jamie held the door for her in one of the excesses of gallantry that she had once found charming but now suspected were fake: all part of Jamie's general duplicity.

'Water,' he gasped, setting down the dregs of his frappé and pouring himself a glass of her Evian. 'This stuff makes me thirsty.'

Jill chose to remain standing while he drank. And when Jamie was done he turned towards her with a quizzical smile: 'What exactly is your problem, Jill?'

'My problem?' she asked, trying to conceal how shocked she was by his tone.

'Yes.' He sat down, legs apart.

'I was going to ask you the same thing. We've just lost a major client, and I get nothing but a one-word email from you.'

'Not lost, Jill. They've passed on one deal.'

'OK, fine, and let's see if they come back to us for another.'

'I can promise you they will.' Leaning back in his chair, Jamie lifted his hands behind his head, expanding his chest.

Jill couldn't let the smugness pass. 'How?' She walked briskly around the desk to face him but didn't sit down. 'I've always admired your confidence, Jamie, but there's a point at which it just becomes rashness. I'd told you your D-list was a bad idea, but you wouldn't listen. And I have got to be kept in the loop more.' The sound the flat of her palm made against the desktop startled her: this wasn't her; she didn't behave like this. 'I mean, you didn't even think to come and tell me when the O'Ceallaighs passed earlier.'

'It was only a few hours ago.'

'They came into the office?'

'No.' A shadow crossed his face. 'No, there was a misunderstanding and ... anyway, this time it was their fault.'

Only now did Jill finally sit. 'What was their fault?'

'They thought we were meeting at their offices, but we had it scheduled for here—'

'Wait a second – you messed up again?'

'No, Jill. They got it wrong. It said right there on the intranet calendar that the meeting was here at BWL.' He shook his head. 'It doesn't matter. We had a conference call instead.'

'I find it hard to believe it didn't matter. Either way, I, like Paul, would quite like to know about these things the moment they happen.'

'Can I finish?'

'Please.'

'Trust me, nobody feels worse about Minerva than I do. But all I can do now is try and line up another buyer for—'

'Right.' Jill couldn't help herself. 'So concentrate on that, not some girl in marketing.'

'Sorry?'

'You know what I mean.'

'Erm.' He made a show of putting his hand to his chin in puzzlement. 'Not sure I do. Seriously, do you hear yourself? Her name is Sophia. And I thought you were the one always saying we should make the newbies feel welcome.'

'I don't give a damn what her name is right now.'

The silence that followed might have morphed into something more hostile had a soft tap on the glass behind her not interrupted them.

'Sorry, Jill – it's your husband again,' her PA mouthed. Of course, she'd muted her phone.

'Thanks, Kellie.' She stood. But all of a sudden, Jamie was beside her, his sheeny brown eyes full of compassion.

'Stan OK?'

She nodded, but he'd spotted her hesitation.

'Go and be with your husband.'

Then Jamie did something he'd only done on a handful of occasions over the years: he hugged her. And rather than squirm, which Jill might have done even half an hour earlier, she felt some of her anger drain away, and found herself hugging him back. These were testing times for them both, so testing for her that she had put everything into question: even him.

He'd been set up with Minerva, that much seemed obvious. And why trust Nicole or Alex over someone she knew far better than either of them, let alone an email that had clearly been sent by someone with a revenge-filled agenda? That she'd actually asked Tara to look into it now filled her with shame. She would tell her to forget the whole thing, then she would go and check on Stan.

'I just really need you to trust that I can handle things,' he said, releasing her. 'That's so important to me with everything you and Stan have going on.'

Jill nodded again, more concertedly this time, and when she went to log out of her computer saw with relief that Tara had already emailed. She was '99 per cent certain that those emails were written by the sender on those dates and times'. She was also 'very sorry if that's not what you wanted to hear'.

CHAPTER 15

JILL

'Are you going to be able to do this?'

Through her fish-eye vision, Paul's questioning face was warped, the open-plan office beyond his glass wall distorted into a nightmarish panoramic curve.

'I don't know.'

'I've drafted something. An email. To go out company wide. The announcement should be along the same lines, don't you think?'

Pulling a sheet of paper from the printer tray, Paul handed it to her.

To: All Staff
Subject: [Company name] mourns the loss of [Insert
job title], [Insert employee first and last name].

Dear [Company name] team,

On [Insert date], our team suffered a terrible loss. Our
[Insert job title], [Insert employee first and last name],
passed away after [Insert cause of death]. He/She was
a hard worker and we will all miss his/her positivity.

Jill looked up from the blur of print and handed the sheet
back to Paul. 'What is this?'

'Shit. That's the sample email.'

Thumbing through the sheath of papers in the tray, he
found what he needed.

'This is the one.'

Jill stared. 'There's a sample email for . . .'

'For deceased employee announcements, yes. HR provided it. Because now that it's out there, on the news . . . and
the police told us they'd need to talk to people, take further
statements. So we need to do this now.'

The right document was there in her hand, but Jill made
no attempt to read it, eyes still on Paul.

'So you filled in the blanks. You inserted Jamie's cause of
death,' she murmured. 'Did you mention that he was still
alive when they found him this morning? That's what they
said on the news. Something must have broken his fall on
the way down, they said, otherwise he'd have been killed
outright. But instead he survived for hours. Hours. Until
they cut him off those railings. That's when he bled out.'

'Jill.'

'But he was a "hard worker". We'll "miss his positivity"?'

'I know this is difficult.'

'No.' She shook her head. 'In answer to your question: no. I can't do this.'

CHAPTER 16

❧

NICOLE

Six Weeks Earlier

'I never told him that, Jen, I swear. I just said that you were single.'

'Only I don't know if I'm looking, that's all.'

'I know, and that's what I said. We can just stay for one drink.'

'Yeah.'

'Maybe two if he's as hot as he looks on Insta. Pass us your mascara.'

Whenever possible Nicole preferred to use the Ladies' room on the third floor. The one she was in now was larger with better lighting, but come 6 p.m. on a Friday night the sinks were cluttered with make-up, the cubicles full of young women changing into ever-tighter clothing – and it grated. Because she'd never done the dating thing in the extended and gloriously meaningless way that these girls were doing it. Christ, she'd been married at their age. And because when she was heading off to meet her husband for dinner at the end of a long day like she was now, she didn't feel that same hot-cheeked excitement. Instead she felt tired – and secretly resentful that they weren't just having a curry in front of the telly.

Still, Nicole had worked late three nights this week, and Ben, whose only adventurous streak involved keeping track of every restaurant opening in west London, had got them a table at a new tapas place on the Fulham Road that had been written up by Jay Rayner. There was no way she could cancel now.

Avoiding the wad of foundation-smeared tissues beside the basin, Nicole leaned into the mirror and began to apply her lipstick. She usually found the process of contouring and filling in what men had always told her was her best feature soothing, but today the lines were ragged, and her trusted shade seemed to leech all colour from her face. Pulling a tissue from the dispenser she wiped the lot off.

'Too dark,' chirruped the woman behind her.

'Sorry?'

'You're so gorgeous. But your lippy – washes you out.'

Nicole was tempted to tell her she'd been wearing it for almost a decade.

'Try this one.'

The peony-pink, lightly pearlescent gloss was too young for Nicole, and she had always found the idea of borrowing another woman's lipstick unhygienic, but she thanked her and took a strange pleasure in daubing it on, picturing the look of surprise on Ben's face when she turned up looking nothing like his wife.

'So go on.'

The two women resumed their chatter.

'He'd asked Sophia if she was seeing someone – casual, like. Then he's all "I hope you've been made to feel welcome here. We should have a getting-to-know-each-other drink after work."'

'He didn't.'

'He did.'

'*Then* – get this – he says, "You should know I don't take no for an answer."'

'Stop it.'

'Apparently.'

A break in conversation was permeated only by the residual rumble of female laughter and the sound of sticky lips being smacked against one another.

'I wouldn't mind a getting-to-know-you drink with him.'

'Wait. Sophia goes for the drink.'

'She does?'

'Yep. And the next day tells Sandra, who told Emma, that he really doesn't take no for an answer – like, as in something that totally weirded her out.'

'Came on too strong?'

'Like, way too—'

A signal, unseen by Nicole, silenced her.

'Who are you girls talking about?' Nicole took care to keep her eyes on the mirror.

The pair glanced at one another, only now registering Nicole as senior.

'I'm just curious.' She added a light laugh. *And if it's a state secret maybe don't gossip about it in the Ladies.*

'Friend of ours in marketing.'

'No, I mean the "welcoming" man.'

'Oh.' Another conspiratorial glance.

'Jamie?'

Both women were staring at her now, clearly appalled at their own indiscretion. 'Well ...'

'God, everyone knows what he's like. And what's said in the Ladies ...'

'Stays in the Ladies,' chuckled the loudest. 'Yeah – Jamie. But keep it to yourself? Sophia's a sweet girl and not been here long. She won't want to cause any trouble. I don't even know if she "does" married men.'

'Right.'

Zipping up her make-up bag, Nicole took one last look at herself, pausing as she opened the door to leave. 'By the way, in my experience it tends to be the married men causing the trouble.'

'Sorry, sorry!'

If Ben weren't always early, she wouldn't always be made to feel late. But he'd got them a good table looking out over the Fulham Road, and she could tell that her husband had been enjoying watching the pretty Chelsea girls and their Ralph Lauren-shirted boyfriends overflowing onto the pavements from the nearby pubs and bars.

Reaching for Ben's nearly empty gin and tonic, she knocked back what was left. 'I need one of those urgently.'

Ben motioned at the waiter for two more, before holding up his glass, now thickly smeared with pink gloss. 'Care to explain?'

He didn't like it. Of course he wouldn't. She had never met anyone more averse to change than Ben, especially where she was concerned.

'Just something I'm trying out. You hate it.'

'What? Give me a chance.' He tilted his head back, taking her in. 'Makes you look ... I don't know, different. Tough day?'

'Just ... long. I had to take some new clients around the old theatre today and then get from there back over Kensington way for another meeting. I spent the whole morning stuck in traffic and that Shepherd's Bush place I took on in March isn't attracting any interest at all.' Shrugging off her jacket, she exhaled deeply. 'Maybe people just aren't buying right now. Anyway it's all dull, dull, dull. Tell me about your day.'

'Well that sour-faced single mum you hate – the one with the eyebrows – was on pick-up today.'

'Oh, she's dreadful.'

'She was actually quite chatty for once. Even mentioned setting up a play date.'

'I don't think so.' Nicole glanced anxiously back inside the crowded restaurant towards the bar.

'Give them a sec, Nic.'

'They're taking their time.'

'The place is heaving.'

'Then they should get more staff.'

'Anyway,' Ben pushed on brightly. 'Chloe said she'd been talking about us at school today. Mostly you, really. Apparently they had to describe their parents' jobs.'

'Really?'

'Yeah. So she said, "Mummy sells buildings – big ones."'

'Is that really what she said?' Her drink was on its way and

Nicole felt lighter. If she could just pretend she hadn't heard that conversation in the Ladies . . .

'And "Daddy looks after me."'

There were so many curdled emotions in Ben's smile, and even in her distracted state she could make out most of them: pride and shame; embarrassment and defiance. The same emotions he must feel every time he ticked that emasculating 'primary caregiver' box on forms. But although he might not have acquired the title entirely through choice, Ben must know how valuable his contribution was and hate the idea that he might be looked down on for doing the most important job of all.

Nicole took his hand. 'I never take that for granted, you know. And Chlo adores you. It's like you two are a unit. To be honest, I sometimes even feel jealous.'

'We're OK as long as we have you.' He smiled. It should have made her feel safe, loved, but instead it bred only a familiar sense of being slowly suffocated.

Nicole took in the sun-glazed temples her husband had acquired from afternoons at the park and the cool blue of his eyes and felt an equally familiar pang of unworthiness.

'I can't even imagine how people manage on their own,' Ben went on, aware that anything resembling slushiness made his wife uncomfortable. 'Now, what are we having?' He turned his attention to the menu. 'Shall I just order a load of "small plates"? Rayner says the tartar is "unmissable". Oh, and there's a tasting menu, but you're never keen on those.'

'As long as we have some squid and some of those croquette things, I'm happy.'

But as Ben began to read out a list of dishes to the waiter, Nicole felt anything but. She couldn't get the conversation she'd just overheard out of her head. Then there was Ben's comment about the single school mum, which had reminded her of Alex. Nicole thought about the woman she'd sat with until the early hours that night: the effort she'd gone to with the new hair and the dark murmurings about 'the things I've seen. The things I know.' Alex had seemed so grateful that Nicole and Jill were giving her the time of day, so keen to ingratiate herself with them. It was as though all she had wanted was to belong. And something about the nakedness of that gratitude had put Nicole on edge at first. But by the end of the night, Nicole could recall feeling not just united with this intense, freckle-faced woman she'd never noticed before but vaguely protective of her. If what she'd said was true, Alex had been used as a scapegoat, and was now navigating life as a single mother, with no prospect of a job to go back to after maternity leave. Maybe she was so immersed in motherhood that she no longer cared; maybe she'd already found another job. Or maybe Alex had somehow found a way to go ahead with her 'wake-up call' alone.

While Ben went on quoting Rayner's review, Nicole cast her mind back to the one and only time she'd been sacked, as a student trying to make some extra cash at a little Bristol sandwich place with pretensions above its station. When the owner had called her into the storeroom one day, citing her 'attitude' as the main reason, along with the fact that she kept 'running her fingers through her hair' while serving customers, Nicole had nodded, taken the cash he owed her and as she turned to leave flung back 'It's pronounced cia-batta, Lee – not "sia-batter".' As an image of his fat ordinary face popped into her mind, she was surprised to find that she still hated him.

'It's bloody typical Oscar went with Westwick for the brand film. Told you he would, didn't I?'

'You heard back?' Nicole helped herself to another Padrón pepper. 'No surprises there. He was always going to go with someone as stuck up as him. His loss. If that were me I'd have taken one look at your portfolio and booked you on the spot. It looked great by the time we'd revamped it.'

Ben blinked.

'Tell me you sent him the one we updated.'

'I just felt like if he really wanted me ...'

'Ben.' Nicole slumped, tired at always being the motor behind her spluttering husband.

'Just leave it, OK? Leave it.'

They ate in silence for a few minutes, pulling shrimps off wooden skewers and spitting bits of shell discreetly back into the palms of their hands, both acutely aware of how tense and joyless they must have looked in comparison with the shrill flirtations happening outside the bars across the road.

'Who's looking after Chlo?'

'Susanna.'

'You think she's got her playing doctors again?'

Was this why couples got themselves dogs when their children left home? So that they'd have something to fill the silences with?

'Probably.'

'I'm sorry.' She leaned in towards him. 'It's all been a bit messy at work and it's stressing everyone out.'

'Messy how?'

'Jill and Paul are pissed off with Jamie after that Minerva disaster I told you about. The clients pulled out.'

'Nothing to do with you though, is it? That was Jamie's mess-up.'

Nicole didn't like hearing his name in her husband's mouth, but she hadn't been able to resist telling him about it. 'It was, but now we're all under pressure to make up for it.'

And although Jamie was the last person she wanted to talk about, Nicole heard herself launch into an account of his recent failures – and how easily he'd managed to shrug them off.

'Can I say something?' Ben frowned. 'You seem to spend way too much time fretting about Jamie Lawrence.'

Nicole put the meatball she'd speared back down on her plate.

'I don't.'

'You really do.'

'Because only a man would get away with this stuff. And every time he gets away with it,' she went on, consciously echoing Alex's words that night, 'he knows he can push things a little bit further the next.'

'But it doesn't sound like he is getting away with it?'

Nicole stared, unseeing, at her husband. She'd felt a certain release after that drunken conversation in the pub, as though telling those women what she had, hearing their own experiences and deciding that Jamie should be punished for his behaviour had been enough to temper her anger. Only it had flared up again as she'd watched him wriggle out of Minerva. And again in the Ladies' room earlier. 'You should know I don't take no for an answer': that was what he'd told that Sophia girl. And Nicole knew all too well how true that was.

Having cleared away the last of their dishes, the waiter hovered. 'Would either of you like to see the dessert menu?'

They replied simultaneously.

'Why not?'

'No thanks.'

What Nicole wanted right now, what she needed more than anything, was to know whether Alex really was behind Minerva. There would be no way to slip away over the weekend, and waiting until next week to find out was out of the question. Because if Alex was somehow going ahead with the plan, it wasn't working. And Nicole knew now how desperately she needed it to. 'Ben, I've got to go.'

She'd murmured it without thinking, but as soon as she heard her own words, Nicole knew what she had to do.

'What are you talking about?'

She focused back in on Ben: Ben who had ripped out the restaurant review all those months ago and gone to the trouble of putting their name on a waiting list. Ben who looked sexiest in summer when he let his stubble grow – something she forgot about and realised all over again every June. Ben who always ordered too much food and liked to extend their dinners into four-hour affairs.

'I've forgotten a file I had to send … and it's urgent. I've got to nip back to the office, but it won't take a minute.'

'What? Why can't you do it on this?'

He tapped the iPhone she kept beside her plate at mealtimes – much to Ben's annoyance.

'It's not on there. It's on my desktop.'

Aware she was making little sense, and that it sounded like lies because it *was* lies, Nicole threaded one hand through the sleeve of her leather jacket and reached for her purse with the other. 'Sorry, Ben. I'm such an idiot. But that was great. Rayner was right.' That wasn't cutting it. 'You didn't want pudding, did you?'

'I thought I might.' Ben glared at her as though she'd lost her mind. 'You're seriously going back to the office now?'

'I've got to. Sorry. Here.' She put her credit card down on the table.

'For God's sake. I can pay for it myself.'

'With what?' she wondered, impatience making her nasty. But the black cab she'd flagged down in a brisk gesture was pulling over and she drew Ben's furious face in towards hers. 'I just need to fix this one thing. It'll drive me mad all weekend otherwise, and I'll be home in an hour, max.'

By the time she'd found the address she needed on BWL's intranet and made it all the way to Acton, it was already coming up to ten. Alex's street was sketchy, with a cluster of young hooded men on the corner clearly in the midst of some transaction, and Nicole had to ask the cabbie to reverse up the street when they zoomed straight past her house number.

She had a moment's hesitation before ringing the unmarked top bell. But she was here now and she needed clarity. Hearing a window go up on the second floor, Nicole took two steps back, forcing herself to smile when she saw Alex's tired face lean out.

CHAPTER 17

≫—≪

ALEX

Soothed by the motorised whir of her breast pump, Alex wandered in and out of the three rooms in her flat, chewing on a chocolate Hobnob. When these two 'express and go' pouches were filled, she would have ten – all dated in marker pen – lined up in the door of her fridge, and the thought filled her with satisfaction.

This time of day, the period between 9 and 10 p.m. when she finally flopped into bed, aware she'd have to be up an hour and a half later, was the only time Alex felt like herself. It sometimes felt like the only time she could enjoy Katie, too. Lying there in her basket, breathing the imperceptibly shallow breaths that had in those first few weeks left Alex panic-stricken, she looked peaceful: released from the tyranny of her constant, unquenchable cravings.

Content that her daughter's face was clear of any bed-clothes – 'soft toys, wedges or sleep positioners should be removed prior to sleep', *First Time Parent* had stipulated – Alex sat down at her desk, and, still harnessed to the pump, double clicked on the BWL portal.

Since that afternoon at Maya's, checking in on Jamie's daily movements had become an evening ritual she looked forward to.

Tonight the corners of her mouth twitched just short of a smile as she took in the tense tone of Jill's emails to her increasingly negligent partner. 'We really do need all three partners present in a finance meeting, J. This one had been scheduled for weeks.' All those months working for Jamie had taught Alex that he responded badly to scoldings. And sure enough his response – 'I was 20 minutes late, Jill. Pretty sure I didn't miss anything' – was as far from contrite as she'd hoped.

Jill had clearly felt she'd gone too far that night in the pub and regretted her openness the following morning. She needed to understand that hers hadn't been an overreaction but the appropriate reaction. And right now she must be seething. Paul, however, seemed relatively unruffled by Jamie's behaviour and, aside from the one gentle post-Minerva chiding, was his usual matey self in emails. As the pump whirred on, Alex ploughed through the rest of the day's messages; she would know what she was looking for when she saw it.

She'd been rereading a furious email from Maya, a forwarded message from Greenleaf nursery school expressing their regret at not being able to offer Christel a place – *When an interview slot is missed without any prior warning, we have to accept that schooling your child at Greenleaf is not your priority* – and was trying to quash a twinge of remorse for the woman whose kindness had disarmed her earlier that week, when the doorbell rang.

Ready to shout down to the Deliveroo guy that he wanted the takeaway-dependent in Flat 3, Alex draped a cardigan over her machine-operated breasts, pushed up the window and stared down at the woman standing outside her front door.

'Nicole?'

Bright-eyed, with a sheen of perspiration along her hair-line catching the security light and something sparkly on her lips, her former colleague looked like she'd been drinking.

'Sorry. I know it's late.'

'What are you doing here?' It came out sharper than intended. 'Hang on a sec.'

Ripping off her Velcro harness and cursing as the milk slopped over the nozzles and down her stomach, Alex buttoned herself up and ran downstairs.

'Are you wanting to come in?' Again, she was aware of how rude this sounded. But seeing this smart and slightly cold woman she knew only in a professional context standing there on her doorstep had unnerved her. Had Jamie been sacked? No. She'd know if he had. Was it Nicole then – had he done something to her? 'You'd better come in.'

Only when they reached the top of the stairs did Alex see how her flat must look to an outsider. Over the first two months, when the NHS health visitor was dropping in regularly, she'd tried to keep things tidy, but over the past couple of weeks the wash basket had disappeared beneath the mound of dirty linen and she'd started kicking dirty clothes into corners.

The crusts of a toasted cheese sandwich she'd made in the early hours of that morning, ravenously hungry from all the pumping, sat on a plate on the sofa, a pile of junk mail and unopened post beside it. On the coffee table, amidst the tangled cords of the pump, sat the two half-filled bottles of breast milk.

'Let me just get this out the way,' she murmured, gathering up the humiliating contraption and taking it through to the kitchen. 'Can I, um, get you a tea?'

'Please.' Nicole had picked up the half-eaten sandwich and followed her through. 'Or – something stronger?'

'You don't need to whisper. Katie's out.'

'Oh.'

In the freezer, Alex located an old bottle of vodka – a present from the Christmas before last that she'd forgotten about. 'Sorry.' Why did she keep apologising? 'This is all I've got. And I have no idea what cinnamon-flavoured vodka is going to taste like.'

'Anything'll do.'

'There's no ice.'

'It's fine.'

'Shall we . . . ?' Alex motioned to the sitting room and the two women sat down awkwardly at either end of the sofa.

'Handy to have a local dealer on your doorstep.'

If Nicole's nervousness was an admission of regret at her silence, Alex was going to let her stew a bit longer.

'Isn't it?' She glanced at the window. 'He must do pretty good business. He's there every other night flogging God knows what.'

'Ritalin.' Nicole cleared her throat. 'That's what all the youngsters are into now, apparently. The "study drug", they call it – helps you pull all-nighters, keeps you awake.'

'Not something I need help with right now.'

'No. And of course back in my day we made do with Pro-Plus and a litre of Coke.'

Alex nodded, and waited.

'Listen, I know this is weird, and that we haven't spoken since Joyce's . . .' She had the grace to look sheepish. Because there had been a closeness that night. Alex hadn't imagined it. They'd made a plan, swapped numbers – and then nothing, for almost two weeks. But Nicole so desperately wanted to be let off the hook.

'We'd all had a lot to drink.' Alex shrugged. 'And look it's not like we . . .'

'Well, no. But I should have checked in – seen how you were getting on.'

A pause.

'Is that what this is about? You checking in?'

'No.' Nicole took a sip of vodka and shivered. 'Weird. Nice, though. No, I came because things have been . . . well, strange at work, since that night. Jamie –' there was a ripple of emotion around her mouth as she said his name '– well, he messed up this huge deal.'

Alex frowned, enjoying the feeling of being the more in control of the two. 'Which deal?'

'Remember that Minerva development? The one near Gunnersbury? It's a long story but we had the O'Ceallaigh brothers primed to make an offer, and he bungled the sell.'

Aware that Nicole was watching her closely, Alex took a sip of her drink before spitting it straight back out again. 'That's disgusting. Tastes like baby powder. That smell . . . it gets everywhere. You've probably forgotten. Anyway, go on – about the development?'

'The D-list we talked about that night. Somehow it made it into his presentation dossier.' She paused, eyes still fixed on Alex. 'And there's been other stuff since. Little things. He's been getting confused about places and times. Turning up late to meetings. And I know Jamie can be arrogant and lazy sometimes but . . .'

'But?'

'But I don't think Jill wants to rock the boat, whatever was said that night . . .'

'Whatever *we* said.'

'Right. About putting him back in his box.'

'Oh, I remember what we said. It's you and Jill who seem to have wiped it clean out of your heads. Which isn't altogether surprising, given you've both got great jobs you'd quite like to keep.'

Nicole shook her head. 'I didn't forget about any of it. I couldn't,' she went on, the words rushing out. 'And listen, I can't speak for Jill – I've hardly said a word to her since that night, and you know how close she and Jamie have always been. But I was out with my husband earlier and telling him how tense things had been in the office, and Alex . . .' Nicole leaned in, her expression moving from concern to curiosity 'Minerva – and the rest. It's you, isn't it?'

Alex traced a drop of condensation down the side of her glass but said nothing.

'God, Alex. I didn't mean to . . . don't cry.'

Until Nicole said that, Alex hadn't realised she was. But it felt good. Because she hadn't cried since the birth itself, and those had been tears of effort, not sadness or even pain, thanks to the drugs. And when she had let herself back into the flat the following day, the weight of Katie in her car seat pulling down on her imploded womb, the words of a *Daily Mail* panic piece – 'carrying new-borns in car seats puts new mums at risk of organ prolapse' – ringing in her ears, all she had wanted to do was curl up in her bed and cry. There was no one else there to carry it, was there? And the person she wanted most was miles away in Portugal, still seeking permission from her husband to fly over. But there hadn't been time to cry because the sheets were still stained a marbled pink from her waters breaking, and when Alex had pulled them off to find that the mattress too had been soaked that desire to cry had been replaced with rage. None of this . . . none of it could be undone.

From the depths of her handbag, Nicole dug out a tissue and handed it to her.

'I moved a few documents around; switched a couple of dates and times. Minerva . . . it was just so easy. Jamie never reads over the presentation files. I was forever putting them out for him on his desk, telling him to have a last check, but . . . ' He'd always get away without doing the work, without taking responsibility. 'So I thought maybe that if Jill and Paul could see how entitled he is, how he makes up his own rules as he goes along . . . '

'That what?' Nicole prompted, but she didn't seem surprised or angry. 'That he'd get fired? We told you about the D-list in confidence. You weren't supposed to use that.'

A high-pitched sound like a siren rang out through the flat.

'Shit.' Alex put her glass down, wiping her nose on her sleeve. 'She's awake.'

'Shhh . . . ' Nicole held up a finger. 'Just wait.'

They both sat in silence for a minute. Nothing.

'If you always go straight to her she'll never learn to settle by herself.'

Alex gave a sodden semi-smile. 'I didn't have you down as an earth mother.'

'Why does everyone say that? And maybe I'm not, but God I love my daughter more than I find bearable most of the time. Only, my husband ... ' She shrugged. 'He's more involved than I am; better at it than me. And all this, what you're going through, seems like a long time ago now. Amazing how quickly you forget. But some things you do remember.' With a few drinks inside her, Nicole seemed so much warmer. 'Listen to me,' she said softly. 'I'm not going to pretend I wasn't glad to see him on the back foot. And after what he did to you, I get why you'd want him to know what paying for something you didn't do feels like. But how did you even manage it? You didn't ... hack into the system?'

Alex met Nicole's eyes, but kept her mouth shut.

'That's a criminal offence – isn't it?'

'Probably,' Alex admitted. It was something she'd deliberately avoided thinking about. 'He'd changed the intranet password, but it wasn't hard to guess the new one. And I only did it because he lied. He lied about everything. I wasn't made redundant; I was fired for "serious misconduct". And how the hell am I supposed to find myself another job now? How the hell am I supposed to pay ... ' She thought of the tremor in her mother's voice when she'd called to warn her earlier that day that 'I might need a bit more time – on that loan.' The dip down into whispering confirmed how important it was to her that Alex's father never found out about the money she'd been lent, and how discovery of the deception alone might set off the kind of scene that Alex had willed her memory to block out, knowing it could never do so while her mother and father were still living under the same roof.

'Sorry.' Nicole pressed her lips together. 'But are you saying you've accessed his emails too?'

Alex decided to play it safe. 'Only once.'

'Recently?'

'I had a look last night.'

Something indecipherable flashed across Nicole's face, and she opened her mouth as if to ask a question before closing it again.

'I know I shouldn't have, and I swear I won't do it again. I just wanted to check that Minerva had . . .'

'Gone according to plan? Well it did. But you can't ever do that again. Seriously. Apart from anything, you'll get caught.'

'I won't. But it's been so . . . hard.' The word came out slow, deliberate and filled with hate. 'I look at him and his perfect family, and I think about how easy it is for them.'

Had the two women not been sitting so close, Alex may not have noticed Nicole flinch.

'Have you met Maya?'

Nicole shook her head.

'Just seen her across the room, you know, at the BWL anniversary bash. And she seemed . . . I don't know. We didn't speak. You?'

'No.' A body language expert would have known that the headshake was a millisecond too late. 'We spoke on the phone sometimes,' Alex went on, omitting the fact that she'd last spoken to Maya the previous afternoon – to schedule another lazy afternoon at her and Jamie's house. 'She actually seemed . . .'

'OK?'

'Yeah. Nice even.'

Was that why Alex had agreed to see Maya again? Was

it as simple as that? Or was it something more malevolent: keeping your enemies close? Until the next time, Alex couldn't be sure.

'I mean I know they're far from the perfect couple. The way he behaved with you – and you won't have been the only one.'

Nicole glanced away. 'No.'

'But they put on a good show.'

Reaching for her iPhone, Alex jabbed at the screen until an image of Jamie and Maya filled it.

'Look at them – look at their perfect Scandi catalogue life.'

She'd wanted to make Nicole laugh, or at the very least smile, keen to alleviate the heaviness of their conversation, but when she glanced up Nicole didn't look amused; she looked queasy.

'What are you even doing looking at that?'

'It's Jamie's Instagram – and it's not private. Here – have a look at this post from last weekend.'

'No.' Nicole pushed the phone away. 'I don't want to see it. All that stuff, his life, it's none of our business. And I've got no problem with Maya. She can't be blamed for what her husband gets up to.'

'Her husband gets up to all sorts, trust me.'

'Meaning?'

'Meaning even when in the doghouse for some pretty major mistakes – and these are just the ones BWL know about – even when he should be keeping his head down, Jamie still seems to find the time to letch over his pretty new employees.'

Nicole seemed to be holding her breath, and Alex realised how insensitive she was being.

'Sorry. What he did to you ...'

'Never mind that. Who are you talking about?'

'There's a new girl in the office, Sophia something. He's been emailing her. I think they even went for a drink, and it looks like ...'

But her guest was on her feet. 'Shit, it's after midnight. Listen I'm sorry for coming here so late. I've really got to go. I told my husband I'd come straight home.' Nicole was looking wildly around the room. 'My jacket?'

'In the kitchen.'

But when she didn't move, Alex guessed that there was more. Something Nicole might never have said out loud before. And she was pretty sure that she knew what it was.

'It wasn't just harassment, was it?'

A beat. Nicole sat back down. 'I'm going to need another drink.'

CHAPTER 18

JILL

The quarterly sales report always made for dry reading, but Jill liked dry – dry soothed her – and as she moved her index finger slowly down the list of potential and past sales, making occasional notes in the margin with the Cartier pen Stan had had engraved with their wedding date for their ruby anniversary, she felt calmer than she had in weeks.

Only when she reached Jamie's sales did she squint a little harder at the page. His outgoings had always been a little elevated, his figures often only loosely tallying. But today it wasn't the usual dismissible discrepancies that caught her eye, but how high his quarterly figures were.

Jill would have expected his numbers to be considerably down thanks to the Minerva mishap, but in the past quarter a sale had gone through that Jamie had never mentioned to her, bumping them up to a decent level.

Why Jamie hadn't immediately bragged about the sale of the pub at the bottom of Westbourne Grove, Jill couldn't fathom. She'd never been a fan of Adrian Spiro, the Greek developer who wanted to turn it into a boutique hotel, but that wasn't what niggled. Then she remembered: Spiro had pulled out, initially, at the last minute. Something to do with planning or historic designation.

She fired off a one-line email to Jamie: *How did you swing the Spiro deal?*

His reply was immediate: *Just did my thing*, adding two flexed-muscle emojis. And although Jill knew this meant insufferable smugness for days to come, she couldn't be churlish, and was bashing out a 'congrats' when another email pinged in.

Raxugdy@sharklaser.com.

Tentatively she clicked on it: another email thread. This time – as though someone had been looking over her shoulder – between Jamie . . . and Spiro.

The Greek billionaire's English wasn't great, and in any case the two men appeared to be speaking in a kind of code it took Jill a few seconds to decipher. The 'carved oak staircase' had been the problem, she remembered, having located the original file on the system. That staircase had become a developer's nightmare the moment a potential building preservation notice had been mentioned.

FYI: the council won't serve that notice for another ten days, Jamie had pointed out in an email responding to Spiro's last-minute cold feet on the deal. *And I know you had been planning to start work on the site early next week. Give us a bell when you get this?*

The following email made no reference to any phone conversation, and was simply confirmation that Spiro had changed his mind, and was prepared to finalise the deal 'asap'. Quite the U-turn.

Jill glanced up at the date the email was sent, then speed-dialled Paul.

'On my way to a meeting with my lawyer, Jill. Olivia's been playing up again. Can you believe she's now saying she wants the Devon cottage thrown in? That's on top of the extortionate maintenance payments she's asking for and custody of Barnaby.'

'Sorry ... Barnaby?'

'Our whippet.'

'Right.' Jill really didn't have time for one of Paul's divorce rage-athons right now. 'Just a quick one: the Westbourne Grove place Spiro bought. I didn't even realise the sale had gone through – and so fast. Do you happen to know when they started work on it?'

'Earlier this week, I think.' He sounded tense. 'I take it the *Telegraph* have been in touch?'

'What? No. Why?'

'I was just going to call to see if you'd heard.'

'Heard what?'

'The staircase, that bloody Shakespearian—'

'Jacobean.'

'Yeah – well, anyway, the whole damn thing came down last night. Apparently the structure wasn't as solid as the workers had hoped and after they started work ...'

But once Paul had said the words 'conservationists are getting into a right state', she stopped listening.

'Paul.' She ran her finger over the three words at the

top of the BWL letterhead – three words she and Stan had agonised over all those decades ago: HISTORY. HERITAGE. PRESERVED. 'Once you're done with your lawyer, I need a chat. Because we're going to have to order an internal review into this – and into Jamie.'

Then she found the original email from Raxugdy@shark-laser.com with the subject heading WITH FRIENDS LIKE THESE? Just before she forwarded it on with three deft clicks, she added a single line at the top of her message: *With friends like these, Jamie?*

CHAPTER 19

NICOLE

'You've got to be joking.'

She was standing with her back to the wall, trying to find the best angle from which to capture on her phone the ornamental pilasters around the stage when the lights went out. They'd tripped when she'd brought Rupert Jones back to the theatre for a second viewing, but the surveyor had managed to get them back on, and although Nicole was pretty sure she could remember where he'd eventually found the fuse box, trying to grope her way there in the dark was going to be a challenge.

It was early afternoon but with only a slice of natural light coming from the windows on either side of the main entrance, the domed auditorium was a mass of shadowy enclaves. That the place could be so silent, with only the occasional muffled siren or horn from Kilburn Lane permeating those crimson walls, was far from reassuring, and Nicole wished she'd brought someone along with her to fill in the missing details Rupert had asked to be supplied with. Nicole's mind went from the ancient fire escapes that opened out onto the building site behind to the homeless men she'd seen lying in their piss-soaked sleeping bags down by the station. If they hadn't already discovered the most spectacular doss house in north-west London, it was surely only a matter of time.

Using her phone to light the way, Nicole walked tentatively up the central aisle of the stalls past the rows of ugly Ambassador chair reproductions that must have been put in in the 1970s or early 80s. To the left of the stage, camouflaged by neoclassical mouldings, was the narrow door she remembered the surveyor pushing through, but where was the handle? Sliding her palm up and down the frame, Nicole found nothing.

'Shit.'

Wincing as a shard of wood slid beneath her skin, she raised her iPhone to inspect the damage. There it was: a tiny black dash just inside the curve of her lifeline. She would have squeezed the splinter out there in the half-light had something else, reflected in her phone screen, not caught her eye. A movement behind her left ear; then the wet white of an eye.

Before she could turn, Jamie had grabbed her by the arm, spinning her towards him.

'What the hell were you playing at, sending Jill that email? You think I wouldn't find out? You think I wouldn't know it was you?'

'Jamie! You scared me shitless.' With a shake she tried to free herself. 'What's wrong with you?'

Something was: that much was obvious. His mouth was dry and scaled and his breath stale. He stared at her, pulling at a sliver of skin on his bottom lip with his teeth. 'What do you think could be wrong, Nic?'

'I haven't got the faintest. Now can you get off me?' His grip was still tight around her arm – too tight for her to shake off without losing her balance, and in an inelegant two-step the pair lurched backwards, slamming into the front seats.

'Ow!'

'You think you're going to fuck things up for me with your little games?' Jamie hissed, backing her so far into one of the Ambassador chairs that she was forced to steady herself on the arm rests to stay upright. 'You think you're going to turn my partners against me by sending them some crap I'm supposed to have written?'

'I don't know what you're talking about.' Nicole hated the wavering in her voice. 'Let go of me.'

'But that's not really what you want, is it?'

Jamie was so close now that when he laughed softly in her face Nicole smelt something warm, bready and beer-like beneath the alcoholic top note. Then her skirt was being hitched up and her knickers pushed aside in a series of matter of fact, semi-custodial gestures.

'Jamie, I'm not joking. Let me—' But his hand had moved up to her throat, cutting off her windpipe, and the last word came out as something between a gurgle and a whimper.

Jamie's laughter then was raucous, ringing out through the dark auditorium. 'What was that? Couldn't hear you.'

And unable to hold back any longer she began to laugh too, wild and hoarse, crushing her mouth into his and revelling, as she always did, in that moment of submission.

Deferring that moment heightened Nicole's pleasure. She'd worked that out early on in their affair. But it was only towards the end of their eighteen-month relationship that she'd understood why: giving in too soon not only banalised what they were doing together but made it feel too similar to what she and Ben did twice a week – once always on Sunday mornings, before Chloe was awake. And there was something else. The darker they'd got, the deeper her feelings for Jamie had become: deep enough to be love – only a feral kind of love she'd never felt for her husband. The kind that over time had ceased to satisfy and left her craving her next hit before she'd even left Jamie's side.

When she'd worked up the courage to voice that thought, five months ago, Jamie had admitted he'd felt the same, promising to leave his wife and 'make it work, whatever the fallout'. And maybe it was Nicole's fault for believing him. But when he'd reneged on that promise, she had been left bitter, broken and sentenced to day after day in conference rooms with a man she now loathed.

That was why everyone cautioned against office affairs, wasn't it? Not because of the risks she and Jamie had taken when they were together – the clinches in the BWL lifts and the frantic, angry sex they'd enjoyed in darkened boardrooms and, that one time, on the floor of the office gym changing room – but because of how impossible work life became once the affair was over.

That theirs had been so different to the average office fling, or any relationship Nicole had ever had, had only made it

harder to forget. Unable to stop herself from replaying their
savage sessions together whenever she'd found herself in the
same room as Jamie, she'd felt as betrayed by her own body
and the desire it continued to feel over the past few months
as she had by him.

'I meant what I said that night in Frankfurt.'

Jamie had raised himself up on an elbow, and she remembered that he always spoke too soon afterwards, whereas she
liked to lie quiet and still, enjoying the aftershocks as they
passed through her.

'The night you promised to leave Maya?' She turned her
face away from his, not wanting him to see the hurt in her
eyes. 'Ah, but you didn't.'

Focusing on the numbers on the back of the chairs – 8A,
8B – Nicole found herself wondering who had sat in them
over the years. Had they got everything they wanted in life,
or had they made do?

'Because look at you now,' she went on, 'still with the lovely
Mrs Lawrence, and busy sharing your happy brood with a
load of strangers on social media. So you can't have, Jamie.
You can't have meant a word of it.'

A few months ago Nicole would have found it hard to
keep her voice as level as it was. All those promises and plans
made as they tore through mini-bar snacks in an overly air-
conditioned Hilton hotel room: she'd taken them seriously.
And maybe he hadn't realised that? Maybe he had her down
as the kind of woman who had affairs, just like everyone else
at BWL seemed to after that first, stupid office fling became
common knowledge. But for Nicole, those plans had been the
promise of a new life. And when she and Jamie had made their

171

pitch to the Zech Group the following morning, Nicole hadn't pushed her leg against Jamie's beneath the conference table as she usually would have, knowing that in a matter of weeks, days, hours, they would no longer need to snatch moments.

Yes, it would be painful before they got there, but Chloe was too young to fully understand or remember a split, and if she and Ben dealt with it well (which they would, her husband being a decent man), they could end up one of those divorced couples who remain close, even sharing the odd grumble about their respective new spouses over coffee.

To have gone from planning that new life and phone conversations with a divorce lawyer she'd found online to it all being over in a single hushed sentence – 'Now's just not the time' – had floored Nicole so completely she hadn't even bothered trying to hide it. The Tuesday before Christmas she'd gone straight to bed, complaining of a tummy bug, and for a week lain there in the same discoloured T-shirt. Then, one morning, Chloe had brought up her copy of *Ant and Bee and the Doctor*, making up the words she couldn't yet read in an effort to cheer her mother up. Once the tears had finally stopped coursing down Nicole's cheeks, she'd managed to say, 'Will you go and get Daddy?'

When Ben had perched silently on the side of the bed, waiting for her to speak first, Nicole had been convinced that he knew. She was going to come clean about all of it, right down to her plan to leave him and start a new life with Jamie. Only before she could, her husband had started recounting the phone conversation he'd had earlier with a friend of a friend: a therapist who thought Nicole might be suffering from depression – 'very possibly something hormonal'. So he'd gone ahead and booked her an appointment.

Her laughter had surprised them both.

'Ben, if you think I'm in some sort of pre-menopausal funk,' she'd croaked, once she'd dried her eyes, 'you're so wide of the mark it's not even funny. I'm forty-one, not fifty-one.'

Hearing the laughter, Chloe had come back into the bedroom, and in a small voice said: 'Daddy says you're not yourself. Who are you then, Mum?'

Which had meant drying her eyes all over again. 'I'm me, ladybird. I'm here. And I'm not going anywhere, I promise.'

That and the distraction of Christmas had galvanised her back into life. This time, Nicole had decided, she wasn't just going to make do, but be the best mother and wife she could be. And apart from the TAG watch she'd kept as a keepsake beneath a pile of jeans in her bottom drawer after he'd left it on a hotel nightstand months ago, she'd successfully managed to eradicate Jamie from her life.

'So all these months – you've hated me?' Jamie was clearing the scattered hair, strand by dark strand, from her face. 'I wouldn't blame you if you had.'

'Good. And yes, I have.'

It was obvious that he found this more flattering than upsetting, which annoyed her. 'You stopped replying to my messages. You cut me dead.'

'You told me it was over! What did you expect?' And when he didn't answer: 'You really thought I'd be happy to carry on the way we were?' Remembering the thousand and one reasons why she'd vowed never to give in to him again, Nicole sat up and began patting the floor beneath the seats for her missing phone. 'Well, no. Sorry. No.' How had she ended up here again? 'I'm going to have to go.'

'Nic, wait.' He pulled himself up to be level with her. 'I need you to believe that I meant it, that night – every word. I'd even mapped out all this stuff in my head. The places you and I were going to go on holiday. Where we might live and how the kids would get on when they were a bit older.'

Nicole shook her head.

'The whole time Maya was pregnant, I kept thinking that we couldn't do anything until she had it, her. But then when Elsa was born . . . and I don't know if it was because she was a girl or because she was so tiny, you know?'

'Two weeks premature. I know.' God, how she hated knowing those things. Maya's due date, the feta cheese Jamie's wife had craved in her final trimester and how jealous Christel had pinched her new sister's thigh hard enough to make her howl when they first brought her home from the hospital. Knowing those things made her feel as though she were standing at a window peering into their life. A life that couldn't be that enviable since Jamie was lying here with her. And although 'What now?' was the obvious question after all these months apart, Nicole loathed that implicit female plea after sex, and wasn't sure she could bear the humiliation of asking it.

Ben was the only man she'd ever met who had made that plea – verbatim – after their first time. And although Nicole knew well before they married that what she and Ben had could never sate her, he was her best friend. So when he'd taken her to dinner at that awful floating restaurant in Bristol the day after their finals she'd stared out of the portholes at the olive-green Severn, waiting for him to produce the ring she'd found hidden in his desk drawer weeks before.

The night Nicole found the ring was the first time she'd

ever cheated on Ben, and she'd genuinely believed it would be the last. She had no recollection of the man's face but she remembered the damp vaulted ceilings of that basement club somewhere beneath Bristol city centre and the pounding on the door of the Ladies as they finished. She remembered the relief too, the sense of closure when it was over, as though now that curious twisted part of herself that longed to be dominated, overcome, could be retired with little to no resistance. Ben was going to ask her to marry him and she was going to say yes. Everything was going to be simpler from now on – above board. And it had been, until Ian. Stupid, meaningless Ian, the 'gateway drug' that had left her with an affair-shaped hole in her life – and led her on to the hard stuff.

'I never meant to hurt you,' Jamie went on. 'Just that Elsa was born and ... I kept wondering who would protect her and Christel if their dad wasn't there.'

Softening a little as she remembered having those same thoughts about Chloe when the idea of leaving Ben had begun to seem real, Nicole nodded.

'And I knew that Maya would find someone else, like that –' he clicked his fingers '– in a heartbeat.'

'OK, I get your wife's a real catch, Jamie.' Nicole started looking for her shoes and buttoning up her blouse.

'I'm not ... it was just the idea of some other guy looking after my girls, when it should be me, you know, because my dad was always working ...'

'And look what a fuck-up you turned out to be.'

'Exactly.'

Pausing, she ran her index finger down his cheek. 'You're not a fuck-up.' And for a moment they both stopped buttoning and zipping and just stared at one another.

'I fucked you up though, didn't I?'

She wasn't going to give him the satisfaction of knowing how badly.

'Come on.' Reaching for Jamie, she pulled her lover to his feet. 'I really have got to get back to the office. But not before I show you something.' Was this why she hadn't told Rupert about the lantern the other day? 'You can't see it from ground level, and on the plans it just looks like part of the roof. It's bonkers: you won't believe it.'

Feeling their way through the hidden passageway behind the stage they climbed a set of narrow, musty-smelling wooden stairs until they reached the heavens. There, rising up amongst a tangle of electric cables, was a Jacob's ladder leading up to a trapdoor in the theatre roof.

'Where are you taking me?'

'Trust me,' she threw back, climbing cautiously on above him, 'it's worth it. Watch your step.'

'Too busy watching something else right now.'

From his perilous position behind her on the ladder, Jamie grinned up, and Nicole felt a twinge of the old excitement as she pushed the trapdoor open, clambering out as gracefully as she could into the domed glass structure on the roof of the building: a kind of bell jar, just large enough to accommodate two seated people.

'You OK?'

Jamie followed, his mouth falling open at the sight that greeted them.

From their position inside this glass lookout post on the roof, was the 360-degree view across north-west London she'd taken in the other day, with the green slab of Queen's Park ahead of them and the thigh-shaped curve of Kensal

Green Cemetery to the left. As neatly plotted as a child's toy village, the city extended out into the Persil-blue spring skies, marred only by a fritter of clouds.

'Isn't it amazing?' Jamie could only shake his head in wonder as Nicole spoke. 'And it gets better.'

Reaching for a hatch at the base of the glass dome, Nicole opened wide a panel of curved window, motioning at Jamie to follow her out onto a small flat expanse of slate roof.

'Come.'

For a moment they sat out there – knees hugged into their chests – lost in quiet contemplation of a soundless London that from this hallowed, secret position seemed to be theirs alone.

'What is this? Where are we?' Jamie spluttered through laughter.

'Told you it was worth it,' she said, watching his smile widen at her detailed description of the structure's mechanics.

'Nerd,' Jamie whispered, reaching for her hand. 'You love this stuff.'

'Don't you?' She turned to him. 'Isn't that what makes us different to those soulless brokers who couldn't care less what they flog, or whether it'll even still be standing a year later?'

'Sure.'

Not wanting to think too deeply about his professional motivations, Nicole turned back to the view. 'All looks so small, so unimportant from here.' She curled her fingers around his.

'Maybe it is.' Jamie leant in to kiss her neck, but the slickness of his comeback brought Nicole back down to earth with a jolt.

Did he think he could spin lines to her, just as he'd done with the new girl, Sophia? After what he'd done to her at the end of last year, she wasn't going to let him think he could have her on any terms. However weak she'd been today, that was no longer the case. Exhausted by the constant push and pull she felt around Jamie, Nicole angled her face firmly away.

'Don't.' Even to herself she sounded unconvincing. 'We can't just go back to how things were. And the way you spoke to me earlier? Accusing me of things? What was that?'

'I know. Christ, I'm sorry. I didn't know what to think.'

'You never even explained what I was supposed to have done: this email I'm supposed to have sent?'

Jamie groaned. 'Forget I said anything. I get that it wasn't you.'

'So talk to me.'

Hesitantly, he told her about the email Jill had forwarded him and the internal review she'd ordered after the *Telegraph* had turned the 'Spiro scandal' into a full-page story.

'This could be serious. But I swear I never wrote the words in that email, Nic. Did I have concerns about Jill? Sure. And I still do. Because she's not all there right now. She hasn't been since Stan got ill.'

'Her husband's got cancer. How focused would you be if Maya had cancer?'

'Listen.' Jamie exhaled deeply. 'I've known Stan and Jill for years. They brought me in, remember? And don't ... don't talk about Maya.'

She bristled. 'God. Sorry.'

'But I wouldn't be stupid enough to write those kinds of things in an email. Anyway, it doesn't matter. But do I think

Jill should take more than ... well, a temporary step back? Yeah. She's of retirement age.'

Nicole pulled a face. 'My dad worked until he was seventy-two. I don't remember anyone questioning it.'

Jamie tried to slip a hand around her waist. 'So, what ... this is some feminist thing?'

The most basic suggestions of equality tended to get 'eye-rolled' by Jamie; it had become an in-joke when they were together. Only right now Nicole's mood felt as precarious as their position on that rooftop, a hundred feet up, and she couldn't bring herself to laugh.

'Come on, I've got to get going.'

'Why do you care so much about this? You don't even know Jill.'

'I really do have to go.' Nicole crawled towards the trap-door. 'But I suppose I care about Jill because I've had enough to do with her to know that she's very good at her job. And for you of all people to be talking about her the way you are behind her back just seems ... then again, maybe loyalty's not your thing.'

They came down that Jacob's ladder in a very different mood, and shoulder to shoulder but in silence headed through the auditorium towards the door. Outside in the stymied fury of London rush hour, Jamie turned back towards her.

'I didn't write that email.'

'I believe you.' Nicole sighed, relieved to discover as she said it that it was true. 'Guess I just thought you might be a liar as well as a cheat.'

'Right,' Jamie said flatly, exhausted now by all this judgement. 'And maybe I deserve that from you. But if you didn't do this, Nic, who did?'

'I have no idea,' she threw back as she turned on her heels and, with a half-hearted wave, walked off down Kilburn Lane. Nicole wasn't about to tell him that this had Alex written all over it, much less the part she'd played in prompting his ex-PA to move ahead with 'the plan'. Everything she'd said that night at the pub had been true – of the preamble to their affair. Only she'd left out her encouragement of Jamie's 'inappropriate' gestures and words. She'd omitted to mention that the day he'd called her 'fuckable', she'd gone home and replayed it over and over while Ben slept beside her, stifling her final shuddering moan with a pillow.

Not one word of what she'd told Alex at her flat that night had been a lie, either. Spurred on by her discovery that Jamie had tried to embark on similar games with Sophia, she'd dredged back that one time – and it had just been one – when Jamie had taken things too far. Whether he'd misread her signals or got off on watching her flail and splutter, Nicole would never know. It had been so close to their split that she'd buried it along with everything else – until that night in the pub. Hearing Alex and Jill talk about their own humiliations at the hands of Jamie, and understanding for the first time just how much he enjoyed power play with women in every area of his life, had awakened the memory. A hotel-room floor: her head painfully angled against a radiator valve; his right hand squeezing her neck harder, harder. As he'd ignored her gasps – 'Stop it' – she'd forced a strangled laugh, hoping it might diffuse whatever aggression they'd worked up together. 'OK. Please. Stop.' They'd never had a 'safe word', never even discussed the idea of one. Would it have made a difference? Remembering the blankness of Jamie's pupils and the slackness of his jaw as his rhythm speeded into angry jerks – then the slump – she couldn't be sure. But the shock on his face when she finally managed to push his dead weight off her and, kicking and cursing, got to her feet – that had seemed so genuine.

'Christ, I really did hurt you!' Jamie had whimpered.

She'd felt grateful that his ongoing apologies and pleas for forgiveness had kept drowning out the question running on a loop inside her head: *But you didn't stop. Why didn't you stop, Jamie, when I asked you to?*

Nicole had never, even to herself, used the word her brain had rejected as inaccurate – impossible? – at the time. And that night with Alex, she hadn't needed to. Because in the madness that seized her after seeing those pictures of Jamie's blissed-out family life and hearing about his fresh office prey, Nicole had gone from wanting to call off the Rottweiler PA sinking her incisors into Jamie's heels to willing that dog to tear him apart.

Only not for a second had Nicole imagined she might find herself back with Jamie. Those wheels she'd set in motion – what if it was too late to stop them?

CHAPTER 20

~≫≪~

ALEX

'Don't you dare take your shoes off! Put them back on.'

'Really?'

Alex was leaning against Maya's hall wall, pushing down on the heel of her right trainer.

'Lexie,' said Maya, laughing, 'we went through this last week. We're not Swiss. Plus I just convinced my husband to get us one of those new Dyson Cyclones or whatever they're called. Looks like a lightsaber, which I know he secretly loves, as all aged *Star Wars* nerds would. Now come through – we'll have some lunch.'

When she'd walked in there the previous week, exhilarated by the risk she was taking even once assured her former boss was at work until late, her first thought had been that Jamie's social media hadn't done their house justice. A semidetached Victorian townhouse, the place had somehow been cleverly reconfigured into an open-plan modern family home, with minimalist furniture and edgy contemporary art lining the walls. Inside, it looked like it was worth a hell of a lot more than the £3,250,000 Zoopla had it valued at.

'Wow. This place is gorgeous, Maya. Doesn't feel like we're in London, somehow?'

'Yeah? It's taken us ages to get it the way we want it. And now I'm already getting itchy feet and thinking of moving further out – but not too far. Richmond or Barnes, maybe.'

After lifting Elsa out of the red scarf carrier she always seemed to have slung around her neck in readiness for her daughter, Maya had set the girls down in the play gym in the far corner of the room, where the kitchen adjoined a trellised conservatory-cum-dining room. There the two girls had gurgled contentedly while their mothers had enjoyed the kind of leisurely afternoon Alex had started to think she'd never be allowed again.

Today, instead of seating her at the kitchen table, Maya led Alex out to the conservatory that looked out onto their garden. In between the two cascading magnolia trees at either end of the lawn stood a swing set and slide: not the ugly plastic kind you found in public playgrounds but a retro, hand-painted wooden set Jamie would have painstakingly put together himself.

The overhead sun was streaming through the glass onto the broad beech table and a heady scent of orchids and baked wood filled the room.

'I'd spend all day in here if I could, but at this time of year the kids find it too hot.'

'Oh Maya, it's amazing. Christel's at nursery?'

'Yes. Our nanny's picking her up. Which means I don't have to drive, and we can have a glass of rosé.'

'Great.' Alex smiled. Only the fantasy she'd been living ever since she'd arrived at Bumps & Babies that morning had just imploded. Because a memory was drifting back: of a cheerful-faced Filipina dropping Christel off with her father at the office at the end of the day, months back. Alex was heavily pregnant at the time, and the two women had had a conversation. What it had been about and whether it had been long enough for her to place Alex today, she didn't know. But suddenly the risk she was running, the madness of being here as 'Lexie the Chiswick mum' in her former boss's house hit her with such force that she stood up fast, catching her wine glass with the back of her hand and sending it crashing down onto the flagstones.

'Oh! Maya, I'm so sorry. Let me ... have you got any kitchen roll?'

'Please – I'll do it.'

In an instant she was back from the kitchen with a dustpan and brush. 'Here I am plying you with wine and you need food, don't you?'

'You know, on second thoughts maybe we should do lunch another day.' Alex's throat was dry and her eyes darting from Katie on the play mat to her bag on the sofa, as she assessed how quickly an exit could be made without it seeming odd. 'You've got little Christel back any moment and ...'

Maya looked up from her crouched position on the floor, where she'd almost finished clearing up Alex's mess. 'They're going to the park after school, so they won't be back until four-ish – relax!'

And as Alex checked the clock on the wall out of the

corner of her eye and saw to her relief that it wasn't yet two, she felt the relief course through her body.

'Now, I'll put us together a quick chicken Caesar – that OK? It won't take two minutes.' Then, from the kitchen: 'I get those blood sugar slumps too – it's the breastfeeding. Doesn't it wipe you out?'

'That and being up five times a night,' Alex called back.

'I don't think men will ever understand what that level of tiredness does to you. And yet we carry on. Jamie's one of the most energetic men you'll ever meet, but he's fetishistic about sleep. Can't survive without it. Anything less than eight hours and the man's a wreck.'

I know – I remember. I was the one who used to have to fix all the work blunders he made when he was jetlagged or had been drinking late.

'My husband's the same,' laughed Alex, calmer now. And it was lovely in this airy, white house with this bright, blonde woman. Yes, Maya was pampered and inhabited another world, but the two women seemed to share many of the same concerns, and there was something soothing about her physical presence: everything from her soft-focus skin and symmetrical Scandinavian features to the flatness of her vowels drowning out Alex's ceaseless inner chatter. Even Katie seemed more peaceable in her company. And as the two women had ambled lazily along Chiswick High Road after their Little Gym class, their conversation jumping from silly ('those plate-sized nipples you've got right now? Don't panic – they'll go back') to serious ('the isolation of those first few months: no one tells you about that'), Alex had felt happier and more relaxed than she had in months.

But it was Maya's kindness that she had found most

startling in the woman who had chosen to marry Jamie Lawrence. Did she have any idea what kind of a monster she was living with? 'I hope you don't mind that I called,' she'd whispered at the start of the class. 'To be honest, I felt a bit worried about you. Like you –' she looked embarrassed '– I don't know ... could do with a gal pal. I know I could.'

Alex could tell that Maya had chosen the cheesiest expression she could in order to lighten the statement. And that in itself was sweet. She hadn't wanted to assume or imply that Alex didn't have friends, but the frustration both of them clearly felt as working-women-turned-mothers wasn't something many admitted to in the easy and immediate way they had the first day they'd met. And however different their lifestyles were, it bonded them. So when Maya had again suggested lunch at hers, this time Alex hadn't resisted.

The curiosity, malevolent in the midst of such a carefree day, had only kicked in once inside Jamie's house. Because until Alex was confronted by those photos of her former boss on the shelves again, it had somehow been easy to forget that there was any link between Jamie and this woman she was reluctantly starting to like. And as she glanced from a picture of her ex-boss and Maya laughing into falling confetti on their wedding day to one of the pair in ironic Christmas jumpers somewhere rich and snowy, Alex was forced to suppress a shudder at the thought of what that gregarious-faced family man had done to Nicole.

Maya had just served up the salad when the slam of the front door made them both jump.

'Hellooo,' came a singsong Filipina's voice from the hall. 'We're back early! Christel not feeling so good.'

'Oh, my sweetheart.' When Maya rushed out to greet her

daughter, Alex, the blood pulsing in her ears, forced herself to think. There had to be a way out of this.

'Are you hungry, my love?' Scooping up her daughter from the play gym and hoping Maya wouldn't remember how recently she'd last given Katie a bottle, Alex ducked out into the conservatory, angling her body towards the wall in the way a breast-feeding mother might.

'Take the bottle!' she whispered, dipping her head in a silent thank you when her daughter did.

There was nothing as distracting as one's own children, and as she heard Maya's maternal murmurings in the next room, she felt reassured that both women might be consumed enough by little Christel to ignore her.

'Did she have a snack on the way home?' she heard Maya ask the nanny, in between nuzzles.

'Just those breadsticks – and some raisins.'

'Do you think she's still hungry?'

'I can make her something?'

Say no. *No thanks. Do head off for the day. We're all sorted here.* Because Katie had decided she'd had enough formula, and her cheeks were turning pink and blotchy in the magnified heat of the conservatory. Any minute now she would kick off, and alert the nanny to their presence.

Alex was still working out a game plan when she heard Maya tell the nanny that no: they would be fine. And why didn't she head off for the day? Closing her eyes, Alex let out a long, controlled breath: someone was looking out for her.

When she opened them again, a small, sleek-haired woman was standing in the conservatory doorway holding out a glass of iced water.

'Thought you might need this? So hot in here!'

187

Her smile was as broad and straightforward as it had been that afternoon at the office, but as Alex took the glass from her hand, the nanny's eyes moved from Katie to Alex's face where they lingered, a question mark implicit.

'Thank you. I . . . I'm Lexie.'

'Maria.'

But the woman didn't move.

'I'm sweltering,' Alex mumbled into Katie's muslin, anxious not to lift her face. 'But I'll just finish off her feed.'

A frown. 'You and . . . Mr Lawrence?'

It was part statement, part question, and before Alex could think of a reply, Maya poked her head around the door and laughed. 'No, this is my friend Lexie. She's a Bumps & Babies girl. Katie here is only a month older than Elsa.'

Alex squirmed as she saw this fact chime again in Maria's consciousness. They would have compared due dates that day in the office; in fact she could remember doing just that.

'Do head off.' Maya was saving her, and she didn't even know it. 'Christel can watch a bit of telly, can't you, my love? Get some rest while Mummy and Lexie finish their lunch? And Katie and Elsa might be ready for their nap.'

Sure enough, Katie looked about to drift off in the heat, and after a barely perceptible head-shake – would it come to her? – Maria gave up and with a wave went on her way.

'I know it's a school day – and I promise I'm not an alcoholic –' clearing their plates, Maya bit her lip '– but we could have one more glass? Unless you have to be somewhere?' And Alex laughed, partly because after what had just happened there was nothing she needed more, and partly at the idea of having to be somewhere. Thanks to your cock of a husband, Alex thought as the two women clinked glasses, she didn't have anywhere else to be.

By the second glass Alex was filled with the same irrational sense of well-being she'd felt in this house the week before. Maya found her funny, or at least she seemed to – throwing her head back and snorting with laughter at some of the stories about Kieran (Alex was proud of how quickly her fictional husband's name had come to her). And when they'd clinked glasses, Alex had surprised herself with an anecdote about her parents.

'My dad doesn't like her drinking. He doesn't like her doing much, actually. He's ...' she searched for the right word, before settling for an understatement, 'controlling. I remember once, he'd let her join a book club. And she'd been so thrilled to be in the company of these other women, to feel free, I suppose, that she'd come back from their first session a bit tipsy. That was it.' Alex shook her head. 'He never let her go back after that. Called her "an embarrassment".'

'Lexie – that's awful.'

'It is, isn't it?' She'd never told anyone these things. 'Their marriage. It's not something I could ever survive. Thank God I found a man like Kieran, right?'

'It's hard though, isn't it?' Maya was saying, her eyes dimmed down to an almost seaweed green by the wine. 'I mean, they worship you for a while but then gradually you can feel yourself becoming, I don't know, irritating, in so many small ways. And there's nothing you can do about it.'

'I think Jamie still worships you. I mean, it seems like it from what you say. And he should, shouldn't he? Plus don't you find him irritating sometimes?'

'Oh I do. But I'm lucky. I married a good man.' Maya put

her hand to her chest. 'So if ever something really bothers me, I tell him and we talk it over and he will pretty much always see my point of view and stop doing it. Take the secret smoking I told you about last week. Once I confronted him and told him how upset it made me he swore never to do it again, and I know he'll stick to that. It's the secrets I don't like, you know?'

'Sounds like he really respects you.' Alex smiled, but inside she was smirking. Yes Jamie respected his wife so much that he kept a pack of Marlboro Lights in his bottom drawer at work. He respected her so much that he raped co-workers.

'In the end respect is the most important thing,' Maya said. 'The rest of it –' she lowered her voice to a sultry whisper '– the intimacy. Well, I know it matters, but when you've been together a few years . . .' Her eyes flicked from Alex's face to her own hand on the wine glass, as though she were trying to assess whether what she wanted to say would be too much, too soon. 'And it's just harder to get yourself in the mood with a newborn around? I remember that with Christel. But now, with two of them and me that little bit older . . .'

'Maya, you look like a twenty-year-old!'

'I wish!' she snorted. 'I'm thirty-six next week. Anyway, it's taking me longer to get back . . . you know . . . into it this time around.'

Alex was liking this. Already an idea of how she could make use of these confidences was coming to her. 'It can't be easy for men,' she prodded.

'No.' Maya's intonation had hardened now, 'but I do think that, given what we go through, they could be a bit more . . .'

'Sensitive?'

'Yeah!'

'Because anything that feels like pressure is only going to make things worse.'

'That's it!' Maya looked relieved. 'Jamie has always been pretty insatiable in that area, which I used to love, but right now ... To be honest, we've fallen out a couple of times over it.'

'I'm sure most couples have. I'm lucky that Kieran has got where I'm coming from.' Alex was beginning to feel quite fond of this fantasy husband of hers. 'And I don't know Jamie, but you have every right to be annoyed if he's being thoughtless.'

'You're right.'

'Maya, can I use your loo?'

Alex headed up, as bidden, to the bathroom on the landing – 'It's nicer for guests' – and had a quick rifle through the small mirrored wall cabinet. There was nothing in there but a spare Diptyque candle and the rainbow 'days of the week' pillbox stuffed full of multicoloured vitamins Alex recognised from Maya's Instagram post, and Alex was about to head out when she spotted something metallic on the windowsill. Jamie's wedding ring.

Hearing Maya gently trying to rouse Christel from her nap downstairs, Alex pocketed it and headed up to the next floor, pausing only to stuff the half-full packet of Marlboro Lights she'd brought with her beneath a towel in the linen cupboard on the landing – where it would easily be discovered – before peering into Jamie and Maya's bedroom. It was dangerous, she knew, but Alex wanted to see where Jamie slept.

Large, sparsely furnished and painted duck-egg blue, their bedroom overlooked the garden from a huge double bay window. Alex stared out for a moment, trying to imagine how Jamie might feel when he drew the curtains in the morning, as Maya lay there in a silk slip like the one poking out beneath her pillow now, lazily planning what they'd have for breakfast.

Did he look from this beautiful, kind and clever woman who clearly adored him to the view from his castle and ask himself how long ... how long did he have until he was busted? Was he even aware that he was a fraud who didn't deserve all this? The answer to both had to be no. Nobody who appreciated what they had could jeopardise it in the way Jamie had been doing for years – professionally and personally. Alex wasn't stupid: she got that the appeal was in that jeopardy, as with the MPs and their researchers, the presidents and their interns. It was the same macho playground taunt: 'You can't catch me.' Only, Jamie was about to be caught out in every way. And maybe then he would appreciate everything he had lost.

Her afternoons with Maya were yielding so much ammunition. But while all that inside knowledge had thrilled Alex the first time she'd been to the house, and switching the time of Greenleaf's interview had given her the same hit of power as tinkering with the location of the O'Ceallaigh brothers' 'last chance' meeting on Jamie's online calendar, her relationship with his wife had quickly taken on an unexpected form: that of a genuine friendship. There was something completely straight about Maya, it had occurred to Alex as she and Katie made their way home that afternoon, stopping briefly to hurl the thin gold wedding band in her pocket into a skip. And the irony of Maya being married to a man who didn't seem able to open his mouth without lying wasn't lost on her.

Alex had been asking herself whether her thirst for pay-back might be close to being quenched when she'd logged onto BWL's intranet to see Jamie and Jill's email exchange on Spiro happening in real time. Had Jill's question on how Jamie had 'managed to swing' a deal that had looked dead in the water – only to be suddenly pushed through at break-neck speed – not been enough to awaken her suspicions, the excessive emoji use would have been. Like his extra-wide smile, these were always a sign of duplicity with Jamie, and Alex hadn't been able to resist blowing his little plot with Spiro wide open, her pulse quickening as her fingers skimmed across the keyboard, as though powered by some external force.

How easy it had been to read back through their emails until she found the one encouraging the slippery Greek developer to take things into his own hands. Whether Jamie had been any more involved than that, Alex would never know, but a quick anonymous call to the *Telegraph* soon had someone with superior investigative skills to hers look-ing into it. And although the piece that appeared was more condemnatory of Spiro than of 'Deal Don Jamie Lawrence', the impact this would have on BWL's reputation could surely not be ignored by Jill or Paul. Given how likely it now seemed that with her gentle rocking of Jamie's world he would be quite capable of capsizing alone, maybe all that was left for Alex to do was sit back and watch.

Nevertheless, as she waited for his inbox to open that night she experienced the usual not entirely unpleasant stomach flutter. Could he somehow have found out what she'd been doing and changed his password? But she was in, and scrolling from one message to the next until she had a complete picture of Jamie Lawrence's day, with all the mounting tensions and micro-humiliations he deserved.

Only, something jarred: too impatient to read the emails in chronological order, Alex had clicked on one sent late that afternoon in which Jamie was arranging to meet a friend for a 'celebratory' pint that evening. In response to his friend's 'What are we celebrating, mate?' Jamie had replied: 'Had something hanging over my head that looks like it's gonna get sorted. Speak later.'

Moving quickly through Jamie's inbox, outbox and trash, and ignoring the bank statements, online purchase receipts and unidentifiable female names she would ordinarily have double-clicked on, Alex felt queasy. She could still smell the Johnson's powder she was sure she'd scoured her hands of earlier, yet still that sickly floral stench followed her everywhere. She was going to need to wash them again in something stronger, but nothing seemed to work. Even the perfume she'd doused them in the other day had only succeeded in reawakening the powdery smell in some curious way. She wondered whether some kind of dishwash detergent might be strong enough to do the job. But first she had to be sure that Jamie hadn't somehow managed to wriggle off another hook.

Up came a brief email from Paul: *Tried my best, mate. She knows every partner needs to agree to a review and I'm not sure she's got the energy to convince me right now, so fingers crossed she'll let the Spiro business drop. Course I believe you had nothing to do with it – the guy's always come across as dodgy as hell. And the fact you've got Ainsley nibbling on Minerva is gonna help, obvs.*

Alex frowned. Paul must mean Harry Ainsley, the tycoon-turned-TV star, which was a coup for Jamie – and a blow for her.

PS. Go easy on Jill? She's been through the mill. But maybe you're right about the other thing.

Good to see the old boys' network was alive and well. And Alex was ready to bet that the 'other thing' was Jill's supposed professional jealousy. Because that's what women were, wasn't it? Jealous and petty.

She spotted a cluster of subsequent emails from Jill: *Paul seems to think we might be able to get this sorted without a formal review. And if we can agree on that and you're able to get your accounts in order for Alan in time, that might be easier all round. Hope you can appreciate that this was never personal – unlike your email of 8 Jan.* To which Jamie had replied: *Think we both know that's a bit of a porky. That you never even bothered to ask whether I wrote it in the first place (I didn't) proves you've had a problem with me way before this. And that feels personal.*

'Don't fall for his crap,' Alex muttered to herself. But Jill had gone quiet and Alex's eye had zoomed in on Hayden's name, which appeared twice in quick succession further down Jamie's inbox: at 11.02 a.m. and 11.14 a.m.

In an act of desperation driven by a conversation with her mother – 'I don't want to pester, but the money … it will be paid back in time, won't it?' – that morning Alex had finally decided to call Hayden before leaving the flat to meet Maya at Bumps & Babies. He'd reacted as expected – with a curt 'No! What happened to leaving me out of this?' – leaving

Alex hating herself that little bit more. And she knew before even clicking on the emails that they would be about her.

Just had the 'bunny boiler' on the phone. She wants money (not happening). I'm still not buying it's mine, for starters.

That's where sympathy fucks get you, mate, Jamie had pinged back.

Alex froze. Was it Jamie's term or something Hayden had used in conversation with him? Surely the inverted commas suggested the latter?

Thinking back to the night Katie was conceived, and how those strong male arms around her had felt like everything in the moment, Alex was dizzied by another wave of anger.

The scent rising up from her fingers now was too much to bear. Alex could picture the particles of baby powder being sucked into her nasal cavity and lungs with every exhalation. There they would attach themselves to those tiny hairs – their name the answer to a GCSE exam question – clogging up Alex's airwaves before eventually suffocating her. But as she leaned over the bathroom sink, scrubbing until any hint of the smell was gone, the idea born at Maya's kitchen table crystallised into a clear plan. She had a whole series of them now, in fact, thanks to the clean air she could breathe and a palliative afternoon with Maya. And the first could be put into practice immediately.

Alex could have spent an hour on the Agent Provocateur website alone, flicking from a cage-like elasticated lingerie set called 'the Whitney', whose 'strategically placed strapped cups' enabled you 'to dress or undress the nipple as desired', to the purple satin 'Clancie', with its elaborate 'cut-out effects'. The Whitney won, evoking, as it claimed, 'a sense of entrapment', which was perfect. And after tapping in Jamie's

Amex number, provided for gift-buying missions just like these, Alex added a note: 'Can't wait to see you in this. Jx.'

Maya deserved better than a man who'd done what Jamie had to Nicole; a man who talked about women the way her husband had so casually in his emails to Hayden – and Alex was going to make sure she got it. Once Maya found out what her husband had been up to, she would never regret kicking him out of her life. And although it might be tough for a while, Alex would be there to help her through it.

CHAPTER 21

JILL

'Jill!'

She was through the turnstiles and about to hotfoot it up the escalator when the receptionist's cries forced her to turn back.

Jill was fond of Lydia, but once that girl collared you, you were there for the duration.

'I'm running a bit late.'

'Sorry! I just meant to give you this.' Lydia handed Jill a small white envelope with her name on it. 'Someone left it on my desk earlier.'

It wasn't until after Jill had returned the calls she'd missed that morning and started on the M&S Greek salad Kellie had bought her for lunch that she remembered the envelope. As she ripped it open and unfolded the A4 sheet within,

Jill stopped chewing and spat out an olive stone into her hand. It appeared to be a screenshot of a formal letter sent by Jamie two days before – and a day after she'd ordered a formal review into his involvement with the Spiro affair – to the BWL supervisory board. Jill read it twice to be sure, but there it was in black and white: the letter was suggesting she should be forcibly retired.

As the co-founder of BWL Ms Barnes is responsible for creating one of the most powerful and important historical property firms in the country. Beyond that, as a partner, she has been an asset to us for over twenty years now and helped navigate the company through occasionally choppy waters. It goes without saying that her market expertise and management abilities are second to none, and I feel honoured to have been able to work beneath and alongside a broker of her calibre over the years.

Regrettably, however, I feel that the complex personal issues she is being forced to deal with at home, tragic as they are, have impacted those abilities as well as my confidence in her to lead BWL through to its next chapter. The markets are changing and with them the cast of buyers and developers – buyers and developers who have more than once intimated that they would prefer to work with someone more in tune with today's outlook.

Much as it saddens me to be forced to point this out to you, my primary responsibility is and always will be to BWL, and it is with a heavy heart and the company's best interests in mind that I write this letter. Although Paul Wilkinson has made it clear to me that he doesn't share my views on Mrs Barnes as things currently stand, I am convinced this will change moving forward, and respectfully ask for a moment of your time in order to discuss this sensitive situation face to face.

Yours sincerely

Jamie Lawrence

Maybe it was events of the past few weeks, culminating in that anonymous email, and the reluctant realisation that you could spend twelve years in close professional and personal proximity to someone you never really knew. Or maybe it was simply that with everything she'd been through with Stan, Jill was becoming immune to nasty surprises. Whatever the reason, all she felt in that moment was bone-tired.

'Jill?' Kellie had popped her head around the door, but Jill didn't look up from the letter.

'Mmm?'

'The meeting? With Harry Ainsley? It's starting now.'

'Oh Christ. Of course it is.'

Grabbing the Minerva file and the battered old Filofax Jamie and Paul were forever teasing her about, Jill strode just fast enough not to draw attention to herself to the corner conference room.

'Harry! Lovely to see you.'

The slight, bearded TV star leaned forward, allowing his cheek to be kissed, and with a small inward sigh Jill took in the forehead, etched into a permanent frown, and shiny custom three-piece suit that had become his leitmotif. Ever since his show *Gazumped!* had become a ratings smash, Harry had started believing his own hype, and today she wasn't in the mood for the rough, gruff shtick his prime-time audience lapped up.

'Shall we sit?' She addressed the question to Harry and his cohorts – all East End boys made good, all circa five-foot-five, and all in equally shiny suits – rather than Jamie, who was stood over by the window, wearing a look of infinite patience.

'Absolutely. We were only waiting for you.'

'Well, here I am.' Jill could hardly bear to look at him – she was still struggling to digest the letter she'd just read – and she certainly wasn't going to apologise for being three minutes late. 'Now, Harry, I know you've been sent the Minerva sales pack and made aware of a JLL sale to Westfield just over the river, just in case you had thoughts of doing anything similar with the site.' Here she made sure to catch Jamie's eye. 'And I believe we've got some footage here that might help boost your imagination.'

'Don't have a problem with my imagination, last I checked,' growled Harry. The cohort tittered in the way that they were required to whenever Harry said anything that qualified as 'vintage Harry'.

'Course you don't.' The words felt mealy in her mouth, her smile pasted on. 'But you'll give us the satisfaction of showing you what the clever folk in digital were able to dream up, won't you? Jamie?'

Jill stared deep into Jamie's big black pupils, and as he shifted in his seat, nervous and jerky in his movements in a way she'd never seen him before, it seemed impossible that he couldn't read the questions she was silently asking him. You really did write that email to Paul, didn't you, Jamie? And the letter – that letter? All these months, you've been trying to get me out. Why? Because you no longer had 'confidence in my abilities'? Or is it because now that I've got you where you want to be, I'm just too much of a reminder of where you once were? You called what happened to Stan 'tragic', which is wrong. Because Stan didn't die, did he? And thank Christ I've never really thought of you as a son, like my husband once said. Because to a mother, you wouldn't just be a disappointment, you'd be heartbreaking.

'Jamie.' She cleared her throat. 'Could you do the honours?'

Once the twenty-two-minute film began and Harry was guided room by room through five possible virtual structures, Jill took a breath and opened her Filofax on her lap, knowing before she started flicking back through her calendar to the first week of January what she would find.

Sure enough, there it was: *J, Ivy – 7.30 p.m.* Stan had been admitted to hospital with acute urinary retention two days earlier. The accompanying infection had been so virulent that when Jamie had visited him that afternoon, her husband had been in a state of delirium. And when Stan had mistaken Jill for a nurse, she'd been so upset she'd been forced to leave the room for a moment to compose herself.

Afterwards, Jamie had insisted on taking her out to supper. 'I'm not having you sitting in that waiting room pestering the nurses all night for updates. You're going to need to eat, to drink wine and to vent.'

He'd been right. At their corner table she'd talked and drunk for hours. And Jamie had listened, speaking only to say all the right things. No one who had ever seen Jamie playing to a crowd would guess that he was capable of that kind of intimacy, always probing deeper with another question. And maybe that was one of the reasons he had always been so appealing to women. Because if there was one thing women loved it was being asked questions. 'How did that make you feel in the moment?' 'What about later?' And although Jill had never considered herself typical of her sex, in that moment it had been exactly what she'd needed. Which may have been why she'd seen nothing odd in what she now saw were carefully planted questions around the idea of retirement.

'Stan's going to need you more than ever moving forward.' 'What's important is that you're there for him now, don't you think?' And: 'You've given your life to BWL, Jill. You and Stan both have. Maybe it's time now to concentrate on you? Take *Lady J* off somewhere and enjoy the spoils?'

But the question that really stood out now, months on, the one that made her wonder whether really, beneath it all, Jamie might not just be casually amoral but one of those 'everyday psychopaths' they talked about on daytime telly, was the one he'd asked as he helped her into a cab at the end of the night. 'You know I'll always be here for you, don't you?'

The film was still playing, and Harry was propping his face up on his elbows, hands pulling his cheeks down into a bull-dog mope. But Jamie was fidgeting in a slightly manic way that was beginning to draw looks from Harry's cohorts as he stared out beyond the glass walls at something or someone. A twist of the neck revealed it to be Nicole, who was bent over the senior surveyor's desk pointing at something on his screen. Her dress, a leaf-green sheath that showed off her defined legs and waist, was straining slightly at the hips with the movement, the curve of a flank clearly delineated beneath the fabric. 'Because in the end women are either convenient to Jamie, or expendable,' Nicole had said that night.

Far from being a bubble of insanity, that conversation – that plan – was turning out to be one of the most lucid Jill had had in years. And maybe while she'd eradicated thoughts of payback from her mind, Nicole and Alex had quietly followed through with it?

'Is there any danger of this thing ending?' Harry's truculent tones snapped her out of it.

'Quite something, am I right?' Grinning nervously, Jamie launched into his sell – only this one wasn't as fluent as usual. In fact, it was garbled. And broken up by pauses during which he ran his tongue back and forth over his teeth, ummed and ahhed, and generally seemed to lose his train of thought. Something wasn't right – and Ainsley could see it. 'Honestly, you could build yourself a whole luxury community on a site that size.'

Jamie always dropped a few Ts and a whole social class when talking to Harry. And although it had never bothered her before, today it seemed significant. Jamie could alter his persona to what was needed in the moment. Whatever it takes to make the sale – wasn't that what she'd always told him? And he'd successfully sold himself to her for years.

'Anyway, at least I hope that now gives you a full idea of what might be available to you,' Jill chimed in. 'And I know you and Jamie have a site visit planned. I'm happy to join if it would be helpful?'

'We're OK.' Harry got to his feet, and Jill didn't bother leaning in this time. 'It's all sorted.'

'Well, good to see you, Harry.'

'Always a pleasure, Jamie. My PA will be in touch to set up the viewing.'

'Good stuff.' There Jamie was with his tongue again. Was

he ... was he wired? 'Now, what about that dinner? Let's set something up, eh?'

Harry's minions had already filed out, but Jamie had stopped to ask the question in the doorway, deliberately blocking Jill's path. He wanted her to hear this. 'We talked about Friday? Maya's desperate to meet Trish.'

Jill tried to busy herself with the file in her hands; anything to hide the annoyance Jamie knew the conversation would prompt. Both she and Jamie had been trying to get Harry to come for dinner for years. If he could manage that, he'd be well on his way to wiping his slate clean in the supervisory board's eyes.

'Yeah. Christ knows how you landed that one, mate,' Harry muttered. 'Punching well above your weight there.'

'Right now I think she'd agree,' she heard Jamie chuckle as he slowly walked Ainsley out, one hand hovering proprietorially between his client's shoulder blades. And was she imagining it, or was he talking too fast, moving too fast? 'In the doghouse, I'm afraid.' This part Jill wasn't sure she was supposed to hear, so she sharpened her ears. 'Actually, you'll like this, Harry. I used to get her underwear from that place, you know Agent Whatever, on her birthday.' He was sniggering like a schoolboy. 'And I didn't this year, 'cause of the new baby and what have you. But somehow the shop messes up and all this stuff arrives.' He lowered his voice. 'Mate, we're talking bondage gear, right? We're talking studded leather. So, understandably, Maya goes spare.'

Jill couldn't believe what she was hearing. Once again here was Jamie trying to pretend his painful lack of sensitivity was someone else's fault.

She could only now see Harry from the back, but he was

a family man, she knew, who adored his wife and observed Shabbat. Jamie had misjudged this, just as he'd misjudged Maya's birthday present – and from the look on his face, he knew it. But he had to finish his anecdote now.

'Anyway it was the shop's mistake, as it turns out, a "mis-order", which was what was so funny . . .'

The two men fell out of earshot here, but Jill thought Harry looked even more nonplussed than usual as the elevator doors closed, and Jamie's final holler, 'Let's make that dinner happen, eh?' had more than a tinge of desperation to it.

The whole episode wasn't just odd, but worrying. Jamie's judgement and intuition were what had propelled him up the ranks, and it was as though everything that had once made him sharper, smoother and better at his job than others was eroding before her very eyes. Unless it had been an illusion all along? But Jill didn't have time to ponder this further. Having grabbed his wallet from his desk, Jamie had left the building, doubtless for one of his sugar fixes, and that meant she didn't have long.

'This you?' Jill thrust the letter before Nicole.

'Sorry?'

It was the first time the two women had done more than exchange a few civilities since Joyce's party, and certainly the first time Jill had ever come over to her desk. 'The letter.' She lowered her voice. 'And the email. I know what you and Alex are trying to do, Nicole, and if this is about everything we spoke about that . . . that night – well, there's no need: the scales have well and truly fallen. But I'm not sure this is the way—'

'Jill,' Nicole cut in. She'd only glanced at the letter, stabbing wildly on at her keyboard instead. 'I don't know what you're talking about.'

'I'm asking you to read this.'

The younger woman stared up at her, and it felt as though she were deliberating over something, although Jill couldn't for the life of her work out what. Finally, having checked to see that nobody was watching, Nicole picked up the letter, swallowed hard and read it.

'This isn't … Jill I've got nothing to do with this.' Jill nodded. That much was clear.

'And I'm not convinced Jamie wrote it.'

'You think …' They both fell silent as the marketing director walked by with a client. 'Then do you think,' Jill whispered, 'that it might be Alex, trying to ramp things up? Have you heard from her?'

Nicole swallowed again. 'No. This is probably just some shit-stirrer. I swear I had nothing to do with it.'

'Despite what he …?'

Nicole looked so mortified that Jill felt guilty for bringing it up.

'I'd rather we forgot I ever said anything about that.'

'Sorry.'

'No, no, I'm just … I've got an appointment with a client.'

'Right. Sorry again. I just … I didn't want you to think I'd stand for any more of that. You'd tell me, wouldn't you? OK, OK, I'll let you go.'

Picking the letter back up from Nicole's desk, Jill saw that there was a picture of a dark-haired, light-eyed girl sitting on her father's lap pinned to the desk partition. She didn't know anything about Nicole, she realised. And yet because of what had been said that night at the pub, there was a strange familiarity there.

'Your daughter?'

Nicole nodded. She was switching off her computer now and reaching down for her handbag. And with the two rosy sweeps that had appeared across her cheekbones while the two women were talking and her eyes as made up as they were, Jill didn't think she'd ever seen Nicole look so beautiful.

'I've really got to . . .'

'Of course – go.'

Jill watched her as she rounded the corner towards the lift, pushing repeatedly on the button as she waited for it to arrive, and it took her a moment to realise that what she was feeling was disappointment. What if everything they'd said that night had been true? What if Jamie did need a helping hand?

CHAPTER 22

NICOLE

B loody Jill. Trust her to be standing there when the message pinged in: *Old Ship at 4?*

Although Nicole didn't think she'd seen; she was pretty sure she hadn't.

How many times had she told Jamie not to write messages in the email subject line? Not to write emails full stop? But having always behaved with impunity, Jamie seemed to believe he was untouchable.

Jill she had no problem with. In fact Nicole had always quite liked the company founder, along with everything she stood for: no kids and yet apparently happy; ambitious and fulfilled by her job alone in a way women weren't supposed or allowed to be. But after what she'd rashly told both her and – worse – Alex, Nicole had started something she now felt powerless to stop. And yet she hadn't heard from Alex since her late-night visit. Maybe with the baby in her life – even after what Nicole had told her – she'd decided to leave Jamie alone?

As she hurried along King Street towards the river, torn between a desire to make Jamie wait and a need to find out what this assignation was about, Nicole wondered whether the letter Jill had shown her might actually be genuine. If so, wasn't it possible Jamie had real grounds for concern? Jill had had a lot on her mind, after all. Then again, given the worrying way Alex had been talking when she'd seen her in that filthy flat, this might well have been her doing. Again, Nicole felt that lurch in her stomach, the lurch you got as a child seconds before the vase or window smashed, when the ball was still in motion. She'd set that ball in motion, first in the pub that night, and then that night at Alex's flat.

It was the first day of what the papers were calling 'our Honolulu heat wave'. School sports days were being cancelled, gardeners encouraged to 'love their brown lawns' in a bid to preserve water. And although it hadn't yet reached the 40-degree temperatures predicted that weekend, the absence of any kind of breeze had imposed a curious stasis on the streets of Hammersmith, as though the whole neighbourhood were taking part in one of those mannequin challenges that had gone viral a couple of years back. Outside the empty vaping cafés and pound stores, staff leaned still and silent against their shopfronts, and even the schoolboys waiting at bus stops seemed unnaturally subdued.

Nicole, in contrast, felt more alive than she had in months, as though her whole system had been jump-started. An old Oasis song she had overplayed and killed at university blared out of a mobile phone shop, and as it climbed into its chorus she felt the beauty of the melody all over again. Maybe that was why people had affairs? That sense of life happening to you all over again, an injection of youth. All Nicole suddenly knew for sure as the echo of her heels against the tiled underpass quickened and she emerged blinking into the riverside light, was that she was no longer prepared to go back to feeling numb.

Swiping a finger beneath each eye, where her mascara would have worked its way into the creases, she adjusted her expression to one less eager. Outside the Old Ship the partially obscured back of a man's head turned out not to be Jamie's, and she tried in vain to remember what colour shirt he'd been wearing in the office earlier.

'Nic!'

There he was, a little way off, back against the low river wall upon which his pint was perched, cigarette in one hand.

'You're smoking again?' she said when they were close enough to touch.

'Sort of. Maya found a pack that wasn't even mine the other day – left by the boiler man or someone – and freaked. Ironically I hadn't touched one in months, but if people are going to believe the worst of you anyway ...'

Although her heart had dipped at the immediate mention of Maya, Nicole was pleased. There was clearly trouble at home, and Jamie smoking was Jamie off the wagon in every sense. Only one thing – the idea of her being something he did when he was playing up, a bad habit – riled her.

'Why am I here?'

She plucked the cigarette from his hand and took a puff, the action awakening vague memories of teenage posturing:

arrow-pierced biro hearts drawn on smooth thighs, bursts of laughter loud enough for boys to hear. And beneath it all that adolescent anguish.

'Forgot how good the real thing tastes.'

'You did?' Jamie sucked the beer foam off his top lip and pulled her to him.

'Hey.' Shading her eyes with a hand, she looked around. 'Anyone could see us.'

'I've done a recce.'

'You have?'

'Relax.'

'I will, as soon you get me a drink.'

'Fuck the drink.'

'Charming.'

Inches apart, they took each other in, and Nicole wondered what it would be like to get to know that face, with all its freckles, furrows and grooves, the way she knew Ben's; to accept it would be a part of her daily life. To watch it age.

'Jamie, why am I here?'

'Why? Because I haven't been able to stop thinking about you and me ... in the theatre.' Nicole felt a contraction in her lower abdomen. She hated the power he had over her body, even when there was no force, no contact, even – just words. 'Because there has got to be a reason why we can't let go of each other.'

Nicole looked out beyond him at the river. A fleet of rowers whooshed cleanly past to the commands of the cox.

'I used to think that. But now ...'

'Now what?'

She shrugged. 'Now I know that it's just a game to you. Because it is, isn't it?'

'No!' His fingers tightened on the green fabric of her dress, pulling her in closer between his legs. And when he was angry or defiant, Jamie looked so young. She'd forgotten that. 'That's not true.'

'But you love your wife.'

Saying it out loud wasn't as painful as she'd thought it would be. In fact it felt quite grown-up, civilised. Only she couldn't be touching him as she said it. She couldn't even be looking at him. Nicole moved to stand beside him at the wall where she stared out at the murky depths of the Thames.

'I really do think you still love Maya. And I know you love your kids. I know that being apart from them . . . well, I can imagine what that would do to you. It's not the same for me, for women. I get that. I could leave Ben and still have Chloe. Still wake up to her every day and put her to bed every single night.' Even as she said it, she wondered how that would work, remembering her daughter's crumpled face on the rare occasions when she had had to take her away from her father, and trying to imagine what it would feel like to tell her not to worry, you'll see Daddy again next weekend. 'I've been thinking since, well, since that afternoon at the Vale. And I thought I had you out of my system. I really did. But going back to the way we were – I can't do that. Not after what happened last time.' She shook her head. 'It's not what I want. I'm not angry any more, but . . .'

'D'you know it'll be two years –' he leaned over and kissed her neck '– next Wednesday.'

'Don't do that!' She turned, angry at him and herself. 'Don't act like this is more than an affair. You and I have both had them before; we don't have to pretend.'

'No, Nic. I want this to be something else. I want us to give

213

it a chance. I can't sleep; I can't function. It's like my mind is just whirring, whirring . . .'

She had to admit that there was something frenetic about his demeanour: his words running into each other and his . . .

'Jamie you're trembling. How much coffee have you drunk today?'

'Because this time I'm ready. Things at home: it's just not working with Maya and me. I honestly feel like I can't do anything right, like she's trying to pick holes in me or catch me out.' He pulled another cigarette from his packet. 'I lost my wedding ring the other day. It literally vanished. And she was all 'I told you that would happen!' and 'Maybe that's telling us something'. I've got no time for that kind of superstitious shit.'

'So this is all about her?' Nicole's mouth felt hard, the resentment making her ugly outside and in. 'Is your dear sweet wife not paying enough attention to you? Let me ask you something, Jamie: will there ever be enough attention for you?'

Taken aback by her tone, he stared at her. 'When did you get so bitter?'

'Oh, I don't know. At some point over the past two years.'

For a moment neither of them said anything.

'Ben wants me to leave. Find another job.'

'What?'

'He can see I'm unhappy. He doesn't know why, he thinks it's the job, but maybe he's right.'

'No.' Jamie shook his head. 'No. You're unhappy because of him, not the job or me. And you can try and resign if you want, but I won't let you. You'll get no pay off. I won't even write you a reference, and I'll make sure you're blacklisted by every property agency in London.'

'Jamie . . .'

'No.'

Firmly, he lifted her up onto the wall. And when he pushed himself between her legs she felt them wrap themselves around him in a way that was instinctive, a way she knew she was too old for but didn't care. They kissed, and it felt as deep and intimate and satisfying as sex. She heard herself moan.

'I love you, Nic. And I want to be with you. You're never going to be happy with Ben, are you? You know that now. And the sooner you can get on with your life . . . with me, the sooner everyone can start to heal.'

'Listen to you, all Zen.'

Jamie didn't smile. 'It's true.'

A tear slid down in a perfect vertical from beneath her sunglasses, and he wiped it away. Nicole had never allowed herself to cry in front of Jamie before and it felt significant that she could now.

'Nic.' He pushed the glasses up to her hairline and held her jaw with one trembling hand.

'You're not OK, are you?'

'No. Look at me. I don't know what's happening to me. These past few days I haven't been able to concentrate on anything. I'm jittery, I can't eat a thing and I . . . Nic: not being with you is killing me. But yes, this time I am ready.'

'I don't believe you.'

'Because of before? Maya was pregnant, for God's sake. You must be able to see that it wasn't the right time?'

She gave the smallest nod.

'But I need to know that you really are serious about telling Ben?'

Out of nowhere an image flashed through her mind: Ben

clasping a weeping Chloe to his shoulder in Hyde Park as her Paw Patrol helium balloon rose ever higher into the sky above. 'Think of all the other balloons that have gone up to balloon heaven,' he'd murmured. 'So he won't be alone.' And at the words 'balloon heaven', Chloe's tears had only redoubled.

'I'm not the one who broke my promise last time.'

'No.' He nodded. 'Then again, I don't remember you making one.'

Nicole knew what he was doing: trying to get her to share the responsibility for what happened – or failed to happen – last time.

'You're not seriously saying you don't trust me to do it?'

'How do I know you will?'

'Jamie ...'

'No, I mean how do either of us really know?' He fingered his pint, pensive. 'But what if there were a way we could both be sure? A way of us doing it at the same time, same place even ...'

'Get Maya and Ben to meet us for some form of group therapy, you mean?'

'There's an idea,' he deadpanned, running his thumb up the inside of her thigh. 'No, I mean we take them somewhere public: a big crowded restaurant. But separately. You book your table, I'll book mine, and we're not allowed to leave until we've both done it.'

Nicole disengaged herself. 'Are you serious?'

'Yes. Think about it: we'd be going through the same thing at the same time. And to help us get through it we could arrange to meet somewhere afterwards – at a hotel. Wherever.'

Nicole looked at him. It was a mad idea, demented. But

it might also be genius. Because however much her whole being shrank from telling Ben and imploding her life with a single sentence, knowing Jamie was there in the room, seeing him go through the same hell – well, that might just give her the courage she needed.

'It's bonkers. And risky.'

'How?' He took a long glug of beer, and not for the first time she wondered whether he felt the reverberations of his words and actions in the same way as other people.

'Well, what if Maya recognises me?'

'You've never even met.'

'We've been in the same room, twice.' The precision was humiliating and she deliberately fudged the next part. 'At a couple of events – some Christmas bash and another thing. And women ...'

Jamie raised an eyebrow.

'Unlike you lot we notice things, people, undercurrents.'

'OK. But I'm not suggesting we go to some intimate little place. I'm thinking somewhere big and rowdy like Angelini's,' he said. Angelini's was a vast banquetted Green Park brasserie favoured by B-list celebs and deal-making city boys. 'And we specify where we want to sit, so we're not on neighbouring tables but can at least see each other across the room.'

It ought to have been preposterous, but the thrill-seeker in Nicole liked the idea. It would give them both a date they couldn't back away from, and it would end the misery she'd nurtured for far too long. Besides, nothing could be worse than the status quo.

'And from that night, we'd both be free?'

'Exactly. Wouldn't that be something?'

Beneath her dress Jamie's hand had worked its way up to the elastic of her knickers.

'Just imagine,' Jamie was saying, 'when we're both free, all the things we could do? We could go away this summer. We could go anywhere you want ... that place in Antibes you keep talking about. Anywhere.'

'Let's go to Biarritz.'

He laughed. 'OK. Why?'

'Don't know. Always wanted to go. The surfing?'

He jerked his head back. 'You surf?'

'No.'

'Me neither.'

Forehead to forehead, they laughed.

'We don't know very much about each other, do we?'

And their kiss then was different: long, lazy and filled with a contained mutual exhilaration at the life-changing decision they'd just made.

'But think how much fun we'll have finding it all out?'

Closing her eyes for a second, Nicole allowed herself a moment of pure happiness. Jamie's warm, solid bulk was there between her legs, the leather of his belt sticky against her inner thighs, and until she chose to release him, he was hers.

A woman's laugh, shrill with alcohol, drifted over, and she guessed without looking that this faceless female was with a man, husband or lover. Behind her another fleet of rowers passed through the water. 'Next stroke!' 'Easy!' A baby's cries drowned out the last words of the cox's command. It sounded like 'full slide', and she tried to formulate a joke – the kind of silly double entendre she and Jamie had always made to one another – but the baby's cries were now wincingly loud, and when Nicole opened her eyes, irritated by the interruption and determined to seek out the source of it, she saw a woman standing a little way off in the sad patch of green by the pub. The woman had a baby strapped to her chest and was staring straight at her: Alex.

CHAPTER 23

❧

ALEX

'You lying bitch.'

She'd waited in the underpass, knowing Nicole would come after her, and when Alex heard her panicked footsteps clicking down the ramp into the cool greyness beneath the Great West Road, she felt a new surge of anger, stronger than the first. Stepping out of the recess in the wall where she'd been lying in wait, she spat the words out into Nicole's face.

For a moment the two women just stared at one another, Nicole struggling to regain her breath, Alex aware without really caring that a string of saliva was hanging from her bottom lip, threatening to drop.

'Jamie thought he'd leave you to it, did he?' There was still no sign of him in the underpass. 'Fucking coward.'

'He didn't see you – thank God. Alex, what are you doing here?'

'That's all you have to say?'

When she'd jumped into an Uber and headed over to the Old Ship, Alex hadn't stopped to think about what she would do when she got there, let alone how she might explain herself. But after logging onto Jamie's email for the third time that day to find his exchanges with Nicole happening in real time, she had to find out what their meeting was about. Why had she agreed? And what did Jamie want from her?

'How did you know we were . . . ' Then Nicole understood. 'You've been reading his emails again.'

'Of course I have. I never stopped.'

Damp-cheeked and dishevelled, her mouth clownishly encircled with pink where the lipstick had been kissed off, Nicole seemed to be struggling with a variety of emotions. From the darting downward glances at her chest, Alex realised that one was a squeamishness at this scene being played out in front of Katie, who Alex had forgotten was still strapped to her, and still howling.

'Your daughter . . . '

'Katie. Her name's Katie.'

'Well, Katie's losing it. Is she hungry?' The concern on Nicole's face only ratcheted up Alex's anger further.

'You're really going to lecture me on how to parent? When you're lying to your husband and child – along with everyone else!'

'I'm not lecturing. I'm just . . . '

Silhouetted against the bright white mouth of the underpass, a couple appeared, their easy laughter dying out as they took in the scene and silently scuttled past.

'You're just a fucking liar, is what you are. You lied to me, and you lied to Jill. Then you came to me, you came to my flat, and you told me more lies.'

Nicole closed her eyes.

'What? You two . . . ' Just saying that made Alex's stomach heave. 'It hasn't just happened, has it?'

'No.'

'How long?'

Nicole looked away.

'How long?'

'Look, I shouldn't have said what I did that night at the pub. And then when I came to your flat, I was so angry I couldn't see straight. But it wasn't . . . ' Nicole broke off, tried again. 'It wasn't a lie. Jamie and I, what we do, how we are with each other – it's complicated.'

'"Complicated?"' It had looked pretty simple from where Alex was standing. 'You told me he raped you.'

'I never called it that.'

But Nicole was no longer meeting her eye. 'Alex!'

Alex followed Nicole's eyeline down to her daughter, who was retching now, mouth in an agonised O, and it struck Alex as strange that she hadn't heard Katie until Nicole had pointed it out, not since she'd found herself frozen on that threadbare patch of green by the river, transfixed by the sight of Jamie and Nicole tangled up like teenagers on the wall.

Alex wasn't sure how long she'd stood there, but it was long enough to take in the wild sensuality of Nicole's laughter and the ease of Jamie's hips between her legs. Those two bodies knew one another well. And that Nicole could have lied about the harassment and made her believe far worse, that she could have sat there on Alex's sofa – 'I said no; I asked him to stop' – when all the time their relationship had been consensual? That wasn't just a betrayal; it was something Alex couldn't, wouldn't accept. They were too far gone.

'Have you got any milk?'

'What?' Rummaging in her bag, Alex found a bottle and plugged it in her daughter's mouth. 'What would you call it, then? What you and Jamie "do"?'

'We're . . . ' Nicole's voice dipped so low it was barely audible. 'We play games. We always have done. Sometimes things get rough. One time – *one time* – I'd asked him to stop, and he didn't get it or hear me or think that I was—'

'You like to play games or he does?' Now this was starting to make sense. 'Because sometimes things can start off as games, only when you want to stop playing the other person won't let you.'

'No.'

'And if that person has all the power, if that person is your boss, then it's still abuse. If that person doesn't stop when you say "no", whether he's your boss, your boyfriend or even your husband, it's still rape.'

'No, you've got this wrong.'

All contrition was gone from Nicole's face now, leaving behind a barely masked impatience. But Alex pushed on regardless: 'I think you told me what you did that night because you knew that what had happened between you wasn't right. Only maybe he'd made you feel it was. Or maybe you're just plain terrified of Jamie.'

Nicole was shaking her head, muttering words Alex could no longer make out.

'Why can't you see what he's doing to you?'

Smoothing her hair back, Nicole sighed. 'Because I'm in love with him.'

Alex stared at her, and that stupid smudged mouth. Then she laughed. 'Whatever you are – and, by the way, therapists will have a term for it – you're not in love with Jamie.'

'I don't know what bad experiences you've had, Alex, and maybe that's what this is about, but me and Jamie . . . it's not what you think. You've got to understand how I was feeling when I told you what I did. If I'd had any idea that we would get back together—'

'"Get back together"?' Alex repeated in a sickly teenage voice.

'I'm trying to explain. I thought I'd have the chance to before you—'

'Found out you were a lying bitch who was sleeping with the guy we were supposed to be taking down?'

Nicole was frowning, but not at the insult. 'What happened to your hand?'

Alex looked down at her right hand, scrubbed raw and yet still, somehow, stinking of baby powder.

'Eczema. Flares up sometimes. Go on.'

'I was so hurt. He'd made these promises in Frankfurt. We'd decided to try and make it work.'

'You two were together in . . . ?' Alex groaned. 'Of course. What else are conferences for if not shagging your boss? You do realise what a fucking cliché this is – you are?'

'Of course it's going to look that way to you.' Nicole shrugged. 'But people don't always get it right first time around. And you can't blame one side or the other for that. You're not married, you can't know.'

'I think I do.' Alex thought of her mother, whose every

move was dictated by her husband. And she thought of Hayden. Nicole was wrong about the blame: it was always clear where it lay.

'Right.' Nicole had pulled herself up straighter now, defiant after the initial shock of being caught out. 'Well, no offence, but at this point I don't care about how it looks to anyone.'

'OK. So let me ask you one last thing: what changed? From before, I mean. From wanting to take Jamie down, from telling me he'd raped you—'

'You're going to have to stop saying that.'

'From telling me he raped you, Nicole,' Alex repeated, louder.

'You're not listening! He was going to leave Maya, before Christmas, and I thought he really meant it.' Alex snorted. 'But she was pregnant with Elsa and then after the birth . . . well, he just couldn't cope with the idea of leaving his daughter when she was that little.'

'Ah – dad of the year is Jamie.'

'I'm not asking you to believe me, I'm just trying to explain why I did what I did – that I wasn't playing a game. I really did hate him as much as you do. And I genuinely thought it was over. Why on earth would I have agreed to what we planned if I hadn't? But then, last week, Jamie and I—'

'Oh, spare me the details.'

Alex started jiggling Katie, who was exuding heat from her nappy.

'Fine.' Nicole attempted a smile. 'Anyway, we've worked things out. Just now. And he's been a mess, Alex. That's how I know this time is going to be different. I've never seen him like this. He says he hasn't been able to eat—'

'Oh really? Having trouble sleeping too is he?'

'Yes. Yes, he is. He's all over the place.'

As furious as she was, Alex couldn't help but smile at this. After all these months running his lucrative little business on the corner of her street and waking Katie up with his sodding scooter, that drug dealer had proved himself useful. Nicole, too, had unwittingly played her part. He might never have had a client with a baby strapped to her chest before, but when she'd asked for Ritalin – 'the highest dose you have' – he'd shown neither surprise nor judgement, reaching into his Fila bag and counting out fourteen anodyne-looking white pills. She'd crammed those pills into Jamie's 'days of the week' vitamin box on her next visit to Maya's house. Let him see how it feels to be up all night every night, heart and mind racing.

'Bottom line,' Nicole was saying, and her calmness made Alex want to scream, *It's not love making your man a mess, love, it's a whopping dose of stimulants!* 'But this is none of your business. We're going to try and do things right this time.'

Alex took a step back. 'Meaning tell your husband, and Maya?'

A flash of something. Concern? Suspicion? Her reference to Jamie's wife had been too easy, familiar.

'You've not ... you've never made contact with Maya, have you?'

'I'll leave that to you. And what a fun conversation that'll be – if any of this actually happens.'

'This is happening.'

'When?'

'Soon.' Nicole looked towards the light streaming in at the end of the underpass, clearly desperate to get away. 'I'm sorry for everything you're going through, just as I'm sorry for keeping things from you. But like I say, this is no longer any of your business.' Nicole swallowed. 'I know you've been trying to get Jill worked up again, Alex. I know about the emails and the letters.'

'Sorry?'

'Stop it. I know it's you – all of it. And it's gone too far. Jamie has his faults, but he wouldn't write that kind of thing without good reason.'

'"Good reason"? I can't believe this!'

'Maybe he genuinely believes it would be right both for the company and Jill that she take a step back . . . '

'And me? There was nothing "genuine" about my dismissal, was there?'

Nicole was scrutinising her in a way she didn't like. At all. 'Did you ever think that there might be valid reasons? Because as harsh as it sounds, from the way you've been behaving, I'm not sure I'd feel comfortable having you around, either. This obsession of yours . . . '

'Obsession?'

'Can't you see that's what it's become? But nothing you do is going to change anything.' Then, more softly: 'It's Katie you should be concentrating on now, not your ex-boss, me, or any of this.'

Not a clue. Nicole didn't have the smallest clue.

'Hey, I wasn't just good at my job, I was the best. Ask anyone. And Jamie took that away from me to save his own skin. He . . . '

But all of a sudden, Alex gave up. She was tired and thirsty – so thirsty. And now that the shock of Nicole and Jamie's affair was sinking in, Alex began to look at it in a whole new light. Jamie wouldn't have the guts to end his marriage, but Maya might. And she would need a friend when she did. Alex could be that friend, help pick up the pieces, make herself indispensable.

Without so much as a last glance at Nicole, Alex began to walk away. 'I've got to get this one home for her nap.'

'Hey!' Nicole trotted after her. 'You're not going to do anything stupid, are you? Alex? I know Jamie's made mistakes, behaved badly – but so have I. So have you! It's time for us to draw a line under all of it now.'

Emerging, blinking, into the bright expanse of the Great West Road, Alex turned to Nicole one last time: 'You stupid woman.'

The sun lit up two white hairs on either side of Nicole's parting, and Alex felt almost sorry for her. 'Those emails I've been reading? I've gone back months, years – before I was even working for Jamie. They're the first thing I read when I wake up and the last thing I read after Katie's bedtime feed. Which is how I know that last Friday he and Maya put a deposit down on a five-bedroom place in Barnes. It's Georgian. Maya's always liked Georgian. And they needed more space, you know, in case she caved and had a third, as Jamie's already begging her to do.'

As the traffic droned past them in sonorous waves, Alex realised that it wasn't just an expression: colour could actually drain from a person's face, sucked out by shock.

'There's a double driveway and "eaves storage", whatever that is. But it was the patio that clinched it for Maya.'

'You'd say anything, wouldn't you? Well, I don't believe you.' Wrapped around the strap of her bag, Nicole's knuckles were white.

'You should.'

'This is over.'

Nicole had started walking away, but Alex wasn't having it. In two brisk steps she caught up with her. But this time she was careful to keep her tone measured.

'If Jamie doesn't turn out to be the man you think he is. If I'm right . . .'

Nicole gave an impatient head-toss.

'Call me. That's all I'm saying. Because I know what it would take to finish him. And it's not much.'

'Get some help, Alex. You need it.' The traffic all but drowned out Nicole's last sentence: 'And don't ever call me again.'

CHAPTER 24

JILL

'Slow down, Harry. You're not making any sense.'
Straightening herself up, Jill rubbed at the base of her spine, where the weeding was beginning to take its toll. Their neighbours had a gardener tend the tiny patch of greenery by their narrowboat, but Stan had always been too proud to do the same. Knowing how upsetting he was finding the overgrown hawthorn and accumulation of litter in the plant pots, Jill, who had never much cared for gardening, had started to spend a few hours dealing with the worst of it on Saturday mornings, while her husband read beside her.

'No, no I haven't spoken to Jamie.'

Up by the fence, the glint of a sweet wrapper caught her eye and she dipped back down to snatch it up. Why were people so disgusting?

'Yes, last night – you and Trish went for supper there, didn't you?'

To Stan's questioning eyebrow, Jill mouthed, 'Ainsley.' Looking up from the hardback copy of *Through the French Canals* she'd given him last Christmas, her husband rolled his eyes.

'That doesn't sound … yes, I can quite imagine … I bet she was. I can't imagine what he was thinking. Jamie's been a bit … well, of course it's not on. Harry, let me call him now, but I'm sure I speak for us all when I say how very sorry I am. Sounds like a total shambles and, if I know Jamie, he'll be beside himself with embarrassment. Listen, I'm going to call you straight back. What? You are? Well can I at least … no? Right. OK. Well please don't let this in any way affect our working relationship. Harry? Harry?'

'What was that about?'

Jill sat down on the end of his lounger and took off her gloves.

'Weirdest thing. Jamie had Ainsley and his wife over for supper last night. You know how long we've been trying to get him on side with us, but he's a tricky bugger so we had a lot invested in this dinner with Jamie. I told you he's been eyeing up the Minerva site, didn't I? Anyway, Ainsley just called to say the dinner was a total shambles. Shambles! Maya served up pork …'

'What? But she must have known that he and Trish are Jewish?'

'How could she not? And not only that, but they'd sent over a whole list of allergies and preferences. I get the feeling Trish is pretty high maintenance, as you'd expect, and Maya basically seems to have ignored the lot.'

'Doesn't sound like her.'

'Stan, she served up white wine with the pork, which apparently gives Harry "chronic 'eartburn".' Not liking the worry on her husband's face, she smiled. 'And just when it seemed like the whole thing couldn't get any worse, Harry goes to the loo and . . . ' Jill put her hands to her face. 'Christ, Stan, he said there was a nappy, a soiled nappy, just sitting there on the floor in the guest loo. Maya must have changed the little one at the last minute and just forgotten to bin it or something.'

At this Stan put down *Through the French Canals* and pulled himself up straighter. 'That's . . . '

'Horrifying. I know.'

'But also completely uncharacteristic. I mean, I've never seen Maya be sloppy about anything. She's so together, isn't she?'

'She is . . . but Jamie's been all over the place, as you know. The other day he was behaving to Ainsley in this manic way in our pitch meeting. I mean, really weird. And maybe this second baby has, I don't know, thrown her – or both of them. Maybe they're having real issues.'

'Well, if he's been harassing women in the office, I bet they are. But you're sure that's all been put to bed?'

'Oh yes.' Getting up, Jill put her gloves back on. 'The woman – Nicole – she's very clear she wants to put it all behind her. But I'm going to keep an eye on Jamie. And if he puts even a single toe wrong in that department . . . but right now I need to find out what really went on last night.'

'Good idea. We really don't want to be alienating Ainsley, do we?' Stan made no move to pick his book back up, she noticed. And, again, Jill felt stupid to have told him about the call.

'It's all going to be fine, you know. Really.'

'Once Jamie's booted out?'

The surprise forced her back down beside him. She'd told her husband about the review she'd ordered once Spiro's antics had come to light, but not about the email and letter, still not certain those weren't somehow down to Alex. 'What makes you say that?'

'Well he can't keep mucking up like this, can he? Look at what it's doing to you, having to clean up his messes. To say nothing of what it's costing the company. That business with Nicole . . . and then Spiro? Bad enough for it to be all over the *Telegraph*, but if it ever came out for certain that Jamie had encouraged him to destroy a listed building, that would be BWL's reputation shot. Our company, Jill, our baby.'

'Shhh . . .' She kissed her husband on the forehead. 'I don't want you worrying about a thing. Now, you've taken your pills?'

'Yes, Nurse Ratched.'

'Good boy.' She held her phone up. 'You have a nap. I'll only be a couple of minutes.'

She was a lot longer than that, pacing alongside the canal all the way down to the Puppet Theatre Barge, with her head down and Jamie's furious voice in one ear. He'd planned the whole thing meticulously – even getting Harry's PA to email over a list of his favourite wines and desserts so that Maya could get it all in for their supper. But things had started to go wrong from the start, he said, with the plates of Parma ham and the Montrachet. And Maya, who had been in 'a weird mood' from the moment he'd got back, late, from work, had reacted badly to being pulled aside and snapped at.

'It's not that much to ask, is it, Jill? I mean I'd given her a list of instructions, for God's sake. And did Ainsley tell you –' he was hoarse with disbelief '– what the woman managed to leave in the loo?'

'Well, if that's the way you spoke to her, I'm not surprised she took it badly. Maybe Maya had had enough, Jamie. Maybe she was sticking two fingers up at you.'

In her impatience to find out whether the dinner really had been as big a write-off as Harry had made out, Jill had forgotten about the opportunism, the belittlings and the letter. She'd set aside her loathing. But that contempt-filled word – 'woman' – had brought it all back. And when, in a sarcasm-sodden voice, he'd begged her 'to put aside the "poor little woman" talk for a sec so that we can deal with this', she'd stopped and taken five deep breaths, just as Stan's stupid NHS support manual had urged them both to do in moments of heightened emotion.

'We?'

When things weren't going well, it was always 'we', 'us' and 'our'. Jamie was generous when it came to sharing his discomfort and spreading the responsibility for his cock-ups.

'D'you know what? I think this one's up to you to sort out. I think I'm done with covering for you.'

'Covering? When have you ever had to cover for me?'

'And how about you stop blaming your wife and take some of the responsibility?'

'I didn't do this!'

'OK, well then at least accept the facts.' Nimbly, Jill side-stepped a map-reading tourist squatting in the shade of Warwick Avenue bridge. 'Harry will be mortally offended by the whole experience, and probably make a point of staying as far away from BWL as he possibly can moving forward. To be honest I'm not sure I can blame him. Which will mean not one but two massive deals scuppered – by you. So the idea that I'm the one not fit to work? Well, that's pretty laughable, Jamie. Because right now I'd say your job is hanging by a thread.'

Elated to the point of drunkenness, Jill gave the little red button a tap and leaned against the railings, arms outstretched, face angled upwards towards the sun. Surely it couldn't be this simple? But frisking herself down for anything resembling guilt or nostalgia, any pinch of the heart, however slight, Jill was relieved to find that the thought of getting Jamie out of her life for good gave her nothing but satisfaction.

CHAPTER 25

※

NICOLE

'Any bags we can help you with?'

Nicole stared at the girl. She couldn't be more than eighteen. This was certainly her first job. The white shirt looked like a school uniform relic and the tiny hole beneath her lip had recently held a stud.

'No.' She swung her Longchamp tote high enough above the reception desk to be seen. 'Just this.'

She might as well have said, 'I'm only here to fuck,' and the girl acknowledged this with a flicker of her eyelids.

'And your welcome glass of champagne?'

'Perhaps we'll have that after dinner, when my . . .' Nicole struggled to find the right word, something she would welcome never having to do again after tonight. 'When my partner gets here.'

The boutique hotel had been Nicole's choice – 'If I know you'll be joining me there that night, it'll make it bearable' – and as she made her way up to the 'superior suite' she'd booked for them on the third floor, she tried to picture Jamie's face when he pulled up outside the white stucco terraced house, partially hidden by its pendulous wisteria, in a South Kensington backstreet.

He'd be surprised, for sure. When, a few months into their affair, Jamie had suggested taking Nicole to Blakes, she'd groaned. Nothing killed sex quite like hotels designed for it, which was why she'd always preferred Hiltons and Best Westerns: beige cubes with strip lighting and humming air conditioners. That's if they had to use anything as trite as a hotel room. Given the choice, Nicole would have opted for a toilet cubicle or an alleyway every time. Only, tonight was different: tonight was the start of their new life.

Fresh and pretty, with tiled mirrors and artfully clashing Ikat cushions strewn across the king-size bed, the room looked like something out of *Elle Decoration*, or the holiday home of the kind of status-obsessed stay-at-home mums who were able to measure how far they'd come by the brand of candle at the four corners of their bath tubs.

It was just past six and Nicole knew she had to shower and change before calling an Uber that would get her to Angelini's for 7.15 p.m. – a full quarter of an hour before Ben. This would allow for any seating mistakes or table moves that needed to be made, although she hoped she had been precise enough over the phone. If she could just catch Jamie's eye beforehand, it would give her the courage she needed.

Instead of undressing, however, she stood at the window,

looking down at the tourists 'taking tea' in the little garden below and trying not to imagine Ben's face and voice when she told him. Her lips moved as she rehearsed the words she'd decided to use: 'I still love you and I always will, but I don't think I'll ever really be able to make you happy.'

It was cowardly to twist it around, as though Ben's well-being was all she cared about, but she and Jamie had to keep their affair out of it for now. A few months down the line their relationship could come out as something that had happened unexpectedly, organically, when they both found themselves single. 'Remember it only ever has to be semi-plausible,' she'd pointed out to Jamie. 'It's just kinder to give them both the option of believing it didn't start sooner.' But was there really any kindness in what they were about to do?

Having yearned for this moment for months, Nicole would now have given anything for an extra week, day or hour. The blue dress she'd picked late the night before felt wrong – too girly, too coquettish. But what did you wear to end a seventeen-year marriage? The trousers and blouse she'd originally gone for had felt cold, transactional. And the dress had the advantage of being relatively new, with no memories attached.

'That's a nice idea.' Ben had smiled, looking up in surprise from his *Guardian* when she'd told him about the restaurant booking that morning. 'Wish you'd said something earlier, though. Still, I'm sure I can find someone to watch Chlo.' Only when Nicole told her husband that she'd already lined up Suzy from over the road to babysit had she felt her cheeks grow hot under his gaze. Ben had always been the one to sort out both childcare and restaurants.

The whole thing was in danger of sounding a little too well orchestrated.

'What's this in aid of?'

'Do I have to have a reason to take my husband out?' was the obvious reply, but Nicole couldn't bring herself to say anything so flippant, and she was grateful for her daughter's whine.

'I don't like Suzy.'

'Course you like Suzy, sweetie. You two always play your Counting Caterpillars game, remember?'

The whole thing was taking on too much weight, and Nicole had turned away from husband and child to make toast nobody wanted. The idea of Ben replaying her lies in his mind when he woke up without her the following morning was making her feel sick.

'So?'

'So what?'

'So what brought this on?'

'I just thought it would be nice.' Nice to have the life you thought you had torn down over a dressed crab? The whole idea was increasingly feeling mad, wrong, but she had to go through with it now. They both did.

'Here you go, sweetie. Eat your toast.'

'Already had some with Daddy.'

'OK.' Nicole swallowed. 'But you have to have a proper breakfast, or you'll be hungry by ten.'

She'd been holding the toast in the palm of her hand like a waitress would a tray, she realised. It was ridiculous. And everything about the scene in that room had struck her as luridly staged.

'Mummy's made it now, sweetie. Eat it.' Folding the toast in half, Nicole had presented it to her daughter.

'But I didn't want it!'

'I don't care. Take it.'

'I don't want to. I'm not hungry!'

Ben was frowning up at her. 'Nic – I think she's had enough.'

'Fine.' Dropping the dry triangle onto her husband's breakfast plate, Nicole had caught Chloe's questioning glance at her father. Rather than make her feel guilty as it might ordinarily, the look had only wound Nicole up further. She'd left the house with the vindictive thought that, however heartbreaking, the next few months might at least give her the chance to claw back some space in her daughter's heart – a thought she felt ashamed of now as she took one last look at herself in the hotel-room mirror and headed out the door.

Angelini's was already bustling by the time she got there. There was no sign of Jamie but a handful of couples bent over menus were scattered about the restaurant and two big groups of businessmen who had clearly been there since lunch were braying on either side of the central bar. The noise levels snapped her out of the trance she'd been in since she'd checked into the hotel: this was real.

'Excuse me?'

The blonde at reception turned towards her, the phone pressed to her ear now visible: 'One minute please,' she mouthed. And Nicole nodded. She didn't have to go through with this. She could walk out of the restaurant right now, call Ben and tell him something had come up. Then everyone involved, from Ben and Chloe to Maya and those two kids, would just get on with their lives, oblivious to the mine they'd just sidestepped.

'New dress?'

His arm was around her waist, his stubble familiar against the side of her neck, and for a moment she questioned which of the two men it was. Then Nicole turned to kiss her husband hello.

'You're early,' she said.

'I know. When the Tube runs on time it throws everything out of whack.'

'Course it does. And no, this is old,' she half-lied, plucking at the blue fabric.

'Pretty.'

'Thanks.'

She wished he didn't look so boyishly excited, and was anxious to be seated. At any moment, Jamie and Maya would arrive.

'Excuse me?'

'Yes.' The receptionist seemed to be hanging up the phone and lifting her eyes to them in slow motion. 'The name? Harper? Ah yes, here you are.'

Snatching up two menus, she showed them to their table. And Nicole was relieved to find that it was the banquette she'd requested in the second part of the restaurant, but with a clear view across the first.

'Remember those long lunches we used to have at that all-you-can-eat Chinese back at Bristol?'

Ben had insisted on sitting beside her on the banquette – 'that way we can people-watch' – and was staring in undisguised fascination at the group of businessmen putting in a vast brandy order.

'I do.' Nicole looked back down at her menu. 'Wish we had expense accounts like theirs. What are you thinking?'

'I haven't even looked.' He put a hand on her arm. 'Relax. There's no rush. Suzy said she could stay as late as we needed.'

'Great.' Nicole's smile felt freeze-dried on her face. She needed a drink. 'Excuse me?' Her voice was a little too loud, too desperate.

The waitress came over.

'A vodka Martini for me please and he'll have a G&T.'

She knew she sounded snippy but didn't care. She also knew what Ben would say as he leaned towards the waitress, anxious as always to mollify any antagonism Nicole might have instigated.

'I'm afraid it's a medical emergency.'

The waitress said something back, something not quite funny or quick enough, but Nicole didn't catch it because Jamie and Maya had just walked in.

She was in an ochre silk dress that shouldn't have worked on a blonde but did – the matt golds and browns of her skin, maybe. He was in jeans and a pale blue shirt she hadn't seen before. Was the receptionist more attentive than she had been to Nicole and Ben? It seemed so. There was something undeniably impactful about the two of them side by side.

'Well, it's got to be the Dublin Bay prawns hasn't it? We're having starters?'

Ben was so engrossed in the menu that he didn't notice her following Jamie and Maya with her eyes as they were led to a table on the far side of the restaurant that was nevertheless in her line of sight. Jamie was right: nobody was going to recognise anyone here.

'Nic?'

'Sorry?'

'The prawns?'

'Yeah – go for it.'

There was a moment's indecision as Maya decided where to sit, and when Jamie finally opted for the chair looking out towards her, with his wife opposite him, Nicole saw that her dress was cut surprisingly low behind and her smooth brown back bared almost to the waist.

Nicole held her breath. This was it. Just as they'd planned. And any minute now he was going to raise his eyes to her.

'Then again the calamari looks good. But thirty quid? A bit much for a starter.'

'Have whatever you like.'

She was scared to look down in case she missed Jamie.

'OK, so here's an idea. I have the prawns and you have the calamari and we share both? Then I might even have a steak ... oh, and let's get some of the sautéed spinach on the side?'

There was something faintly ludicrous about her husband's interest in restaurant food.

'Perfect.' She snapped her menu shut. 'Where's my Martini?'

As though on command, the waitress appeared with their drinks, hovering expectantly in front of them and obscuring Nicole's view.

'Do you have a nice Sauvignon Blanc?'

'Yes the Pouilly-Fumé Domaine Chatelain is one my favourites, but if you're after something a bit more bracing, there's the CRUX Marlborough ...'

As the waitress leaned forward to point it out on the menu, Jamie finally lifted his eyes to meet hers. He was smiling along to something Maya had said but his eyes were intense, aroused, and as Nicole squeezed her thighs together beneath the table she felt a crackle of pleasure travel up her body. In just a few hours the worst would be over – and her real life could begin.

'That one sounds great.'

'The CRUX?'

'Yup.'

'Not the Pouilly?'

'Sorry?' How complicated could it be to order a bottle of wine? 'We'll go for the CRUX.' Ben laughed. And then, once the waitress had left, 'Bracing?'

'What?'

'Can wine be "bracing"?'

She managed a small laugh, but it wasn't enough to smooth away the concern on his face.

'You OK? This morning you seemed a bit . . .'

'Yeah, sorry about that. I've had so much on at work and I slept really badly last night for some reason.'

Ben started his usual refrain about her working too hard, one she usually found galling on account of it being her hard work that kept them afloat as a family. Tonight, though, it didn't seem to matter and she found herself nodding along to everything he said. Two glasses of champagne were being taken over to Jamie's table, and Nicole thought it odd, in bad taste, that he should have agreed to drink something so celebratory at a time like this.

A younger, prettier waitress came to take their order, laughing at something Jamie said, and Maya seemed to be asking a lot of questions. She would be one of those women, wouldn't she? The ones who ask how things are cooked and what's in the sauces: all the things Nicole had always been so blokeishly unconcerned with. Was that what Jamie liked about her? How different she was to his wife? And would he miss the whimsical, delicate mother of his children once he was waking up every day to Nicole?

She turned to Ben, already heady from the Martini. 'Do you think I'm too dominant?'

'What?' He spluttered a little on his G&T. 'Er, no.'

'You know what I mean. The career thing.' She paused. 'You never like it when I order your drinks for you, do you?'

'I like pretty much everything about you if you must know.'

'Such as?'

'You want a list? OK. So I like that you're clever and decisive. I like that you always fill in those travel form thingies I can't be bothered with and how good you look in those weird neon-panelled leggings you run in. I like that you're such a great mother, even if you've never, ever been known to carry a pack of Wet Wipes in your handbag.'

'I'm not.'

'What?'

'I'm not a good mother. At least I never feel I am.'

'Don't talk rubbish. Is this about this morning? Chlo worships you.'

'I know. But sometimes I can't help but feel ...' Nicole looked up in alarm as what seemed like an unnecessary amount of food was placed on the table. None of this would get eaten. Because she couldn't sit here filling her face and then tell Ben that their marriage was over. And they sure as hell weren't going to eat it once she'd said what she brought him here to say. 'Jeez, Ben – why do you always over-order?'

From the way his soppy smile faded, her tone had been harsher than she'd thought.

'It's just ... it's too much, isn't it? It's always too much.'

'Nah, I haven't eaten a thing since lunch.' He smiled,

raising his wine glass to her, and it was such an eager gesture that she felt something inside softly implode.

'Ben . . .'

But his mouth was already full of calamari.

'This is so good,' he managed from a chink at the corner of it. 'Here – try some.'

Nicole dodged his loaded fork – 'I'm OK' – and allowed herself another quick glance at Jamie, making the kind of superstitious pact she'd relied on as an indecisive teenager as she did so: *If he looks over now, the next words out of my mouth will be 'It's over'*. But Jamie didn't look over. And he wasn't looking at his wife, either, but down at his plate as he listened intently to whatever Maya was saying.

Pulling her eyes away, Nicole went on: 'It's not just Chloe I always feel like I'm letting down. I sometimes feel . . .' Was this the way to preface it? Was there any way to preface 'I'm leaving you'? 'Well, actually most of the time I feel like I'm a pretty crap wife to you, too.'

'What are you talking about?'

At this point Ben would still be thinking that this was one of those marital regrouping sessions couples had when they were finally able to spend an hour or two without the kids. Then again, he knew her. He'd noticed that she hadn't touched her food but was on her second glass of wine, and Nicole caught a flicker of animal fear in her husband's eyes.

'Just that I know I've been so bound up with work, and the truth is that I love the work, you know I do . . .'

'But it means you're strung out a lot of the time? And tired. What I think you need – what we both need – is a holiday.' He leaned forward. 'Why don't we spend an hour on Expedia tonight, looking up all the places we've never been and wanted to go?' He was panicking and it was agony to watch. 'Checking out the good late August deals and, you know, just book something? We can even—'

'No.'

'What?' Ben laughed. 'No to which part?'

'No to the holiday. No to all of it.' Look at me, Jamie. I need you. 'We can't carry on, Ben – not as we are.' And it felt like coming up for air after having held your breath too long. But the relief didn't last. As her husband stared at her, still holding his fork but oddly, as though he'd forgotten what it was for, Nicole realised something that made her wince with sadness: Ben had been expecting this for the past twenty-one years.

'Nic . . .'

'I'm sorry.' She opened her mouth to say, 'I tried' before thinking better of it. 'I do love you. But I don't . . . it's not in the way that . . . it's not enough.'

He smiled, but it was the nasty smile of someone who would never stop hurting. 'You don't love me *enough*?'

'I don't think I feel . . . the way I should.'

'How should people feel after seventeen years of marriage?'

Ben had a bullish streak, Nicole remembered, which only emerged when something threatened his wife or daughter – and in any other circumstances would be admirable. Had Ben only been able to harness it for work or life, the two of them might have stood a chance.

'I think they should feel more than I do.' There was no way of tempering that. 'I'm not saying that to hurt you. I'm just being honest.' She took another sip of wine. 'Ben, we were so young when we got together, and we still are. You can't be . . .' She tried again. 'We don't have to spend the rest of our lives with the feeling that something's missing.'

'I don't feel anything's missing.' His face was hard, obstinate. 'I have everything I want.'

'OK.' And then meekly, in a whisper: 'But I don't, Ben. And I wish I did. I wish you were enough, but . . .'

'You're not trying. You're saying all this because you've reached an age where—'

'Oh, please don't start with that. It's nothing to do with my age or my "time of life" or "the grass is greener" or any of that stuff.' She stole another sideways glance at Jamie, who could surely be in no doubt from their expressions and body language that Nicole had kept to her end of the bargain. But he was still listening in silence to his wife. And because Nicole knew that Ben wouldn't give up trying to change her mind until she said something that would make him hate her, she looked him straight in the eye and said: 'Chloe's my daughter: I love her and need her in my life. But us, Ben . . . there's no future for us.'

'I can be different.'

'It's not about that. And I don't want you to be different.'

'I can get a job. I know you hate that I'm not working. I know you think I'm just sitting around the house—'

'Ben! I do not think that. What you've done for Chloe and for me . . .'

'So what then? There's got to be a way.' He reached for her arm but she pulled it back.

'There isn't. There isn't because there's someone who—'

'Oh Christ.' Ben turned away from her, and finally put his fork down. 'You brought me here, to this place, to tell me you've found someone else?'

'I wasn't going to tell you like this,' she murmured. 'But you weren't listening. You push and you push, and it's like you—'

'Who?'

'It doesn't matter.'

'Who?'

'I just think . . . '

'You're seriously not going to tell me?' Ben cut in, putting his napkin on the table. 'What I think is that I want to go home.'

You know those moments are going to be pure pain, but nobody ever tells you how, above all, they're just plain awkward. Ben was semi-standing, bent at the knees, but boxed into the banquette by other tables and diners.

'Excuse me,' he murmured. But the place was so loud, and nobody moved.

'Ben.' She felt she needed to say it – after all, there was Chloe to think of. 'I'm not going to come back to the house tonight.'

'Course you're not.' And a little louder: 'Excuse me.'

'I think if we both just take a bit of time to—'

'Yup. And what am I supposed to tell your daughter, out of interest?'

'Let me help.'

A waiter had finally spotted him and come to help pull the table out. 'The Gents is downstairs, sir.'

'No.' Ben had a hot pink dot on each cheekbone. 'No, I just want to leave.'

And finally released, his napkin falling to the ground, her husband crossed the restaurant floor, right past Jamie and Maya, and walked out the door.

In a smaller restaurant it might have caused a stir, but although the diners on either side of Nicole threw one or two curious glances at her and the scarcely touched food on their table, nobody else even seemed to register what had happened. Nobody but the waitress, who had seen too many carefully contained marital disputes to count – or care.

'Are you still working on these?'

'Erm – no.' *Working on.* Why did people say that? 'And we should probably cancel our mains. Sorry – my husband had to rush off.'

'Got it. You'd like the bill?'

Nicole glanced at the half-full bottle of wine sitting in its ice bucket by the table. Then she looked over at Jamie, who still didn't look like a man ending his marriage. In fact, from their body language the pair of them looked more like they were out on a date night.

'No.' Nicole had been on too many business trips to feel self-conscious in a restaurant alone. And she had a morbid desire to watch Maya suffer like Ben just had.

Gesturing at her wine glass, she said, 'I'm going to stay and finish this.'

Whether or not the waitress found this odd, Nicole didn't care. She was too busy watching Maya, who had now picked up her clutch bag from the table and was leaning towards Jamie, as though about to leave. Was she angry? In tears? Nicole couldn't see her face. But when she finally stood, turning back to Jamie with a final word, Nicole caught a flash of white teeth: Maya was smiling.

Something was wrong. Everything was wrong. And as she watched the receptionist point Maya in the direction of the Ladies, Jamie finally lifted his eyes to hers. She raised her chin a fraction, asking the question, begging and imploring, but there were no signs of comfort or solidarity on his face, and it took her a moment to read both his guilty expression and the words he was mouthing: 'I can't. Sorry.'

CHAPTER 26

ALEX

'Don't. Just don't.'

'Hey,' chided Alex, parking a sleeping Katie in her buggy by the table. 'I'm not here to say I told you so. I'm not even going to ask what happened tonight. I'm just here to tell you what I tried to the other day.'

Pulling up a chair, she took in Nicole's vacant eyes, the silt of mascara that had accumulated in the fine lines beneath, and her bare mouth. She'd never seen her without lipstick before, and there was something indecent about the nakedness of her face. 'If we – you – get this right, you never ever have to see Jamie again. He's gone; out of the picture.'

Low-ceilinged and sticky-walled, it wasn't the sort of pub you brought a baby to – especially not past nine o'clock at night. But when Alex saw Nicole's name flash up on her phone she guessed what had happened. 'I can be in Victoria in half an hour. Find a pub and sit tight.' Just over thirty minutes later, in she'd walked, ramming the pram into ankles and ignoring disapproving looks until she spotted Nicole sitting, two vodka tonics in, in the corner.

'Look at me. Jamie's good at this stuff – he specialises in screwing people over, remember? I'd have thought that was pretty clear by now. But please, please don't feel stupid.'

Nicole threw her a watery smile. 'Hard not to feel stupid when you've just ended your marriage for someone who doesn't give a damn.'

Alex thought about this. 'I actually don't think it's that. Jamie probably does give a damn. You two wouldn't have lasted this long if he didn't. He just . . . '

'Gives more of a damn about Maya?'

'I did try and tell you that.'

Elbows on the table, Nicole gripped her face in her hands. 'And I knew! I knew there was something wrong when I saw them in the restaurant. The way she was just talking and he was listening, when it should have been the other way around.'

Alex shrugged. 'I don't think he ever had any intention of leaving her.'

Nicole stared. 'Then why . . . ? What kind of a sick fuck does something like that?'

Another shrug. 'You're better placed to answer that than me. Maybe the whole restaurant thing was sort of foreplay to him? A turn on? From what you told me, Jamie's, well . . . a sick fuck.'

Nicole made a noise, part sob part bleat, and Alex thought it best to press on.

'But what turns him on isn't just sick – it's illegal, isn't it?'

Nicole looked up blearily from her vodka and tonic, uncomprehending at first, then weary. 'I told you ...'

But Alex silenced her with a finger. 'Let me finish. If what just happened tells us anything, it's that you've got one hell of a blind spot where Jamie's concerned. And I get that your relationship is "complicated", as you put it, but if what you told me that night at my flat really happened between you ...'

'It was just once, and ...'

Alex sat back forcefully in her chair, arms crossed. 'Do you hear yourself? Just once is *one too many times*. So why protect him? Especially when you now know what kind of a man he is, and what he's capable of?' Alex leaned forward across the table. 'When you know that he has it in him.'

Nicole blinked. 'So what do you want me to do?'

'It's not about what I want. It's about doing what you should have done months ago to protect other women from men like Jamie. And yes –' this was going to be the tricky bit '– it would mean a bit of exposure for you. People would find out what Jamie did to you; well, HR would. But they would never have to know about what came before.'

Nicole was shaking her head. 'No, no. That can't happen. You see, I told Ben tonight that I was seeing someone else. If I then come out and accuse my boss of ... no, I can't have Ben hearing that stuff.'

'He won't even find out about it. Do you know how sealed up complaints of that nature are? The moment you make them you're a victim: protected. And that's as it should be. So even if Ben did somehow hear about it, he'd never in a million years think you'd had a consensual relationship with him.' She hadn't meant it to sound snide, but Nicole gave a dry laugh. 'Look, I don't care about what you did any more. We were all taken in by him – seduced and then scammed – weren't we?' Alex gave a small smile of encouragement. 'But this will finish him off, no question.'

'I see that, but . . . ' Nicole's eyes had fixed on something at table level, and Alex took it for alcohol-induced wooziness before remembering the state of both sets of knuckles now, where another bleaching session had burned through the thin skin. 'Your hands!' Nicole slurred. 'Alex, your eczema. You need to go to the doctor – that's bad.'

'Like I said –' Alex pulled her shirt sleeve down as far as it would go '– looks worse than it is. Nicole, I need you to focus.'

'I am.'

'Good. So listen: you're pretty exposed already, aren't you? I mean, if I know about you and Jamie, then other people might?'

Nicole inhaled sharply, then nodded.

'OK. And you can't realistically be thinking that after what happened tonight you can carry on at BWL, looking Jamie in the face every day, sitting across from him in meetings, clinking glasses at the Christmas party? And when he starts another affair, which he will, probably has already, right under your nose – let's say with that girl, Sophia . . . '

'He won't,' said Nicole quietly. 'From what I hear she won't be having much more to do with him.'

Alex raised an eyebrow.

'He took her out . . . and did something, came on too strong. Anyway, it freaked her out. And maybe . . . ' She trailed off, tried again. 'Maybe it wasn't an accident. Maybe he gets a kick out of pushing things. But Alex: I'm not leaving. Not when I've put everything, years, into getting where I am. Not when I deserve to make partner at BWL. I'm not going to let him take away everything I have left.'

Two young men standing at the bar threw Nicole a glance before turning back, too quickly, to their pints. And Alex watched this woman who was on the cusp of going from male fantasy to ghost digest the perilousness of her position in life. Alex had nothing to lose with age – she had always been invisible. And for all the pain this had caused her in her teens, she was grateful that she would never have to experience the kind of loss Nicole was facing now. A loss that, beneath her disgust at the notion of a woman's 'last good years', she'd be all too aware of.

'They'll be needing to find another partner,' Alex went on. 'To replace Jamie, I mean.'

Nicole stared at her. 'Right. And then what, they give me Jamie's job? What about the police? What if he gets arrested and I have to give evidence or something?'

'I promise you'll be protected. No way are BWL going to want the whole thing made public, or the police involved. Only you can decide if you want that. They don't legally have to, remember? Not unless you want to press charges – which you won't. And whether you decide to call it what it was, or something less explicit – assault, maybe – Jamie will be booted out, which he should have been long ago for reasons a lot of people are already aware of. But the real reasons for his 'exit' will be kept hush-hush. Trust me, it's not only perfect but the right thing to do.'

When Alex was done explaining the rest, Nicole simply nodded: 'I need to lie down.'

Nicole was silent as Alex escorted her out of the pub and helped her into a waiting Uber. But after the door had been slammed shut and Alex had turned her attention to Katie, tucking the blanket a little closer around her twitching body in the cooling night air, she heard the whine of the window coming down behind her.

'After this we're done,' Nicole called out. 'You have to promise me that. No more plots, no more plans. Done.'

Alex was glad that a single brisk nod was enough to assuage the panic in the other woman's eyes. She might never understand Nicole, but she had grown fond of her, she realised. And she wouldn't have wanted to tell her an outright lie.

CHAPTER 27

JILL

'What do you mean you can't tell me? How are you not able to tell me?'

Well before Jamie's muffled outrage had permeated the glass walls of his office, Jill knew that something was up. Like birds on a wire, the row of junior surveyors were twisting left and right in the long line of desk space they occupied opposite the lifts, swapping information with nods of certitude and peeps of disbelief. It was a scene she'd witnessed before, but only ever the morning after big office bashes.

Perhaps because she had never, even as a young woman, been the subject of gossip herself, Jill didn't object to it as much as Paul and Jamie. In fact she'd always secretly enjoyed it. A few shrill assertions elevated themselves above the collected twittering – 'Amy says he's always been a complete perv with her, even grabbed her arse once'; 'Sorry, total bollocks – don't believe a word!' – and she made a mental note to find out from Kellie which of the novelty-sock-or-tie-wearing brokers had been misbehaving.

That turned out not to be necessary. As she neared her office, she heard Jamie's raised voice and established at a glance that it was indeed both Ross and Jayne from HR seated opposite him.

'They've been in there nearly an hour,' Kellie whispered. 'Paul's been trying to get hold of you. They're saying someone's accused him of harassment.'

Jill pulled her phone from her bag: four missed calls. She'd forgotten to unmute it when she'd left the hospital that morning. Her mind went back to Nicole's crimson lips, bitter and thin: 'I'm not going to report him. End of.' Only, if she hadn't, it looked like someone else had.

'Damn it.' Then, aware of the hush and the faces turned towards her: 'Cancel my calls, will you? Where's Paul now?'

'In his office.'

'Christ almighty.' Paul didn't move from his position at the window when he heard her come in, but stood there with his back to Jill, staring down at the ugly grey tangle of Hammersmith flyover beneath. 'This is a mess and a half.'

'Yup. Sorry. Phone was switched off.'

'What do you know?'

'Nothing. First I've heard.'

He turned. 'They're suspending him – effective immediately. He's being told now.'

Jill could only nod.

Plonking himself back in his chair, Paul stared into the mid-distance. 'This is bad Jill, really bad. The words HR are using ... We need to distance ourselves and the company from this. Pronto.'

Whatever Jill had expected, it wasn't this. Paul had always supported Jamie, defended him.

'I thought you and Jamie ...'

'Me and Jamie what? Go for the odd pint together? Play the odd game of golf? Well, I'm not getting dragged into his tawdry mess, I'll tell you that for nothing. Do you realise how toxic these kinds of allegations are?'

'I'm aware.'

'The papers get a hold of this and suddenly they're using that word "endemic", talking about a "culture of harassment" and passing BWL off as some kind of "old boys' club". It's all right for you, Jill, you're a woman.'

In any other circumstance, she would have laughed at this statement. 'I don't follow.'

'I'm the only other old boy in the partnership, aren't I?'

Jill didn't have time to marvel at how egocentric fear can make people, how quickly that instinct of pure self-protection kicked in, expunging every prior loyalty.

'Even if I don't get drawn in on that level,' he went on, 'if this gets out, who's going to want to do business with us? I can't afford to take a hit right now. Not with the divorce all set to clean me out.'

'Do we know who the woman is?'

Paul stared at her. 'It's Nicole Harper. I thought you knew.'

She tried to swallow. 'No. I ... right.'

'But Jamie doesn't know that. HR are holding the specifics back until he's safely off the premises, at which point they'll put the allegations to him, I suppose. But for the moment only you and I are to know there has been a complaint.'

'People already know – Kellie and others. I heard them on the way in.'

'Shit.'

Was this her fault? Her fault for not reporting the harassment Nicole had told her about – harassment that had led to assault?

'At the moment it's clearly a case of her word against his. But we do know she doesn't want to press charges, which is ... helpful – from our perspective, I mean.'

They fell into a sombre silence.

'Were HR able to share anything else?' she said eventually.

'Until they've fully investigated the claims, they can't tell us much more. But Ross did say that there's often a pattern of behaviour in these instances, where after one woman makes an allegation ...'

'Jesus.'

'So we've got that to look forward to.'

Paul picked at a dry patch on his scalp. 'I mean this is someone we've both known, trusted and worked with for years! You ...' He pointed at her, and then realising how accusatory it looked, let his hand fall to the desk. 'Well, you know him better than I do. You two were friends, proper friends. And I know he likes the ladies, but ... Jamie's not the kind of man who does this, is he?'

'I have no idea what kind of a man Jamie is.' Not so long ago, Jill would have been unable to keep the sadness from her voice. Now she felt like she was talking about a stranger. 'I haven't said anything to you but over the past few months Jamie's behaviour's been pretty out of order. Things I'd previously ignored have surfaced.' She thought back to the email. 'Incompetence. Disloyalty. Then there was the review. And I suspect he's been pretty frank to you lately regarding his feelings about me. But all that pales. We should have seen it coming, shouldn't we? Maybe we just didn't want to.'

But Paul was shaking his head. 'Nope. Not taking the blame for this. This is what I mean! And we both know that *this* you don't come back from. Whether it turns out to be true or not, it doesn't matter. Shit doesn't just stick, it stains. We've got to get Jamie out of the picture. Gone.'

What would the old Jill do? The Jill who could handle even the worst professional 'surprises' in the most rational and efficient way possible. 'I think we've got to push our personal feelings to one side and get on with putting together a statement in case we do need to say something publicly.'

It was as they were on their first draft, both still fervently hoping they'd never have to use it, that the sound of Jamie's raised voice pulled them both to their feet. There had been one or two audible outbursts since she'd been sitting there in Paul's office, but this one came from the office floor.

'Here we go. But listen, I think it's best that neither of us gets involved here, that we let Ross do his job.'

Too distracted by the very public confrontation now taking place between Jamie and Ross outside on the office floor, Jill could only nod.

The whole scene would have been comedic – the HR director was a good foot and a half smaller than Jamie and a lot rounder – had the situation been any less serious.

'It's a simple question. What's Pete doing here?'

The two men were outside Jamie's office door, and craning her neck Jill could see that the largest and most benign of BWL's three regular security guards was hovering a little way off beside Jayne, Ross's more imposing blonde deputy.

'Can we please have this conversation inside your office?'

As though to remind him which way his office was, Ross held an arm out, and Jill was surprised that the stab of dislike she felt in that moment wasn't for Jamie, but their officious HR director. All those years he must have spent watching this handsome, charismatic man lord it about the office. This was his moment. This might even be fun for him.

'We've had a conversation, Ross,' she heard Jamie counter, 'and I'm none the wiser on anything, except that I'm supposed to have assaulted – assaulted – an employee.'

Whatever the HR manager said next prompted a fresh outburst.

'You can't wait till I've left? You've got to do it now? No. Sorry. Anyway, I want my jacket.'

There were over a hundred people on their floor, but apart from the odd ringing phone and whirring photocopier, the place was silent, every neck artificially taut, every eye glued, unseeing, to its screen.

'You're seriously not going to let me get my jacket? What do you think I'm going to do in there?' Jamie looked from Ross to Jayne. 'Delete all my porn?'

On some murmured command Jill couldn't hear, Pete moved briskly into Jamie's office, got down on his knees and disappeared beneath the desk – reappearing seconds later with an electric cable in his hands.

'Right, that's it – I'm calling my lawyer. This is ... unacceptable.' There was that pathetically overbearing language again, as though Jamie believed he could save himself or some semblance of dignity with professional formalities. And Jill felt the creeping unease she'd fought off throughout her meeting with Paul earlier reassert itself. Something about this was wrong – and not in the obvious way. No, it was Jamie's reaction that was wrong. Because as much as she'd started to question how well she knew this man, right now Jamie was genuinely astonished by the claims being made against him.

'Ashley, can you get me Simon Oliver on the phone? Now. And I don't care if he's at lunch or the club. Tell him I need an immediate call-back.'

But his PA's eyes were fixed on Jamie's computer as it was carried out of his office.

'Ashley?'

As the poor girl blinked at him, then Ross, Jill wondered if she might burst into tears.

'I – am I . . . ?'

Ross shook his head at her.

'I can't call my lawyer?' Jamie looked around wildly. 'Is this actually happening? Hey, girls, help me out here?' Jamie had moved to the central hub, arms outstretched. 'It must be one of you. Don't be shy. Unless – hang on a sec – unless you don't remember it, either. Because I don't remember assaulting anyone. And that's not the kind of thing you forget, is it?'

Jamie's shirt had become untucked at the back and his hair ruffled into a peak.

'Was it you?' he asked a junior broker, peering intently at her screen. 'Did I open the door in a way that made you feel "uncomfortable" or tell you I liked your skirt? It's a very pretty skirt. Am I allowed to say that? Is it "verbal assault"? Probably.' When there was no reaction, Jamie began waving his hands around in front of her face – 'Hello! Hello! I'm talking to you!' – causing her to jolt back in alarm and every woman nearby to freeze, lest they too should be noticed and picked on.

'Come on! Is nobody going to 'fess up to being attacked by me? One of you comes forward with some bullshit story that I'm not even allowed to hear, by the way, and suddenly I'm Harvey fucking Weinstein? Where's the proof . . . where's the proof of anything?'

Out of the corner of her eye Jill saw Ross, flanked by Pete, walking fast in a straight diagonal towards Jamie.

'Oh – I forgot – we don't need proof any more do we? 'Cause if a woman says it, if it's her truth, it's the only truth.'

'That's enough now, Jamie,' Ross said, adding something else she couldn't make out.

'Worse? How could it get any fucking worse? You make out I'm some sort of predator who attacks women – not just women, but my employees – and then I'm supposed to just quietly disappear without knowing who I'm supposed to have done this to?'

'Jamie.' Ross reached forward to tap him on the arm before thinking better of it, and for a second Jill had the absurd thought that Jamie might take a swing at him. 'As we explained, the allegations will be made clear to you in due course.'

At Ross's signal, Pete moved in closer and clamped a paw on Jamie's arm.

'Come on, pal, time to go.'

'Pal?' Jamie took a theatrical step back. 'Am I still your pal, Pete? I was your pal when you gave me your daughter's CV and asked me to look into an internship, wasn't I? I was definitely your pal when I got her that summer job in the post room. And now I'm not. In fact, you wanna throw me out in the street.'

'You need to go and cool off.'

''Cause everything's going to look better in the morning? I don't think so. But I will leave – after I've got my jacket.'

Jamie took a step towards his office and so did Pete, barring his boss's path.

'Let's not let this get silly, Jamie.'

'Pete's right. That's more than enough. I appreciate that this is upsetting – for everyone. But right now we're going to need you to leave.'

Despite everything, Jill felt a flush of embarrassment for her one-time friend as Pete, a hand clamped on Jamie's arm, 'saw' him into the lift and out.

At this point the whole floor seemed to exhale in unison. And after the murmurs had subsided – a proper post-mortem would take place in the pub later – everyone got back to work. Everyone except Jill, who was still standing there, one hand on the doorknob, in Paul's office.

'Paul?'

'Yeah.' Her partner was slumped at his desk, head in his hands.

'I didn't ask before because I was embarrassed. Because I was pretty sure I knew the answer, and that someone was playing pranks on me. But Jamie didn't send you an email, a while back, referring to me as "YKW" and –' she cringed '– "senile", suggesting I was no longer "a good look" for the company, that sort of . . . ?'

The way Paul shifted in his seat, his refusal to meet her eye, stopped her short. 'We had a brief exchange about four or five months back in which he, um, told me he was worried about you and felt you should take some time off. But "senile"? He's never used a word like that on any email to me. And "YKW"? What does that even mean?'

The relief made her smile. 'Never mind. It must have been . . . a prank.' Alex. It must have been Alex.

Of course Paul hadn't engaged with Jamie's crude language in that email, because that language had only been added afterwards, when the email was being edited – by an ex PA with a grievance.

'But I should tell you –' there was that shifty look again '– that there was a letter to the supervisory board, suggesting you be . . . '

'Retired?'

'I tried to talk Jamie out of it, and I refused to have any part in it. But he was concerned about Stan's illness taking its toll. He'd mentioned it a couple of times to me.' Paul flushed. 'And others, I'm afraid. I just put it down to his ego: always wants – wanted – to be top dog, Jamie, didn't he?'

Maybe it was that simple. Jamie wasn't the man she'd believed him to be, and that he'd actually written that letter was beyond treacherous; unforgivable. But if the words in that email had been manipulated to make him look worse than he was, could Jill really be sure that Nicole wasn't doing the same thing now? Because if her claim had been exaggerated, didn't that make the punishment they had decided to inflict on him worse than the crime?

She was already halfway back to her office by the time Paul called out, 'Jill, why are you asking?'

Once at her desk she fired off an email.

To: Raxugdy@sharklaser.com
From: Jill Barnes

I know that you doctored that email. What else did
you do, Alex? What else?

The answer pinged in minutes later: a chilling reminder
of the tie that bound them.

From: Raxugdy@sharklaser.com
To: Jill Barnes

Here's to putting a not-so-good man down.

CHAPTER 28

NICOLE

'Still not quite visualising it?'

Rupert Jones moved slowly and wordlessly around the gallery, kneading the side of his neck with his knuckles as he gazed up and down at the four tiers of boxes arranged in a semicircle around the stage. These, and the *trompe l'œil* ceiling that continued to catch her out no matter how long she stared at it, had always been the theatre's most impressive features in her eyes. But after their meeting with the council's planning department the previous week – a meeting in which an alarming number of unforeseen limitations had been placed on the property's structural development – Nicole had felt a sharp downturn in Rupert's enthusiasm.

It was up to her to get his excitement levels up again, but after a sleepless night in the hotel and the call to HR she'd finally mustered the courage to make that morning, Nicole wasn't sure she had it in her. And yet she needed to close this deal.

'Originally the boxes would have had their own entrances on the north and south sides,' she volunteered with a brightness she found physically painful to muster. 'Apparently theatres from the period were always laid out that way – one entrance for the king—'

'And one for the Prince of Wales,' Rupert murmured, gazing down at the proscenium arch. 'Yeah. I read the paperwork, too.'

'Course you did.' Nicole wished she'd stopped to buy the Nurofen she so urgently needed on the way here. The back of her skull ached from all the booze she'd got through the night before and she hadn't had anything but black coffee for breakfast. 'It's all pretty fascinating stuff, isn't it?'

Fascinating stuff? Her phone buzzed loudly in her handbag. She'd put it on vibrate after the first two missed calls and now regretted not muting it altogether. 'Sorry.'

'Answer it.'

'No, no. Anyway, you heard what planning said about pushing the stage back, so that's a big plus even if . . . '

'That's basically the only structural alteration I'm allowed.'

'Well, they didn't quite say that,' she countered, smiling – although they had. 'But they could have been more helpful, I agree. Still I'm convinced . . . '

A more insistent buzz as a voicemail pinged in.

'Someone really wants you.'

He turned away and Nicole took the opportunity to reach into her handbag and check whether it was Ben, finally returning her calls. But Rupert chose that moment to speak: 'I'm not going to lie: that sit-down last week has changed things.'

'Of course it has.' She felt repetitive and slow-witted, incapable of doing her job and yet acutely aware of how important it was to clinch this deal before they left the premises. If she didn't, Rupert would pass, she was sure of that. And yet there was something humiliating about this part of her job, reminding her as it always did that she was no more than a sales girl, zooming in on that crucial moment's indecision before it hardened into a 'no'.

'Listen, I'm sure you of all people can find a way around these things. And, actually, keeping a lot of this the way it is – with the restoration needed, granted – will really add to its charm?' She was flailing and he knew it. 'The originality of this place, though! I mean, I've never seen anything like it.'

Rupert's facial expression was immovable. Time to up the ante. 'And I should tell you that I have had a call from another potential buyer. Now of course I can manage to hold off on allowing anyone else to see the property for, well, a week – ten days if need be?' She feigned a professional embarrassment she would have felt, had any of this been true. 'But at a certain point I will have to let them know whether or not it's still available.'

Rupert held her gaze a second, amused by the clumsiness of her tactics. 'Another potential buyer, eh?'

'That's right.' Lies: the more you told, the easier they were. And right now every sentence Nicole uttered seemed to be filled with them. 'But I can hold off. I mean the second I saw this place I thought, "This has Rupert written all over it." And I came to you first because I know that you've been looking for a north-west location for, what, eighteen months now – longer?'

Over the balustrade she caught the curve of the first row of Ambassador's chairs. 8A: that was the number – white on black – she'd stared up at as they'd lain there afterwards. And for a moment she saw them both from above: panting and pleased with themselves on that fusty carpet. The place felt airless, prickles of damp beneath her arms and in between her breasts awakening the smell of yesterday's sweat. She hadn't thought to bring a change of clothes to the hotel, thinking only of getting through that dinner. Because after that nothing would matter: after that there would only be her and Jamie.

'And as I said …' Distracted by the acidity of her own breath, Nicole had forgotten exactly what it was she'd said. It didn't help that Rupert was scrutinising her the way he was.

'You OK? You seem …' He made a vague hand gesture in her direction, and she felt a stab of shame at how much of a mess she must look in her crumpled blouse and Tube-applied make-up. Being well put together was part of who she was; today Nicole felt like she was coming apart.

'Sorry, Rupert. D'you know I'm … I'm actually not feeling that well. Do you mind if I just pop to the Ladies? Let you have a bit more of a wander?'

In the dimly lit toilets she searched for a stall clean enough to allow her to sit, even for a second, before giving up and sinking to the floor, her back against the wall. With trembling fingers she pulled out her phone, staring at the screensaver image as though the two people in it had nothing to do with her. Syon Park, one freezing Sunday seven … no, eight months ago. Chloe on Ben's shoulders, the bubble pipe she'd bought her on their way in just visible in her daughter's hand. Ben's affectionate rebuke to his wife, when she'd insisted they do the gift shop first: 'You can never wait, can you?' And her guilty interpretation of it, knowing she'd sent Jamie a text proving exactly that on the way there: *Tell me you can get away tomorrow? Need you.*

Ross, the HR director, had called twice and left a voice-mail she didn't have the strength to listen to. The third message was a WhatsApp from Anita, a colleague in Project Development. Their relationship had always limited itself to vaping breaks and celebrity bitchery exchanged in a rubbish-strewn Hammersmith backstreet behind the office. They'd never been for a drink together or contacted each other on anything other than email. *OMG – you heard?* Anita had messaged. *Jamie's been suspended!*

She'd known he would be. From Ross's silence at the end of the line after she'd strung out the nonsensical preambles as long as she could and finally managed to utter that sentence, recite it really, because that was what it felt like she was doing. Just get that first sentence out and the rest will come, because it has to: you won't have any choice once those first words have been said. 'Ross, I'm calling you to report an assault: Jamie – he assaulted me.'

She'd known he'd be suspended, and yet only as she nodded silently along to Ross's instructions to write him an email, a written statement 'including as much detail as you can remember about the assault', had the permutations started to filter through. 'I realise that might be hard for you,' he'd said, businesslike rather than soothing, as a woman in his position would surely have been, 'but it's also vital in terms of how we proceed from here.'

'I don't want to press charges, though,' she'd flung back, panicked. 'I don't want the police. I can't ... go through with any of that.' Alex had sworn that wouldn't be necessary, but she had to be sure. 'I don't have to do that, do I?' She'd been standing at the hotel-room window watching the same tourists as the afternoon before scraping up the last of their eggs Benedict as she made the call. While they'd been at their West End show or doing whatever the hell it was that people came to London to do, she'd been capsizing her life. And now she was going to do the same to Jamie's.

'At this point the report really is for our eyes only,' Ross had stressed. 'And an investigation will follow. But Nicole: we're going to need you to stay out of the office today while we deal with this.'

'Of course.'

Ross had then gone off on a whole spiel about the confidentiality of the process and 'minimising co-worker speculation', and all the while Nicole had had the curious sensation of falling down a bottomless shaft.

'Nicole? You still there? '

'Yes.'

'It goes without saying that there is to be no direct contact with the accused.'

'Yes,' she said again. 'I mean, no. I won't make any contact with him.'

The accused. Like this was some TV drama. She thought of the CEOs, ministers and actors who had been dismissed at the first mention of 'impropriety', let alone assault, in the heady first months of Me Too. 'They wouldn't even tell me what I was supposed to have done,' one MP had said. And back then she hadn't believed that could be true. In the casual rush of thoughts news stories can prompt, she'd wondered about the wives and kids: were they blindsided? Were the whisperings at the school gates bad enough to make them change schools or were they too considered victims and deluged with sympathy?

That word – accused – forced her to consider the person she'd pushed out of her head from the start: Maya. How soon would she find out? And was she one of those women in denial about who their husbands really were? The kind you saw proudly clutching the hands of paedophiles outside courts in the papers? Of course, Jamie might confess to cheating. Tell her he wasn't a saint and it didn't matter who the woman was because it never meant a thing, but he was no monster – and he didn't do this.

Alex had warned her that there might be pangs of guilt, but to force herself to remember, every time she felt one: 'I said no.'

And if she could make Jamie feel even an iota of the pain sluicing through her now, then this was the purest form of justice.

Rupert would be wondering why she was taking so long. Pulling herself up by the basin, she leaned over the tap and splashed water on her face. Too late Nicole remembered her eye make-up and stood there a moment transfixed by the drops running down her face like muddy tears.

By the time she'd cleaned her face and taken two deep breaths in the mirror, Rupert was done in the galleries and was waiting for Nicole outside in the theatre atrium.

'Rupert I'm so sorry. I really was feeling a bit off, but I feel much better now.'

He glanced up from his phone, trying to mask his irritation. And she wondered when Rupert Jones had last been kept waiting.

'I'm thinking maybe I could take you for a bite? It would give us a chance to work out a game plan that we could take back to the council and . . .'

'I don't think so.'

He said it so quietly that for a moment Nicole hoped she'd misheard. Because it wasn't just no to lunch, she knew. It was no to the sale – no to all of it. And why it mattered so much right now she couldn't be sure, except that the falling sensation was back, with everything that mattered now slipping from her grasp.

'Rupert . . .'

In its persistency the whirring seemed to be getting louder, and while she reached into her bag and scrabbled to find her phone in amongst the detritus of her life – the lipsticks, pens, compacts, dead batteries and mysterious electric leads – Rupert turned with a wave and let himself out of the door.

Had anyone else's face appeared on her phone at that moment, Nicole might have thrown it against the wall, but it was her husband, it was Ben, and the relief made her light-headed.

'Ben. Finally. I've been trying you all morning. Please – please – can we talk? Where are you? Can I come and see you now? And Chloe, how is she?'

She would have kept on going if Ben hadn't cut in in low, measured tones: 'Your boss, Jamie, is sitting in our kitchen. And he's rolling drunk.'

CHAPTER 29

✦

ALEX

'He's out. Gone. Suspended until further notice.'

Alex had been waiting for Nicole's call all morning, checking her phone so frequently throughout the first half hour of Little Gym that the instructor had finally told her off for 'taking herself out of the mum moment'.

When there were still no missed calls by the end of the class, Alex had started to question whether Nicole had been able to go through with it. Yet Maya's soothing effect was such that, as they ambled back to the house for lunch, she'd forgotten about the phone in her jacket pocket – until that first muffled tinkle; until the words she'd been waiting not just hours but months to hear.

'Good news?' Maya had asked after the brief exchange in which Nicole had passed on the news alongside one other fact: 'He's out – and drinking his way through the pubs of Hammersmith by all accounts.'

'The best,' Alex had smiled back. 'I won't bore you with the details. But isn't it great when a plan actually comes off?'

Maya no longer bothered inviting Alex back for lunch after Bumps & Babies. It was understood that twice a week almost without fail they would go back to the house together, often by way of Turnham Green Terrace. Sometimes, when Maya had errands to run or Alex had ascertained that Maria was due over later, Alex would stay only an hour or two, aware that a second meeting with the nanny was all that might be needed to spark a definitive memory. But other times she would spend the whole afternoon at the house.

Today she was more grateful for the distraction than ever, having finally forced herself that morning to tell her mother that she wouldn't be able to pay back her loan in time: that she'd lost her job, that she was as big a disappointment as her father had always intimated. She could still hear the panic in her mother's voice – 'What am I supposed to do? What am I supposed to tell him?' – and the limpness of her own reply: 'Sorry, Mum. I'm so sorry.'

But she couldn't think of that now. All that mattered was that Jamie was gone. The plan had worked. And this: the clattering of the lunch plates being tidied away by Maya in the kitchen, the naps the girls would take in a moment, and the lazy hours of wine and conversation they'd be left to enjoy.

She wasn't worried about Jamie coming home. She'd seen him on boozing missions before, and this one was bound to be more protracted than most. Since Maria was also taking Christel to a birthday party after school, that meant that Alex had most of the afternoon before her, and she lay back on the rug Maya had thrown down on the lawn for them and the girls, trying not to think of the heart dip she'd experience when she stepped out of that house and back into her empty life and flat. Because increasingly that dip would descend into something darker, with sobbing Katie clearly feeling the same, and Alex somehow unable to do what was necessary to comfort her.

Looking over at Maya now as she bent over the girls, the low-cut rose-pink summer dress she wore gaping as she did so to reveal tidy breasts encased in a white cotton bra, Alex marvelled again at that preternatural tranquillity. She'd met serene and grounded women before, but those attributes usually came at the expense of others, making them boring or priggish.

'I don't know how you do that – calm Katie down just by being around.' Alex moved herself over an inch or two so that her face was in the shade. 'I've seen her about to go off the dial and then she looks at you and ...' She shook her head. 'It's like you're some kind of baby whisperer.'

Maya sat back down at the table, steadying herself on Alex's shoulder as she did so. 'What a nice thing to say. I think she's just had a spot of colic? But she's over the worst – aren't you, little one? I'm more worried about those burns of yours, Lexie. And do you know what? I've nearly done exactly the same thing and been about to reach into the oven without gloves on.'

Alex had forgotten about the gauze she'd started wrapping around her hands in an effort to stop the looks and the questions. She'd forgotten too exactly what burn story she'd told Maya a week ago was.

'Oh, it's actually healing nicely. I can't even feel it any more. I think maybe your French grape juice might be helping.'

A case of Maya's favourite rosé had arrived at the weekend – an impromptu gift from her 'sweet but naughty husband, who's got some making-up to do' – and Alex had allowed herself to get a little tipsy over their long lunch. 'What do you mean you've never had Minuty?' Maya had cried when she pulled the bottle from the fridge, popping a couple of ice cubes in each of their glasses. 'It'll change your life!' And in anyone else's mouth it would have been such a ghastly Chiswickism but in Maya's – and said with her faint accent – it had the charm of a phrase borrowed from grownups by a child. And yes, the wine was good, but it was the woman who had changed Alex's life.

A gentle breeze blew a flurry of pink petals down onto the girls, and the two women looked at each other and laughed.

'I wonder what they think about it all,' Maya murmured at the tail end of that laugh, wrapping the maroon baby sling, like a scarf, about her shoulders. 'About life.'

She shook her head, embarrassed by her sudden seriousness. But Alex nodded, eager to reassure her that she had had similar thoughts, even if she hadn't. Still it seemed like a natural continuation and proof that she was the right kind of mother to suggest that they too lie down beside their girls and stare up at the world – that they too try to see it anew. Because something about it did feel new to Alex, now that Jamie had successfully been brought down and Jill had guessed that it was down to her – well, all of them, really. Not that the email the BWL founder had sent Alex's anonymous account that morning had bothered her. They'd planned all this together, so nobody would be saying anything to anyone.

'Ahhh.' Maya exhaled as she let her soft blonde head fall back on the rug. 'Head rush.'

'Well, we finished the bottle, didn't we?'

'We did.' Maya closed her eyes. 'But rosé . . . doesn't count, does it? And it's nearly the end of the week.'

'Wednesday?'

'Whatever.'

Maya went quiet and for a moment Alex wondered whether she might have fallen asleep, but when she looked over at her friend she saw that her eyes were open and fixed on that cloud of magnolia above.

'Lex?'

Alex pulled herself up onto her elbows.

'That your phone?'

The chirping was just audible from the kitchen table, where she'd left it.

'Think I drifted off for a sec.'

Alex padded off indoors, half hoping she'd miss whoever was trying to reach her. And she had. But no sooner had she logged the words on her screen – 'Missed Call: Nicole' – than the chirping started up again.

'Hey.' She was groggy from the sun and the wine, and, wedging the phone between ear and shoulder, Alex located a glass on the draining board and filled it with cold water from the tap. 'Listen I'm in the middle of—'

But Nicole wasn't going to listen. 'He's . . . at my house . . . husband?'

Broken up by violent bouts of wind static, as though she were moving at high speed through a tunnel, Nicole's phrases were coming out in fragments. And Alex thought about cutting her off and blaming the bad connection.

'I can't hear you. You what?'

While Nicole continued to make difficult-to-make-out

noises on the other end of the line, Alex gazed out of the kitchen window into the quiet sycamore-lined street beyond, imagining herself the owner of the blue Conran tumbler she was filling with water, this house and this life. Everything but the husband. She didn't want him. As of today, nobody would.

'Nicole? Where are you?'

An Ocado van pulled up opposite and the driver got out, earpod leads dripping from ears to pocket, mouth moving silently along to his music. As he began hoisting red plastic crates out of the back and piling them up outside the neighbour's front door, Nicole's words finally began to join up.

'... in my house.'

Alex was prepared to bet she could list every item in those Ocado crates: the inevitable avocados and almond milk catering to some kind of spurious allergy; the organic steaks and the Manuka honey.

'Who's in your house?'

'Jamie was in my fucking house. Two hours ago.'

Alex set her glass down. 'What?'

'Two hours ago. Ben called me. Apparently he was trashed. He'd clearly gone out boozing before deciding to confront me. He knows, Alex. He must do.'

Glancing out of the open patio doors into the garden, where those three figures were still horizontal on the grass, Alex lowered her voice and managed a limp 'He can't – not so soon. But obviously they will have to tell him the details of the allegation moving forward.'

Whatever Alex had assured her, Nicole must have known that?

'That's not what you said last night. And why the fuck did

he go to my house? Ben hasn't told me what was said, but Alex, I'm losing it here.' Nicole was sobbing now.

'Calm down. Like I said, HR won't have told him it was you – for now.'

'I just … I thought I'd have a moment in which he would cool off and I could sort my life out. You promised me this was safe.' Nicole's tone had swerved from plaintive to accusatory, and it was starting to annoy Alex.

'Just sit tight. It'll all be over soon.'

Out in the street a blonde in ripped jeans she was too old for was signing for her Ocado delivery.

'I should never have gone along with this.'

'Nicole.' Alex took a breath. 'Nobody forced you. And don't forget,' she added, dropping her voice down to a whisper, 'that last night you were sitting in a pub telling me how badly Jamie had screwed up your life.'

A pause while Nicole seemed to give in to a rush of tears. 'My daughter was there! Chloe was there in the room!'

There was a blaring of horns and an expletive from Nicole, then the background noise seemed to abate. 'I mean, how dare he? How dare he come into my house, my life, after what he did?'

'Well, I bet that'll be the last we see of him.' Any minute now Katie was going to wake up and howl. And Maya was going to wonder what was taking her so long. Alex really needed to end this call. 'Listen I'll call you back later, OK?'

'Yeah.' Nicole sounded a little deranged. 'You go. I'll call you back later, once I've found him.'

'Great.' Relief – then a sudden tightening of her chest. 'Found who? Nicole?'

The Ocado man was stacking his crates over the road, and as she waited for Nicole to respond Alex lost herself in his methodical movements. Then she followed the direction of the man's eyes as they logged the arrival of something or someone in that quiet street. A woman approaching with fast, purposeful steps; a woman with a phone to her ear, standing less than three feet away from Alex, now, on the other side of the kitchen window. A woman whose words, when they finally came out, weren't muted by the glass between them but shockingly loud in her ear: 'Jamie,' said Nicole, staring in at her. 'Once I've found Jamie.'

For a second everything sealed itself over, as though a membrane were protecting her from the sudden atmospheric pressure. Then Alex's ears popped and everything happened at once: the doorbell, Katie's cries, Maya at the patio doors, holding her pink-faced daughter, her mouth a tragic mask. 'Think someone's hungry.' Again, the doorbell.

'Here.' Handing over Alex's daughter, Maya headed towards the front hall.

'Wait.'

Maya half turned.

'Don't . . .'

But it was too late; in a second all of this would be over.

'Hold that thought.' Maya smiled. 'Let me just get this.'

'Hello.'

The wall separating the hallway from the kitchen was thin, and from her position at the head of the kitchen table Alex could hear a multitude of inflections in that one word. Recognition, first and foremost, because although the two women had never met, they had seen each other more than once across rooms. Confusion: Nicole's was probably one of those faces that only made sense in a professional context.

And something else: a tension that suggested some form of prior knowledge on Maya's part.

'Maya – I ...' Whatever courage had propelled Nicole on seconds before seemed to have deserted her. 'I don't know if you remember me. I'm Nicole Harper.'

Were the two women shaking hands?

'We haven't actually met before, but I work with your husband and we've ...'

'Of course I remember.' Perhaps Alex had imagined that strain. 'Come in.'

The sound of high-heeled boots in the hallway, the kind that do irreparable damage to hardwood floors like these; the kind that leave divots in carpets.

Katie – who had been quieted by the implication that she was about to be fed – broke out into a new wail of impatience and, spotting her bag on the side, Alex reached for a bottle with fumbling fingers.

'Sorry.' Nicole's still unsteady voice from the hall, where the footsteps had stopped. 'You've got your ...'

'No, no. It's a friend's. My little one's just napping. How can I help?'

Maya's coolness had spilled over into something brisker now, and a wild hope flared up in Alex: Nicole must have guessed that if she was here, Jamie wouldn't be. Maybe she wouldn't make it any further into the house. Maybe Maya would get rid of her before she had the chance to say much more. Then Alex could find a quiet place to call Nicole and explain her presence.

'I'm looking for Jamie. We haven't been able to locate him. And after what happened today ...'

'Sorry – you've lost me.'

'You don't . . . ? He's not here?'

'No.' Maya gave a frustrated laugh. 'I thought he was at the office. What happened?'

'There's been a . . . situation. And I've tried him on his mobile. Sorry, I thought you knew. Jamie's been suspended.'

Silence. Then a murmured 'You'd better come in.'

As the two women appeared at the door, Maya, ever the graceful hostess, ushering this woman she barely knew into her kitchen before looking around for her phone, Alex felt herself divide into two. Part of her wanted to run away from the inevitable confrontation, and part of her – the part that increasingly stepped outside of herself – was just curious to see how Nicole would react.

'This is my friend Lexie. Just going to wake up my daughter. Then we'll try Jamie on his mobile.'

Leaning against the counter, Nicole silently took in the scene: Alex sitting there at Jamie's kitchen table, her daughter across her lap; the bowl of fruit salad on the table and the empty bottle of wine.

'*Lexie?*'

Maybe there was still a way out of this; maybe Maya didn't have to know. But Alex was going to have to speak fast.

'I was going to tell you. And I know you said Maya was off limits.'

'Off limits?' Nicole hissed. 'Alex, "Lexie", what the hell is going on?' A pause. 'Tell me that's a nickname. Tell me she knows who you are.'

Shaking her head, Alex put a finger to her lips.

'This is completely fucking insane. You do know that, don't you?'

'It was all supposed to be . . .' Beneath the table, Alex

pushed her wounded hand up against the jutting join in the wood, soothed by the flood of pain through her veins as the hard edges dug through the gauze into the bloody crust beneath. 'It was part of the plan.'

'Christ,' moaned Nicole – and she really was going to have to keep her voice down.

'I know, I know. But the things I've been able to do and find out from here. It's been so useful – for us.'

'Oh no, no, no. I don't want any part of this. I never wanted Maya dragged into things.'

'Will you keep your voice down!' Nicole just wasn't getting it. 'All that office stuff – the email to Paul about Jill that I doctored – that wasn't going to be enough. Don't you see? I needed more access. How do you think I've managed all these months? The cigarettes, Jamie's ring.' Alex had been longing to claim the credit, she realised. 'That was all me. His wedding ring will be landfill by now, and I spiked his vitamins with Ritalin, to put him on edge, work him up into the state he left us all in. As for Ainsley . . .'

'The dinner was you. Of course it was.'

'It wasn't hard. A few edits to the menu Jamie's PA had drawn up for Maya did the trick. And while Jamie was off on a pre-dinner livener with Hayden that afternoon –' she paused before delivering her triumphant punchline '– I left one of Katie's nappies in the guest loo.'

But Nicole didn't look impressed: she looked sort of aghast.

'It worked, didn't it? It worked! Maya never even figured out it was me. She'd been so busy getting the place ready she thought she'd left it there herself.'

In the garden, Maya had finally managed to rouse Elsa and was making her way back, the rug draped over one arm, towards the conservatory. This gave Alex only seconds to explain something crucial: 'But I like her, Nicole. A lot. We're friends. Because Maya's nothing like him. She's warm and funny and a good, solid person.'

Both women fell silent as Maya came back in with a yawning Elsa, and Nicole forced a smile.

'Now let's just try and give Daddy a call, shall we?' Maya shifted Elsa from waist to shoulder level and back again as she dialled.

'Voicemail,' mouthed Maya. Then: 'Darling, I've got Nicole here from the office. She told me what happened. They've been trying to reach you. So if you could just call me back?'

Alex snuck a sidelong glance at Nicole, whose eyes were darting around the room, taking in the details of her lover's life.

'Can I get you a tea or—'

The landline rang.

'Ah – here we go.'

Whoever Maya was talking to, it wasn't Jamie.

'He ... what time was this? Of course you should tell me.' Then, more stridently this time: 'What do you mean they won't say? OK. Thanks, Jill.'

All three women were still. And Alex was relieved to hear Katie's cry fill the silence. That Maya was unable to disguise a tetchy glance in her daughter's direction was a shock.

'Lexie, do you mind just ... ' She gestured towards the play gym, the implication clear. 'I just need to get my head around this and I can't with that ... '

'Of course. Want me to take Elsa, too? Let you—'

But Maya made an involuntary move away from her. A blotchy triangle had appeared at the part of her throat left exposed by the wrap that looped loosely around her neck like a scarf, and she looked around the kitchen, momentarily disorientated.

'Actually, do you know what? I think I'm going to need you both to leave. Sorry, I've got ... ' She turned to Nicole. 'When you said my husband had been suspended earlier, you didn't say why.'

Lips pressed together, Nicole looked around awkwardly. 'I was out on a viewing when it happened. But there was ... an allegation. Jill told you? But listen, I'm sorry I troubled you.' She gestured towards the hall. 'I'm going to leave you to it now.'

'Right.' Maya was staring out of the kitchen window at a street and a world that must now look very different. 'Sexual assault,' she added, jolted out of her stupor and turning to face Nicole. 'That was what Jill said. That some woman at the office is saying he ... he assaulted her.'

'Maya.' Alex was by her side in an instant, a hand raised but not quite touching her friend's arm.

'I just can't ... ' Maya scratched a temple.

'Let me take Elsa.'

'No, no – I'm OK. I just need to be on my own.' Then to Nicole: 'In answer to your question, I'm hoping my husband is with his lawyer.'

'OK.' Nicole nodded, with a last murmured 'I'm so sorry' as she left the room.

Were it not for the absence of any incidental noise at that precise moment – no lawnmower next door, no van pulling up outside or baby's squawk – Nicole might not have heard the two words Jamie's wife, eyes still on her phone, said next: 'Stupid bitch.'

Alex stopped stuffing wet wipes and sun cream back into her bag and stared over at Maya. She looked like the same kind, bright and wholesome woman she'd got to know so well over the past two months, but that voice, those words, belonged to someone else.

Nicole reappeared in the kitchen doorway. 'What did you say?'

Maya moved towards her, Elsa still in her arms, and for a moment Alex had the dramatic notion that she might slap her, but instead she sat squarely down at the end of the kitchen table, legs slightly apart, Elsa across her lap, and began to unbutton her dress. Then, with a small sigh of irritation at having to repeat herself: 'I called you a stupid bitch.'

The two women stared at one other, Nicole so astonished that a current shivered beneath the surface of her skin, Maya cool, borderline amused. Crouched down beside Katie in the corner of the room, Alex had been forgotten.

'You're not asking why?' Glancing down at Elsa, Maya slipped a sleeve down over one shoulder to reveal that bright white bra. 'It's coming, my sweet. It's coming.'

A second dip of that same shoulder allowed the strap to drop, and sitting back, making herself comfortable, Maya tugged one side down, scooping up a hard, blue-veined and brown-tipped breast and pulled her daughter's fretful head towards it. All the while, her eyes never left Nicole's.

'You're not asking why I called you a bitch?' she went on, her tone ponderous. 'I'm guessing because you think a wife is allowed to speak this way to the woman who's fucking her husband.'

Only a very occasional jumble of words – in particular a

confusion with 'this' and 'that' – told you that English wasn't Maya's mother tongue. It could be charming or give her statements the severity they had now. And as Alex looked from Nicole in the kitchen doorway, handbag dangling from the tips of her fingers, to majestic Maya and her suckling child, she wondered what on earth would keep her there in her lover's house, listening to his wife spew venom at her. Why didn't she leave? The moment she heard Maya say those words, why didn't she leave? Jamie wasn't here, and he was the only reason she'd come. She was ruining their afternoon, and now she really needed to leave.

'Allowed?'

It was a challenge – one Maya countered by donning a faintly puzzled expression.

'Yes, allowed. Surely it's to be expected, even.'

Nicole swallowed, visibly trying to reassert control. 'Listen, I don't know what you think you know, or what Jamie's told you.'

'Oh, please.' Maya cocked her head to one side, saddened. 'Can we assume I know everything? The theatre, the naughty little texts when you're supposed to be enjoying family days out with your little girl. The Best Westerns and the Hiltons and then that silly, silly Angelini's idea. So when I say everything, I mean *everything*. How? Because I set the whole thing up. I chose you.'

'What are you talking about?'

Gently, Nicole lowered her bag to the floor.

'Does he call you Nikki? No. No, he calls you "Nic", right?' She smiled; shook her head. 'Doesn't matter. You're married, aren't you? That was always part of the deal. Anyway, the point is that you know – about the boredom, I mean. Same thing with the same person, year after year. We're all bored. And I don't think it's that men get bored first. I think they just give into it first.'

'What are you—'

'Jamie was bored. So was I. But I wasn't about to let our marriage break down and put the kids through a divorce over a few minutes, a few seconds of what? Nothing. And, well.' Maya narrowed her eyes and again Alex wondered who this woman she thought she knew was. 'I started to think that maybe I liked the thought of him with someone else.'

'You two are . . . you're messed up.'

Maya considered this. 'I don't think so. I was upset – the first time, I mean, when I found out about his PA, years back. She was trashy, for one thing, and because it was such a cliché it meant people would be more likely to notice. I don't like people knowing about my cheating husband. I don't like pity.'

'Jessica?' Nicole's voice was hoarse.

'Was that her name? I can't even remember. But it stung. And I was never going to go through that again. So if there was going to be anyone else, it had to be on my terms.' Maya paused, gently repositioning her daughter's head. 'The Christmas party two years ago – you in that black dress with the fussy neckline and those shoes. I've got the same ones in nude. Which is why I noticed them. Then I noticed you.'

The rise and fall of Nicole's chest quickened.

'I guessed Jamie had already logged you, you know, as someone he'd like to fuck. Probably already even imagined it when he was with me, and in the taxi on the way home I told him you were unlikely to make it hard for him.'

Nicole flushed. 'You don't know anything about me.'

'Oh, I think anyone could see that. And once we'd worked out that you were right, and that you were never going to leave your husband.'

'You really don't know what you're talking about.' Somehow Nicole had mustered the strength to fight back. 'Because I did leave my husband, so your little game didn't work, did it?'

Ignoring her, Maya went on. 'But really there were only two rules: that he would tell me everything, every time. And that when I said it was over, it would be over.'

Her grey-green eyes raised themselves once again to Nicole. 'You must have known he wasn't going to be *that* man? The one who ups and leaves and starts again? After all, you were the only one stuck in an unhappy marriage, Nicole. We're both fine; always have been.' She gave a small shrug. 'But he gets –' she thought about it '– overexcited, carried away. So maybe he promised you things? Things he couldn't – didn't want to – deliver. But that's part of his charm, isn't it? And secrets are fun. Only Jamie's not very good at keeping them.'

'I don't ...' Nicole stared. 'There's something wrong with you two.'

'Maybe.' Elsa had finished feeding and was slumped in a milk stupor against the breast Maya was slowly covering up. 'In which case, why don't you get out of my house?'

'I'm going.' Nicole took a small step, but couldn't seem to bring herself to leave. 'But for the record I'm not buying this. Because if I was just some ... some game, then why would Jamie show up at my house a few hours ago?' Maya made a tiny head movement betraying her surprise at this. 'That's the only reason I'm here. To tell him that if he went there to humiliate my husband even further, then there was no need.' The words were broken up by sobs now. 'There was no need! Because he'd already been humiliated. I'd left him, just like we planned.'

Nicole was an ugly crier, Alex noticed with detachment, her eyebrows pulling the skin of her forehead together into a ladder of lines, the corners of her mouth twisting into a rictus grin. And perhaps she knew it, because within seconds, Nicole was angrily wiping her tears away.

'And if he didn't actually want us, me, to go through with it, then why set up that Angelini's plan to start with? Who does that, if they're not planning to go through with it?'

Maya nodded almost sympathetically. 'That, I'll admit, I didn't know about. And to say that I was surprised when he told me what he'd brought me to the restaurant to do . . .' It was the first time since Alex had met Maya that she'd seen her look rattled. 'Not that we lasted long: we'd only just ordered when he came out with it. And when I looked over and saw you there with—'

'Wait,' Nicole interrupted. 'You knew I was there?'

'You're not listening, are you? Yes, I knew you were there – you and that poor husband of yours. So I made a few things clear. Firstly, that he wasn't going to leave me and the kids – not then, not ever. And secondly, that if he ever wanted to see his kids again, oh and didn't fancy being kicked out of BWL for all those little, well, shortcuts he was taking at work – because, yes, I'm well aware that Jamie sometimes likes to speed deals up in a way Jill and Paul wouldn't be too happy with – then he would eat his steak and drink his wine and leave you to get on with it.'

'You knew and you let me end my marriage?'

Alex flashed back to the conversation she and Nicole had had in the pub the night before: her saying that something about this husband and wife's 'power dynamic' had been wrong. This was why. All this time they had both seen Maya as the wronged wife, when it had been she, not Jamie, calling the shots.

But none of that really mattered right now. What mattered was getting Nicole out of the house. Because all this drama was eating up precious time, and Maya would be holding it together out of pride. You couldn't break down in front of the woman your husband had been sleeping with, but she pictured her friend's serene features collapsing the moment Nicole left, and knew how badly she'd need Alex then. It was why she'd ignored Maya's request to be left alone.

'Nicole.' From the startled looks on both women's faces as Alex stood, they really had forgotten she was still there. 'You've said your piece, but Maya's asked you to leave.' The glue ear was back, and although she could her hear own voice it sounded like someone else's. 'She's too nice to say it again, but I'm not, and you need to get out now.'

To her amazement Alex saw that Nicole was smiling – with disbelief maybe, but still a smile. This annoyed her.

'I said get out.'

Nicole shook her head. 'Don't worry. I'm going. And by the way, Maya,' she called out as she headed into the hallway, 'your new friend's name isn't Lexie; it's Alex. Alex Fuller. Which should ring a pretty loud bell, since she was your husband's PA until a few months ago – when he fired her for misconduct.'

As Nicole left, Alex's ears finally unblocked. And from the look on Maya's face, the way she was holding little Elsa's head – protectively, as though she were … wait, was she scared? – Alex knew she had to act fast.

'Maya.'

Running over to her, Alex knelt at her feet, burying her face in the fresh, clean, redemptive fabric of her friend's dress.

'Get out.'

Maya's voice wasn't right. Nothing about this was right. It was as though the woman she knew was being played by a stand-in.

'You don't understand. When we first met, I was …'

'Get out!'

But Alex wasn't going. Not until she'd made her understand. She'd tell her about Jamie – what he did to her. And why she'd found herself at Bumps & Babies that day. Because now more than ever they needed each other.

As Alex tried to envelop mother and child, Maya's voice wavered into a whisper, then died, before coming back stronger. 'Get off me or I swear to God I'll call the police.'

With a single shove she pushed Alex back, and was on her feet in an instant, clutching Elsa to her chest. Which gave Alex no other choice. Maya had to calm down. If she could just stay still, Alex could make her understand. She launched herself at her friend, grabbing at the baby wrap Maya always wore loosely, like a scarf – that stupid, overcomplicated wrap that only uber-mums like her could master – and clinging tightly to it.

'These past few weeks,' Alex sobbed as Maya gasped for air and tried in vain to loosen the wrap that had crossed around her neck, 'they've been some of the best of my life. Because you don't care who people are or where they come from. And you see me. You see me!' She peered into her friend's eyes but there was no sympathy or understanding – just fear. And as Alex's grip tightened Maya seemed to be slipping away from her, the whites of her eyes turning pink, until she slumped to the floor.

'They're on their way! They'll be here any minute,' came Nicole's voice from behind her. Wait: Nicole was still there? Her voice seemed unnaturally shrill, agitated, like the sirens that were getting louder outside, and all of a sudden, Alex felt very tired. Maya had stopped saying all those vicious things. She wasn't saying anything at all now – just lying there, immobile, on the tiled floor. And Alex would make her understand, but not now. What she needed now was to get home and lie down.

Wincing as the sirens grew louder, closer, Alex grabbed Katie and walked out the front door.

CHAPTER 30

JILL

'He's tall. Light brown hair.' Jill paused. 'Probably pretty drunk.'

Another headshake. Her third since she'd started working her way down King Street, scouring every darkest pub corner for Jamie.

'Do you think he might have been here earlier?' she called out, but the barman was already serving another customer.

There on the busiest stretch of the high street up by the station, Jill stopped, edged a foot out of the pumps that had rubbed a hole in her pop socks and felt a flood of suppressed pain release itself. It took a second to find Jamie's home number in her contacts, but as her thumb hovered over the call button, again she decided against it. What if Maya answered? What if he hadn't told her yet?

She tried his mobile again, only to get the same: 'Hello you've reached Jamie. I'm available – just not right now.' That cheeky chappie mockney lilt that only ever came out on his voicemail and in meetings: she'd once asked him about it. 'Buyers like it,' he'd flung back. 'Makes you sound like a good guy, you know? Solid.' And at the time she'd thought, 'Why try and make yourself sound like something you are anyway?'

Anxious to catch their trains and start drinking, people jostled past her. There was still Belushi's on the corner, but would Jamie really go to a sports bar? She didn't know the answer to that or any other question in the 'What would Jamie do' vein any more. And yet here she was, against her better judgement and Stan's, who had been uncharacteristically terse when she'd called from the office earlier to tell him she might be late because she wanted, needed, to track Jamie down.

'Why not let him be?'

'Because . . .' she'd started, unable to tell her husband about Alex and the confirmation she now had of her involvement – all of their involvement. 'You should have heard him earlier. He was so angry.'

Over in Jamie's empty office a cleaner had started hoovering.

'You realise you're still, even after everything, making excuses for him,' Stan had said with an exasperated laugh.

'You don't get it.'

'No,' he'd sighed. 'I don't. He brought this on himself.'

And how could she explain that she wasn't sure of anything any more? Yes, the letter had been genuine, but not the email, and maybe not the claim that had got Jamie suspended. How far had Alex and Nicole gone to bring him down?

As Jill pushed through the doors of Belushi's, aware as she asked the punters the same questions that she was being mistaken for an angry wife come to retrieve her husband, it occurred to her that the guilt she'd been burying had morphed into a kind of superstition. As though purely by having that stupid drunken conversation the three of them might have prompted bad things to happen: double, double toil and trouble. 'Excuse me,' she called out to the bartender across the din. 'Can I have a G&T? Make it a double.'

She'd downed it in three gulps, hoping it might sharpen her mind, but when she emerged blinking from Belushi's just minutes later it was almost six and the sun was bleeding into the pink evening sky. Unable to decide whether to try Jamie again, yomp along to whatever that pub halfway down Hammersmith Grove was called or just give up and go home, Jill stood for a moment in a cloud of second-hand smoke outside the door. Then she called Maya. If Jamie was home, then at least she could give this up and make contact in the morning. It could all be sorted out then. Only he wasn't. And when Maya picked up on the first ring sounding both tense and hopeful, Jill knew she had to tell her.

After assuring her that was all she or anyone other than HR knew, she urged Maya to sit tight. Jamie would be home once he'd finished drinking himself into a stupor, and tomorrow he could thrash out a plan with his lawyer. Jill had kept it short, upbeat – she'd got the feeling Maya had company in any case – but when she'd rung back seconds later to assure her that of course if she located Jamie first she'd send him home, there had been no answer. Which Jill had taken to mean that her husband had just crashed through the door. Until she saw Jamie's name flash up on her mobile.

'Where are you? Christ, Jamie. I've been calling and calling. Everyone's worried about you.'

'Everyone?'

Jill extricated herself from the pull of commuters and put a hand over one ear. Wherever Jamie was, there was a lot of background noise, and his words were running into each other. 'Well, Maya, for one. Why didn't you call her?'

'And say what?'

She was going to have to tell him. 'Listen I just spoke to her. I thought you might have gone home, and she sounded so worried. I had to say something.'

'Course you did.'

'I was only trying to help.' A burst of song in the background drowned her out. 'Just tell me where you are.'

It took her less than fifteen minutes to get to the Crown & Sceptre, a triangular end-of-terrace pub in which they'd celebrated Paul's birthday years ago, but the place was already rammed with boozers in QPR shirts. Of course, there would be a game on. Craning her neck she saw him, hunched over a full pint at the end of a long table of men in blue-and-white-striped scarves.

'Sorry. Excuse me. Can I get by?'

Relief at finding a chair and finally being off her feet buried any initial awkwardness, and they sat there in silence a moment.

'Why are you here?' His eyes were glassy and disconnected.

'Stan asked me the same question.' She attempted a smile. 'The way he sees it you've made your bed. And part of me feels the same. I know about Alex, Jamie, about you using her as a scapegoat for your bungles and scams. I know that you've cheated and lied and used Stan's illness and my distraction to push yourself ahead. And I know about the letter you sent to the board. The email was doctored, yes, but the letter was all you.'

A flicker of something. Not contrition, more annoyance at being caught out.

'And you may feel no loyalty to me, Stan or your employees, for that matter. You may be comfortable with the lying and the scheming, but I'm not. *That's* why I'm here. Because you deserve to be disciplined – but only for what you've done. And I'm worried that there's been some kind of . . .' she was on shaky ground here ' . . . vendetta against you.'

Sucking the beer foam off his top lip, Jamie widened his eyes and laughed. 'You don't think I know that? You don't think I've spent the past few hours going over and over what's been happening in my life lately – and putting two and two together?' Jill wished she had a drink in her hand. 'Because let me tell you that when you get sacked—'

'Suspended.'

'Let's call it what it is. When you get sacked for something you didn't do, and the woman you had an eighteen-month affair with not only doesn't call you but is uncontactable, it's not hard to do the maths.'

'You and Nicole?'

'Ha! It *was* her. I knew it was her!'

The men sharing their table glanced over.

'Christ, Jamie, I'm not supposed to say anything. HR are in charge of this now.'

'Well thanks for the heads-up. And yes, Nicole and I were together. We were in love!' Jamie squealed out the words, one hand to his shirt front. 'And we were going to try and make it work.' He paused, frowned, drank some more. 'But I let her down. I couldn't . . . go through with it. And now she's accused me of assault. So I guess Biarritz is off.'

He'd stopped making sense, but Jill knew enough to work out the rest. Of course the two of them had been together. Something about them – a hardness, an inner darkness – made sense. She didn't know why she hadn't seen it before.

'I should have guessed. Maybe I just thought you'd be mad to cheat on Maya.'

He smiled at that. 'My saintly wronged wife. You have no idea. Nicole wasn't the first. I did something stupid a few years back.'

'Your PA.'

'Yeah.' He met her eye. 'Always thought you might have twigged.'

Jill thought back to the conversation she and Stan had had by the canal the day after Joyce's leaving do: the PA who had left suddenly, without explanation.

'It was irrelevant; she was irrelevant. But Maya's never let me forget it. And let me tell you, she's been the one calling the shots ever since. Nicole was her idea . . . to start with. But then it got out of control, hers and mine. You know what?' He leaned forward. 'We're meant to be the bad guys, but women are twisted, manipulative – fucked up. Nic liked our games. Least I thought she did. Then everything started going to shit: the "mix-ups" at work, and at home. I don't know how I didn't see it, and God knows how she was doing it, but all the time it was her . . . '

Jill put a hand up to stop him. 'No. No, Jamie, it wasn't all—'

He wasn't listening. 'This is going to destroy everything. Maya will never be able to forgive me.'

Jill pictured pretty blonde Maya at the school gates – the

Celia Walden

sidelong looks, the whispers. No, she wouldn't forgive him.
And despite everything, she felt for Jamie. He might not have
been the man she'd thought he was, but he wasn't the man
they'd conjured up in the pub that night, either.

'There will be a full investigation, and I'll make sure you're
dealt with fairly.'

'Big of you – thanks.'

'Hey. I'd take it. Your behaviour to me, after I brought you
in, after I taught you everything, promoted you and had you
at my dinner table ... We've been on holiday together, for
Christ's sake.'

He made a face: not this again. 'Does any of it matter now?'
Jill shrugged.

'No,' he answered for her. 'So I'll speak frankly.' Having
lost the ability to pronounce his Rs, the word came out a
feeble 'fwankly'. 'I'm gone. I'm out. But you should go, too.
You've been at the company forty years,' he slurred. 'Isn't
that enough?' He was staring at Jill, eyes unfocused, head
swaying loosely on his neck, like an articulated doll.

'Right. I think we've both said our piece.' She reached for
her bag beneath the table. 'Let's get you an Addison Lee.'

'Always the grown-up, eh Jill? Do fuck off.'

The curse landed like a slap, and this time when the QPR
supporters looked over, they weren't laughing. But Jamie
was oblivious to the attention he was attracting, his mouth
twisted into a snarl as he raged on: 'We're not in the boardroom now. And we both know there's nothing "fair" about
what's going to happen to me now. BWL are never going
to clear my name, are they? Only Nic can do that – but she
won't, not now. I knew it was her, that's why I went to her
house, had a word with her wet husband.'

'You spoke to Ben?'

'Damn fucking right. I went over there. Had a cuppa with Mr Harper. Saw the house. Met Nicole's little one. Very cute, by the way.'

Jill's hands flew up to her face. 'No, no, no.'

'He's a nice bloke, Ben. Or he was until the moment I told him that his wife had just got me fired. And that if I did assault her, she must have really liked it because she just kept on coming back for more. Even planned to leave him for me.'

This was Jill's limit. 'I'm off.'

'Wait.' As Jamie stood he toppled his pint, sending it crashing to the floor.

'Mate!' The man beside him leapt to his feet, staring down in disbelief at his soaked jeans. 'What the . . . ? Are you even going to apologise?'

But Jamie was non-reactive, scarcely even registering what he'd done.

Jill looked from him to the man. 'Sorry. He's . . . pretty out of it. Let me get you a—'

'I'm not fucking out of it.'

'Hey! Instead of talking to the lady like that, how about you apologise?'

Jill didn't like this and began to look for an exit pathway through the bodies. Stan was right: this had been a bad idea.

'Sorry about your fucking jeans.' Reaching in his back pocket for his wallet, Jamie pulled out a twenty-pound note and tossed it at the man. 'Primark, I'm guessing? Here. Buy yourself two new pairs. Jill – where are you going? I thought we were going to talk?'

She hadn't thought for a minute that Jamie would try

to stop her, but his hand was on the strap of her handbag, pulling her down.

'Stop it. You're embarrassing yourself.'

Whipping out her phone, she clicked on the company Addison Lee account app and called Jamie a car. That was her kindness used up for the night. 'The car will be here in six minutes. Get yourself home to your wife.'

'Yeah, 'cause that's a conversation I can't wait to have,' he leered. 'Just one last thing: I was being loyal. I was being loyal to the company when I told people you'd be better off at home. You were a mess, you are a mess, and you're going to be a mess long after he's gone.'

The words hovered there between them: *after he's gone*. It sounded like the title of a book by that Aga saga woman, whatever her name was, about some well-heeled Buckinghamshire woman who learned to live and love again. After.

'Stan's not going anywhere. You know that.'

As they stood there inches apart, eye to eye, she watched Jamie register her vulnerability. And she watched him home in on it.

'Is this some weird denial thing? Or has he seriously not told you yet?'

She tried hard to focus on the pain in her right foot, but that, along with everything else, seemed to be muffled by something so huge and heavy it would eclipse everything.

'Stan's not going to make it past Christmas. He told me that in January – that day I came to see him in hospital. You'd left the room and ...'

'No.'

'He didn't want you to know, back then, that it had spread

to his spine and his lymph nodes. But I thought he'd tell you, when he was ready.'

'No.' She put her hand up to protect herself from his words, and Jamie grabbed her wrist and held it firm.

'Why would I make this up?'

Everything happened very fast, then. The freckled arm that came from behind Jamie, jamming him in a headlock. The distant shout of 'You'd better get your hands off her now, mate.' People parted as two, no, three of the men in blue and white scarves, led by the one in beer-sodden jeans, hauled Jamie through the pub towards the door, his damp shirt ruckled to expose a few inches of soft white belly, the heel of one of his suede shoes pulled free as he was dragged along the floor. And although Jill knew she should stop them, she waited until the first and second punches landed, the third flooring him, before begging the men to stop.

Jamie was still lying by the pub bins, his lips slick with blood, when the car pulled up, and Jill pressed a twenty into the driver's hand – 'help him into the back and home, will you?' – before walking away. All she was thinking about as she headed off in search of a cab, ignoring the persistent ringing of her phone in her bag, was 'after he's gone.'

Only when she saw the back of her husband's neck rising up from his armchair, did the tears come. Without a word Jill pressed her wet face into that neck, and after a small movement of surprise she felt Stan's body slump as he registered what Jill must now know.

Even as she was sobbing – 'How did you think you could keep this from me? Why?' – Jill understood why. It was seeing his wife reduced to this that Stan was trying to avoid. Had it been the other way around she wouldn't have been able to bear it. 'Hearing it from Jamie, Stan, having him know that, and not me . . . but there are trials you can go on. There's a hospital in Bordeaux with an incredible success rate . . .'

Her husband said nothing, shaking his head and pulling her to him in an awkward embrace. And for a while the two of them just sat there, Stan stroking her hair and Jill waiting until the heaving gave way to shudders.

Then – because there was nothing else to say: 'Camomile?' And Jill had nodded and cleaned herself up before joining Stan in the kitchen, where they stood shoulder to shoulder waiting for the kettle to boil, the way they had a thousand times before – before today, after which nothing would ever be the same again.

Spotting her laptop in its usual place on the counter, Jill surprised herself with the thought that she should check on Jamie, ensure he'd been dropped off safely.

'After everything he's done?' Stan murmured, peering over her shoulder as she started to track his car on the company system.

'I know. But he ended up getting into a brawl.'

Stan blew softly on his tea. 'Don't you think he had it coming? He's a liability, love. Let Jamie take care of himself from here.'

'I will. This is just for my own peace of mind.' As if to reinforce her husband's pleas, up came the twirling rainbow wheel on her screen, and Jill was hit by a wave of weariness.

'Come on.' Stan took her hand, and with one last glance at the open laptop, Jill let him pull her off the kitchen stool. 'Let's get you to bed.'

*

Later, under the cover of darkness and blurred by the sleeping pill Stan had insisted she take, Jill allowed herself to cry again. She had hoped her husband was asleep and was dismayed when he reached over to her, his hand warm against her thigh.

'My love . . .'

'Sorry. I just wish you'd told me – not him. And I know you and Jamie had become close over the years, but . . .'

Stan turned on his hip to face her in the darkness. 'It wasn't that. I was so out of it that I didn't know what I was saying. So I told him what the doctors had found: how far the cancer had spread . . . the prognosis. And afterwards, I suppose I hoped I'd dreamt it up in the haze. I certainly never thought he'd betray me – us – the way he has.' He took her hand beneath the covers. 'But forget about Jamie.'

Jill wanted to tell him that she couldn't, and why she couldn't. She was ready to do that now, and admit that although her former partner had been guilty of so much – infidelity, opportunism, double-dealing and a disloyalty so shocking towards both her and Stan that it had rocked her very foundations – she too had played a part in something full of lies and deceit.

'Stan, there's something you should . . .'

Only, before she could go on, Jill's eyes flickered shut.

CHAPTER 31

NICOLE

Because none of the mums had mentioned Ben, Nicole knew that they knew. It had been less than a week since she'd moved out, but somehow they knew. And somehow the fact that she and her husband were splitting up had made her popular in a way no previous attempts at ingratiation with these women had been able to.

Since they'd arrived at Bella Boos, the sickly pink kids' café where Chloe's school friend was having her birthday party, a steady stream of mums had come to ask how she was, and the hostess had refilled her cup with Prosecco twice.

'They say it's the white make-up,' the birthday girl's mum announced now, sitting back down beside her after a loop with the sandwich tray.

'Sorry?' Nicole spoke over a blare of party horns.

'Clowns: they say it's the white make-up that scares the little ones – even grown-ups. So when Annie mentioned she'd used Trudy Tickle for her eldest, who's got that condition, coulrophobia – coulrophobia?'

'A fear of clowns?'

'That's it. Anyway, I thought she'd be perfect for Lizzie's party. They should all be a bit less scary-looking, don't you think? Given how easily spooked they are at this age?'

As she moved on to the 'night terrors' Lizzie had experienced that autumn, Nicole nodded and sipped her Prosecco. She didn't care that it was tepid and too early to be drinking. She didn't care about whether or not clowns were whited-up, either. She just wanted the normality and purity of this pink balloon-filled moment to last for ever, for these women's inconsequential worries and chatter to drown out the memories of the last twenty-four hours and silence the noise – that stomach-churning noise – of Maya's head cracking like a nut on the kitchen tiles. How had this never been enough for her? Why had she courted excitement and danger when everything she needed was right here?

When Nicole had called Ben that morning, begging him to let her take Chloe to the party that had popped up as a reminder – and a reprieve – on her phone, she hadn't expected him to say yes. But after the scene she'd witnessed in Maya's kitchen the previous afternoon, and the hours spent talking to the police and in the hospital waiting room – where only after midnight had she been assured, 'Mrs Lawrence is OK: shocked and sore but stitched up and OK' – she needed to see her daughter.

Ben had let her second 'please' hang there, enjoying the humiliation, turning it back on her, before finally muttering:

'OK. But I want Chloe back here by six. If she eats any later she gets hyper and it takes hours to put her down.' As though Nicole were already an outsider who needed to have her daughter's foibles explained to her. 'And actually I got that gig with the software company in north London, so I could use the time to start prepping for that.'

When she'd tried to congratulate Ben on the job, he'd cut her off and hung up. She didn't get to be surprised or pleased for him any more. Not after everything. Not after Jamie had turned up on their doorstep drunk out of his mind. And although her husband had said that their conversation was brief and Jamie 'too out of it to make any sense', Nicole still felt sick at the thought of what could have been said. What could have happened in Maya's kitchen, if she hadn't been there and called the police?

When a traffic accident is narrowly avoided, it's only afterwards, when one pulls, trembling, to the side of the road, that the imagined impact is felt. Nicole was at the side of the road now, relieved and grateful that the worst hadn't happened – that Jamie hadn't told Ben and that Maya was going to be fine – but still trembling at her own recklessness.

She'd done everything she could to put it right. She'd filled in the police on Alex's obsession with the man who had sacked her and given them her address – surely by now they would have found her? But there was one thing she hadn't summoned the courage to do yet, and that was tell Jill. Nicole had got as far as bringing up her number, finger hovering over the call button, before turning her phone off, unable to bring herself to describe yesterday's events. It was she, not Jill, who should have noticed how unstable Alex was, and yet her violent behaviour implicated them both.

'What's this game?' Her phone was buzzing in her bag, but she had no desire to answer it.

'You know – giggle coin.'

Nicole shook her head. Why did she always feel like these women were speaking a language she didn't understand?

'It's basically pass the parcel, only you pass a coin around and ...'

Nicole smiled and nodded, but again she was back in that Chiswick kitchen, trying to pull Alex off Maya, her limbs heavy and movements nightmarishly ineffectual. And as she'd crouched by Maya's body, waiting for the ambulance to get there and watching the blood trickle from the back of her head, filling the grouting between the Silestone tiles in orderly crimson right angles, her single thought had been: 'This is all my fault.'

They hadn't let her ride with Maya to the hospital and for one ghastly moment Nicole had pictured Jamie turning up to find her there, holding his baby. The sound of a key in the lock had made her heart dip, but then a tiny Filipino woman had appeared in the doorway, holding a little girl – Christel – by the hand. Remembering the blood, so much blood, Nicole had blocked their path. 'Something's happened – they've taken Maya to St Mary's,' she'd told the nanny. And as she'd handed her Elsa, trying to ignore the collapse of Christel's face, Nicole had experienced such a yearning to escape this toxicity and breathe in the clean soapy smell of her own child's hair that she'd felt dizzy.

'I'll go there now,' she'd assured the ashen-faced woman. 'And call as soon as I know anything.' A pause. 'Can you ... will you call their father?'

While Lizzie's mum went to 'check on the cake', Nicole

took advantage of a brief moment alone to glance at her phone. Two missed calls from an unknown number. Would it be the police, telling her they'd found Alex? Even if they had left a voicemail, she wouldn't have had the courage to listen to it.

No matter how many times Nicole had turned it over in her head that night, looking for an absolving loophole, she couldn't absolve herself of responsibility when it came to Alex, and she had seen Alex's instability developing at close quarters. She'd even spotted the warning signs, but had chosen to ignore them because Alex's fixation with Jamie, with revenge, had suited her.

'Need another top-up?' How long had the hostess been watching her? Long enough to see Nicole drain what was left of her Prosecco in one, eyes closed. The question was all too clearly going to lead on to ... 'Been a hard week?'

And there it was.

'Yes.' Nicole was too tired to put on any kind of front. 'But I think you know that. Everyone seems to know that Ben and I have split up.' It seemed an adolescent way of describing the smashing up of two lives – three, really, although she couldn't bear to think about that. 'It's been tough. It's going to be tough.'

'I bet.' Out of nowhere another mother, probably one of Ben's little admirers, had joined their conversation, and was nodding sympathetically along.

Nicole took a breath. 'I'm just grateful he's being so civilised about it all.' And she was.

Taking in the translucent skin of her daughter's neck now as she sat with her back to Nicole – so innocent, so exposed by those two bunches – brought tears to her eyes. Where had that freckle come from? Was it a freckle or a mole, and how much more had she missed? All those business trips she'd been on, they'd seemed manageable, enjoyable, even, if Nicole was being honest with herself. But maybe only because she'd known that her daughter was there whenever she wanted, needed, to hear her prattle on about Peppa Pig. And every day without Chloe, Nicole had woken up feeling like she had a limb missing.

'She's adorable,' Lizzie's mum murmured in her ear, eyes lingering on Nicole long enough to make her want to turn and say, calm and still smiling, 'Yes, this is what a woman whose marriage has broken down looks like.'

But instead Nicole heard herself laugh. 'She is. Am I allowed to say that? I never know.'

And maybe it would all be OK? Painful and long drawn out, but OK.

'I'm getting so awfully confused!' boomed Trudy Tickle, looking down, hands on hips, at the circle of enraptured faces. 'But I think it might be time for the cake!'

Again, Nicole's phone buzzed in her bag. This time, she knew she would have to answer it.

'Hello?'

'It's . . . ' A pause. 'It's Jill.'

'One sec.' As the party blowers honked, Nicole covered one ear, and headed for the door. 'Sorry, who?'

'It's Jill.'

She would be wanting an update, but Nicole had nothing new to tell her.

'Sorry, I'm at a kids' party with my daughter. They're about to bring the cake out. Can I call you back?'

'No.'

Afterwards, Nicole had fixated on when. At which point exactly did she know that Jamie was dead? Was it with that 'No'? Was it in the congested silence before Jill spoke again? Because by the time she said it – 'Jamie's dead' – Nicole somehow already knew.

'They found him this morning. The police want to talk to me. They'll want to talk to you, too. And Nicole –' Jill's voice dipped down '– I can't get hold of Alex.'

Leaning against the pink-painted door frame, Nicole doubled over, the shock fluid as it ran through her.

'How?'

They'd found him behind the Vale Theatre that morning, Jill went on. He'd been alive, then, kept alive by the railings he was impaled on. But he'd bled out in the ambulance. Jill's voice was high-pitched with fear: 'We've got to find Alex.'

Nicole tried to speak.

'Nicole, are you there?'

'Yes. The theatre,' she managed. 'There's this little glass hut on the roof. No one knew about it but us.' That she was still able to form coherent sentences was surprising to her. 'I took him up to see it. We . . . Jill? Jill?'

But the line had gone dead.

CHAPTER 32

ALEX

From her upside-down position on the bed, the painting looked like a cat. A cat or maybe a tiger, painted in the kind of watery style that leaves traces of brush marks on the canvas. But if Alex twisted her head around to look at the picture the right way up it looked more like a girl with deep-set, feline eyes. Her mother's eyes.

'That,' she asked the woman who had appeared beside her. 'What is it?'

'What's what?' She didn't look up from the clipboard in her hand.

'The picture. Is it a cat or a girl?'

As the woman's eyes flicked briefly to it, Alex saw that she was very young, sullen-mouthed, and ... why was she wearing scrubs?

'That? That's a fox.'

Alex tried to focus her eyes, but the lids felt heavy and the corners gunged up, as though she'd fallen asleep in full make-up.

'Where am I?'

The hard horizontal of the woman's brow softened slightly, but her tone remained detached. 'You're in hospital –' she looked down at her clipboard '– Ms Fuller. You've had a very long sleep. Almost two days. How do you feel?' Then, without waiting for an answer, 'The doctor's going to come in and explain a few things now that you're awake.'

'Hospital?' But the nurse was already on her way out. 'Two days? Hey!' Her voice was weak from disuse. 'That's not a fox!'

Attempting to stress this with a hand gesture, Alex heard something heavy and wheeled dislodge itself from behind her left shoulder and turned to find an IV stand beside her. She followed the progress of the pee-coloured liquid in the bag down to the catheter implanted in her inner forearm.

'Hey. come back!'

By pushing and pulling the IV stand against the metal-framed bed, Alex succeeded in making enough of a clattering to bring the nurse back.

'Can we stop that please, Ms Fuller. I said can we stop that!'

'Why am I here? Where's …' A memory, shadowy but growing sharper, came and went. Something vital she'd forgotten. 'I need to get out of here.'

But the nurse had disappeared and sent in a small bearded man, who seated himself at the foot of the bed.

'I'm Doctor Chua.'

Her mouth felt metallic: the drugs. 'What's in that drip? Can I ... can I have some water?'

The doctor handed her a paper cup and waited patiently as she drained it. He seemed like a nice man, not like that bitch of a nurse.

'You were very dehydrated when they brought you in,' he explained with a nod at the IV.

'But Doctor ... ' Again, that suspension of breath: something had been forgotten, left behind. But what? Catching sight of a strip of redness across her knuckles where her fingers were wrapped around that paper cup, Alex remembered the scrubbing, the smell of the baby powder: Katie. A sound rang out that was so high-pitched she thought it might be an alarm in the street below. Only when Dr Chua's face loomed, concerned, over hers did Alex understand that it had come from her.

'Katie,' she whispered. 'Where's my baby? What have you done with her?'

'Ms Fuller ... Alex.' Dr Chua had taken her hand. 'Your baby's safe and well and with your mother.'

'With my ... ' Deep pockmarks scored the doctor's cheeks: childhood acne. 'That's not ... no. You don't understand. She's in Portugal.'

Wordlessly, Dr Chua went to the large rectangular window by the door, and with a sharp tug pulled open the vertical blinds to show the corridor beyond, before resuming his perched position on her bed.

It took Alex's brain a few seconds to make sense of the face staring back at her through the white slats.

'Your mother got here the morning after you were

admitted. Apart from taking your daughter for fresh air and formula runs, she's been here the whole time.'

'Mum,' Alex mouthed, as their eyes met through the glass. Her mother was pressing her lips together the way she did when she was trying not to cry, but her eyes were smiling. She blinked once, twice, three times, and Alex recognised it as the form of Morse code they'd developed when she was a little girl: a way of silently reassuring one another after the worst of her father's outbursts. Three blinks meant 'I love you'.

'She can come in. But first you and I need to have a chat.' Dr Chua regarded her calmly for a moment. 'Do you have any idea why you're here?'

Alex couldn't take her eyes off her mother – her mother who had come and stayed. But how? Wouldn't her father have found out about the loan by now? She didn't want to think about how dearly her mother had paid for that secret. And yet, somehow, he'd allowed her to get on a plane and come here.

'You've not been doing so well, have you?' Dr Chua raised a sparse eyebrow. 'Can you tell me a bit about that? Did it start when Katie was born, perhaps, or soon after?'

'Because you think . . . no, no. This isn't some post-natal thing.' Whatever they'd given her was making her nauseous. She swallowed hard. 'I wasn't getting much sleep, and doing it all alone – well, it hasn't been easy.'

Dr Chua was nodding as if he understood.

'I just thought that if only I could get it right, you know? Be as good a mother to Katie as I was at my job.' Her stomach dipped as she remembered. 'But then they took that job away.'

One after another, the memories began coming in, like

phone messages held back by a bad connection, and then Alex began to cry so hard that she lost control of her features. Embarrassed, she turned away from the doctor, burying her face in the pillow.

'Alex, sometimes when a person suffers a trauma, like the loss of a family member or a job that means a lot to them, it can awaken or exacerbate an issue that has been there, dormant, for some time. It's also possible for that issue to rear its head postpartum. Either way, we believe that what you experienced was a psychotic episode.'

Alex stared.

'In the build-up to that, reality can sometimes feel distorted or even taken over by paranoias, manias and fixations on things or people.' He paused, but not long enough to be expecting an answer. Which was just as well, since she had no idea what he was talking about. 'But they tend not to come out of nowhere. And we'd like to explore various contributing factors: the impact of the job you lost . . . ' He paused, glancing through the blinds at Alex's mother. 'Your father, possibly.'

'My father?'

'Your mother and I have spoken. She's given us a bit of background, told us of the problems you experienced growing up, that you were fearful of your father, often with good reason.'

'She said that?'

Dr Chua nodded.

'Did she . . . ' Alex glanced back at her mother. 'Did she tell you anything else? Did she tell you it wasn't just me?'

'Your mother's not my patient,' said the doctor firmly. 'So it's not up to me to discuss any experiences specific to her. But I will say that domestic abuse in any form is rarely restricted to a single family member.'

'Domestic . . .'

'I think you two have a lot to discuss. Because this . . .' He gestured at her, and although he'd spoken warmly, compassionately, Alex felt a flush of shame at the reductive nature of the pronoun. 'This isn't you, is it, Alex? And I'm guessing you haven't felt like you for some time. But once we have a better idea of exactly what has been going on in here –' he tapped his temple lightly with his index finger '– we're going to be able to get you treated. OK?'

What could Alex do but nod?

'Now I'm going to step out and give you and your mum a moment alone. But just a moment, because there are things – pressing things – you and I need to discuss.'

Again Alex nodded, desperate now to hear her mum's voice and to bury her face in the warm, ruckled crook of her neck. But when, after some low murmuring in the corridor outside, her mother appeared in the doorway, all Alex could think of was how badly she'd let her down, how furious her father would be about the money – and now this.

As her face crumpled, she managed: 'I'm so sorry, Mum. I'm so sorry.' But her sobs were muffled by her mother's jumper, and for what felt like a long time the two women just held one another. When Alex again tried to speak – 'Katie?' – her mother explained that her daughter was safely back at home with a baby nurse, and not to worry. Further questions were shushed, as her mum continued to run a hand down the back of Alex's hair in long, rhythmic strokes.

'My love.'

'Mum ...'

'It's going to be OK. It's all going to be OK.'

At that, Alex wrenched herself away from her mother's chest. 'How? How is it going to be OK? I can't get you that money, Mum.'

'I don't care about the money. None of that matters, love. All that matters is getting you treated – getting you better.'

'But Dad ... the new house ... '

Her mother's jawline hardened. 'There won't be a new house – not for us. Not for me.' She cradled her daughter's cheek with one hand. 'I should have put a stop to his behaviour years ago, decades ago. And I would have if I'd had any idea what it had done to you. But I was so weak. I was ... '

'You were scared.'

Her mother nodded, and Alex watched her wrestle with tears before her face assumed an expression she'd never seen before: part anger, part iron determination.

'When we got the call ... when we found out what had happened to you, and he actually tried to stop me from getting on a plane ... ' She shook her head. 'Neither of us will ever be scared or controlled by him again, I can promise you that. And I'm going to stay here with you –' her mother pulled her in for another hug '– for as long as you'll have me. It'll be just you, me and that precious little girl.'

'Sorry to interrupt.' Dr Chua was back so soon.

'Can we just have a few more minutes?' Alex pleaded.

A silent message passed between the doctor and her mother.

'My darling, I'm going to check on Katie. But I'll be back in an hour or two.'

Alex clung to her, but her mother gently disengaged herself before kissing her forehead.

'Just a couple of hours, I promise. And if Dr Chua here thinks it's all right I might even bring the little one with me.'

This time Dr Chua pulled up a chair.

'The sedatives we've given you might be making you feel a little woozy. Longer term we're going to need to put you on an antipsychotic and an antidepressant. Finding the right mix can take time, so you'll have to bear with us, but it's important you understand that we're dealing with something a little less predictable than depression or even post-natal psychosis here, and therefore harder to manage.'

'My mother . . .' Alex cleared her throat. 'She mentioned a phone call, and something happening. What happened? What did I do?'

'I'll get to that,' he said quietly. 'We've spoken to friends and colleagues who have told us that you've been focusing quite intently on the man who let you go over the past few weeks and months. Unhealthily so. One described it as an obsession.'

Flashes, as though her brain were going in and out of signal again: Jamie holding Katie, surrounded by cooing women. How could she have let him touch her? And when did that happen? Jamie behind a desk reciting sentences from some HR manual. Jamie in a pub, full of bonhomie, lapping up the applause. Jamie's weekly schedule, with all its colour-coded blocks.

'We think that this fixation culminated in the episode.'

Alex felt nauseous again.

'You became violent, Alex.'

'No. That can't be.' She'd never lifted a finger to anyone in the whole of her adult life. 'I'd never . . .'

'You went to your boss's house, and you attacked his wife.'

Maya. Oh God.

'Her children . . . ?'

'Her children are fine. But Maya needed medical treatment.'

'No. Maya's my friend. I would never hurt her.'

'But you did. You put her in hospital.'

'No, no . . .'

Alex tried to pull herself up. She needed to get out of here: find out how much of this, if any, was true.

'I need you to calm down and focus, because this next part is important.'

Exhausted, she fell back against the pillows.

'You were lucky. Your boss's wife is going to be OK, and I'm told she doesn't want to press charges. But it could have been much worse.'

Maya's blue-veined breast, exposed. Magnolia petals falling like confetti. A plaid picnic blanket and Katie on her back, tiny arms raised at right angles. Nicole was there, and Jill. No, not Jill, just Nicole, who was about to ruin everything. And throughout it all the monotonous rise and fall of sirens.

'You're sure . . .' Alex swallowed and tried again. 'You're sure it was my boss's wife that I . . . ?'

'I'm sure. And my only concern is your health and treatment, but the police want to talk to you. I'm obligated to tell them that you're now conscious. Because they have been trying to establish where it was that you went after.'

'After?'

'After.'

The sirens had kept getting louder. The only way she could block them out was by dipping down into the nearest Tube station. That was where she'd gone afterwards.

'I got the Tube home. With Katie.'

'We know that you went home first. And again, this is not my concern. But that's not where you were found later on that night. Your daughter, Katie, she was found at the flat, alone. She was OK. She is OK, I need you to understand that, but the police found other things, Alex: printouts of your former boss's schedules, private emails of his. And what they're trying to work out is whether you went somewhere that night, whether you saw Mr Lawrence.' Dr Chua leaned forward. 'These are questions the police are going to ask you. Because Jamie Lawrence is dead, Alex. And they seem to think that you had something to do with it.'

CHAPTER 33

JILL

7 AUGUST

'It's a formality, as I said on the phone, Mrs Barnes. We're just crossing our Ts. So if you could read through your statement and sign right there at the bottom, that's us done.'

It was the same DI she'd spoken to forty-eight hours earlier, DI Silver, but a different room – brighter, airier – and a very different atmosphere.

'Can we get you a cup of tea, water?'

He'd left her alone, then, to relive the nightmarish details of Jamie's final hours – details Jill could hardly even remember providing, so distraught had she been on her last visit to the station. And, taking a breath, she began to read back through the curt, clumsy and often barely grammatical string of sentences on the paper before her.

'On the evening of Wednesday 4 August I'd left Mr Lawrence outside the Crown & Sceptre pub in Shepherd's Bush around 9.15 p.m., where he was being kicked and punched by three men in QPR shirts. The men had been annoyed by his behaviour inside the pub. He had spilled a drink on one of them.' She took a sip of tepid tea and pushed on.

'We had had a row about his behaviour over the past few months, and his suspension [prompted by an allegation of assault made by BWL's special projects supervisor Nicole Harper].' Here Jill paused. She'd said nothing to the police about Nicole and Jamie having had a consensual affair, unwilling to get into the murky details of a relationship that she would doubtless never understand. That both Nicole and Maya had enjoyed some kind of sordid game-playing was now clear to her. But with both women instantly eliminated from the police inquiry, Jill had left it up to them to decide how much of that, if any, needed to be shared.

'Mr Lawrence was very drunk, so I'd called him a company car on account – we use Addison Lee – to take him home. I gave the driver an extra £20 to get Jamie home safely. Then I went straight home myself.'

Stripped of all the conflicting emotions she'd felt that night – rage at Jamie's behaviour towards her, pity at what he'd been reduced to, shame at the part she'd played in a downfall that in retrospect was perhaps inevitable, and lastly the visceral pain of her discovery that Stan's diagnosis was terminal – the statement read like someone else's account of an evening she, Jill, could never possibly have lived through.

'I had been going to check that Jamie had indeed been dropped off safely at home on the BWL system. I was worried enough about him to think of doing that, but once home I got distracted by my husband, who has been unwell.' Unwell. A mental image of herself clinging to Stan, tears matting the wool of his jumper. A slam of the pain that might lessen over time, but would be part of her life for ever now.

Had she followed through with the check-up on Jamie's journey that she'd started – even going so far as to log on to the system before abandoning her open laptop on the kitchen counter – could his death have been avoided? Would she have been concerned enough by the realisation that her partner had changed his destination to the Vale to send for help? Or would she – more likely – have snapped her laptop shut and left the man responsible for so much hurt to his chaos?

'On the following morning, the morning of Thursday 5 August, I decided to take the day off work to look after my husband. Then at around 1 p.m. I got a call from my partner, Paul Wilkinson, who told me what had happened.'

Still woozy from the sleeping pill Stan had given her the night before, Jill had emailed Kellie to say she wouldn't be in. Then she had sat down and drawn up a 'to do' list. Anything to slow the unspooling in her head, restore a semblance of order.

One last Grand Union trip was what they needed. One last wander down the flight of locks near Tring to Marsworth and back up past the reservoirs. One last steak and ale pie at the Half Moon pub – if the doctor gave them the go-ahead. Early September would be ideal. Any later and the nights would get chilly aboard *Lady J*. But first they were going to have to sit down and discuss Stan's burial plans, the ideas they'd tossed about after funerals over the years being no more than moments of self-indulgence. And Jill had been thinking about how to broach this when the call had come in.

In a curiously clinical monotone Paul had managed to get across what she needed to know – that Jamie was dead, that he'd been found that morning at a building site behind the Vale, that they didn't yet know how it had happened – and she'd felt behind her for a bar stool to sink down on.

The timeline had become sickeningly clear later that afternoon, when Nicole had described the scene in Maya's kitchen. Obsessed, deranged Alex attacking first Jamie's wife at home, before somehow tracking him down at the Vale, and carrying out her final act of revenge? *Here's to putting a not-so-good man down.*

'How are we getting on?'

DI Silver popped his head around the door.

'I'm, um …' Jill glanced down at the last words on the statement, and the dotted line beneath. So much had been left out, and yet the facts listed in black and white above were true and correct. All she needed to do now was put her name to them, sign off on Jamie's death.

'You say this is just a formality.' She looked up at him. 'Because you know? You know how he died.'

DI Silver pulled the door shut behind him and took a seat opposite her. His eyes were kind but tired, and his shirt front bore the faint satiny imprint of an iron. Perhaps there was no Mrs Silver at home to take care of him.

'The coroner will give the official verdict.' He paused. 'But yes, Mrs Barnes, we're confident we've now pieced together what happened.'

'So you've spoken to Alex? She's conscious?'

'We have, and she's still in pretty bad shape, but being looked after.' The sympathy in his voice was unexpected. 'Ms Fuller was nowhere near the Vale Theatre on the fourth: we've had that corroborated by neighbours who heard her shouting and saw her looking disorientated in the streets outside her home late that evening.'

'What? But ...' The question died on her lips. 'Jamie killed himself.'

DI Silver nodded. 'We've heard a voicemail he'd left Mrs Lawrence while she was in hospital. It was –' he pressed his lips together, perhaps anxious to spare her unnecessary pain '– pretty conclusive. He spoke of feeling things were "stacked against" him, and it's not uncommon with men in these situations to feel there is no way out, to spiral out, especially when under the influence.'

Jill nodded, thanked him – and signed on the dotted line.

Of all the emotions vying to be heard within her as she made her way out of the ugly red brick building onto Salusbury Road, she was surprised to find that the loudest was anger. How fitting that Jamie would make such a selfish final gesture. That he would betray Stan, devastate her life – and then make it all about him.

CHAPTER 34

JILL

'Jill? Come and have a look at this.'

Stooped over the low, sprawling branches of an ash in Mortlake Crematorium's Garden of Reflection, Stan began to read out the messages inscribed on little silver leaves by the bereaved. 'You were my world, Ted.' 'JJ, I will keep you in my heart.' 'Love you to the moon and back, dearest Anita.'

In grief, human emotion reduced itself to song lyrics. And maybe there was nothing wrong with that; maybe in the end platitudes were people at their most honest. But there was nothing honest about Jill being here today, about pretending to 'celebrate the life and mourn the passing' of James Edward Lawrence, when she couldn't, in good conscience, do either.

'I don't think I can do this.'

The ceremony was due to start in ten minutes – and Jill felt her ribcage tightening like a vice.

'Of course you can.' Stan straightened. 'You were up until silly o'clock writing it.'

'I know. But I should never have agreed to give a eulogy. It's not ... my place.'

From her husband's pause, she realised with mounting panic that he felt the same. And there was something else.

'You shouldn't have to be here today.' Jill slipped her arms around her husband's waist, alarmed by how easily her hands now met across his stomach, how quickly the very substance of him was dwindling away. 'You shouldn't have to ...'

'Stare death in the face?' Turning to his wife, Stan tilted her chin up towards him. 'Hey. Me and death, we've been on first-name terms for a while now. I know it's too much to ask, but I wish you could make peace with it the way I have. Or somehow ... go back to not knowing.'

How could she? It was the first thing Jill thought of when she woke up, patting the covers for her husband's warm, reassuring shape before she even opened her eyes, and the last thing she thought of at night. So no, she couldn't suspend disbelief. But if Stan wanted her to be brave, that's what she would be.

In the days after that final police interview, the postmortem results and the coroner's official ruling of suicide, Jill had swung from culpability to fury and back again. Unlike Jamie, her husband didn't get to choose how or when he was going to die. He hadn't even got to tell his wife how long he had left: by blurting out what he had that night in the pub, Jamie had robbed Stan of that. And yet ... how desperate Jamie must have been to do what he did. How certain he must have felt that the world was closing in on him. A world she, Nicole and Alex had manipulated to do just that.

Beyond the rose bushes and crab-apple trees lining the Garden of Reflection, the glint of a hearse appeared.

Stan was right. She was here now, and she had to go through with it. 'We'd better go.'

As they rounded the hedge to see a tiny figure in black stepping out of the car behind the hearse, however, Jill nearly turned back and fled. 'Those children,' she murmured. 'I can't bear it.'

'I know, love.' Her husband's voice was no longer as steady as it had been. 'Come on.'

There was Maya – straight-backed in a plain square-necked black linen dress, Elsa on her hip – nodding to the assembled mourners as she passed through the crematorium's arched entrance. But as they approached, Jill's eyes snagged on another figure: a woman in a wide-brimmed black hat and sunglasses, standing alone, a little way off.

'She came.'

Nicole looked up from the Order of Service in her hand to meet Jill's gaze, her incredulity at what she'd just read mirroring Jill's own.

'Maya wasn't up to the eulogy,' Jill pre-empted defensively. 'She asked me and I ... I couldn't say no. Jamie's father's doing the main one. Mine is short. Just a ... anyway. But you?' Jill thought back to the headlines that had appeared after Jamie's death. TOP PROPERTY BROKER PLUNGES TO DEATH AFTER ME TOO CLAIM; DISGRACED PROPERTY BROKER FOUND IMPALED ON RAILINGS. 'Did Maya see you?'

'She was the one who asked me to come,' Nicole replied

quietly, swaying a little on her heels. 'And I couldn't ... not be here.'

Something in Nicole's over-painted face released itself then, and as the two women held each other's gaze, Jill felt her own anger and recriminations drain away along with Nicole's. All this bitterness, all this hate, had left them both so very tired.

'Stan?' After a brief chat with Paul, her husband had joined them. 'This is Nicole.'

'We've met before.' Stan: always measured and polite, even in the most testing circumstances. 'I think I'd already taken more of a back seat when you started?'

'That's right.'

Theirs was the banal introductory exchange of any social gathering, with the same 'where do we go from here?' silence, once concluded – a silence Nicole filled by asking Stan about his health. But as the niceties went on it became evident to Jill that having any kind of conversation at all was proving an enormous strain for her colleague. Something curious had happened to Nicole's mouth, the fuchsia lips unnaturally hard around vowels, and in that moment she understood how much it was costing Nicole to be here, despite the shades, the hat and the lipstick. It had been more than an affair. Maybe losing Jamie would be the tragedy of her life.

From the first few bars of Vaughan Williams's 'The Lark Ascending', people cut their conversations short, rearranging their faces into suitably sober expressions and adjusting their jackets and ties. Stan's hand was warm on Jill's back, guiding her forward along the nave of the crematorium. And when she turned to give her husband one last imploring look, he responded with a small nod.

'In an hour, all this will be done,' he murmured as they took their seats.

That he understood without knowing what she'd done that Jill would want to distance herself from anything connected with Jamie after today was miraculous. And as a crop-haired minister with a rapturous expression assured the room that the Lord would 'hear their cries and comfort them', 'light a lamp for them' and 'be there through the darkest valleys', Jill watched little Christel, three pews ahead, walk a tiny plastic fairy back and forth along the polished wood of the pew.

Had Maya bought it especially? 'Your daddy killed himself. He's lying in that casket a few feet away now, because he couldn't be bothered to wait around for you to lose your first tooth, become a woman and go on your first date. But here – have this.' At that moment, the gulf between her and mothers felt larger than ever. Jill only had herself and Stan to think about; the pain of losing him and surviving life without him. How could Maya remain strong not just for herself today, but for Christel and Elsa for ever?

With heavy steps Jamie's father made his way up to the front of the chapel and stood before his son's raised coffin at the lectern. Jill noticed that his black suit looked relatively unworn, but not new – the kind bought by men in their sixties once they'd started to lose a few friends and were conscious there would be more to come. A 'funeral uniform' no father ever imagined wearing to bury his son.

His hair glowed white against the russet tan of his face – a wide, honest face – and Jill remembered the pictures of the Alicante condo Jamie had once shown her on his phone, proud to have been able to give his parents the retirement they'd dreamt of. Too snobbish to visit much – 'the weather and wine still don't make up for the chavs' – Jamie hadn't mentioned his parents a great deal in conversation, but on the rare occasions he had, Jill remembered, his tone had always been suffused with love.

Ted Lawrence must have become a father in his late teens or early twenties. In stark contrast to his hair, Ted's face was youthful and unlined, his eyes the same soft velvet brown as Jamie's. He was probably mischievous, too, under normal circumstances. He'd been something to do with central heating. Boilers – that was it: Ted had been a boiler repair man in Sevenoaks, where he and his wife Laura had been based until their retirement. She was there beside Maya, her uncontained sobs audible to all. Jill couldn't bear to look at her.

'Seeing so many of you here today – hearing how much you loved our boy – is a great comfort to myself and my wife,' Mr Lawrence began slowly, pulling a crumpled sheet of paper from his inside pocket and smoothing it with a palm as he placed it on the lectern. 'But I'm standing here with a broken heart.' He faltered, and Jill willed him to get through it, before remembering there was no way through this kind of grief. 'Laura and I, we never thought we'd have to deal with the loss of a child: our only child. I dare say nobody does. But losing a child like this. Knowing he felt like he had no alternative, no one he could talk to.' Mr Lawrence shook his head. 'Because Jamie had all these plans, you know? For the future. And he was well on his way to making them all come true. So this . . .' Nodding at his wife, Jamie's father's eyes filled with tears. 'This just makes no sense. Jamie's always been a glass-half-full man, since he was a little boy. He'd never let us sleep in at the weekends. He'd be in there at the crack of dawn, bouncing on the bed, telling us to "get up!" – wouldn't he, Lau?'

His wife's only response a strangled gurgle, he pushed on.

'And it was always the same thing – 'What are we going to do today, Dad?' As though every day had to bring some new adventure. And I knew then that the normal his mum and I were happy with wasn't going to be enough for Jamie. He wanted something special, and he got it. He got his beautiful wife –' Ted smiled at Maya '– and children and house, and a job that was better than anything we ever hoped for. A partner in a top ...' his voice cracked, '... top London firm – mentioned in magazines and newspapers.'

From the corner of her eye Jill could see Jamie's mother nodding vehemently through her tears. She had a vision of framed articles on walls – a kitchen fridge papered with 'hasn't he done well' mementos – and a contrasting vision of the pieces that had appeared after his death. 'I know that success was smeared at the end, or, or ...' Jill winced at the poignancy of this man scrabbling around for the right word to describe what happened to his son at the end of his life. 'But today we don't think about that. Today we think about everything Jamie achieved. And it wasn't a surprise to us. Because I'd take him along to local jobs as a lad, you know, and I'd be there explaining to a client that more than likely the whole boiler was going to need replacing, and they'd get annoyed, you know: "How much is all this going to cost?" Well, right about then Jamie would always show up. "My dad can fix anything – you can trust him," he'd say. And even then he'd have this effect on people. The men loved him, and the women.' A curl of the lip, a hint of macho pride at his son's success 'with the ladies'. 'And despite what he did, I know he loved us, too.'

When Mr Lawrence's chin dropped to his chest and his shoulders began to jolt up and down, the minister came and whispered a few words in his ear.

'No, I'm … I just want to say one last thing: we'll always be proud of you, son. And we hope you've found peace.'

Throughout the passage from Ecclesiastes and the whole of Ed Sheeran's 'Supermarket Flowers', Stan kept hold of Jill's hand, giving it a little squeeze just before she made her way up to the lectern.

'Mr and Mrs Lawrence, Maya, I'm sure I speak for all of us when I say that if I could take any of your pain from you, I would. But I hope there's some comfort in knowing that everyone in this room shares it.'

Nicole was there at the back, third in from the aisle, as dark and distracting as a smudge on a lens, and behind the lectern, Jill shifted her weight from one foot to the other.

'Everyone here has known Jamie in different capacities …' Keep to a work context, she'd told herself the night before, and you're safe. 'And as someone who spotted his potential twelve years ago, brought him into BWL and worked closely with him throughout that time, I watched him grow professionally and personally. I saw him turn into a loving husband and father to little Christel and Elsa. I saw him work his way up from junior broker to partner.' She cleared her throat. 'But that thirst for adventure you spoke of, Mr Lawrence, was always one of his most distinctive features.' Because you always wanted more, didn't you, Jamie? Why? Was there not enough excitement for you in adulthood? Or did you just get spoilt – by your parents, women, success, me? 'Then there was Jamie's charisma, his magnetism, which was –' exhausting, devastating '– noted by all who met him. When he was speaking to someone, anyone, they always felt like they were the only person in the room. That's a rare gift indeed.' And one you abused, Jamie, time and time again, to get what you wanted. 'In a job like ours, where charm is so important, it gave him an energy and a power that propelled him forward.' And made it all too easy for you to trample over others. She paused. 'That beneath that glittering façade was a tormented soul is not something many of us ever suspected. But Jamie made his mark on everyone in this room while he was with us. And again, I'm sure I speak for all of us when I say that he will never be forgotten.'

CHAPTER 35

❧

NICOLE

December

'He's coming for you, he's coming for you!'

The warning came too late. 'Suzie Pong', the stinking washerwoman Nicole had no memory of being in the original *Aladdin*, was already leaning across her and reaching for Ben's hand.

'Up you get,' she screeched, the stubbled chin and smear of lipstick on her teeth visible up close. 'I'm going to need an apprentice at my launderette, and you look just the ticket.' Spinning Ben around from the waist to face the audience, Suzie Pong fog-horned: 'Do we think he looks just the ticket, ladies, gents and non-binary friends?'

A chorus of yeses and a wolf-whistle drowned out her

husband's protests, and Nicole shrank back in her seat to allow Ben to be pulled out into the aisle and up on to the theatre stage.

'Something tells me Daddy's going to be made to look very silly,' she whispered in her daughter's ear. And when Chloe broke out into one of her manic cackles, baring that joyful jumble of mismatched teeth, Nicole felt her eyes well up.

All those years of listening to girlfriends cringe at the seasonal sentimentality that would floor them in Westfield or at the ice rink, when the first few bars of Wham!'s 'Last Christmas' came on, Nicole had never understood it. Until this year. Until she'd almost lost everything and had to claw it back, piece by piece.

When she'd first moved back home, those emotional swerves had derailed her several times a day. Strong enough to feel like vertigo, they came out of nowhere: when she was laying the table for three or trying to find a mate for a tiny star-print sock in the tangle of laundry still warm from the drier. When she picked up letters from the mat addressed to Mr and Mrs Harper. When, as she made her way up to the guest bedroom Ben had made her sleep in for over a month, she glimpsed the back of her husband's neck as he edited content for the production company he was now contracted to.

All the things that had once made her feel trapped were now tangible reminders of what real happiness was. Because it wasn't seeing her name go up on that reception wall alongside Paul and Jill's after all those years or the first letter written on BWH writing paper, as it turned out, but something far subtler. And when, on a pub night out celebrating her partnership the previous month, her new PA had shown Nicole a tattoo she was in the process of having removed, she'd found herself fascinated by the fragments of black ink you could see being carried away, dot by dot, feeling that same purifying process was taking place within her. And that with Ben and Chloe beside her, the toxicity in her bloodstream would eventually be washed away.

Because of that, Nicole had felt none of the usual tightness across her chest when Ben had brought up their yearly pre-Christmas trip to the pantomime.

'Of course we're going,' she'd insisted.

And how could Nicole explain that its banality was what made it so significant? More so even than their first night back in the same bed together, when despite the three glasses of Merlot Ben had perhaps deliberately downed at dinner, it had felt as though he'd had to force himself to go through with it, keeping his eyes fixed on a distant point on the bed post until he was done. But that Saturday afternoon at the panto – with all the bickering over whether or not Chloe was allowed Maltesers and the mad dash to the Ladies in the interval – Nicole felt that they were almost like everyone else.

'Oh dear – this doesn't look right, does it?'

Laughter filled the auditorium, and Nicole looked up at her husband on stage. Pinned to a washing line by two giant clothes pegs pulling his shirt shoulders up like a ventrilo-quist's dummy, Ben was trying his best to look like a good sport. 'Two worst words in the English language?' he'd joked on one of their first dates. 'Audience participation.'

Yes, Ben would be hating every second of this. In the way that couples who have been together a long time are able to catch waves of each other's emotions, she could actively feel the loathing emanating from him. But knowing how much

Chloe was loving seeing her father up there, Ben would grin and bear it. And bearing with humiliation, Nicole now understood, was the greatest proof of love.

Just as gracelessly as he'd been yanked up on stage, Ben was propelled off again – 'Let's give it up for my apprentice! And send 'im off to the job centre' – and whatever he whispered good-humouredly in her ear as he took his seat again was drowned out by a reprise of the Prodigy's rave-rant 'Firestarter', the cast assembling on stage for their final scene.

'Mummy, I'm hungry!' Chloe whined as they filtered slowly down the theatre stairs and out onto the packed pre-Christmas streets of Hammersmith.

'How can you be hungry?' she marvelled, crouching down to zip up her daughter's coat. 'You've just put away a whole box of Maltesers pretty much on your own.'

'She didn't have much of a lunch. And there's always the Christmas market?'

Following her husband's eyeline and breathing in the sweet and savoury smells – churros, roasted meat and something hot, fruity and alcoholic – Nicole looked over at the colony of stalls across the road.

'Let's do it,' she agreed. Then, spying a postbox, 'I'll catch up.'

The Christmas card had languished in her bag all week, and smoothing out its dog-eared corners, Nicole took a last look at the address – 'Alex Fuller, Oak View Cottage, Albion Road, Marden, Tonbridge' – and pushed it through the slot. 'It's just a rental, and tiny,' Alex had told her. 'So Mum's got the bedroom and I'm on a sofa bed in the sitting room, but as soon as the divorce money comes through she's going to buy us somewhere bigger. And it's so peaceful out here,

Katie's even sleeping through the night! You must come and visit.'

Nicole had promised she would, knowing it would never happen, that it was the last thing either of them wanted or needed, and that anything more than an occasional call would only reignite painful memories. A little girl in black at her father's funeral; two little girls who would be spending the first of many Christmases without their father.

But Nicole had developed a series of deflection tactics to banish Christel and Elsa from her mind, whenever they appeared. And taking Chloe's gloved hand, they headed towards the steaming little encampment of Christmas stalls.

'Do you remember last time,' she said, grinning at Ben, 'I got that crazy sense of smell?'

'Remember? You'd know what I was making for supper before you were even inside the front door.'

And when their daughter asked 'Last time what?' they both knew she'd never let it go.

Pulling Chloe into a doorway, away from the fast-moving throng, Ben cupped her flushed cheek. 'How would you feel about having a little sister – or brother?'

Their daughter's eyes moved from Nicole to Ben and back again. Then the faintest shadow flickered around her brows. 'And we would all live together? You, me, Mummy and my sister or brother?'

'Of course, Chlo.' Over their daughter's bobble hat, Ben's eyes met hers. 'I'll never let anything change that.'

Watching the pleasure in her husband's face spread to their daughter's, Nicole prayed for the millionth time that this baby would be just a few weeks late.

CHAPTER 36

JILL

'Fifteen thousand hours – that's how long these new energy-saving bulbs are meant to last.'

Lowering her *Sunday Times*, Jill glanced up at her husband from her curled position on the sofa. Stan hadn't moved in the past half hour, and was still facing the house-boat wall, tinkering with the wire-filled hole above his head. Beside him, on *Lady J*'s mantelpiece, was the defective sconce he had determined to fix.

'Which is great, but they're never bright enough. So if that's fifteen thousand twilight hours …' She scanned the opinion page for her favourite writer, only to find him replaced by a suspiciously young 'guest columnist'. 'Anyway, the bulb's never been the problem, has it?'

'Nope. But I think I've finally worked out what was,' he

muttered, screwing the light's rectangular backplate to the wall before taking a step back. 'Only took me three and a half years.'

'It hasn't been that.'

'It has.' Stan turned to her with a smile. 'Remember that weekend Prue and Alan came on board and we went down to Milton Keynes?'

'And she kept losing her hearing aid.'

'And we spent most of that last afternoon looking for the damn thing.'

'Before finding it down the side of the sofa.' Jill's frown lifted. 'Oh!' She put a hand to her mouth. 'You're right. It was that weekend! That last night when it was raining and we had supper in here – you couldn't manage to turn the damn lights on.'

'Exactly. Been bothering me ever since.' Stan nodded at the switch behind the sofa. 'Do the honours?'

Reaching across the patchwork of papers surrounding her, Jill flicked it.

Nothing.

Stan groaned.

Jill chuckled. 'Leave it. Come here.' She patted the space beside her. 'I'll make a cuppa.'

'No, no.' Her husband had already turned back to the wall and started unscrewing the sconce. 'I'm getting this sorted now. Those fifteen thousand hours are starting today.'

Jill reached for the property section, rolling her shoulders rhythmically back as she flicked through it in an attempt to ease the tightness across her chest: anything to stop her mind doing the involuntary sums. Fifteen thousand hours was what? Well over a year and half. Probably nearer two. That light had nothing to do with Stan's annoyance or crossing something off his to-do list; he was doing it for her.

Accepting her husband was dying had turned out to be easier than talking to him about the life they were still living, and the first few slips – 'We need to remember to prune that clematis early May, before the leaves start clogging the drain-pipe', 'Remind me to invite Steph next year' – had been enough to make Jill leave whichever room she was in and lock herself in the nearest toilet until she could breathe again.

It hadn't helped that Stan was able to laugh off these slips, and she'd warned him weeks back that any form of black humour wouldn't just be lost on her but repulsive. Yet as Jamie's death receded into the past, along with all the ugliness leading up to that single life-changing week, Jill's orderly mind had found a kind of comfort in acknowledging that there would simply be a before – and an after. By the time the next home insurance bill came in and the gutters next needed cleaning; by the time that stupid fifteen-thousand-hour energy-saving bulb went out, Stan would be gone. And God knows he had long ago made his peace with that.

That her husband had defied all expectations and made it to December was 'a credit' to her, Dr Jacks kept saying – although she was more inclined to put it down to the healthy life they'd shared: good food, long walks and all those decades of waterway air. But when they'd finally been given the go-ahead to take their Grand Union trip, three months after they'd planned, the doctor had taken her aside, handed her five pages of medical instructions and added, 'You know people can be lulled into a false sense of security in cases like Stan's – start believing we got it wrong.' Here he'd paused. 'Believe me when I say that I wish we had. But ... ' He shook his head. 'You know Stan's very unlikely to make it to Christmas, don't you?' She'd nodded, swallowing the lump in her throat, and asked: 'But the trip? You're not saying we can't go?'

Why that trip mattered as much as it did, Jill only realised on the first morning, when she and Stan awoke in a misty stretch of waterway near the Tring Summit. In the summer, the water was cluttered with 'all inclusive' three-day cruisers, but only hardened boaters like them would think to go that way in December. And apart from a single houseboat that looked as though it had fused with the riverbank it was moored to, so overgrown was one slatted side with moss and lichen, there was just *Lady J.*

Yes, the weather was far cooler than they'd hoped, cool enough to wake them both shortly after six that morning, but after filling a thermos with coffee, helping Stan into his thickest fleece and heating up two croissants, they'd sat out on the rear deck beneath a blanket watching the orange wash of sky lighten to a nursery pink.

'Isn't this blissful?' Stan had murmured.

And it was. But it wasn't easy to live for the moment when every one of those moments was already a memory to be greedily stashed away: from jokes her husband made to mental snapshots of his speckled hands. Because if she could just amass enough, those memories might last her the rest of her life.

They'd drawn up a list of rules before they left London. No death talk was allowed – the last of the funeral details having been dealt with before they'd left, in any case – and no medical nagging permitted from Jill. Stan was a big boy who could remember his pills unprompted. He didn't need Jill to fuss. Apart from a single pint with his steak and ale pie at their Half Moon lunch, there was to be no alcohol for him (the doctor had advised against it). And other than a half-hour mid-afternoon window during which Jill was allowed to check her emails and call the office if need be, no work was to be done or discussed. Before starting up *Lady J*'s engine, they'd shaken on this, and left Little Venice determined to stick to those rules.

Of course by day three and that Sunday, every rule but one had been broken. Jill had nagged Stan about his pills within hours. Had he remembered to bring them all? Even the ones by the kettle? Her husband had enjoyed his first beer before they'd even passed through Brentford, and as the waitress had taken down their lunch order at the Half Moon that day, Stan had looked over the menu at his wife: 'You're not seriously going to stop a dying man from enjoying a nice bottle of red, are you?'

That pretty, snub-nosed blonde, all of seventeen and certain this was a joke, had laughed. Because the idea that ordinary people who ate Sunday lunch in pubs then went off and died was laughable. So Jill had asked the girl whether they still had that nice Ribera, 'the Vega something we had three years ago and loved', and they'd polished off a bottle over their four-hour lunch, before ordering two more glasses to drink with their apple crumbles.

It had been raining when they left the pub, and Jill had been pleased this cancelled out plans of a walk and gave them a languorous late afternoon in which to work their way through the papers together, wordlessly swapping supplements in the order decreed decades ago. Only instead of curling up with her, Stan had fixated on that sconce.

'Oh.'

For a period after Jamie's death had been made public, Jill had got used to seeing his name in the news. But the case had long ago been closed – ruled a 'clear-cut suicide' – and it had been weeks since she'd last come across anything pertaining to either her former colleague or the Vale. So the impact of those two words destabilised her almost as much as the grinning portrait beside them.

'What?' Still engrossed in his wires, Stan didn't turn around.

'There's a piece in the *Times* property section about the Vale sale to Creighton Mackintosh. A big piece.'

'The sale was always going to get out. Roger Creighton is a big name. You're worried they think we leaked it?'

'No, no. There are quotes from him. He says he wants to make it "the biggest working theatre in west London".'

'Good for him.'

Jill nodded, her eyes drawn back to the paragraph on Jamie, the 'site's tragic recent history', and that defiantly vital face pictured alongside it.

'They've gone and rehashed the whole thing.' She shook her head. 'It's the last thing Maya and the girls need.'

Seeking some indistinct form of reassurance, Jill looked up at her husband, but still he didn't turn, and she took in the dwindling trails of fuzz Johnny the barber had shaved down to what Stan called 'a tapered number two' before they left.

'That was always going to happen. As soon as the assault claim came out … Then you've got the theatre with its forgotten lantern – manna from heaven for journalists, isn't it?'

Wishing she'd never bought the paper that had allowed Jamie back into their lives, even for a moment, Jill turned the page. But it was too late. And like a door that won't quite close, no matter how hard you slam, something jammed.

'You knew about the lantern?' She spoke more to herself than Stan, remembering even as she did so that in all the press coverage of Jamie's death there had been no mention of the concealed glass structure on the theatre's roof. In fact the only person who had ever mentioned it to her was Nicole.

Beneath the 'three for two' M&S polo shirt she'd bought him, her husband's shoulder blades were rigid, the tendons in his neck taut beneath that 'tapered number two' – and there was still time to take the question back. But when Jill saw her husband's shoulders slump, she knew it was too late, and the whisper of fear inside turned into an inner howl.

'What he did to you … what he did to the company we spent a lifetime building.'

'Shush.'

Out jabbed Stan's elbow as he inched his screwdriver round and around. 'Jamie had no respect for that.'

'Shush.'

'No respect for women and that poor sick girl he used as a scapegoat. No respect even for my death.'

Her eyes still on her husband's neck, Jill was taken back to the last time she'd seen Jamie. The truth he'd spat out at her. The laptop left open on the kitchen counter as she'd given up tracking his journey home on the company database. The sleeping pill her husband had given her: that same neck dissolving into soft focus as it took effect.

'He was so drunk when I got there.' Stan went on in a low voice she didn't recognise. 'Drunk and desperate to show me the Vale's little "oddity".'

The sconce was back up, and Stan laid his screwdriver gently down on the mantelpiece.

'He would've fallen anyway.'

For a second, neither of them moved.

Then Jill heard herself speak, brisk and schoolmistress-like: 'That's enough.'

Freeing herself from the paralysis that threatened to engulf her, she reached behind the sofa for the switch and flicked. It was bright, too bright. And in the moment that Stan finally turned to meet her eye, she yearned for those old shadows to hide behind. But there was no going back, and grateful that her limbs could still carry her, Jill went through to the kitchen and pulled out their *Nicholson Waterway Guide* from the drawer.

'Now that we can see again, let's work out where we're headed next.'

Because it was all about making those new memories. And if they could just keep moving, slow and steady, some of the old ones could surely be forgotten.

ACKNOWLEDGEMENTS

This book came into being thanks to the infinite patience and razor-sharp eye of my agent, Eugenie Furniss. Every scribbled 'brutal!' from you, Eugenie, made me happier than you know, and my late, great friend and agent, Ed Victor, would be so pleased to know that you took over where he left off.

My editor, Rosanna Forte, provided the best advice any author could wish for. Thank you for believing in *Payday*'s plot and characters to the extent that Jamie's comments sometimes left you fuming – and I was forced to remind you that 'he isn't actually real'.

Thalia Proctor, Laura Vile, Stephanie Melrose and the whole Sphere team at Little, Brown have been so brilliant and tireless, and I'm excited to work with you all again on the next book.

I owe a special debt to Alexandra Kordas at 42 Management & Production, whose energy and enthusiasm lit up many a bleak, locked-down day. I'm also deeply grateful to Malcolm Ward, for taking the time to read some of the most sinister passages that will ever have landed in his inbox; to Simon Raw, for putting me in touch with Her Majesty's Theatre's wonderful Stage Manager, Stewart Arnott, and to Emily McCullagh, for her expertise and rapid email response time, despite having far more important things to do.

Much gratitude to Mike Beveridge of Canal and River Cruises Ltd for providing me with insights no amount of research could have yielded; to John Goodall for sharing his vast knowledge of all things architectural, and to Vincent Galea for his legal prowess. It doesn't go without saying that any mistakes are my own.

Thank you to my friends Darryl Samaraweera, Jessica Fellowes, Kate Johnson, Caroline Graham and Alice Evans for their help, support and time, and to Paul Paolella, for being the inspiration behind 'that scene'.

It's only because of the *Telegraph*'s generosity – in allowing me to take a sabbatical – and with the assistance of Maria Flor, that I was able to find the time to write. That you then read *Payday* over a single sleepless night, Cory, meant so much to me.

I'm beyond grateful to my family: Olly, Frank, Mum and Dad. Elise, you were more helpful than any nine-year-old should have been in coming up with ever darker twists and turns. And Piers, thank you for putting up with my random and often gory questions – 'Should Jamie survive being impaled on railings or be killed outright?' – mostly late at night when you're trying to get some sleep. You're right: my pillow talk does need work.

Known for her wide-ranging articles, opinions and commentaries on everything from current affairs to health, fashion and motoring, *Daily Telegraph* columnist Celia Walden has written for *Glamour*, *GQ*, *Elle*, *Porter Magazine*, *Harper's Bazaar*, Net-a-Porter's *The Edit*, *Grazia*, *Stylist*, *Standpoint*, *The Spectator* and Russian *Vogue*. Born and raised in Paris, Celia studied at the University of Cambridge. She and her husband now divide their time between London and LA. *Payday* is her first thriller.

When you've got a house to die for,
Be careful who you let in.

Colette spends a lot of her time at Addison Square.
She knows the place and the people better than anyone.
But the wealthy residents she works for can barely
remember her name.

Which is unfortunate, because Colette knows
all about them.

She sees all their secrets.

Even the ones they'd kill to protect.

Pre-order now

Exclusive Additional Content

Including author interviews, reviews and much, much more!

Richard and Judy ask Celia Warden

Obviously you've worked for ghastly men like Jamie! Tell us all!

I fear every woman has come across a Jamie variant in her working life. I had some pretty revolting bosses in my late teens and early twenties when I was doing part-time jobs in bars and restaurants. One in particular served as partial inspiration for Jamie, although he didn't have his charisma. But I think charm, wit and/or good looks can make predators and opportunists even more toxic because it gives them their power.

Because those men can only thrive if the women they prey on are constantly asking themselves: 'Am I over-reacting?'

Despite the overt sexual harassment and the bullying, however, it was this one little 'party trick' of this particular boss that I remember most clearly. At the end of the night when he was drinking with his friends, he would ask me to come over, take the Zippo out of his breast pocket and light his cigarette for him. I think I only realised later why it was so vile: because the intent was to humiliate.

Do you think women make better conspirators than men?

Definitely. It's why (stand by for outrageously sexist comment) we always guess 'who did it' before men. I think women are better plotters in general because we tend to be more observant, and we've certainly got over-active imaginations.

Whenever my husband and I go out to a restaurant or stay at a hotel, I'll point out people and invent whole fantasy lives and dilemmas for them. He finds it concerning, but I always enjoy myself.

Are male bosses better behaved towards women today, or just cleverer at hiding their innate misogyny?

The reality is that most male bosses are not Harvey Weinstein-size villains. I genuinely believe that a lot of them won't have realised that some of their behaviour and comments were misogynistic until Me Too, when many adjusted their behaviour accordingly.

The problem is that the innate misogynists won't have had that wakeup call. They will just have got better at hiding it: never putting anything in writing, implying rather than saying things outright. And we all seem to have avoided the question of what happens to a woman after she calls her boss out at work, don't we? Did her career flourish? Or did she have to pay a price?

You're a journalist by trade, dealing in facts and opinions. How do you find writing fiction?

After twenty-five years in journalism, I find writing fiction incredibly liberating. The combination of the two is perfect for me. But there is this incredible moment with fiction when one gets stuck on a logistical detail such as 'but it wouldn't take an hour to get from my character's house to the crime scene…' Then you realise that you can just change where he or she lives. You are God in your story! Honestly: being able to escape to my study and conjure up a whole dark, twisted world during the longest days of the pandemic was heaven.

Listen to our podcast, available across all major platforms. Just search "Richard and Judy Bookclub"

To find out more visit our website –
www.whsmith.co.uk/richardandjudy

Richard and Judy ask Celia Warden

The Richard and Judy Book Club, exclusively with WHSmith, is all about you getting involved and sharing our passion for reading. Here are some questions to help you or your Book Group get started. Go to our website to discuss these questions, post your own and share your views with the rest of the Book Club.

Q1 Jill, Nicole and Alex are all very different from each other. Did you sympathise with one more than the others?

Q2 Would you and your two closest friends agree on how to deal with a man like Jamie?

Q3 Did you guess the ending? Who did you think killed Jamie throughout the book?

Q4 When, if ever, do you think it's acceptable to take justice into your own hands?

To find out more visit our website –
www.whsmith.co.uk/richardandjudy

Read on for an exclusive sneak peek at
Celia's next addictive thriller . . .

When you've got a house to die for,
Be careful who you let in.

THE
SQUARE

Celia Walden

COVER TO BE REVEALED

PROLOGUE

It had stippled the blinds, marbled the wall, and run in ragged rivulets to the skirting board.

It had formed crimson trenches in the plastic sheeting laid out across the floor, pooled in the swirls and twists of the floorboards.

It was beautiful, in a way. Like a piece of conceptual art. Like the young woman herself, even in her soaked silk dress – even in death.

CHAPTER 1: COLETTE

'I'm going to need a few more minutes.'

From her crouched and cramped position beneath the desk, Colette angled her face up at her client and forced a smile.

She needn't have bothered. He was back to pacing up and down his study, and as she returned to the tangle of cables wedged between desk and wall, Colette did her best to ignore the rhythmic stick and wheeze of his soles against the hardwood floor.

Those slippers summed up everything she disliked about Adrian Carter. There was the pomposity of the oxblood velvet, and the pretension of their pointed tips. Paired with the middle-class, middle-aged West London summer uniform of linen shirt and chinos, they were obvious in their intent, banal in their cultivated eccentricity: *I'm not just an off-duty suit. I've got kooks and kinks. Layers.*

She'd seen similar slippers in Shepherd's Bush market, laid out in rainbow stripes. But these were more likely to have come from a real Moroccan medina; one of the exotic conferences the TV agent was forever jetting off to, and

Colette pictured Adrian, the statesman-like patron, slowing to survey the footwear in a souk: 'Aren't these jolly!'

'You OK with me switching off the master plug?'

'You what?'

'The master plug. I want to check the software's done its thing, but you should now be bug free.' Hitting the right tone – one that was clear but never patronising – was the hardest part of being an IT consultant.

'It means switching off this lot,' Colette stressed, holding up the overloaded extension lead.

'Do it.' He didn't look up from his phone.

'At some point we should really transfer some of these to another power outlet . . .'

'At some point,' Adrian's tone was so tetchy it bordered on amused, 'we will. But not at this precise point, when I've got seven, no, six minutes until an urgent Zoom call it's not currently looking like I stand a hope in hell of making. I'd assumed this would get sorted hours ago.'

Adrian liked his passive tense. How or by whom didn't matter, just that it 'got sorted.' And 'hours ago'? Given he'd only called Colette two hours ago, when after a quick attempt to fix the problem from her flat – using RemoteViewer – she had been forced to drive over to Addison Square, this seemed unrealistic. But now wasn't the moment to point that out.

'Bloody thing's had a mind of its own this past week,' Adrian muttered. 'How the hell did I get this bug anyway?'

Without waiting for an answer, he made a call.

'Dom? It's me. Listen I've been floored by some bug.' A laugh. 'No. Worse. The tech kind. And I've got our person on it but I'm going to need you to host the meeting until I can join . . .'

Our person? How about *Colette*? The same "person" who retrieved eight years' worth of your family memories – two sets of ultrasounds included – when you thought you'd deleted them all. The 'person' who dug out that work file you thought you'd overwritten, has painstakingly talked you through every TV glitch you've ever had and just sped over here, at 8pm on a Friday night, to deal with your "emergency".

Beneath the desk Colette exhaled slowly. The smack, stick and wheezing had resumed, closer now, louder, and she swivelled on her haunches to find herself blocked in by two chino-clad calves, the points of Adrian's preposterous babouches inches from her own feet.

It wasn't personal. Reaching for something on his desk, Adrian had forgotten the woman wedged beneath it in the way one might forget a sleeping collie.

'Adrian?'

'Mmm ...'

'I'm going to need to get out.'

With an exaggerated side-step her client let her through and hoisting herself upright Colette slipped back into his chair and pressed 'refresh' on one of the open tabs at the bottom of the screen.

It took her a moment to make sense of the image that sprang up: a fleshy blur of pinks and browns, with what she first mistook for a wound, glistening crimson at its centre. Doubtless some Netflix gore-fest Adrian had been watching. Then the freeze frame released itself.

There was male grunting, panting, thrusting and a high-pitched female whine that was more animal than human. Two, no, three men. A woman spreadeagled on a leather sofa. Her hands were tied above her head; her lower limbs being manipulated like a doll's. Male laughter, raucous, from behind the camera; jokey comments exchanged in a Slav language she couldn't identify.

Colette froze, waiting for Adrian to lunge forward and stab at the keyboard in the way clients did when some shameful little proclivity was exposed on a job. But he stood perfectly still, head tilted to one side, eyes on hers: 'Not your thing?'

His gaze moved dispassionately down the length of her body, from her cropped hair and glasses right down to the Velcro straps of her sandals. There it lingered, as though tickled by these final details. All the while, the grunting and whining seemed to be growing louder, perforated now by the sound of a palm against bare flesh. 'Hard to tell what you're into.'

What felt like minutes must only have been seconds. Finally, with one last glance at Colette's face, Adrian tapped a button on his keypad. The grunting and bleating stopped. The image vanished. And as though the whole thing had been a mirage, as though she'd imagined it all, her client deadpanned: 'We sorted?'

'I just need ...' To her irritation Colette found that her voice came out hoarse with embarrassment. Gluey with shame. All the shame Adrian hadn't felt she had somehow taken on. '... to do one last reboot.' He was smiling now; he was enjoying this. 'Then we're done.'

'How's it going?'

Colette turned to see a pretty, full-faced woman peering through the crack in the door: Adrian's long-suffering wife.

'Slowly,' he groaned, leaning in to follow the white oblong's sluggish progress across the screen.

'Hi Emilia.' She managed to raise a stiff hand in greeting.

'A cuppa, Colette, or some iced water?'

'Not now, Em,' her husband snapped. 'For fuck's sake not now.'

The spasm of hurt on Emilia's face was swallowed up immediately by her smile: too broad, too bright. A smile adept at papering over cracks.

'Sorry,' she whispered, pulling the door shut. 'Let me know if you need anything.'

As they both stared at the screen, Colette could feel the heat exuding from Adrian's damp torso, hear the impatience pushing through every nasal whistle, and in silence they both followed the line: 6 minutes remaining; 5 minutes remaining; 4 minutes . . .

'Come on. Come on . . .'

Abruptly, as though tired of its own teasing, the screen brightened into a familiar seascape, and although the last thing Colette wanted was to extend her time at Number 46 Addison Square by another second, part of her felt dismayed that the device hadn't seen fit to torment him a little longer.

'We're in.'

She was packing up her things when the Mad Men theme tune rang out: Adrian's cretinous ring tone for as long as she'd known him.

'Yup?'

Maybe it was the length of the pause that followed, or her client's sudden stillness, registered out of the corner of her eye – but his reaction was curious enough to make Colette glance up.

Whoever was calling wasn't just unwelcome but

unnerving. The levity in his face had drained away along with the colour, and his voice dipped to a murmur as he spat out: 'How did you get this number?' Then: 'No. Sorry. Not going to happen. Hanging up now.'

For a moment Adrian stood there staring at the phone in his hand, as though it were an unknown quantity – or a threat.

Colette cleared her throat.

'I'll let you get on.'

Zipping up her mobile briefcase she pulled it out into the hallway. 'And you'll remember to log out of RemoteViewer, bec . . .'

But already Adrian was kicking his study door shut: 'Will do. You're a star, Lynette.'

For a moment she just stood there. Then, to no-one: 'It's Colette.'

Our latest Book Club titles

RICHARD & JUDY
BOOK CLUB
EXCLUSIVE TO
WHSmith
EST·1792

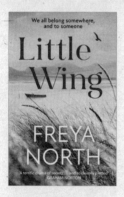

We all belong somewhere,
and to someone

LITTLE WING

FREYA NORTH

'A terrific drama of secrets... tender but keenly plotted'
GRAHAM NORTON

'A hugely impressive page-turner'
ASHLEY AUDRAIN

'A knock-out twist'
GILLIAN McALLISTER

Two best friends.
Two opposite opinions.

THE HERD

Try picking a side.

'Will have book club across the country in hot debate'
CLARE MACKINTOSH

EMILY EDWARDS

'Totally gripping'
SUNDAY TELEGRAPH

'Impossible to put down'
HELEN FIELDING

'I adored it'
GILLIAN McALLISTER

PAYDAY
Celia Walden

They all wanted to destroy him.
But which one *killed* him?

'A must-read'
JANE CORRY

'Impressively entertaining'
LOUISE CANDLISH

'Cracking'
DAILY MAIL

'A twisisted little tale
of a thriller'
SUN

WHAT HAPPENS WHEN
NO ONE
IS WATCHING?

'Terrifyingly
real'
CLARE MACKINTOSH

'Totally
page-turning'
LINWOOD BARCLAY

ONE STEP TOO FAR

LISA GARDNER

THE SUNDAY TIMES BESTSELLING AUTHOR

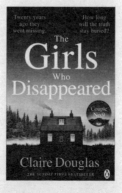

Twenty years
ago they
went missing.

How long
will the truth
stay buried?

The Girls Who Disappeared

Couple
No.9

Claire Douglas

THE SUNDAY TIMES BESTSELLER

THE NUMBER ONE
BESTSELLER

Linwood BARCLAY

A MISSING
WOMAN.

A HUSBAND
SUSPECTED

THE TRUTH WILL...

TAKE YOUR BREATH AWAY

'A suspense master'
STEPHEN KING